THE OTHER SIDE
OF
TENDERNESS

THE OTHER SIDE OF TENDERNESS

Diane M. Zimmerman

Tendernesspub

Dedication

For my daughter, Danielle, whose encouragement shielded me from the storms of doubt.
You will have my love for all eternity.
My life began the day you were born.

Please be aware that this story contains scenes of mafia violence and profanity which may be upsetting to some. It also contains explicit male/female consensual sexual situations.

PART ONE

The Color Red

1979 Las Vegas

"C'mon man, finish up. We're gonna miss the bus," Antonio yelled.

"Yeah, yeah, I'm almost done, hold on," Manny shot back, annoyed by his friend's impatience. He was exhausted, wanting only to get home to his wife and baby but it had been another long night at the Jugs and Suds Lounge, a popular Vegas strip club featuring nonstop music, $1 beers, and 'the friendliest lap dancers in town' — or so the handbills claimed. Tonight, had been standing room only and the din of raucous tourists and conventioneers had given him a migraine.

With just ten minutes to closing time, the bouncers were tossing the last of the drunks out the front doors and Manny could hear the protective voice of his boss as he escorted the girls to their cars. Bernie was like that. His nostrils filled with the stench of the alley as he made his way toward the dumpsters with the last two overstuffed bags of trash.

The shrill cry of an alley cat pierced the silence and a pair of yellow eyes careened toward him. He swerved, narrowly avoiding the furry dumpster diver before losing his balance and tumbling forward into a puddle of viscous dark liquid. He cursed his clumsiness seeing his hands and pant legs covered with the sticky red substance. Groping for leverage, he forced himself upright and peered into the dumpster just as Antonio stuck his head out the back door again.

"Come on man, move it."

But Manny was frozen, his voice garbled, "Ca… call 911, CALL 911 NOW!"

LVPD Sargeant Mike Branigan, and Officer Harvey Epple were first on the scene accompanied by a baby-faced rookie named Joe Sinclair. The alley was swiftly cordoned off in hopes of maintaining evidence.

Lying atop a sea of black plastic trash bags was the badly beaten body of a female, her vacant eyes staring up at the veteran sergeant. Branigan held tight to the rim of the dumpster observing the savage mutilation of her torso while forcing an ocean of bile back down into his stomach. Epple stood beside him, jaws agape and rookie Sinclair was already choking up vomit in a nearby corner.

The victim was between the ages of 18 and 25, stripped bare of all clothing, with deep cuts to her left cheek, arms, and legs. Her right breast had been viciously severed by a sharp instrument and a deep gash across her abdomen revealed a mass of bursting entrails.

Red satin ribbons adorned her neck, wrists, and ankles, possibly a calling card or just part of the once pretty girl's ensemble and the only possible identifier was a newly inked tattoo above her left pelvic bone — *Daddy's Girl.*

With twenty-five years on the force, Branigan had seen his share of gruesome murders but this was the most savage. He shook his head hoping to regain composure. Retirement couldn't come soon enough, he only needed to make it another thirty days.

The broken body of the victim was carefully lifted revealing a blood-soaked royal blue dress, and a pair of silver stilettos. A coin purse was also retrieved, slithered down between the bags in a deep corner of the dumpster, empty of cash but containing an employee parking badge from the Royale Casino — a lead.

Epper shifted foot to foot, "What do you think, Sarge, could be a waitress or a dealer? Maybe she was stealing and some Mob boss had her whacked."

"Nah, not their style. They're old Mafia, they don't do body dumps. Even so, send the rookie over to the Royale. See what he can find out. Tell him to ask for Nick Rusano."

Cruel Baptism

Atlantic City, 1961

"Is the boy ready?" Don Rusano checked his watch before donning his overcoat. He did not want to be late; it was important that his entrance be observed.

"Yes, he's right here but I still don't understand why you will not be taking Dominic, he would like to see the movie too," questioned his wife.

"Mama!" Her husband raised his hand, abruptly ending the discussion. The Don had two sons, both complete opposites. He had little tolerance for Dominic, his youngest, viewing him as a whining, sniveling mama's boy cowardly hiding behind his mother's skirts. Whereas Nicky was strong, tough, never afraid to use his fists.

Tonight was a treat for Nicky alone, a father-son bonding activity to celebrate the boy's tenth birthday. Nicky had a passion for superheroes, devouring every book and comic book available, and this weekend the Empire Theater, a nostalgic venue featuring only films from the 1930s, 40s, and 50s was showing a classic film, *Superman and the Mole Men*. The Old Don was gleeful, viewing the auspicious timing as the first test of his son's loyalty. Would the boy question his father's actions, would he show emotion?

Don Angelo Rusano was a handsome figure towering over most men by several inches with a solid muscular build, piecing dark blue eyes, and hard massive fists; but it was his hair-trigger temper that caused men to quake in his presence. He ruled Atlantic City with an iron grip ensuring all profits from the city's numerous clandestine poker games, horseracing, bookmaking, loan sharking and extortion were directly channeled into the Mob's east coast coffers. Having immigrated from Sicily as a teen, he viewed America as a land of opportunity proudly displaying the red, white, and blue flag while still holding fast to his Sicilian heritage and maintaining strict adherence to the Cosa Nostra's code of conduct in both his household and his business dealings.

Young Nick stood proud whenever summoned to his father's office, listening from a shadowed corner as the Old Don conducted business, forbidden to speak, or make noise. If he obeyed the rules, he could stay. He viewed his father as kind and generous, but also a tough negotiator demanding unquestioned loyalty from his constituents. A favor granted today might need to be reciprocated in the future. Nick had also overheard his father order violent actions, which he knew to be necessary for the greater good of the family business.

#

Atlantic City was home to two burlesque theaters owned by the east coast Mafia. Burlesque was a lucrative and business was booming. Don Rusano needed more venues, and the Empire Theater was the perfect choice, located mid-city and surrounded by pawnbrokers, souvenir junk shops and custard vendors, all paying percentages to the Mob. The Porters, an old Atlantic City family, owned the Empire and even though Don Rusano had made many reasonable offers for the property, the family still refused to sell.

Don Rusano entered the Empire Theater flanked by his lieutenants, Big Julie and the Turk, plus four additional bodyguards. He introduced young Nick to Michael Porter, the theatre owner, and Aaron Goldburg, the theater's manager, insisting that he shake hands with both men. The boy found it curious that Big Julie and the Turk chose to remain in the lobby throughout the film but didn't dare question.

When the film ended, the moviegoers filtered out, happily opining, and departing. Nick observed the Turk whispering into his father's ear before their group returned to their cars. Big Julie lagged behind. All sat quietly as the lights of the parking lot and the theater marquee faded.

An additional fifteen minutes passed before Big Julie hurriedly emerged, taking his place in the front seat of their gray sedan, but still the entourage did not move. Another ten minutes passed before the theater owner and manager exited the building accompanied by two employees. Nick remained quiet, staring into the darkness, his father at his side. No one moved, no one started an engine.

Minutes later an ear-piercing boom reverberated from inside the theater, shattering the silence. Bright orange flames shot into the sky and thick black plumes of smoke rose from the roof as the ground shook beneath Nick's feet. The air quickly filled with floating red acrid cinders and he could feel the heat of the fire on his cheeks even through the tightly sealed car windows. He watched in **paralyzed horror** as the plastic marquee melted; its neon lightbulbs popping in the darkness. The massive letters curled and twisted, spiraling to the ground below, **each embodying the flailing cape of his defeated hero**. The windows and doors of the theater squealed as extreme heat buckled the exterior and glass shards rocketed into the air, blanketing the parking lot with oxygen robbing clouds of thickening smoke.

Nick gulped down the rising ball in his throat, plunging his balled fists deeper into his pockets and pushing back his tears. He would not cry, he refused to cry. Tears symbolized weakness and his father detested weakness.

The Old Don observed his son, but young Nick only stared straight ahead, never blinking an eye. "Did you enjoy the movie, Son?"

"Yes, sir," he replied unflinching, his eyes transfixed by the horror.

The Old Don nodded, signaling the driver to start the car, but as they slowly pulled away, he lowered his car window making a special point of tipping his hat to Michael Porter.

No one was injured in the fire, the cause of which was undetermined. Don Rusano bought the property the following month. The building was gutted, and a new theater was built in time for the upcoming season.

But for young Nick that outcome bore no victory and he struggled with his conscience while trying to justify his father's actions. Evil had triumphed over good and night after night he was tortured with dreams of towering flames, shattering glass, and melting marquee letters. There was no one to comfort him, there never had been. He would battle his nightmares alone.

Seeking His Father's Approval

Nick Rosano leaned against the wall of the White House Sub Shop, vigilantly scanning the street for unfamiliar faces or vehicles. This was his assigned turf, serving as lookout each day after school while earning a few dollars to supplement his pinball addiction. Tall with black hair, dark blue eyes, and rolled shirt sleeves accentuating his already muscled biceps, he was the neighborhood tough guy.

His focus today was the entrance to Vic's Corner Candy Store, ensuring that no overzealous feds dropped in on Vic's back-room poker game. The local cops were never a problem, his father paid them to turn a blind eye. It was the pretty boy feds in their shiny suits that worried him— always looking to get their name in the paper, always hoping for that big bust.

"Nick, Nick, help me!"

He turned toward the scream, watching his younger brother barreling toward him–shirt untucked, tie askew, papers flying from his open bookbag – with four neighborhood boys in hot pursuit.

"Whoa, whoa," halting Dominic's progress. "What's this about?"

"He stole my Mickey Mantle baseball card," screeched a breathless Butchie Genova as the pursuers abruptly pulled up.

"Did not," Dominic blurted out. "I didn't steal your stinkin' baseball card. Mickey Mantle is a loser anyway. No one wants his stupid, old card."

"He did too, Joey saw him," yelled Butchie.

Nick turned to his younger brother, "Did you take his card?"

"No, Nick, honest, I swear to the Blessed Virgin, I didn't take his card," he answered, sidling closer to his brother.

Nick turned back to the accusers. "He says he didn't take it, now get lost."

The boys continued to protest until Nick raised his fist punching Butchie square in the nose. "I said beat it!"

All four fear-filled boys quickly turned, tripping over each other, and retreating in the opposite direction. Butchie's loud sobs could be heard throughout the block, his hurried exodus leaving a trail of blood from his dripping nose onto the pavement.

Just then Vic came hurrying across the street, tossing Dominic a roll of comic books, and a bag of penny candy, "Here, kid, enjoy."

Reaching for Nick's hand, he stealthily pressed a folded $20 bill into his palm for today's services and a sealed envelope, "For your father." A silent nod passed between them. The envelope would contain the weekly percentage of Vic's numbers racket, bookmaking, and afternoon card games. "Listen kid, I got a whale coming in from New York Saturday, game will probably go all night. You up for that?"

"Yes, sir."

"Good boy!" Slapping Nick on the shoulder, he retreated back across the street chuckling to himself. *The Don's son just called me sir. In a couple years I'll be calling him sir.*

"Can I see the whale?" Dominic innocently asked.

"It's not that kind of whale, silly; a whale's a high roller, lots of money. Now go home, tell mom I'll be late."

Nick knew he would remain at his post for another few hours. A second, more lucrative game was occurring simultaneously above Connie's, the bar opposite Vic's. Things were calm so far, no one had come crashing through the third-floor window at least, unlike last week.

He watched his baby brother skipping gleefully toward home as the hairs on the back of his neck alerted him to danger. The usual din of the busy street quieted. Something was happening. He spotted the unmarked black **Ford Fairlane turn onto** Arctic Ave. **two blocks away,** slowly cruising in his direction. THE FEDS! He vaulted inside the foyer of the sub shop, grabbing the counter phone. Two rings and hang up, that was the signal. Within seconds, four harried men rushed out the side door of Connie's, disheveled, hats in hands all heading in different directions.

Nick returned to his spot, just as three overzealous FBI agents jumped from their vehicle to carry out the raid on the now empty upstairs room. Outsmarted, disappointed, defeated within minutes.

Agent Mazur stood with arms akimbo, blocking the entrance as his underlings piled out empty handed. He scanned the passing pedestrians before crossing the street to confront Nick.

"You tip them off, kid?"

"Don't know what you mean, Agent Mazur," unable to mask his sarcasm.

"You're Angelo Rusano's kid, aren't you?"

"I'm just an innocent citizen waiting for my pal. We're gonna split half a regular inside. You know how it is, White House Subs are so stuffed with meat, you can't wrap your mouth around a whole one. Your wife don't have that problem though, does she? I mean wrapping her mouth around that much meat," defiantly taunting Mazur.

"For a 14y/o, you got a filthy mouth, kid."

"Yeah well, I *was* with your sister last night."

Mazur's face turned purple as he lunged forward, "Why you little…."

"Hey Nick, your sub's ready."

"Thanks Moe, be right in," Nick replied, grinning up at the hapless agent.

"Mark my words kid, someday I'm going to put your father behind bars and you with him."

#

That night both boys lay in their beds, laughing and sharing the comic books. Dominic reached under his pillow, winked at Nick, and proudly retrieved the Mickey Mantle baseball card.

"Is that Butchie's card?" Nick asked, eyes wide in disbelief.

"Yeah, how 'bout it?" smirked Dominic.

"What 'cha go and do a thing like that for? Why'd ya lie?" Nick shook his head, unable to comprehend his brother's blatant disregard for the truth. "Don't you know, your word is your bond?"

Dominic only rolled over.

High Hopes

Running from threatening creditors and mounting debt, Steve Sullivan arrived in Atlantic City hoping for a fresh start. The Brooklyn electrician moved his family into a small row house on California Avenue. Plans for a new luxury hotel had been announced in the Atlantic City Press, the city's newspaper, instructing interested parties to submit bids to the city's planning committee. Steve was naive, unaware that his bid would never even be considered. Publishing the notice was simply a legality.

The project manager, George Montgomery, was also new to the city, new and stupid; not understanding the politics of this booming town. Steve Sullivan's bid for the work came in sizably lower than the local union bid. Montgomery pressured the committee to accept Sullivan's offer thinking it only logical and unaware of the futility. Contracts were signed. *Big mistake.*

On the first day of construction, Sullivan's men were met by a thirty-member union picket line. Twelve crossed the line, returning to flat tires and broken windshields. The next day, only four dared cross, and on the third day, not one of Sullivan's employees reported for work.

Don Rusano sat in his office fully aware of the Montgomery/Sullivan situation. He spoke to his underboss, "This needs to be resolved tonight. Give the job to Rudy… but have him take Nicky along. First time out, let's test the kid's balls."

Young Nick was summoned to his father's office, escorted by Rudy Becks, one of his father's capos. Becks stood 6'4", with massive shoulders and chest, and a jagged four-inch scar on the left side of his ham hock neck from a long-ago knife fight. Rudy explained the plan.

The Old Don then asked, "Do you understand, Son, that this is business?"

Nick nodded.

"Good enough," his father replied.

#

Rudy drove with a stone-faced Nick at his side. "You know what to do, right, kid?" he asked, looking at the teen. "You'll be okay, just do it exactly like I showed you."

Nick nodded, stoic eyes staring straight ahead, showing no emotion.

As dusk fell upon the city on a cold April night a young Nick Rusano, a mere high school sophomore, tossed a Molotov cocktail into a beat-up 1962 station wagon belonging to the Sullivan family outside their California Avenue home. The vehicle was quickly engulfed in bright orange flames, destroying it along with two neighboring cars within minutes.

Rudy and Nick witnessed the tragic scene unfold from across the street. Ensuring that the message was adequately received, Rudy nodded to Steve Sullivan as he rushed onto his front porch holding a wailing toddler in his arms. No one was hurt but the following week the defeated Sullivan family returned to Brooklyn. George Montgomery also left town, replaced by a Mob friendly project manager that knew how to play by the rules. The local electrical union was awarded the contract.

Determined to please his father, young Nick completed his assignment quickly feeling no remorse and fueled by the enormous pride he saw reflected in the old man's eyes., He vowed to harden his heart against even the slightest hint of compassion.

His broadening tough guy reputation circulated quickly throughout the neighborhood and a small group of teens: Enzio, Little Paulie, Petey, Rico, Benny and Freddy Zee became his eager enforcers. He had been resolving disputes in the neighborhood for years, preferring negotiation of course, but when that didn't work, his fists served the purpose.

Following the flawless firebombing, Don Rusano decided that he should be given more responsibilities. *Time to bring the boy into the family business.* He assigned his son to protection extortion. Nick would visit the local mom and pop stores throughout the city collecting their weekly payments along with a percentage of the profits.

This newfound power exhilarated him, delighting in the fear of his victims. The proprietors didn't want trouble, nor did they want to suffer the wrath of the young mafioso. They easily fell in line avoiding any disruption to their businesses. Broken windows were costly, broken bodies even more so. The Old Don sat back happily observing his son's penchant for violence. He planned on increasing the boy's responsibilities in the future.

The Laundry

Nick entered his father's office, trepidation causing his heart to race. This was the first time he was requesting his father's intervention. The self-confident seventeen-year-old had been part of his father's crew for the past two years; accompanying his father's capos on several jobs, fulfilling his role without question. The Old Don was proud; the boy performed well.

"Dad, I need your advice."

His father sat behind his desk, his consigliere and several of his men surrounding him.

"Son?"

"Dad, you know my friend Bennie Bianchi, right?"

"I do, is the boy in some type of trouble?"

"No, nothing like that. Let me tell 'ya. Bennie is dating a girl, Emma, from Pitney Village. Her mom works at the sewing factory on Arkansas Avenue. Bennie's girl is fourteen and she took a job to help her mother with the bills."

"Go on."

"Well, this man she works for, this Cork Deamhan, he's a real pig. He owns this junk shop on the boardwalk. This Deamhan guy, he's old and he preys on young girls, 14-year-olds like Bennie's girl. This guy is always touching them, coming up behind them and rubbing himself against them. You know what I mean, Dad? He catches them in the basement and touches their breasts and stuff, tries to kiss them. It's disgusting!"

His father interrupted, "Bennie's friend, where is her father?"

"He's dead, Dad. Hit by a car a couple years back. That's the thing, this old guy likes to hire girls that don't have fathers, no one to fight for them."

His father nodded. "Why doesn't she go work somewhere else?"

"She's tried but places tell her she's underage, something about child labor laws."

The Old Don raised his hand to silence his son, eyebrow cocked, his glare intense. He stood slowly, both hands on the desk, then turned his back to stare out the window as the others waited in silence. When finally he turned back to them, he asked, "How would you handle this, Son?"

"I don't know, Dad. That's why I came to you. This old guy needs more than just a roughing up, but I wanted to talk it over with you before I did anything."

His father nodded, "You know we don't get involved with these boardwalk grifters. They peddle their cheap trinkets and tee shirts to unsuspecting tourists down for the day. They are not our people; we stay out of their business."

"But Dad, this guy is a pig! We can't let a piece of scum like that keep doing what he's doing."

His father raised his hand again, summoning his son to silence. "Let me look into this, do nothing."

#

Three days passed before Nick was summoned by Big Julie, his father's most trusted enforcer. Julie was a giant of a man with a jagged scar across his 23" neck from a failed garroting attempt. He was said to have killed a man with his bare hands in his last boxing bout before retiring from the ring.

"Come with me kid, we got a job to do."

Nick followed Julie to the car, surprised to see Bennie in the back seat alongside the Turk, his father's second in command.

They drove uptown toward the jetties weaving through a series of dimly lit streets filled with dilapidated houses and vacant factories on the north side of town. No one spoke. Bennie's eyes were wide as saucers, but Nick remained quiet, staring straight ahead.

Big Julie turned down an alley alongside an abandoned brick building with boarded up windows. "This one's for you, kid," he beamed, looking at Bennie through the rear-view mirror.

The Turk unlocked a side door, releasing the smell of rotting meat and death that immediately assaulted their nostrils. A dozen crackling florescent fixtures flickered eerily from the ceiling above, each casting moving shadows across the gloomy warehouse. Several carcasses of decomposing cats littered the concrete floor and rats scurried nervously into corners, their shiny eyes peeking out through the darkness. Bennie's nerves were jumping but Nick had full trust in his father's men. Big Julie was like an uncle to him.

A rusted metal folding chair sat in the middle of the dank room. Its occupant securely tied to the back with metal straps; head covered by a bloody burlap hood. The moaning figure was slouched forward; the floor beneath covered with a mixture of blood, vomit, and urine causing a putrid stench to envelope the occupant.

The Turk ripped off the hood, grabbing the victim by the back of his hair and forcing him to face his torturers through swollen eyes. The man had been savagely beaten; his face distorted by fractured orbital bones, a broken nose and misaligned jaw.

"Say your name," the Turk bellowed.

"Cork… De…," his reply barely audible, blood spluttering through broken teeth.

"Again," the Turk roared, this time louder.

"Cork, Cork Deam…."

Big Julie smirked, stepping forward, his voice melodic. "We understand you like little girls, Cork Deamhan. Now is that nice? You must have a tiny cock if you like little girls. Either that or you can't get it hard enough for women your own age. Can't please the ladies so you go after little girls? Which is it, huh, little man?"

Turning his attention to Bennie and Nick, Big Julie continued, "What do you think boys shall we take a look at this scum bag's cock?"

Deamhan's entire body quaked as Julie approached with a 10" blade and swiftly cut away the trembling man's pants revealing a tiny, shriveled penis and even smaller testicles.

Big Julie released a loud, echoing belly laugh. "Should have been a girl," he screeched, as everyone joined in laughing while staring at the pitiful sight. Everyone that is, except Cork Deamhan.

"Enough!" Julie boomed, raising his hand and halting the laughter. "Time for business. You two, front and center," he ordered, pointing to Nick and Bennie. "Pick up that car battery and put it right about here," directing the boys to a spot on the floor. "Good, now I want to introduce you both to one of my favorite little toys. Step over here." Hoisting a leather case onto a nearby table, he grinned proudly ceremoniously undoing the zipper and revealing the deadly contents within. "Ahh, my beauty," he drooled, his eyes overflowing with admiration. Both boys watched in awe as he reverently lifted the ominous device, cradling it in his beefy hands then lovingly stroking the barrel before planting a wet, sloppy kiss on its protruding wires.

"This, boys, is what we call a picana." Big Julie held up the long metal rod similar to a cattle prod. "We are going to attach this lovely darling to this here car battery and then to the stinkin' balls of this scum bag, if we can find them," he chuckled. "Then, my fine, young apprentices, the fireworks will begin... so to speak." Julie shot a knowing wink to Bennie. "This here car battery has enough juice in it to shock this sucker's balls into infinity and you, my friend, will get to do the honors since this is about your girl and all." Bowing with a flourish, he placed the picana in Bennie's hands. Droplets of sweat rained down onto the floor as Deamhan gulped for air, fighting to escape his restraints.

The Turk quickly stepped forward releasing a sadistic laugh that echoed against the walls before assisting Bennie to affix the rod to Cork Deamhan's shriveled testicles. Julie then directed Nick to attach the connecting wires to the car battery and, within seconds, Deamhan's head jerked back in torment as he released a horrendous tortured scream. The purple cords on his neck bulged, grossly stretching the skin; the sclera of his blood reddened eyes rolled back in his head, and his entire body violently shook as his fractured fists futilely gripped the chair. His body convulsed in rapid succession, foaming blood poured from his eyes, ears, and mouth, and the air filled with the putrid stench of burning flesh.

The four men stood back watching the gruesome spectacle before Big Julie turned to Bennie, "That'll keep the chump busy for a while. You satisfied kid?" Bennie nodded in agreement, smiling broadly before sending a wad of spit at Deamhan's blood-soaked face.

"Great, let's get out of here. Wet work always makes me hungry, I'm starving," announced Big Julie. "How 'bout we stop by White House Subs for dinner, best subs in town?"

Archer

Following high school graduation, Nick Rusano pursued a degree in economics from Princeton University and joined its prestigious champion crew team. Tall with dark blue eyes, the facial features of Adonis, jet black hair, and a wide hard chest, he easily honed his reputation as a ladies' man and educated himself in the ways of the upper class.

Archer Macland hailed from Brownsville, a poverty-stricken, crime laden area of Brooklyn, NY. He was a ward of the state, raised in foster care from the age of five and was attending Princeton on full merit scholarship. He and Nick were dorm mates, both rowing on the same crew squad. They worked hard, they played hard, and they developed a strong bond that would last a lifetime.

Knowing that Archer would remain on campus during semester breaks and holidays, Nick insisted he accompany him home to Atlantic City where he quickly became aware of the inner workings of the family business. The Don viewed Archer as a levelheaded young man that could bring balance to his reckless playboy son. He encouraged Archer to pursue a law degree and promised him a lifetime of lucrative employment serving the Rusano family.

Rise to Power

The leaders of the major crime families meet in one of several cities throughout the country every five years. This has been an established practice since the days of Charles "Lucky" Luciano when the renowned Commission was first formed in 1931. Members of the east coast Mafia attend along with various other branches throughout the country. The purpose of the meeting is to resolve disputes among the members, reorganize territories when needed, and to strategize means of increasing earnings for the families. Currently there was turmoil within the Philadelphia organization and equal upheaval was simultaneously occurring in the New York syndicate.

Angelo Rusano had proven himself in Atlantic City, running the town like a tightly wound clock, allowing for no nonsense. Money flowed uninterrupted. Nick worked alongside his father, now fully immersed in the business since his graduation from Princeton. Serving as one of his father's most effective enforcers, he had an appetite for violence, resolving issues quickly and efficiently.

The suggestion was made that Don Rusano take control of Philadelphia or New York, perhaps both, to enforce stricter control. But it was decided that he would instead supervise Mafia interests on the west coast where his violent management skills could be better utilized.

The political climate across the country was changing and the Mob sat in its crosshairs due to the blatant greed of a few Las Vegas casino owners. The Mafia's control of the town was weakening, replaced by flashy corporations and criminal groups from Asia, Russia, and Eastern Europe. But the Commission had a dilemma, they had purchased a massive property on the Vegas strip and they were not about to be deterred. Management of the newly built Royale Resort would now fall to the Rusano family. A straw company would be established and figure heads would be put into place. Archer Macland, a man with no criminal background, would serve as CEO but the man pulling the strings would be Nick Rusano.

Archer had returned to the Rusano family following his graduation from Harvard Law School. His loyalty to Nick remained steadfast, their bond growing stronger with each passing year. He would serve as Nick's consigliere when the Old Don passed. He married Daniella, a highly intelligent, strong-willed graduate of one of Philadelphia's exclusive female colleges. Having overcome the gender bias of Harvard Medical School, Daniella was now a respected physician at Sunrise Medical Center, specializing in the otherwise male dominated field of cardiology. She also managed the Rusano family's medical needs, being available 24/7.

Ten years passed with the Rusano management of the west coast proving to be both successful and efficient. Profits poured in; the Commission had made the right decision.

The Queen of Hearts

Details of the new assignment were rather odd, but she eagerly signed the contract. *Who wouldn't grab a chance to spend 90 days in Las Vegas?* She had just completed an exhausting two-month assignment in New Mexico fraught with too much illness, despair, and poverty. She needed some R&R, Vegas sounded perfect. She did, however, wonder about the unusual circumstances of this contract. The agency was adamant; Alaina must agree never to disclose the name of the patient nor his physical condition. If she did, she would be immediately terminated from this and all future assignments. She was told only that the patient was an older gentleman recovering from cardiac surgery.

Alaina McGovern was a green-eyed Irish beauty with long, wavy brunette hair and a sprinkling of freckles. She relished the nomadic lifestyle. Working as a traveling nurse for the past two years fed her independent streak allowing her to jog every day through crowded streets and isolated roads of each new city while mentally cataloging the sights and sounds of its people.

But today she questioned her recklessness staring up into the hardened face of a Goliath holding her credentials hostage in his mammoth hands. *What have you gotten me into, Cora?* The house was a fortress hidden behind twenty-foot stone walls with armed security manning the ten-foot wrought iron gate. Additional armed men were stationed along the one-hundred-foot stone driveway. A cold chill ran down her spine as she reached for the bell at the servants' entrance seeing visions of Jane Eyre waving a foreboding finger.

Angelo Rusano, a 50-year-old Sicilian gentleman had undergone open heart surgery five days earlier and had been discharged from the hospital after a shortened stay by request of the family. The early release was unusual. The family had contracted round the clock nursing coverage. His personal physician, Dr. Daniella Macland, visited daily allowing for the best concierge care money could buy.

Alaina was assigned the 3-11 pm shift, six days a week. Her duties were simple: care for his surgical site, monitor his vital signs, administer his medications, immediately report any signs of distress or infection, and make him as comfortable as possible.

Mr. Rusano was noticeably quiet at first, saying little. He did, however, ask several pointed questions about Alaina's family, experience, and employment history; never replying to her answers, only nodding. He grew friendlier as the days passed and his strength increased, often watching as she moved about her duties and chuckling as she transferred him from bed to chair, his large mass towering over her. When she pushed him to increase his daily steps, he huffed and puffed but inwardly smiled through his empty complaints. They soon fell into a routine playing a daily chess or checkers game and watching television then ending each evening with Alaina reading from a novel she had toted along, allowing him to drift into a peaceful sleep.

Mrs. Rusano also warmed to Alaina, delivering tea each evening. The Rusanos had a son, Nick, who visited his father daily. The two men frequently discussed business matters, conversing in Sicilian and during those times Alaina was politely asked to leave the room.

Nick Rusano was tall and handsome with dark hair, a Las Vegas tan, a broad toned chest, and penetrating blue eyes that a girl could easily fall into. His excellent physical condition was proof of his dedicated daily workout. The bulge of a shoulder holster ominously protruded under his suit jacket. He was always friendly, self-assured, and charming— a little too charming— but Alaina liked him.

Each day he consulted her about his father's progress, leaning in close so as not to disturb the old man's slumber. His hand would rest on her arm, her back, her waist until one day he gently leaned in and kissed her lips. Those blue eyes melted through hers and she quickly turned away in embarrassment, but his touch was electric sending vibrations to areas of her body that had been asleep far too long. She craved his kiss, desired his touch but at what price? She needed to maintain a professional relationship with the son of her patient. *Nick Rusano is a dangerous man.*

Despite that, she looked forward to his visits, their bodies growing closer, kisses more emboldened. She shivered wantonly as his fingers caressed her neck, her cheeks, her hair.

Hello Dominic

Nick barreled up the stairs toward his father's room but stopped short seeing his brother, Dominic, leaning on the door frame. Alaina was preparing his father's medications, her back to them both, unaware of their presence.

Chuckling, he quietly whispered, "No, no, little brother. *That* is mine, let me show you." Approaching Alaina, he slipped his arm around her waist, and leaned in close, "Hello, beautiful. Want to be my nurse tonight?"

Alaina laughed, looking into his soulful eyes, "Only if I can put you in traction."

"Hmm, sounds kinky," he laughed, pecking her on the forehead and sighing, "but unfortunately, I need to go to work. I'll check in later, gorgeous." Triumphantly he turned to face the door, finding Dominic already gone.

\#

Nick smirked as he drove down Las Vegas Boulevard. Girls were so easy, especially girls that didn't work in the business: nurses, waitresses, salesclerks. A fancy dinner, some empty words and they fell right into bed. He enjoyed the game. Love them and leave them. His bed was never empty. There was only one problem, girls like that had little experience, never knowing how to correctly position their mouths or their hands. He needed to stick with girls that worked for him. They were no innocent flowers, and they certainly appreciated his talents. Sicilian men had huge cocks and his was bigger than most.

#

Later that evening, Alaina lowered the lights so that her reading didn't disturb her sleeping patient. Dominic appeared in the doorway, crossing the room, and kneeling beside her. "Hello. Alaina, right? Mama sent me with your tea. I'm Dom, Dominic Rusano, Nick's brother."

"Oh, I didn't know Nick had a brother."

"Yeah, I'm the handsome one," he grinned.

Dominic was shorter than Nick, not as good looking but with the same dark blue penetrating eyes and a small scar on the left side of his chin.

"Huuuh," the Old Don tossed fitfully, murmuring incoherently, balled fists in the air fighting an unseen assailant.

"Shh," warned Alaina, putting her fingers to her lips, before rushing to quiet him.

Dom nodded, giving her a wink before leaving.

The Date

Calm down, girl, calm down; but Alaina was too excited, feeling like a teenager on her first date. Nick Rusano had asked her to dinner at the Adventura, the Royale's finest gourmet restaurant. She twirled in front of the mirror admiring her image in the sleek blue dress. *Perfect!*

Nick was not only handsome, funny, and charming, but his simple touch sent her imagination spinning into overdrive. She longed for his caress, for his body next to hers. *What was it you always said, Mama? 'Never fall for a man that's prettier than you?' Well, he sure is that!*

He sent a car at nine and when she descended the escalator onto the casino floor, there stood Apollo in black tux and tie, ripped right from the pages of GQ; his eyes making her melt, his smile caressing her soul.

The maître'd greeted them warmly, steering them to a secluded dimly lit alcove overlooking a manmade waterfall, its mist dancing upon the air of the shimmering pool below. Alaina scanned the room, admiring the sparkling crystal chandeliers, and art deco sculptures filling every corner and reflecting off the black and silver mirrored walls. Puccini's *O Soave Fanciulla* added soothing sounds to the ambiance.

"So, tell me about this traveling nurse thing," Nick began as his fingers gently stroked her wrist sending her nerves into overdrive. "I don't understand it."

"It's simple really. I work for an agency that supplies nurses all across the country. We're sent wherever there is a temporary need, as in your father's case, or wherever a replacement is required by law." Seeing his intense glare, she continued, "it boils down to a numbers game. Hospitals today are severely short staffed because fewer people are enrolling in nursing schools. Federal regulations require a set ratio of nurse to patient but while those regulations look good on paper, they are impossible to enforce. Traveling nurses fill the gap; we are in high demand, but we are only a band-aid to an ever-growing problem. I could work every day, double shifts if I chose to; that's how bad the situation is. The company I work for keeps us moving. I've never been unemployed."

"I was unaware there was such a problem."

"It's decades old, seemingly unfixable."

"Your travel must be hard on your family."

"I have no family," she stated bluntly.

Nick's eyebrows shot up, questioning.

"My mother died; I never knew my father, no siblings, just me. It's a perfect career for someone with no obligations. I get to see the country, and eventually I'll know where I want to settle. In addition to taking care of your dad, I also pick up extra shifts at Sunrise. I like to stay busy. I don't like to be alone, especially at night."

Again, Nick's eyebrows shot up as he burst into laughter.

"Oh, geez, I didn't mean it like that," she sputtered. "Oh dear, um… sometimes I not only put my foot in my mouth, I swallow my whole leg," she appealed, stumbling. Scorching heat quickly traveled from her shoulders to forehead, painting her face bright red.

Nick attempted to stifle his laughter while continuing to stroke her wrist. "Tell me more, where were you before Vegas?"

Inhaling deeply, she tried not to sound the fool again. "Before Vegas, I worked a sixty-day maternity assignment in New Mexico, and before that, three months on a critical care unit in Compton. Vegas… is my perk for Compton."

"Your perk?"

"Yes, my perk. The company I work for prioritizes the wellbeing of their nurses which, in turn, benefits their retention. Each assignment is rated for its level of stress or hazard. If I accept an assignment in a hazard zone for instance, they guarantee me a future perk; something more relaxing. Your dad is a cushy assignment, not much to do for him. Vegas is my perk, fun in the sun. But… sometimes even a perk is not as enjoyable as one might think."

"Really… interesting. Explain."

"Well, once a client requested a private nurse for his wife. She was a brittle diabetic who required constant monitoring. They were cruising to St. Lucia on their *seventy-five-foot yacht*. Turns out she was a first-class bitch. Oops… sorry. She didn't want to be within two feet of her husband. Just proves money doesn't buy happiness," pausing she added, "but my saddest assignment was during last year's Super Bowl. A nice older gentleman, sweet as can be, requested a nurse as more or less a companion."

Nick raised his eyebrows again, enjoying the faux pas.

"No, no, not that type of companion! Nick, you're not helping. Anyway, the patient was recovering from spinal surgery and needed a nurse to accompany him. We traveled to Tampa in his private jet and watched the game from his VIP box. Very swank. He was a perfect gentleman, but it was sad. Imagine having all that and no one to share it with."

"I've been to some beautiful places, too," she continued. "Colorado is breathtaking but doesn't compare to the beauty of the Northern California mountains. It is so peaceful there; a person could lose themselves among those tall, majestic trees. I ran every morning and sometimes I would just sit under the trees for hours, lost in thought. Alaska is also stunning, but I could never live there. That was the only assignment that ever frightened me, not a good place for a single woman."

"Alaska attracts many different types of people, some looking to disappear," Nick inserted.

"Yes," she replied, diverting her eyes.

He noted her discomfort and changed direction. He would probe Alaska later. "Did you always want to be a nurse?"

"It was my dream. I was that typical little girl playing dress up in my white uniform and cap, plastic stethoscope around my neck, even had an old-fashioned blue cape passed down from a great-aunt. I put band aids on my teddy bears, headwraps on my stuffed animals. Had a make-shift ambulance crate, too. My poor cocker spaniel suffered endlessly as I rushed him back and forth to my pretend operating room." She paused as he laughed at her tale before continuing. "And what about your childhood aspirations, did you always dream of Las Vegas lights?"

He scoffed, "No, no. I dreamt of being a Superhero!"

"Superhero? No, really?"

"Yep, saving the world from dastardly evil villains, cape and all."

The conversation was easy, relaxing, his eyes never left hers even as the sommelier poured the wine; but he shared little about himself, always turning the conversation back to her.

"Mr. Rusano, excuse me." A sinister looking gentleman with a cold, tight-lipped expression interrupted them, leaning down, and whispering in Nick's ear. Alaina spotted a shoulder holster as he bent forward, his gray suit straining to conceal the weapon.

"Excuse me, honey," Nick turned, briefly touching her arm, and sending chills down her spine. He stepped away and both men spoke head-to-head.

The easy calm of the previous few minutes vanished as a much more serious Nick returned to the table. "Sweetheart, I must take care of something. I apologize. I'll send you home in a car."

"Really? I've never been stood up *before* the meal came."

"Hon, it's not like that, this can't be helped. It's *business*," he said, looking coldly into her eyes before quickly departing with the interloper.

Within minutes, a spry older gentleman approached. "Come with me, Miss, I will see you home." The return ride was silent but when they arrived, the driver insisted on taking her to the door and checking the interior, "Orders, Miss."

#

Penthouse suite, Royale Casino

"What the FUCK, Junior!" Nick roared.

Junior McCain was the reigning middleweight champion in town to defend his title in a multimillion-dollar fight in the Royale's arena Friday night. He had arrived three days earlier with full entourage and had been partying in the top floor penthouse from day one.

Boxing is highly profitable for any casino and the McCain/ Lewis bout was the biggest event of the year. Wagers were pouring in by the minute; the betting boards couldn't keep up.

Nick surveyed the area. The room was trashed: used condoms, cocaine lines, drug paraphernalia, toppled liquor bottles, and miscellaneous clothing lay everywhere. A dozen girls in various stages of undress stood off to the side, barred from leaving by a hotel heavyweight blocking the door. Five of Junior's cronies paced the floor, stealthily eyeing each other, and trying unsuccessfully to distance themselves from the gruesome scene.

Sprawled across the silver carpet in the middle of the room, lay the twisted nude body of a young blond female, her wrists and ankles bound by leather straps. White tinged vomit trailed from her mouth; an area of dark red blood pooled beneath her skull; and an ugly purple gash crept above her right eye, possibly from being struck by a heavy object. Obviously, this was a night gone terribly wrong.

It was customary for the Royale to supply (entertainment) girls to high rollers on request. Several were employed for just that purpose. This one Nick didn't recognize. She was too young.

Junior sat dazed, his voice barely audible. "I, I don't know. I don't know what happened," he stammered, bloodshot eyes pleading with Nick. "I don't even remember her... ugly bitch! One minute, we were all partying, the rest... I don't remember. I must have passed out."

Nick knew the situation had to be quickly contained. The police couldn't be involved and, most importantly, Junior had to be ready to fight. The money must continue to flow uninterrupted. He turned to one of his men, instructing him to escort the girls to the gray room, a private interrogation area in the basement level of the casino. "Make sure no one leaves." Each would need to be interviewed, threatened, and paid off for their silence. He then had to handle the coked-out entourage and, of course, Junior. The body would also need to be disposed of. That was the easy part. After all, this was Vegas. No one would miss another party girl; people disappeared every day. Finally, the rooms had to be scoured.

#

By 6am, he was finally on his way home for some much-needed sleep. Junior would fight tonight, and he and his buddies would be on a plane out of town as quickly as could be arranged. Couldn't come soon enough. Junior would win the fight, of course. The fix was in weeks ago.

As he passed his father's bedroom the Old Don called out, "Everything okay, did you have a good night?"

He would brief his father later, months from now, maybe never. "Yep, no problem, Dad. Just another night. I'm gonna grab some sleep."

Yep, just another night in paradise he thought, as his head hit the pillow.

Negotiation

Nick entered his father's sick room the following afternoon, noticing Alaina reading quietly to her dozing patient. "Hey, I owe you dinner," he whispered in her ear, warm breath making her pulse race.

"No, it's ok." She pursed her lips, not wanting a repeat of the previous night's humiliation.

"No, it's not ok. How about tonight?"

She turned, looking between both men, palms up.

"Next Thursday then? You're off on Thursdays, right?"

"Really, it's ok."

"Alaina, please. What happened last night couldn't be avoided." Taking her hand in his, he raised it to his lips, his pleading stare causing her resolve to falter.

"Um… all right," she relented cautiously, "if you're sure." She knew she was falling deep but drowning in his eyes might be a pleasant death. "But I'm a traveling nurse, I only have one dress and you've seen it."

His eyes twinkled with laughter, "I'll buy you a dress."

"You certainly will not," she replied indignantly. "What kind of girl do you take me for?"

He quickly stifled his laughter trying not to wake his father as he evaluated her reply. *Other girls would have jumped at my offer.*

"All right, I know a little Italian place, casual, great lasagna."

"Okay… sure, sounds nice," she nodded, looking up into his eyes.

With that, he bent, wrapping her in his arms and kissing her full and hard on the mouth, tongue probing. His release was slow, his eyes never leaving hers. His fingers rose to gently stroke her temples, and with one final kiss on her forehead, he was gone.

She sighed, watching his taillights fade away, still feeling the warmth of his lips. "Last thing I need is some arrogant Romeo with a gun strapped to his shoulder. Better run, girl," she murmured as the Old Don snored.

The Touch

Mario's Italian Restaurant was a small, remote hideaway known only to the locals, just ten minutes from the Strip. Crystal wine glasses, flickering tall black tapers, and starched white tablecloths adorned the dimly lit dining room. A fresco of Trevi Fountain adorned one wall while another was covered floor-to-ceiling with upscale wine bottles sheltered in a temperature-controlled glass case. Tonight, a scant handful of couples sat head-to-head languishing in the intimate atmosphere.

"Mr. Nick, welcome!" A short, rotund gentleman with a broad smile and open arms ambled toward them. "No, Mr. Archer tonight?" he questioned, looking beyond them.

"Not tonight, Mario, but let me introduce my companion for the evening, Alaina McGovern."

"Ah, bellissimo, bellissimo, lovely." Mario kissed his fingers in approval, smiling his satisfaction.

"Yes, you may be seeing more of her, she has no clothes," Nick replied with a devilish grin.

"NICK, OOOH!"

Mario looked quizzically between the two, confused by the exchange.

"Something in the back, Mario, quiet," Nick directed as the little man escorted them to a darkened secluded corner.

Alaina surveyed the room. "The furniture is very unusual. Is this a wine barrel?" she exclaimed, running her hand across the curved wood.

"Yes, it is. Mario appropriately calls this the barrel room. He designed the furnishings himself from refurbished barrels purchased from Napa vineyards. They're solid oak. We are actually sitting in a barrel that's been cut in half. Beautiful, aren't they?"

"Oh, yes. So unique, how innovative! I must compliment him before we leave."

He beckoned Mario, allowing Alaina to fuss and ask questions. The little man flushed with pride, strutting about the dining room like a peacock for the remainder of the evening. She had received his approval.

Nick ordered a bottle of Hundred Acre Dark Ark Cabernet Sauvignon. "Do you know anything about wine?" he inquired when the sommelier departed.

"I do, I was a bartender in college." She raised the glass, swirled its contents, and took a small sip. "This wine has wonderful long legs indicating high alcohol content; it is boldly aromatic with hints of … hmm, blackberry, I think; and it's silky tannins continue to exquisitely linger on… the tongue," she winked enticingly. Alaina also knew the bottle's value, well over one thousand dollars.

"Bravo, my lady. I compliment you on your knowledge," he replied, enjoying her play.

"A girl can learn a lot in a bar, not just about wine but about people," she continued. "A bar stool is the equivalent of a psychiatrist's couch. People pour their hearts out, tell their darkest secrets. Do you have dark secrets, Nick Rusano?"

His gaze snapped bluntly, becoming sharp, bordering on danger. "Darker than you know, angel," he replied, each word slow and menacing.

She shuddered, feeling a coldness emanating from his body, his expression frigid. Several silent seconds passed before his controlled veil chased away the ominous shadow and a lecherous grin transformed his lips, his words dripping with mockery.

"I've always found dining with a female companion to be a sensual experience. It is especially pleasurable to watch a woman wrap her lips around something she finds… delectable."

Searing heat raced through her, painting a crimson blush along her face, neck, and shoulders. He had bested her. She heard him chuckle and watched as his dark eyes softened, skillfully ensnaring her in their trap, making her his willing captive. She allowed herself to tumble into their depths, paralyzed by their spell. *Those eyes, those gorgeous eyes, eyes I could easily drown in.*

"Enough play," he murmured, having measured the naive girl's feeble attempt at fencing with a master.

His hand reached for hers across the table, and it was then that she noticed the flash of his cuff links, causing a sea of warm memories to wash over her. She gently traced the diamond initials embedded in platinum with trembling fingers.

"My grandfather wore cuff links; he owned a pair remarkably similar to these, marcasite of course, not diamonds. I've always thought cuff links to be so classy on a man." Seeing him listening intently, she continued, her voice gentle and meek. "I have such good memories of my grandfather, you see. When I was little, I would sit with him in the evening as he dressed to go out. He was so dapper, so handsome. I enjoyed watching him shave, then he would slap on his Old Spice after shave. I still love that drug store scent, smells heavenly to me. Little did I know at the time that he was cheating on my grandma and going to meet one of his lady friends," she whispered, eyes big with merriment.

Nick laughed heartily, enjoying her story. She was easy to listen to, no pretense, a quality unseen in the women he normally dated. He pressed her more about traveling about the country, the different cities she'd been to. They shared stories of their childhoods and college days, of east coast vs. west coast. They had both attended strict Catholic schools. He spoke of his humiliation when the vice principal cut his hair in the stairwell because it's length touched his collar. She told him of being sent to the *bad* table every day for giggling during prayers. They compared literary taste and culinary taste. They were both avid readers—he read crime novels; she enjoyed historical romance. He hated sushi, she loved it. They even touched on politics.

#

When they approached her front door, he held out his palm, requesting her keys and insisting on checking the house before leaving.

"Thank you for tonight, dinner was lovely."

"Thank *you* for the conversation," he replied.

"Did I talk your ears off?"

"No, not at all. My ears are still here," he grinned, playfully checking. "But regretfully, I need to get back to work. I'll call you in the morning." And with that he lifted her chin to his, softly brushing her ear with one hand, never releasing her eyes. Slowly, ever so lightly, his lips grazed hers. Heat rose between them as his fingers traced her chin and inched their way behind her neck. He gently pulled her toward him encasing her in both arms before kissing her slowly until she felt herself quiver. *Stay, please stay.* But he was already pulling away.

Concern

Call from Nick to Alaina:

Nick *"Can u meet tomorrow at 2? Want to review a few things."*
Alaina *"Sure, is everything alright?"*
Nick *"Just want to talk."*
Alaina *"Okay."*
Nick *"Good, drive past the house on the right side, first guesthouse in back. I'll make coffee."*

Nick thought about their recent interactions. She was hot and he wanted her in his bed, but she was different from his usual taste. She was genuine, honest, innocent, able to hold an intelligent conversation. She made him laugh, decreased his tension. He found himself analyzing her words, independent and self-assured at times but also vulnerable. He hadn't been able to control his laughter when she said she didn't like being alone at night and he regretted his callousness. She almost shut down at that point, but he coaxed her to continue, inserting the subject again at Mario's. She had been afraid in Alaska, creepy landlord, felt she was being watched. She stayed out as much as possible, working seven days a week, bracing a chair under the doorknob for added security when sleeping. She said he wouldn't understand because he was a man; maybe he didn't but he wanted her to feel secure. Had more happened in Alaska than she revealed? Was she still fearful? He knew she didn't live in the best of neighborhoods. It was low income, cheap housing abandoned by the military years ago. The agency should have done better.

#

Alaina drove past the main house, spotting three cozy guesthouses stealthily hidden in the tree covered alcoves. The front door sprang open as her finger reached the bell as though he were anticipating her arrival. He was clean shaven, dressed for work minus his suit jacket and tie. His rock-hard muscles stretched every fiber of his shirt, its collar still open, his body holster hanging from one shoulder, not yet buckled. His smile was almost boyish, his eyes once again imprisoning hers. Taking her hand, he invited her inside and she was swept away by the warmth of the space, *his space*.

The guesthouse was artfully decorated with dark hardwood floors covered by lush forest green carpets. Natural light filtered through the floor-to-ceiling windows of the living room's east wall and a large stone fireplace covered the opposing wall, faintly scenting the air with burnt cedar. Heavy masculine furnishings of burgundy leather, brass, and dark wood filled the room. He led her through to a bright sunny kitchen with gray marble countertops where a small table was tucked into an elevated corner, surrounded by tall bay windows overlooking a shrub filled garden of red roses and pink azaleas.

"I had no idea these houses were here, no idea you lived back here," she said.

His eyes filled with merriment, "Did you think I still lived in my boyhood bedroom at the Big House, Legos still strewn across the floor?" Playfully mocking her, he laughed, "I'll show you my collection of action figures later." Handing her a steamy cup of coffee, he joined her at the table, "black, no sugar, just the way you like it." Pausing, he measured his words, "I was thinking about something you said last night and because of that, I've decided to send a driver for you every day. The same driver will return you home and ensure your place is secure before he leaves."

"What? Oh, Nick, no, no. You don't need to do that."

Gently taking her hand, he leaned in close. "Sweetheart, I'm aware of what I *don't need* to do, it is what I *want* to do. You're taking such diligent care of my father and I want that to continue. This is my way of thanking you."

"Nick, no, really. You don't even know me," she protested.

Flashing his playboy smile, he continued. "After last night, I know you, I do. I want you to feel safe."

"Please, I'm fine; I'm sorry if you thought..."

"Shh, that's not what I thought. Believe me, I wouldn't be doing this if that's what I thought. I've already made the arrangement. I think you will like the driver; he's been with me a number of years. Name's Bobby, here's his number if you need to change dates or times. He is at your disposal, day and night, double shifts, whatever you need."

"Nick, this is really not necessary."

"End of discussion," he replied, gently squeezed her hand, "*end* of discussion."

She was unaware of his strict policy to never give a woman something she asked for. Many had tried to take advantage of his wealth, requesting outrageous gifts: BMWs, townhouses, jewelry. Their greed being their ticket goodbye. He chuckled inwardly. *This one doesn't even want a driver.*

The hour passed quickly and before long they were saying their farewells at the door. He held her more firmly, kissed her more passionately. His hands gripped her back and buttocks as the heat rose between them, and she feverishly returned his kisses. But then somewhere a clock chimed three intruding on her Cinderella moment. She needed to relieve the day nurse.

"This is no way to send me off to work," she whispered, feeling his tongue travel toward her shoulder.

"Yeah... same here." His reply was muffled, his warm mouth still lingering, unmoving. He slowly released her, reaching down to adjust himself, but his eyes never left hers. For a moment they stared at each other, hesitating.

"You better go before I throw you on the carpet," he sighed.

Fire

After Mario's, the intensity of their passion only increased, its fire burning hotter each day as they stole minutes outside his father's sick room. They both knew only one remedy would satisfy their need. Thank goodness the Old Don was a sound sleeper.

"You know we have a problem," he whispered, his lips hot against her ear. "I don't get nights off. I want this to be right, unhurried. We deserve time, *you* deserve attention."

She heard the Old Don stir and tried to break away from his embrace, but he held fast, pinning her against the wall.

"Stay with me tonight, I need you too much," he said, guiding her hand to his swollen organ. "I'll figure something out."

Again, the Don stirred, fighting off a bad dream, causing Alaina to inch closer to the door.

"Later," he whispered, his hands trailing hers as she rushed to attend the Old Don.

11pm, end of shift

"Hey lady, need a lift?" Nick sat behind the steering wheel of the gray town car; Bobby was nowhere in sight.

Alaina laughed, positioning herself on the front seat. "You don't look like Bobby, and you don't feel like him either," playfully putting her hand on his cock.

"Oh, have you been feeling Bobby?" he joked, devilish eyes dancing.

"How did you get away?"

"I didn't, called in a favor. I'm still attached to this damned beeper so let's hope for some of that Irish luck of yours." Pulling her toward him, he gently lifted her mouth to his, tracing her lips with the tip of his tongue. "I need you too much tonight, baby," he murmured, tugging at her bottom lip with his teeth. "I. Want. To taste. Every inch. Of you."

The heat of the fireplace blanketed them when they entered the guesthouse, but she knew the flame he had lit within her was already blistering hot. They stood face to face; the few inches that separated them alive with static energy. Her body cried out for him, craving his touch, igniting long suppressed desires.

His dark eyes consumed her, **reading her thoughts as his fingers grazed** her temples, hair, and the nape of her neck before lifting her face to his, and placing soft airy kisses on her forehead, eyelids, cheeks, and finally, her lips. His breath was warm, his lips gentle, barely touching, teasing, sending smoldering pulses through her entire body. Tilting her head, he ran his tongue from neck to shoulder, his velvet mouth an opiate to every nerve and muscle. She was floating on an ocean bathed in his intoxicating scent, quivering in sails of hard muscles. Could he sense her ecstasy? Could he feel her temperature rising?

"Let me look upon you, Bella," he whispered, hot breath searing her ear as he moved his hands to her shoulders and stepped away.

No, lover, no. Don't move a muscle, don't change a thing, her body screamed but the spell was broken, and she looked up seeing a pair of sultry eyes welcoming her back, their faces inches apart.

His scorching fingers skipped along her waist, lifting her shirt, and sending it floating to the floor. He moved to trace the outline of her bra, releasing her breasts into his palms, his eyes lingering. "You are beautiful, amore mio. Truly beautiful, more beautiful than I envisioned."

"You make me blush, love."

"I'll make you blush later," he teased, lips curling into a lecherous grin before leaning down to lick each nipple, each stroke titillating like a demon's tongue.

Her fingers raked through his hair, holding him in place until she was no longer able to bear the smoldering intensity. After weeks of bringing him to heel, she also knew his weak spots. Trailing her fingers down the nape of his neck in slow rotation, she heard him shudder within seconds.

"I need to touch you, love. I need to feel you," she whispered as he raised his molten eyes. Breathlessly, she slid her hands down the hard contoured muscles of his back, ridding him of his shirt before snaking her fingers upward from waist to shoulders, burrowing into his downy tree of hair from navel to pecs.

"No, beautiful, control is mine tonight," he warned, waving a warning finger before crushing her breasts to his bare chest as the heat from his body seared through her skin. His mouth devoured her, rendering her breathless with kisses deep and passionate before he dropped to his knees, masterfully disposing of her remaining clothing. Intense heat rocketed through her body feeling his fiery tongue lapping at her navel and softly sucking a path down her stomach. She gripped his shoulders then, feeling her balance slip as her knees weakened from her heightened euphoria. Cupping her buttocks, he drew her closer teasing the crest of her mound with his smoldering tongue. Then in one swift move, he rose, his eyes ablaze with passion, sweeping her off her feet and cradling her against his chest. She rested her head against his wall of massive muscles as he carried her up the stairs, heart pounding with anticipation.

"Let me worship you," he whispered, laying her onto a bed of cool silken sheets but once again she halted his motion, firmly pressing commanding palms to his chest. Had he read her wrong?

But her welcoming eyes met his, vanquishing his confusion before she looked upon his hard, tanned torso with hunger, her voice raspy with lust, "Don't rush me, love. I've longed for this moment; longed to touch you, to feel your body next to mine. Each day that desire went unsated as I watched your taillights fade down the driveway, leaving me empty."

He sighed feeling her soft palms slide across his chiseled shoulders, inspecting every inch, reveling in the firmness. Slim fingers traced his clavicles, mapping each curve, valley, and notch. Her touch felt like satin floating across the surface of his body, and he sat unmoving, mesmerized by her motion, every move a stroke of decadent admiration.

Then suddenly her facial expression changed, her gaze grew intense, her brows furrowed, and her lips tightened as her fingers inched toward center, gliding over his sternum.

And it was then, at that very moment when her two hands met directly above his heart, that he first experienced her haunting power.

A soothing warmth radiated from her fingers, each pulsing with a curative energy that penetrated his skin. An immediate sense of calm coursed through him, and his heartbeat eerily slowed, its usual thundering pace quieting within his chest. The ever-present pain in his shoulder strangely dissipated and lingering thoughts of his day vanished; all pressures seeming to lift.

His mind stumbled. *Did that happen? No!* **But he knew it did, seeing her briefly raise her eyes to meet his, erasing all doubt.**

She continued her exploration then. The spell now broken. Her palms fanned out, pressing into his granite pectorals, devouring their strength, and fueling her desire. His muscles flexed, responding to her silken touch, and causing them both to laugh before her spidering fingers returned to his deltoids, squeezing the rock-hard muscles of his upper arms, and guiding him toward her with a satisfying murmur.

Awkwardly remembering his role, he returned to the present, snaking an index finger from her throat to her navel and surveying every curve of her nakedness. "You are beautiful, truly beautiful."

His words sang to her then, stealing seconds of oxygen from her lungs as she watched the devil dance across his darkening eyes. He released a hungry growl, slipping his palm beneath her back and bringing her body flush to his. Hot kisses christened her breasts, sucking her nipples with ferocious need. His fingers traced the curve of her side; his lips inching lower, searing her skin. She heard herself moan, caught between a pendulum of pleasure and pain as his teeth gently nipped at her side and his scorching kisses wrapped her in wave after wave of titillating ecstasy. Her breath hitched making him smile at her obvious rapture as his teeth bit harder one last time, and she cried out before he smothered the area with soothing strokes of his tongue.

Moving to face her; his brow furrowed. "Did I hurt you? I never want to hurt you."

"Hurt?... No, love, hurt was the last thing I was feeling," she whispered, placing her hand upon his cheek. "This may sound old fashioned but... you leave me breathless. Your lips are dangerous, Nick Rusano, like a weapon, paralyzing me. Your kisses shatter me, your touch weakens me."

He stared immobilized for several seconds, basking in her sincerity. *Who is this creature?*

"Your words caress my soul, Bella," he whispered, bending to softly graze her lips before tugging playfully on her lower lip. "Surrender to me, beautiful. Let me hear your gasps; don't play a lady, don't stifle your moans. Let me suck away your breaths. Let me be your oxygen. Let me fuck you like no man has ever fucked you. Let me be your master."

The devil strummed his fiddle in those obsidian eyes, and he lowered his mouth to her throat, his savage desire pouring forth. "I want you, Bella. I've wanted you from the day I first saw you. Let me ravish you tonight."

Her wanton hand trailed his arm as he moved to the far end of the bed and once again his eyes flashed black, fueling her desire.

"I want to taste every inch of you, my love. I want to own your body," he whispered, coaxing her back down onto the pillow. "Close your eyes. Submit," he ordered, before cradling her calf in his palm and dancing his fingers across her thigh in a titillating glissando. She shuddered feeling his velvet tongue softly grazing her toes, the arch of her foot, her ankle before his torrid lips traveled to her calf, her knee, and then her thigh, lingering. Her breathing grew uneven, every cell in her body electrified with each sweep of his tongue. She thought he would stop when he reached her center but instead, he moved to her opposite thigh, teasing, kissing, caressing, driving her mad with longing. Every nerve in her body tingled and just when she was about to beg, he placed one hand beneath her spine and lifted her to his lips playfully tugging on her clit with his teeth before licking her already soaked core, devouring every drop. Then his tongue began to circle, each movement increasing in intensity, slowly taking her to the brink until she thought she would explode, swept up in a vortex, whirling out of control.

It was too much! She tried to bolt, moving her leg, but he held her fast.

"Easy, baby, easy, not yet," he whispered, briefly breaking his connection. "Wait."

"My God, Nicky."

"One more minute, baby," he murmured but she could no longer hear him, her tension was too high. He then increased his movement, sending her gasping for air as a torrential orgasm shattered her very core.

"Float, my beautiful angel, float. Come back to me when you can," he softly whispered, moving beside her and wrapping her still shaking body in his arms. She was trembling, consumed by breathless ecstasy and wanting only to melt into his hard shoulder.

Through slit eyes she saw him cover her hand with his and center it atop his chest while his other hand stroked her back, fingers barely touching. She lay paralyzed as crazed thoughts bombarded her. *What kind of man waits; what kind of man takes so much time to please a woman?* She knew he was ready when he returned to the head of the bed, feeling his hardness pressed against her thigh but still he waited.

Quiet minutes passed; her body cradled in the Nirvana of his embrace before the featherlight touch of his fingers stroked her temple, and his lips skipped a delicate trail of kisses across her cheek. His tongue circled her ear as she continued to quiver, and his burning lips brushed her neck, making her moan with pleasure. He found that spot he knew so well, that spot that made her his. She was drifting again, helpless beneath his touch, feeling his fingers trace her shoulders and cover her breasts in soft caresses.

He hovered over her then, locking one elbow, allowing her to fully appreciate his body and she nervously drew in a breath, seeing his cock for the first time. He was huge, rock hard. She had never been with a man this large.

He heard her frightened gasp as he entered her, causing him to hesitate. *She's too small, too tight. Move slow.* Watching her eyes, he allowed her to adjust knowing he could pull out before hurting her. But then he felt her body relax, accepting his girth, enveloping his every inch. He smiled with satisfaction knowing what his size had made her feel, slowly pushing deeper, responding to her tightening pulse on his organ. She gripped his shoulders as they watched each other, moving together in rhythm, increasing speed. She knew she was ready to come again when he slowed.

"Wait, baby," he whispered, "it will be better if you wait."

She nodded, surrendering, allowing him full control of the thrusting, the speed and within minutes she felt herself rising again, wickedly throbbing, and convulsing as he too gave into his own seismic orgasm.

His lips were moving, but she couldn't hear his words, the echo of her frantic heartbeat blocking out all sound. She couldn't even feel the sheets beneath her as her body still pulsed from their lovemaking. They rested together, breathless, wrapped in each other's arms, the room gradually coming into focus.

"Move that leg next time, and I'll tie it down," he teased as he held her.

"You wouldn't?"

"No, you don't think so? Try me."

4am

Alaina tried to quietly disengage from his arm. They had fallen into a light sleep after a night of continuous lovemaking.

"Hmm." Feeling her move he tightened his grip, firmly pressing her to his side.

"Nick, honey, I need to go. I'm due in work at 7."

"What? Crazy woman, it's Thursday, you're off."

"No, I picked up an extra shift at Sunrise 7-7. I need to go home and shower."

"Hmm, shower here,"

She hesitated, "*Okay.*"

"I have a shower, woman." He looked at her, still sleepy before grabbing his phone and setting the timer for one hour. "Go back to sleep," he whispered, pulling her closer.

The steamy water tumbled down upon them as his hard chest encircled her. His tongue traveled to her neck causing an involuntary shudder within. He already knew every weak point on her body, each nerve on her neck responding to his lips. His huge cock pressed firmly against her stomach as his hand moved to her breast, kneading her nipple, her body already begging. He ran his other hand through her hair, their eyes meeting, hearts beating, need increasing. His strong arms slid beneath her buttocks, lifting her, and pressing her firmly against the tiles as she wrapped her legs around his waist. He plunged his cock deep inside relishing her gasp, then pausing for just a moment as they both enjoyed the fullness before lowering his lips to hers. His kiss was gentle at first then grew more frantic, at pace with the thrust of his cock within her. They were hungry for each other, devouring each other, their need desperate. His thrusts grew more forceful, and she met each with equal fury, luxuriating in the hardness, feeling the power equaling her mounting orgasm. Her hands gripped his shoulders and she moaned with pleasure as he bit her neck, bringing her to near ecstasy.

"Baby, baby now," he cried breathlessly as his final thrust pushed deeper, and they both burst forth in thunderous climax. They were trembling, their hearts pounding, still entwined. She clung to him tightly, her fingers numb, unable to release him as their lips locked together in a final violent kiss. She faltered attempting to lower her legs, still captured in the rapture and he sensed her weakness, quickly moving to support her then staring deep into her vixen eyes. Both were unwilling to break the spell, standing breathless against the wall, fully sated.

7am

A chill coursed through him as he stared at his solitary reflection in the bathroom mirror, the memory of their lovemaking fresh in his mind. He could still feel the tenderness of her touch seeping beneath his skin, calming his heart, and piercing his soul. Her haunting presence remained, floating in the shadows.

She frightened him.

He shook his head, *crazy!* He'd send flowers, which would end it. He had bedded her; he didn't need to see her again. He would push her off, give her some lame excuse. He was an expert at the game but… he wanted to see her again.

Afterglow

Nick raced his Ferrari across the hospital parking lot, quickly finding a spot before staring up at the bright sun-streaked windows of Sunrise Medical Center. His hands lingered on the steering wheel, his grip tight with insecurity. *Why am I here? What am I doing?* He knew better. This type of woman hopes for more, dreams of a deeper relationship and that was not how it worked with him. *Drive back to the Royale, down a glass of Macallan, line up a cocktail waitress to bed tonight and get back to your usual routine.* But there was something, something in the way Alaina McGovern looked at him, something in her touch, something he had never experienced before. He shook his head. *Stop being a fool.*

Instead, he headed for the elevator.

"Good morning, gorgeous. How are you this morning?"

Alaina startled, not hearing his approach. He was dressed impeccably in a dark navy Desmond Merrion suit tailored to define every muscle. His blue eyes sparkled, and his wanton playboy smile mirrored their lust causing her pulse to race as his hand lightly fell across her back.

She glanced at the two dozen long stemmed red roses delivered earlier with the simple message—*Alaina, Enchanted. Nick.* Blushing momentarily, she diverted her eyes before turning to face him. "I'm fine," she stammered, her voice cracking.

His eyebrows shot up, "You're fine?"

Scenes of their lovemaking flashed through her mind remembering her total surrender to his expertise, and she was unable to control her embarrassment.

"Yes, I'm fine. Thank you for the flowers, they're beautiful," still unable to mask her nerves.

"Their beauty does not compare to the woman standing before me."

Once again she felt herself falling, her surroundings dimming in the background. The sincerity in his voice encircled her; the kindness in his eyes entrapped her.

His fingers lightly grazed her chin as he leaned closer, "Have dinner with me tonight."

"I can't, I'm here until 7."

He cocked his head, "How about 9, I'll pick you up?" Then, whispering in her ear, "I promise I'll be gentle. Say yes."

His eyes were holding her captive, awaiting her answer as bright red danger signs flashed before her, *don't give in; he's a player, you'll get hurt.* But she wanted him to touch her again, wanted to lay in his arms, to feel him deep inside her.

"9 would be perfect," she replied, bravely returning his smile, and feeling heat march across her cheeks.

"Alaina, do you have room 4?" Dr. Khaleel walked into the nurses' station, looking up from reading the patient's latest EKG strip.

"Yes."

"Decrease his drip to q12."

"Of course."

"Later, sweetheart," Nick murmured before turning to depart, his cologne lingering and sending an involuntary shiver down her spine as she anticipated their upcoming evening.

"Hmmm, hmmm, honey, if that were my man, I'd never let him out of my sight. I'd tie him up in a nice tight bow and take him straight home; wouldn't let him out of bed for a week. Hmmm, hmmm. You need to keep him, honey." Nevaeh, the unit clerk had been sitting at the nurses' desk, witness to the entire exchange.

#

Vegas is beautiful at night especially when seen from above. The casino facades dance and spin in sparkling neon glitter, sending trails of color up into the heavens, and mesmerizing the viewer. Standing high above this oasis of light, Alaina couldn't help but appreciate its enchantment. She inched closer to the floor-to-ceiling windows of his private suite drawn by the breathtaking panorama, barely hearing him as he called downstairs to one of the Royale's restaurants.

"Pork chops okay, gorgeous?" he asked.

She nodded, thinking they could not have wished for a prettier backdrop for dinner.

Nick beheld her beauty reflected in the glass. She had the striking elegance inherent to Irish women, her features etched with fiery strength. Her dark silken hair floated upon snow white shoulders begging for his touch while her haunting emerald eyes danced a demon's waltz luring him into her web. He reached for her, immediately feeling the welcoming flow of her tranquil sedation. Her soothing salve pierced his skin, mysteriously evaporating the tension from his shoulders and shedding their weighted burden as her vixen eyes gazed upon him. Thoughts of fleeing engulfed his thoughts, but her connection was viselike, cradling his heart in her hand and gripping his soul. *Was she a witch come to spar with the devil?*

Turning toward the window, she guided his arms around her, leaning her body into his. He bent to kiss the nape of her neck allowing the scent of her hair to seduce him like a welcoming drug as fireworks exploded across the night sky. *Was his pulse slowing? Was the tension melting from his body?*

Even their lovemaking changed, as *she* orchestrated every move. There was no lust filled madness, just the calm appreciation of each other. They drifted, relishing soft caresses and sweet kisses, cradled in a sea of surrender. He no longer knew who was in control and he didn't care, content to be swept along in her mystifying spell.

The shrill sound of his phone broke through the quiet as they lie holding each other, abruptly interrupting their serenity. He was needed downstairs. He turned with immediate regret, apologetic.

"I need you to stay, promise me you'll be here when I return. I'm uneasy sending you home in the middle of the night. Stay, I won't be long," he begged, leaning in to stroke her face and melting her willpower with his eyes. Then a boyish smile crossed his lips. "*We* will order mountains of fluffy french toast and gallons of bellinis and I will feed those pretty little lips of yours," he teased, before kissing her one last time and rushing to dress.

The Over-Turn

Nick was greeted by two of his employees, Steve Corson and Binx Sacco. Steve was the Royale's floor manager. His job was to ensure that all gaming ran smoothly during third shift. Binx was a trusted ten-year employee and the pit boss of a small group of no limit blackjack tables.

Both men wore a look of satisfaction knowing tonight they had undisputable proof that Kenny V., one of the Royale's dealers was cheating. The cat had finally caught the canary. Kenny was employing a scam known as the Over-Turn when a dealer teams up with an outside player commonly seated in the middle chair of the blackjack table. That player uses a hand signal to alert the dealer that he is holding a weak hand. The shady dealer then discretely eyes the next card in the deck to determine if that card will cause his friend to bust (go out). If so, he deftly passes that card to another player allowing his partner to stay in the game.

Corson and Sacco had been monitoring Kenny for weeks to no avail. The eye in the sky and table cameras weren't giving them the necessary proof nor were the boys on the catwalk able to catch the sleight of hand. But tonight, Kenny had slipped up and he knew it. He was sweating like a pig, complaining of stomach pain, and requesting a break. His co-conspirator, sensing the danger, had already left the building.

Nick reviewed the evidence, wanting to wrap things up as quickly as possible and return to Alaina.

"Bring him down to the garage," he ordered, "and grab a sledgehammer." Steve and Binx knew what was coming. Nick Rusano had a reputation for being the toughest boss on the Las Vegas Strip; his penchant for violence being no secret among his employees.

#

Administration conveniently used the Royale's parking garage for what might be labeled behavior modification due to its many blind spots and areas lacking surveillance. Most employee discrepancies could be easily handled simply by dismissing the offender and banning them from future work on the Vegas Strip, but dealer cheating was different. If a casino were lax in monitoring dealers, they would shortly become a magnet for scammers intent on robbing the house. Constant vigilance was required.

When Nick exited the elevator to the garage, he found Kenny shackled to a rebar enforced concrete barrier by a thick leather harness, sobbing and sweating profusely, blood streaming from his freshly battered face. He shook violently upon seeing his boss, instantly losing control of his bladder, and sending a putrid stream of urine onto the concrete.

Nick threw up his hands in exasperation, "Kenny, Kenny, Kenny, is that nice? Where are your manners? Now we will need to call housekeeping."

The little man began to plead, "Please, please Mr. Nick, I didn't do anything, honest. I didn't do anything. Please, please," he sputtered through broken front teeth, his sobbing increasing with every word.

Nick circled, "You didn't do anything? Did you steal from me, Kenny?" Nick paused before circling his prey again, awaiting an answer. "Did you steal from me?" he boomed, his volume echoing off the concrete.

"No, no, Mr. Nick, I swear. Please, I have three kids at home, please."

"No one steals from me, *NO ONE*, especially not some two-bit worm like you!" Nick's voice rang out as he slowly removed his suit jacket. His men eyed each other predicting their boss's next move and watching Kenny helplessly follow Nick's movements through swollen eyelids, fear building with each turn of his head.

"Hold his arms," Nick bellowed, directing his men to step forward and press Kenny's forearms to the concrete. He nodded and, in one swift move, he hoisted the sledgehammer and slammed it into Kenny's left hand. The little man's terror filled scream was deafening. His hand was shattered, revealing ugly flattened bones protruding through broken purple skin. Nick circled again, oblivious to the sounds of his victim. Twenty seconds later a second blow destroyed Kenny's right hand causing him to sink into unconsciousness.

Nick stood assessing the damage as Corson and Sacco waited, unmoving, knowing their boss might not be finished.

Finally, Nick released the hammer to the blood-soaked floor. The loud clang reverberated sending a cold chill up Sacco's spine. He watched as his boss retrieved the handkerchief from his jacket pocket, wiped his hands and discarded the soiled cloth to the floor.

A bolt of lightning ripped the sky and thunder boomed. "Storm's coming, gentlemen," Nick announced, but Sacco knew the storm had already arrived staring down at the broken victim. In just a few short minutes, Nick Rusano had stripped the little man of his livelihood. He would never deal blackjack again.

#

Nick returned to the suite to check on Alaina, finding her deep in slumber wearing one of his faded Princeton tee shirts. He stood watching her breathe, recalling the passion they had shared just hours earlier. That welcome sense of calm had pulsed through his body; his fury dissipating as she rested her palm atop his heart. Her delicate fingers had miraculously erased the tension of his day as she stroked his chest. But dealing with Kenny had ratcheted up that fury again and he contemplated waking her, longing to return to that state of Nirvana. *Ridiculous! What kind of spell is this?*

Looking down, he noticed a single speck of blood on his cuff. Damn it, he thought, before tossing the shirt in the waste bin. Turning to take a shower, he formulated a plan to wash this witch out of his mind. He would stay at the Royale for the next week, line up a few showgirls to warm his bed and get out on his boat each morning. That would surely clear his head.

But that plan lasted a mere three days before he succumbed to the beckoning memory of her touch.

The Playboy Stumbles

Nick Rusano knew how to romance a woman. He never failed to send flowers after bedding them, always following up with the empty, meaningless sentiments their egos required. Women came easy for him, always had. He enjoyed the game.

He also knew how to make love to a woman. Most couldn't keep pace with his sexual appetite, they were unskilled, boring and he quickly lost interest. He used them then sent them on their way, never wanting a meaningful relationship, moving from one to the next. One night worked best for him, a week at the most, no involvement, no commitment. He was too busy to let someone into his life. Currently, he and Dominic were splitting the casino hours, Nick working 4pm through 4am and Dominic the reverse. He was also conducting family business meetings at the Big House several days a week during his father's recovery, ensuring that no one knew of the Old Don's condition. Sickness showed weakness and business associates viewed weakness as an opportunity to move in on someone's territories.

His current problem was Alaina McGovern. She was different, far from his usual taste. He tried to reason the attraction; he came in contact with her daily when checking on his father. She wasn't a gold digger—he had certainly run into plenty of them—heck, she didn't even recognize the family name. He also knew she was discreet. Alaina had not broken the NDA. Even her neighbor, who was also Nick's employee, didn't know the name of Alaina's patient, proving integrity. Perhaps that was the attraction. That, and the kind way she cared for his father. Nick often heard her laughter as he climbed the stairs each afternoon, sometimes listening at his father's door before entering. It was obvious the Old Don liked her. She was patient, cajoling him to be more independent while treating him in a grandfatherly manner. One morning as she was shaving his father he walked in, astounded that the old man was allowing a stranger to hold a razor to his neck. Nick jumped, grabbing her wrist but his father simply waved him off. She had no idea she was holding a blade to the throat of the most powerful man on the west coast. He laughed when she said his father was such a "sweet man." That was never a term anyone used to describe Angelo Rusano.

One thing Nick was sure of, his father's contract with the nursing agency was ending. Alaina McGovern would be moving on, and he would return to his old lifestyle. But as the days slipped by, that thought only increased his confusion, bringing little comfort.

#

3am Alaina's apartment
BANG, BANG, BANG.
She stumbled from the bed, disoriented and frightened.
BANG, BANG, BANG.
"I'm coming, wh… what is it?"

"Miss Alaina, it's Bobby, please open the door. The Old Don fell, they need you at the Big House."

Twenty minutes later she was battling her very belligerent patient as Daniella Macland sutured a jagged three-inch gash on his forehead. Adding to his humiliation were his wet pajamas. He had fallen in the bathroom after his cries went unanswered from the nurse asleep in the corner. Nick was pacing the room, spewing thunderous expletives, having already dismissed the woman.

The Old Don's recovery would soon become dangerously impossible to conceal and for the first time in Nick's life he was forced to recognize his father's frailty. Thoughts of his own future weighed heavily and the burden of conducting his family's business while still fulfilling his responsibilities at the Royale swiftly caused fatigue to take hold. He began to question his decision making, seeking refuge in Alaina. She became his drug; his craving for her increasing each day, unable to withdraw. When his stress level soared, his body begged for her soothing touch; her hand upon his heart instantly calmed him.

But time and sleep had always been his enemy and conventional dating was never an option. Stealing hours together became routine. There were times when he had Bobby drop her at the Royale after her shift allowing them to share a boozy milkshake at Holsteins, grab a quick dinner at the Royale, maybe catch the lounge act. But it was on the nights when she stayed with him, entwined in his arms before the crackling fireplace, that brought him the most comfort, nights with no expectations, just simple conversation where he learned more about this mysterious woman.

She grew up in a small town, the type where everyone knew each other. "The bank was on Bank Street. The church was on Church Street, post office on Post Street," she explained. She talked of the annual Halloween parade and Christmas bazaar, of 4H fairs and homecoming queens, of downtown shops open late on Wednesday nights. He couldn't imagine a more idyllic place, taking shelter in that utopia and, as with Scheherazade, he encouraged her stories, finding strength from the simple sound of her voice, her words a salve to his soul, her touch a healing sustenance. She was his window into normalcy, a world he had dreamed of, a world that had been stolen from him.

Enchantment

Each day before leaving for the Royale Nick checked on his father, but family business often kept him from crossing paths with Alaina. On those days he would send a message inquiring after his father's health. Tonight, he questioned her about her driver, wanting to ensure the arrangement was still working. She replied with heartfelt gratitude, exhausted and thankful not to battle Vegas traffic.

"This is your stop tonight, Miss," Bobby announced, jostling her from slumber.

She heard the car door open and felt strong arms lifting her from the seat. Did her heart really flutter when he touched her?

"Nick?"

"Were you napping, my little Sleeping Beauty? Hope you were dreaming of us."

"Hmm, does that mean you're my handsome prince?"

His eyes twinkled. "Let me wake you for just a little while." He put his arm around her waist, pulling her in close before giving her a quick peck on the forehead. "I thought you might like to take a walk. Want to show you something, something as beautiful as you."

She was confused but happy, feeling the warmth from his body pressed against her. They stopped at a food cart for coffee and continued strolling down the Strip, hand in hand, winding their way to their destination — the breathtaking Bellagio Hotel.

Several times each night the brilliant Bellagio engineers mesmerize visitors with a thrilling outdoor water show where thousands of fountains dance to music and flashing lights while shooting water four hundred feet into the air. Viewers stand in awe welcoming the break from the sometimes-frenzied Strip and allowing the spectacle to instill in them a sense of peace and romance.

Nick held her firmly, pulling her to his shoulder as they watched the show. When it ended, he turned her body into his, crushing her to his chest and kissing her passionately, oblivious to the passing crowd.

"Happy?" he whispered, gently tugging on her earlobe.

"Oh yes, it was beautiful. You are *so* sweet. You make me feel like a princess."

"Good. Go home and dream of dancing waters, my little Aurora. *I* need to get back to work. I'll call you in the morning."

Alaina McGovern was swept away by the enchantment of that night, surrendering her heart forever to Nick Rusano, the fairy tale complete.

Family

Nick listened as the perky blond smiled into the television camera promising perfect weather for Thursday morning. It had been a horrendous week with multiple annoying incidents chipping away at his patience and he was itching to get out on the water.

Most of what occurred could be rectified by his department supervisors, but some required his personal intervention. On Monday, a beloved veteran roulette croupier had suffered a massive heart attack in the middle of the casino floor. Later it was revealed that his wheel was rigged. Nick was hoping to avoid a government investigation.

Yesterday, his most histrionic chef had a screaming tantrum about shortages in this week's Kobe beef delivery. Was the beef walking out the door before or after it arrived at the Royale's kitchens? The investigation was ongoing.

More disturbing was the need to disprove an accusation made by one of the Royale's guests, an aging Hollywood actress claiming the theft of her prized Russian sable coat. She made it quite clear to Nick that nothing would satisfy her until he was personally in her bed. His father would have laughed it off as the price of doing business, but he knew better than to stick his dick into crazy. *That* wasn't going to happen.

He was proud of his little cabin cruiser, it was small but comfortable, the perfect respite to escape the chaotic din of the city. He vacillated, unsure whether to invite Alaina, having never asked a woman to join him in the past.

He picked up the phone.

#

They piloted west up Lake Mead into a breathtaking sunrise–a palette of yellows, pinks, and oranges–while sharing steaming mugs of strong, hot coffee. He planned on showing her his favorite spot, a private little cove where they could skinny dip unnoticed and, before long, they were jumping off the back of the boat holding hands, him laughing, her screaming as the icy water hit them both. They played freely like children, chasing, racing, and dunking each other; while kissing and hugging with her legs wrapped tightly around his waist. Later they snuggled under towels, drinking wine and whiskey, watching the sun reflect off the water and sharing the conversation of new couples.

"Tell me about your family," he prodded.

"What do you want to know?"

"Tell me more about your grandfather. You said he was a boxer, right?"

That made her smile. "He was and I was his little princess. He would tell his friends, 'Ooh, she's a pip.'"

"His name was Jack McGovern, and he was a horse soldier in World War I. His platoon was struck by mustard gas; his horse died, and my Pop lost all his hair. Prematurely bald, but to me he was *so* handsome, a real ladies' man. When he returned from the war, he made his living as a professional boxer in Philadelphia, and whenever he spoke of those days, he was sure to tell me that he was one of the lucky few that had an honest manager. I have his picture at the apartment if you want to see it."

"I would," Nick assured, "tell me more."

"Well, he married and had four children. One of the girls was sickly and the doctor advised my Pop to move closer to the ocean for the salt air. The grandma I knew was his third wife, and I knew a few of his girlfriends too," she shrugged. "He worked at the racetrack, and he would sneak me back to the stables and sit me atop these awfully expensive horses. He would take me to bars, and we would watch baseball together on tiny corner TVs as he drank beer, and I had my very own Shirley Temple with whipped cream and a cherry, of course. Very grown up!"

"But my best memories were when he would show me treasures from his dresser drawer. It was stocked with all these *suspicious* weapons, making me fantasize that he was really an undercover spy with a secret double life." Her eyes grew large, a conspirator's smile spreading across her face, "There was a well-worn leather blackjack, a set of brass knuckles, knives, even a gun; super cool stuff to a kid like me."

Nick couldn't help but laugh at her animated expression, thoroughly enjoying her story. "Sounds like good memories."

"Oh, they are. How about you?"

"No memory of my grandparents. My father is all business. He's responsible for the lives of many people, a good man." Turning the conversation back to her, he asked, What about your mother?"

"My mother never married; I was a burden. No worries though, I worked past all that psychological baggage years ago. I'm just naturally unstable," she joked but he noted her momentary tension. "Do you have a big family?" she asked.

He nodded, "Pretty big, you met my brother and I have plenty of aunts, uncles, and cousins."

"Do you like it, having a big family, I mean?"

"Nah, sometimes they argue over such petty things, especially my brother."

"Funny, isn't it? People always think they want what they don't have. If they come from a small family, they long for a larger one and vice versa. It's like with women, blonds want to be brunettes, brunettes want to be redheads. Fat, thin, rich, poor, we're never happy with what God gave us."

#

It's amazing how a two-minute phone message can ruin a previously perfect twenty-four hours. That was the thought replaying in Alaina's mind as she sat alone in her apartment on her one night off. Nick had taken her home, coming in to check the house as gallantly as always. They stood wrapped in each other's arms passionately kissing goodbye, ignoring the persistent ringing of the landline until….

"Hi Alaina, it's Cora from the agency. I've lined up your next assignment at Northwest Medical in Tucson just as we discussed. Call back to confirm."

Ginny

Working as a Las Vegas showgirl is not the glamorous job it appears to be. It is highly competitive work requiring strength and stamina. Many flock to Las Vegas hoping for a chance at one of those coveted spots. Most never make it. They fall into the more obvious jobs: cocktail waitresses, topless dancers, call girls and sometimes worse.

Ginny was one of the lucky ones, having worked for the past three years as a member of the Royale's EXTRAVAGANZA dance troupe. Every night she donned her feathered headdress and pranced across the stage allowing thousands of tourists a glimpse of her perfect body. She was proud of what she did. Glamorous? No, but it paid well, and she had a rambunctious five-year-old to support and a never-at-home, womanizing husband who traveled the rodeo circuit.

Today Ginny was curious about her new neighbor. The girl seemed friendly and hardworking, rarely taking a day off. Ginny always made a point of making conversation at the community mailbox whenever they met. What she knew thus far was that Alaina McGovern was a nurse, useful information especially if her boy wasn't feeling well. She came from some small town back east, single, no children. She jogged every morning. Ginny thought about inviting her to the gym where her fellow dancers worked out.

Everyday a gray town car arrived to drive Alaina to work. *Curious, must be some nurse.* But today, there was a hot little silver Ferrari in the driveway. Ginny kept watch from her living room window; she had to know who sweet, little Alaina had brought home. Thirty minutes later, her curiosity was satisfied, *big time.*

After the Ferrari pulled away, Ginny rushed over and rang Alaina's bell. "Oh my God, are you fucking him?"

Alaina hesitated, "I'm… dating him," shocked by the intrusion.

"Do you even know who that is? That's Nick Rusano!"

Alaina nodded, "Yes, that's right, Nick. He works at the casino."

Ginny roared with laughter, "Oh girl, you are a hoot! Nick Rusano doesn't just work at the casino. He owns the casino. His family owns this entire town."

My Sweet Roy

Weeks slipped by with boating quickly becoming their favorite activity; they could speed down the highway in Nick's Ferrari and be on the water in twenty minutes. Today the little cabin cruiser bobbed peacefully in the tranquil cove where they lazed away the morning making love and relaxing in each other's arms. Both were awaiting phone calls; he needed to reschedule a meeting and she was hoping to work an extra shift at the hospital. They indulged in one last swim before heading back to town. Unfortunately, her phone began to ring while they were still in the water and that's when a loud, crazy, voice from her past echoed through the speaker as Nick stared, astonished.

"Ah, my Midnight Angel, it's Roy Nutaaq. I still have your number, sooo I thought I would give it a try. Want you to come up again this year. We will laugh more, we will drink EVEN more, and we will work little, eh, maybe more than little. I promise to pick you up if you fall on your face again and I will tuck you in every night. Call me, you have my number."

"Oh my God." She covered her mouth to stifle her laughter, averting her eyes.

"What the hell was that?" Nick demanded.

"Just a crazy, old friend, it's nothing. I'll call him later." Her laughter was breaking through as she noted Nick's incensed glare. He had grown increasingly possessive over the past few weeks, and it worried her. "Relax, it's not what it sounds like," she cajoled.

"Really? Oh, sweetheart, you don't even want to know what *I* think it sounds like." Nick's eyes widened, his temper already beginning to flare. "Let's get back on board and you can explain it to me." He hoisted himself onto the boat without offering his usual assistance, and by the time Alaina climbed up, he was holding her phone, staring at the number. "Who is Roy whatever?"

"Roy Nutaaq, he's a doctor in Tuktoyaktuk. I worked with him last year."

"Tuktoyaktuk? *Where* is that?"

"It's in the Northwest Territories in Canada." Unfortunately, the absurdity of the situation caused her to burst forth with another badly timed giggle.

Unamused, he fired off another question. "You drank so much you fell on your face, *and* he tucked you in?"

"Please, honey, let me explain."

"And what did he call you, Midnight Angel? What is that?"

"Nick, calm down." Alaina sensed his anger rising quickly, his hands tensing, eyes raging.

"Alaina, you know I am a jealous man. Explain *now!*" his voice a measured calm, his stare icy cold.

But she was still giggling, tears welling, and, hard as she tried, composure escaped her. She inhaled deeply, trying to steady herself, "Alright, hear me out," erroneously thinking she could diffuse the situation, "Last year, I took an assignment with a doctor in Tuktoyaktuk. They call it the village hopper."

"Tuktoyaktuk, Canada?"

"Yes, Tuktoyaktuk, Canada."

His brow furrowed; his angry eyes penetrated hers. "What exactly is a *village* hopper?"

Taking his hands in hers, she began to explain. "Every year a small group of doctors and nurses volunteer to travel north into the remote villages of Canada's Northwest Territories. Their goal is to administer care to those residents that are unable to travel, whether due to personal reasons, maybe a disability, transportation, or even financial reasons. So, doctors travel to *them* instead of the reverse. Get it?" She spoke softly, trying to deescalate his ire. "Every doctor travels with one nurse, moving from village to village in his assigned area. Doc Roy closes his clinic in Tuktoyaktuk each summer and volunteers as a member of the team. Last year I was his nurse."

Nick looked confused so she continued, "Some areas of Canada are not easily accessible by car or jeep and require the teams to be dropped into their assigned village by a small plane or helicopter. They stay for three or four days seeing everyone, sick and well. The people know the doctors won't return for another year, so they line up: whole families, pregnant mothers, babies, everyone in the village. The biggest obstacle is the weather; it can play havoc with the schedule because it's so unpredictable. Sometimes the chopper can't land, maybe there's too much mud, or the pilot has a short weather window for drop off, forcing the team to jump out. First time, I slipped and *fell* on my face."

"You jumped out of a helicopter?" he asked, incredulous.

Alaina laughed, "Only about a foot, I slipped off the landing skid and Doc Roy had to pick me up. That's what he's talking about, I *fell on my face.*" She laughed, eyes wide. "I was covered in mud and needed an immediate shower."

Nick remained serious, "How old is this Doc Roy?"

"That's your question?" she smirked. "He's about sixty, a really good person, very dedicated. The people love him, and I admire him. I felt privileged to work with him."

"And he has a *pet* name for you?" Nick's voice was beginning to elevate again.

"He's talking about the sunsets. Each night we would sit at the cove and watch the sun go down before bed. Nick, c'mon, lighten up."

"You're kidding, right? Some guy with an accent, French, I don't know, calls you. Talks about you drinking with him and tucking you in. What do you expect me to think?"

"Nick, stop. You're making something out of nothing."

But he was not laughing, his angry eyes fixed, their cold daggers boring into her.

She sighed, finally understanding. She knew she had to placate him, but at the same time, she was annoyed that he was questioning her character, her own ire building. "OK, that's enough. Give me this." Snatching her phone from his hand, she spun around, quickly lobbing it into the water. "My phone messages seem to cause friction between us." Her angry eyes clashed with his, all laughter gone. "I did not sleep with Roy. You are jealous of a man you have never met; an old man that does nothing but good work for extremely poor people. Do you think I'm a whore fucking every doctor I work with, crisscrossing my way across the country with a *fuck* in every port?" she challenged, hands flying, rage growing.

Turning her back to him, she gripped the counter before inhaling deeply, allowing her voice to soften. "My heart belongs to you, Nick. Don't you realize that?" But her admission was met with cold silence and after several seconds she spun back to face him, tears welling, "Take me home!"

Nick's eyes remained dark with rage as he turned to start the engine; the heavy shadow of anger enveloping them both.

#

When Alaina arrived the following day, Don Rusano was seated in his chair awaiting her visit. After all these weeks together, they had come to enjoy each other's company and today they had planned a busy afternoon. He was to teach her a new chess move and she, in turn, promised to read the latest Nero Wolfe novel she had purchased at the used bookstore.

Each day she pushed him; "Five more steps, Mr. Rusano," her voice demanding but kind. His strength had improved and his weight bearing ability had also increased, now able to move from bed to chair without becoming short of breath. Today she planned for him to descend the stairs to the kitchen, with her help, of course. "I expect you to make me coffee," she warned with a smile.

"My son left you a present. Is it your birthday?"

Wrapped in metallic pink paper with a gauzy white and silver ribbon, the package sat on the table aside the Old Don. He handed it to her with expectant curiosity. Inside sat a brand-new phone, the latest model, with a simple written note— FORGIVE ME.

Alaina rewrapped the phone, returning it to the table. Her anger was still too raw. She would weather the storm if needed.

The following day Nick was waiting, looking stern like an angry father about to reprimand an errant child.

"Need to talk to you," he said, backing her into a corner outside his father's room. "Why did you leave the phone?"

"I don't need it; I bought a new one," she defiantly replied, producing the replacement from her pocket.

He swiftly grabbed it, snapping it in half before pocketing it in his jacket.

"Nick!"

"Should I call the agency and say I can't reach you?" he boomed.

"You wouldn't do that."

His eyebrows shot up in anger, his eyes black with rage. He inhaled deeply causing his chest to expand before cupping her chin and moving her face six inches from his. "Look, you are stubborn, and I am a jealous man. Probably a toxic combination for a relationship but I know we can resolve this *miscommunication* tonight. I'll be outside at 11."

"*NO!*" she countered, her angry glare clashing with his in a war of wills as she wrapped her fingers around his wrist and forced his hand from her chin. "I picked up an overnight shift at Sunrise. I'm going straight there after your father."

"Ah, there's that fuckin' defiant look I've come to know." Nick's darkening stare pierced her as he slammed the wall above with his palm. But she stood firm, unflinching, her eyes narrowing. "Is that supposed to frighten me? Try for some control, big man."

Taking another deep breath, he drew back, standing tall and assessing her mettle. He was not accustomed to someone challenging him, especially a woman.

"Oh, little girl, you're going to fight me on this every step of the way, right? Okay. Okay. I'll wait, I'll wait until you get past your stubbornness... maybe."

Turning abruptly, he retreated down the stairs; not allowing her to reply, knowing she had bested him.

Alaina's hands were shaking as she entered the Old Don's room; but she regained her composure, cementing her smile and feigning sunshine before taking her seat beside him. Gently reaching out, he placed his hand atop hers as to steady her, never looking up from his game of solitaire. He had obviously heard the entire exchange.

#

She halted abruptly seeing the gaily wrapped present atop her bed when she arrived home the following morning. *Clever, guess breaking and entering should be counted in your skill set.* But she was too desperate for sleep to confront him now. *I will deal with you later.*

Mid-Morning

Bbring, Bbring. Her landline was ringing, jolting her from a deep sleep.

"H—hello," she answered in a haze, trying to bring the clock face into focus. *"Hello."*

"Honey, it's Ginny. You ok?"

"Yeah, yeah, I-I worked a double last night, just got home a few hours ago."

"Well look, honey, Nick's been sitting in your driveway for the past hour."

"Wh-what?"

"Yeah, just sitting in his car."

Sigh, *"Thanks."*

"If you need help, call me, Nick has a temper."

"I'll be okay, he won't hurt me."

She stumbled to the front door, shielding her gaze from the blinding Vegas sun before making eye contact with him and retreating back inside, leaving the door ajar. Without words he entered, avoiding her stare as she stood immobile in the foyer. Slowly he removed his suit jacket and holster, methodically placing them on the hall table before turning to her, anger still emanating from his eyes. She watched him inhale before he strode toward her, firmly placing his hand on her hip and gently backing her against the wall. Their faces once again six inches apart as he looked down into her eyes.

"This is about my reaction to a phone message on *your* phone. Am I right?" he questioned, pausing briefly. "Now, normally with any other woman, I would not put up with such childish nonsense. I would walk away from your little girl tantrum and never look back…."

"No!" She stormed, cutting him off, her ire rising again. "You have it wrong. I am angry because you questioned my integrity. You immediately assumed that I slept with Roy, which I never did."

He hesitated for one split second, before placing his hand over her mouth. "Shh. Stop your fighting. I came here to tell you that I do not believe you slept with a sixty-year-old man. I do *not* believe you are crisscrossing the country with a fuck in every port. By the way, nice language from *your* mouth."

Feeling the hot sting of humiliation, she turned from him as flames of embarrassment erupted from neck to forehead.

"Look at me, Laina," he said, gently turning her face to him. "I came here to apologize; I know I overreacted, and I'm sorry for losing my temper and … obviously jumping to the wrong conclusion. Let go of your anger with me."

"Nick…," her voice trembled, her eyes brimming with tears.

"No more," he whispered, wiping away an escaping tear.

A silent moment passed between them before he lowered his mouth to hers; kissing her fiercely and, with equal violent force, she returned his kiss. Valiantly lifting her in his arms, he swiftly crossed to the bedroom, tossing her onto the bed, their need for each other unrestrained. There was no gentleness now in their lovemaking, only mutual dominance and submission, both rough and uninhibited. They couldn't kiss each other hard enough, hold each other tight enough. He pressed her wrists to the pillow, ravishing his way from neck to nipples with blazing lips until she squirmed in ecstasy beneath him. His unshaven face caused her every nerve to jump, its coarseness chaffing her skin. He continued going lower, releasing her hands as he tore at her panties before slipping his fingers deep inside her core. She couldn't breathe, every part of her body was tense, pulsing with need. His tongue circled her stomach, wickedly teasing and biting. She was his wanton prisoner, rocked in the motion of tongue and fingers. She bent her leg, grinding her heel into the sheets, and she heard him growl before he slapped her soundly on the thigh.

"Behave, woman."

"I can't, I need you now," she begged, seizing his shoulder.

His eyes met hers, their lust for each other bursting forth. "Now… or always?" he asked, before entering her in one swift move. Her entire body shuddered as he plunged deeper with each inward thrust, both lost now in the frenetic cyclone of their desire until they collapsed in each other's arms.

"I never want to let you go," she breathlessly uttered, refusing to release her tight grip on his body.

"Oh, baby," he declared, "you won't."

Bruised Porcelain

Big Larry Mazzone called upstairs asking to meet with Nick on a matter of 'utmost importance.' He paced nervously, at wit's end, seeing no plausible resolution to his problem. He needed to meet with Nick NOW!

His primary responsibility as Showroom Supervisor was to ensure that the Royale's EXTRAVAGANZA, the casino's nightly production, was flawlessly performed six nights a week. Larry was a perfectionist and he prided himself on being close to his people—knowing the name of every stagehand, every gaffer, every best boy. With his unlit cigar forever in place and belt straining on its last notch, his gruff demeanor could be intimidating but beneath the layers, he was a gentle teddy bear. Nick trusted Larry and Larry was loyal to Nick.

Larry's responsibilities also included the supervision of the Royale's troupe of fifty showgirls and dancers. He was tough, allowing no absences from practice sessions or shows. Choreography had to be exact, no one out of step. Costumes had to fit precisely, accentuating every curve. Repairs went immediately to tailoring, every feather and sequin in place, makeup, and hair perfect.

"Smile like you mean it," he would yell, "the guests expect to see perfection and you, ladies and gentlemen, *ARE PERFECTION.*"

Peggy, Nick's secretary, was welcoming when Larry arrived, but he remained nervous, sweat dripping from his reddened face.

"Go right in, he's waiting for you."

Nick stood, greeting him warmly before motioning him to sit. "Larry, it's good to see you. What brings you upstairs? Everything all right, family good?"

But poor Larry could only clench his hands together, eyes searching the carpet, sweat increasing.

"Larry? Larry, what is it?"

"Boss… never mind, sorry to bother you. Everything's good," he stammered, already looking to exit.

"Wait, sit, tell me what's wrong." Nick had never seen his supervisor in such a state. He walked to the bar and poured him a double whiskey, hoping to calm the poor man's nerves.

Larry shook, reluctantly settling back into the creaking chair and emptying the drink in one swift swallow.

"What has you so upset?"

"It's the girls, no, no, it's not the girls. It's your brother, Mr. Dominic," his voice quaking.

"My brother!"

Larry gulped in a deep breath before nervously making eye contact with Nick's already troubled glare. "Mr. Dominic, he… he likes the ladies, and I get it, I really do. We have some extremely fine ladies but he's, ah, he's not nice. I don't know how else to say this, so… let me just put it to you." Larry held up a shaking hand and began ticking off several incidents. "I have one girl, Lily, she has a black eye. He broke Barbara Jean's arm and she's in a cast, can't work. But the worst was two nights ago, Mr. Dominic beat the crap out of little Sylvia. Left her in a room on the fifth floor, two of the girls came to get me and I ran up there. She was a mess, she's has broken ribs, a broken nose, her face is caved in," he stammered, downing a second glass of whiskey.

"What! Why didn't I hear about this?" Nick asked, astonished.

"Boss, these girls are afraid to report him. They need their jobs, he's your brother, for God's sake. He's like the boss, too, or… at least he acts like it. They tell me it's a sex thing with him… rough and all. I mean, I know, Boss, you like the ladies too, and they like you. You treat them nice and all. Never heard a single one of your girls complain but this...," Larry's voice trailed off.

Nick was shocked but remained quiet, encouraging Larry to continue.

"Look, Boss, it took everything I have to come up here, but I think we know each other a long time. I'm not the only one having a problem, ask Cheryl in food and beverage. Dominic's going after the cocktail waitresses, too. This is bad, Boss. I'm sorry, I know he's your brother and all, but this is bad, really bad."

Nick ordered Larry to immediately send him reports of all incidents past and present, then he sent for Cheryl, who also recounted numerous incidents confirming the problem.

The next day he confronted Dominic and their meeting quickly grew ugly.

"What, now you're telling me who I can fuck," screamed Dominic, "you, the great Nick Rusano, who's had every dancer in the place."

"I don't beat them," Nick roared back.

"They deserve to be beaten, they're nothing but whores."

"Listen, you want to beat someone up, go down to the gym. These girls are not playthings, they're human beings, for God's sake. Get yourself under control."

"Don't tell me what to do, I'll do what I damned well please," Dominic yelled, slamming out the office door. Nick shook his head, exasperated; his brother was a ticking time bomb.

Two weeks later, Dominic Rusano chose the wrong dancer to harass. Lisa Marie had been rebuking Dominic's advances for several days to no avail. Not all dancers are single, and Lisa Marie was married to a burly, no-nonsense good old boy from Texas who didn't appreciate what his wife was telling him.

At 3am on a Friday morning Dominic phoned Nick begging to be picked up from the Sunrise Medical Center Emergency Room. That Texas husband had exacted his revenge in the form of five broken ribs and a fractured eye socket.

The Clarity of Confusion

She was tense, not her usual self. Last night she had stayed with him, their lovemaking passionate and exhilarating. Nick knew he had satisfied her, and she him. It wasn't that. But this morning, she was pensive.

He watched as she checked her messages when they first left the bed. That had to be it. He was curious, especially when he witnessed her angrily toss the phone back into her bag, unaware of his presence. She was working a half shift at the hospital 11-3, before returning to care for his father so he planned for them to breakfast at the Veranda Cafe beforehand. For now, they were having coffee, listening as the tv newscaster reported on a violent crime in Juneau, Alaska.

"So, you ever going to tell me about that creep landlord in Alaska?" he asked casually.

"No, it wasn't anything," she answered, blowing him off and avoiding his eyes.

"No?"

They were sitting knee to knee allowing him to place his hand under her chin and gently turn her face to his.

"Don't push, Nick, please." Looking away, she immediately regretted her raw response.

"Look at me, angel."

"It wasn't anything, really, not even worth talking about. I wasn't mugged or raped, nothing like that, I think I told you that." She paused but his hand remained in place, persistent. "Damn it, I know you want to be my knight in shining armor, but I don't need a knight."

He jerked back, stung by her brash response, his jaw tightening, the muscles of his neck taut and pulsing. He lowered his hand.

"Let me help you, baby. Talk to me. Let me help erase this from your mind."

His dark blue eyes held her captive, knowing there was no escape. He would have his answers, but her heart raced into panic mode, having locked away this fear long ago.

He gently reached for her chin again, stroking it softly before giving her a nod.

Inhaling deeply, she stammered, his eyes urging her to continue. "I'll… I'll try. The landlord was friendly, too friendly, entering the apartment unannounced with lame excuses of looking for a leak, checking the radiator– stuff. My danger sense would signal whenever he was near. Once I turned around and he was right behind me, close—too close. When I returned from work in the evenings, I would feel a presence yet there was no one there. An item would be slightly moved, a dresser drawer left open the tiniest crack. At first, I thought it was my imagination and I blew it off to single woman paranoia, but it happened a second and third time. Then a pair of my panties went missing. That tipped me over the edge, I was frightened." She saw compassion in his eyes, but her anger flared again not wanting to appear the weak, helpless female. "So, what did I do? I picked myself up and checked into a motel near the hospital. Wasn't the best that Juneau had to offer but I felt safer. End of story so you see I don't need to be saved by Sir Lancelot," her tone brusque. She turned from him, clumsily retreating to the kitchen, knowing he was only trying to help. But the last thing she wanted was his pity and that was exactly what she saw. Her demons had been poked…a buried memory surfacing.

He threw back his head in frustration, raking his fingers through his hair. *Why the hell am I bothering? I don't need this drama.*

Her phone rang again, and he retrieved it, following in behind her. *Who was calling? What was she hiding?*

She reached for it, hoping to silence the damned thing, but he kept hold, suspicion written on his face. He hit the speaker button, handing it to her but remaining close, allowing him to hear the conversation.

"Hi Alaina, it's Cora again. I don't mean to keep bothering you, honey, but I need to FAX you this contract so I can get it to Tucson before close of business. Can you get to a FAX machine today?"

Nick nodded, jotting down a number for Alaina to repeat.

"Great, I'll send it right away. Get it back to me today, please. And, honey, where have you been? I've called several times; I was beginning to worry. I have so many great opportunities coming up and I want to review them with you. Canada's coming around again, the Doc up there requested you specifically. You okay, girlfriend?"

He was intensely watching, that angry parental expression emanating from his eyes.

"I'm good, Cora. Let me go get that contract so I can fax it back. I'm off tomorrow. I promise to call in."

#

He was quiet on the drive into town, making no further comment about Cora's call. She had signed the contract and he immediately faxed it back but not before looking at the salary. He never realized nurses were paid so little. He wasn't concentrating on his driving now having just passed a tractor trailer at a risky speed. He saw her grip the handrail and silently reprimanded himself knowing speed was her fear. His mind was still on the morning. She would be leaving soon, and it was for the best. They never talked about her staying, they had some fun, that was it. He would miss her calming touch, the power of her fingers was still something he couldn't explain, but he had let her get too close. He knew she was in love with him. He needed to walk away. Better to back out now, get back to the different-girl-every-night philosophy that suited him best. Good that she was moving on.

Alaina's mind was racing too. The contract for his father's care was ending and she desperately wanted him to ask her to stay. *Foolish, foolish.* She had let herself fall in love and Ginny's words of warning echoed, *'Nick Rusano is a player, he'll leave you broken.'* Dark visions of Rhys crept into her mind, too. Dr. Rhys Ravikumar, superstar of the emergency room, hot jock of her hometown hospital. She had fallen for his smooth lines four years ago. He had also played her, married with two kids. *What a fool I am! Canada is sounding better and better; at least I won't fall in love with a moose.*

Breakfast went quickly, awkward small talk, no commitments. She admired the view; he spoke of the number of conventioneers expected to arrive this weekend. Festival season was also beginning, and Las Vegas would be crowded with partygoers. He would be spending more time at the suite instead of the guesthouse. She knew he was saying goodbye.

After breakfast, he helped her into the car, directing the driver to take her to Sunrise Hospital. "I'll call you later," he said, bending in to briefly kiss her forehead. Then, lifting her chin so they were eye to eye, he added, "And, sweetheart, maybe sometimes I *want* to be Sir Lancelot." He then angrily slammed the car door preventing her reply, banged on the roof and signaled the driver to pull away.

With balled fists and a deluge of tears, she admonished herself. *Why can't people just say what they mean? Why didn't I just tell him I love him?*

"Well, good morning, handsome. You're early today." Nick turned, seeing the tall redhead tugging at his sleeve. It was Mina, one of his cocktail waitresses, delivering a tray of drinks to a nearby blackjack table. Mina was knock out gorgeous, he had bedded her before, and right now she was exactly what he needed.

"Hey, baby, how are you?" he smiled, working his way down from eyes to breasts.

"I'd be better if I could see more of you," she replied, flirting invitingly as her eyes traveled to his groin. "I miss you, Nicky. I'm off at 7 tonight. You haven't forgotten me, have you?" she asked, moving closer and batting her false eyelashes.

"Of course not, baby. Come see me then, my suite, 7 o'clock." *Yep, back to one a night, no baggage.*

A Voice in the Dark

Alaina was worried. Nick had sent a driver for her every day without fail, Bobby was always reliable but today he did not show. *Maybe there was a mix-up, maybe he thinks I'm off.* She called Bobby but there was no answer. *Better drive to the mansion myself.* But when she approached, she immediately noted the increased security at the front gate.

"Hi Cliff, I know I'm a little late," she called to the guard.

"Sorry Miss, I can't let you in."

"You can't let me in? Why not?"

"Orders, Miss."

"Orders? I don't understand."

"You need to back out of the driveway now, Miss," he replied, abruptly turning away without explanation.

Cliff had always been welcoming but today his attitude was cold. *Why such a change? What was going on?*

Alaina sped back to her apartment and placed a call to Cora knowing she needed to explain her absence.

"All nursing services for the Rusano Family have been cancelled," Cora stated, assuring her she would be assigned another position as soon as possible.

She immediately called Nick, hoping he could clear up the confusion, but her call went to voicemail.

"Nick, it's Alaina. Is everything all right? When you didn't send the car, I drove over to the house. They wouldn't let me in, I don't understand. Is something wrong? Please call me."

Nick's phone was buzzing nonstop as he lay motionless in the hospital bed, lost in a haze of heavy sedation. He had been rushed to surgery earlier that morning with a gunshot wound to his side. Fortunately, the bullet traveled clear through causing only muscular damage. He had been lucky. It still hurt like hell.

Replaying the incident in his drug induced fog was useless. *Geez, how much pain medicine are they pumping into me?* So much was unclear. He remembered getting off work around 4am and stopping in to check on his father. The nurse wasn't in the room, which was unusual. *Maybe she went to the kitchen for coffee.* Suddenly a male figure emerged from the shadows calling his name, 'Nick Rusano.' A shot went off and pain shot up his left side as he jumped to deflect the gunman's arm, unable to reach his own holster. A second shot fired and struck his father as the old man lay sleeping, unaware of the scene unfolding around him. Nick remembered his feeling of dread seeing a pool of crimson blood spread across his father's pillow just before the room went black.

He thrashed fitfully within the confines of his hospital bed, repeating the same nightmare; futilely reaching out to his father each time but being reeled back by the unrelenting grip of sedation. *Think, clear your head, open your eyes.* His hands flayed, reaching aimlessly for the tray table, the room fading in and out.

2 hours later

"I want security doubled outside this room. You hear me? No one gets in or out!"

Nick heard the voice of his friend as he struggled to open his eyes.

"Arch, what the hell happened? Where's my father?" he mumbled, slowly coming out of his stupor.

"Your father's okay, buddy, don't worry. He has a minor flesh wound on the side of his head. Daniella treated him last night and she checked on him again just now; she assures me he'll be fine. In fact, he's planning to go down to the office today. You took the worst of it, pal."

"Tell me what the fuck happened!" Nick yelled, now fully awake.

Arch turned all business, summing up the event. "This is what we know so far. The gunman gained entrance to the house through the side service door. He laid in wait, obviously knowing your schedule because we think it was an assassination attempt on both you and your father. Probably Dominic would have been hit too but he was sleeping out with some dancer from the club. Bottom line, you saved your father's life, pal. We think it was the LeBritzzis out of Chicago. Word is they believe we're responsible for high jacking their freight trucks. It was definitely a takeover attempt. You want me to send some boys to Chicago?"

"FUCK!" Nick's temper raged. "No! I'll take care of Chicago. Keep digging. Double security around my father and find the breach. How did this thug get past our security? Who sent him? *Find him!* Fuck!"

"Nurse, nurse! Get this thing out of my arm," he screamed, yanking the IV free and sending blood flying as he stumbled out of the bed, sending both he and Archer tumbling to the floor.

"Restrain him before these stitches pop! Get some Benzo into him, STAT!" a doctor screamed, rushing in with two orderlies and hoisting a combative Nick back onto the bed.

Later that night

"Nick, Nick, wake up." Archer was standing over him, shaking his shoulder.

Everything was still hazy, but Arch's face came slowly into focus. Nick chuckled to himself; *Arch never looked so good.* After a minute, he tried raising himself up in the bed, wincing in pain but more coherent.

"What do you know? How's my father?"

"Your father's fine, no ill effects, up and about. We've doubled security just as you ordered, no one going in or out. One of LeBritzzi's men was seen boarding a plane to Chicago but we didn't intervene. We suspect one of the nurses unlocked the door allowing the gunman access."

"Nurses, what the fuck!" Nick put his hand on Arch's shoulder, raising himself further up, pain pulsing through his side before releasing a defeated sigh. "Find out everything you can about the nurse angle," shaking his head in disbelief. "God damn it, I'm fuckin' one of them."

"Well, there you go, want me to pick her up?"

"No, no, not yet." He smirked, his eyes scheming, "This one is *all* mine. I'll strangle that little bitch with my bare hands. I want to look in her eyes as the breath seeps out of her body. I want her to *know* who's killing her."

Arch nodded and left.

Nick fell back onto the bed, mind racing. *That little bitch, she knew my schedule; she knew the house; even knew the alarm codes. I'll make sure she pays for this. I'll kill her… slowly.* Sleep began to overtake him then, his dreams filled with bloody revenge.

The next day

"Well, it wasn't your girl; at least, I assume you weren't sleeping with the 50-year-old!" Arch was chuckling having returned to the hospital with more news. "We rechecked the backgrounds of all the nurses. Day shift nurse was clean. That brought us to the 3-11 nurse, Alaina McGovern, and the overnight, Emma Fielding. The Fielding woman entered the complex at 10:50 pm going into the house through the service door. Your girl left at 11:20 pm, leaving through the same service door. However, the driver you had so graciously provided was waiting. He checked the door after she exited, ensuring it was locked and drove her home. The nightly perimeter rounds at 2am showed all doors secure, evidenced by the electronic printout. Records show the keypad was accessed at 3am from the interior, unlocking the door. And the ultimate proof of the overnight nurse's guilt is this." Arch handed Nick his cell phone showing a picture of Emma Fielding's bullet ridden body on the floor of a downtown dive motel, bloody $100 bills strewn across her torso.

"Seems Mrs. Fielding needed money," Arch concluded.

"Find the shooter and change every damn alarm code," Nick seethed falling back onto the pillow. *Nurses! Goddamned nurses!*

He blamed himself. His father was hurt and even though it was only a flesh wound, it should never have happened. No one, absolutely no one, should be able to get near his father. *Fucking nurses, we let them in.* He never wanted to even look at another nurse.

His phone buzzed again. Alaina was calling. He hit delete.

Chicago

Archer's investigation confirmed that the LeBritzzi brothers were behind the assassination attempt of Don Rusano. Moe Cifarelli, an independent hitman had been hired for the job. The plan was to eliminate the Rusano family and take over all Rusano holdings. Since Don Rusano was a high-ranking member of the Commission and rules state that no one can kill a ruling Don unless all other Commission members agree, a major breach had been committed and needed to be rectified. The event triggered anger throughout the organization, and everyone held their breath waiting to see what retribution would unfold. Moe Cifarelli immediately went into hiding fleeing to his hometown of Cincinnati, but his location was quickly disclosed.

Nick arrived in Cincinnati one week after being discharged from the hospital, accompanied by two of his father's men and three from his own crew. He was greeted by a capo and soldier representing the Cincinnati crime family. Sincere apologies were offered to the Rusano family since the scum bag was currently residing in their fair city.

Cifarelli was scooped up and delivered to an abandoned warehouse in the Avondale section of town. He was chained to a twelve-foot concrete wall, arms and legs splayed crucifixion style. Urine and feces stained the floor below.

The group of onlookers stood silent reverently watching as Nick Rusano commanded the room; his reputation for violence preceded him but some had never witnessed its ferocity.

Nick surveyed the area, evaluating the readily available tools of torture. Just shooting this SOB was too easy, too quick; he needed to pay for his violation of the Don. Nick removed his jacket, slowly pacing back and forth, eyeing his victim like a bird of prey. Cifarelli shook with fear, struggling against his unyielding chains as he watched his torturer walk to a nearby wall, carefully selecting a sledgehammer from the offerings.

Nick inspected his choice, caressing it, admiring the workmanship; all within view of his victim. Then he slowly turned, his eyes black, his face a demonic mask of terror. He quickly hefted the sledgehammer and, in one swift motion, slammed it into Cifarelli's right knee followed within seconds by a duplicate blow to the left. Cifarelli's screams bounced off the ceiling, his pain unfathomable. Not one of the onlookers spoke, eyes wide with fear as they inched back secure against an opposing wall.

Nick sneered; his face cloaked in shear evil. He then signaled two of his men to retrieve the unmarked container they had brought with them, watching as they lifted it on to a nearby table, grumbling under the weight. The audience dared not move from their positions as Nick opened the case, removing the ominous demolition jack hammer within. The onlookers gasped, their jaws slack staring mesmerized as he methodically attached the 15" chisel point bit to its end. Cifarelli began to quake, sweat dripping, eyes bulging.

The group remained silent, not a murmur, not a sigh, as all held their breath seeing Nick remove his shirt and don a pair of safety glasses and a waterproof surgical gown. Two of his men followed suit, stepping forward and firmly securing their shaking victim with head held upright assuring that Ciferelli would clearly see his coming retribution.

Cifarelli began to plead, screaming at high pitch, "No, no, please God, no!"

Then, in one swift move Nick Rusano hoisted the immense jack hammer with both hands and moved forward. "This is for my father," he calmly announced as he centered the drill over Cifarelli's heart.

The sound of tortured screaming was deafening as the deadly jack hammer pounded into the shooter's chest, echoing throughout the room. The sternum bone protecting the heart cracked first with a hollow eerie clap, followed by flying bits of jagged mutilated dark red cardiac muscle and profuse arcs of spurting blood. Within minutes, Cifarelli's decimated body hung lifeless from its chains; chest wall crushed—ragged pieces of membrane now dripping hideously from the surrounding perimeter. Those present had never witnessed such inhumane brutality. It would become a recurring nightmare burned into their memories for a lifetime.

Nick lowered the machine to the floor as Little Paulie raced to his boss with a towel and clean shirt. Turning to the shocked onlookers, he simply said, "Thank you for your cooperation, gentlemen."

#

Word of the butchery quickly spread so that by the time Nick and his men arrived in Chicago, the LeBritzzi brothers were waiting—and quaking. Armed members of their own crew assembled at their waterfront warehouse in anticipation of the coming assault.

Once again Nick was greeted by representatives of the local crime families, expressing their regrets. They offered assistance, but Nick refused all help and prepared his men for battle. This would be a gunfight.

At 10pm on a biting cold Saturday night on a darkened South Side pier, the group stormed the LeBritzzi warehouse, killing eight men. Nick was adamant that the LeBritzzi brothers not to be harmed but instead held for him personally.

When the fighting was over, he moved deeper into the warehouse in search of the brothers before finding them shackled to two industrial steel columns courtesy of his smiling crew. He stood calmly, never speaking, the same demonic mask of revenge staring into his victims' eyes. Raising his Glock, he casually emptied the magazine six pack fashion, striking knees, ankles and elbows—purposely maiming but not killing. Before exiting Nick ordered his men to torch both warehouses leaving the barely breathing LeBritzzi brothers within. They would be burned alive.

Nick called his father when the carnage ended to apprise him of the result. The only causality was Little Paulie, his childhood friend from the old neighborhood, who caught a stray bullet during the battle. His death would haunt Nick for life.

Humiliation

Skyler Macent was Hollywood's current male heartthrob starring in the popular television series, *The Troubled Donan Clan*. He was young, muscular, and a poster boy for raw sex appeal. He was also a compulsive gambler with a weakness for craps and poker. Skyler was heavily in debt to the Royale Casino, with management refusing to honor additional markers; however, the Royale had agreed to decrease a sizable amount of that debt if, in exchange, Skyler would host a rooftop champagne party for hotel VIPs and special guests. Skyler would be required to sign autographs, pose for pictures, assist the DJ, mingle, make nice, etc. The event was the hottest ticket on the Strip and would be a mega moneymaker for the Royale. Profits from private cabanas and VIP bottle service would be sizable but even that would not alleviate Skyler's bottomless debt.

The party kicked off at midnight. The rooftop was packed with celebrities, sports figures, and scores of seminude women. Champagne was flowing, and tables of marijuana, cocaine and other drugs were on full display for the partygoer's pleasure.

Since Ginny was dating one of the bouncers, gaining entry was easy; she invited Alaina to join her. Both were enjoying the music and champagne when, without warning, Alaina felt a pair of strong hands on her waist, spinning her around and slamming her face first into a wall of hard male pecs. She found herself staring up into a pair of familiar dark blue eyes. Dripping wet and wearing only a towel, Nick Rusano stood before her, muscles rippling as he moved both hands to her shoulders. The wound on his side was clearly visible, making him even sexier and the outline of his cock showed provocatively beneath the towel. She shivered, remembering the feeling of his huge organ deep within her and she shamelessly longed for him again. The sclera of his eyes were bloodshot, and she thought she detected the smell of marijuana. He had obviously begun to party early. He had not contacted her for over a month, never bringing closure to their relationship. It had hurt her deeply.

"Whoa, angel, what are you doing here?"

"Just enjoying the party," she replied, smiling up at him.

"Oh, no, no, no, sweetheart, not this party. This is not your kind of party," he countered. "How did you even get in here?" But as he spoke, he spied Ginny across the aisle. "Never mind, I know. You need to go home."

"Why? I'm enjoying the entertainment. What woman wouldn't appreciate a chance to admire Skyler Macent's body?" she retorted, pointing up to the stage.

Nick looked amused. "Skyler Macent's body? Honey, at this type of party *you* are the entertainment, *he* is just the noise. Go home now like a good little girl before things really kick off."

"Nicky… hurry. We want to play some more." Alaina's eyes followed the syrupy voice, spotting a trio of topless beauties in a nearby hot tub. "Bring another bottle, baby," the purring voice continued.

"Looks like you're needed elsewhere, *baby*," Alaina mocked.

"Ohhh, little girl," he replied, noting her sarcasm, "Take that fuckin' defiant look off your face, and listen to me. You need to go home *now*. You don't belong here, trust me. In fact, let me walk you to the door," he scolded, taking hold of her elbow.

But Alaina stood firm, unmoving. "So now you're my father telling me what to do? Oh, that's right, I'm not a good learner, am I? Guess I didn't hold my mouth at just the right angle. No, I think I'll stay."

He stared coldly at her for a few brief seconds, stunned by her retort. He couldn't answer, she had cut him, and she knew it. A fiery rage pulsed through his veins, eyes darkening, before he abruptly turned and stormed away.

He was right, of course. She should have gone home. As the night wore on, the alcohol and the drugs took effect and inhibitions slipped away. She might have been the only one *not* enjoying the party anymore. As she gathered her things to leave, she heard him call out. He was still in the hot tub now surrounded by three different women.

"You coming in, honey?" he taunted, champagne bottle in hand. "The water's fine, right ladies? Come join us, party girl, lose that dress and climb in. The girls will take care of you, too. Myra will do you. Won't you, Myra?"

A young redhead leaned out the side of the tub, smiling and slowly licking her lips. "Absolutely, been looking forward to it."

Nick laughed; his venom filled eyes never leaving hers.

The heat of embarrassment quickly crept up her neck as she returned Nick's stare knowing he was purposely humiliating her. "Maybe another time."

Myra raised her eyebrow, "Your loss."

He watched as she moved toward the exit, his rage still boiling. She had shamed him, and he had retaliated.

A Reckoning

He chastised himself knowing he had acted like an immature fool. But Alaina had contributed, this was her fault, not his. She had provoked *him*, he argued. *What a bitch!* She didn't belong at that party. She didn't belong anywhere near that party.

Why did he even care? He was done with nurses, all nurses. He could have any woman he wanted, always had. *Why am I feeling protective of the little country girl?*

He knew she was drunk. He had watched as she took that fourth glass of champagne. Had she tried any of the other party offerings? He should have escorted her out, sent her home in a cab. The problem was he didn't actually *see* her leave. That's what bothered him this morning. *What if she was picked up by some lowlife... or worse? I should have taken her home, been her Superman.*

Superman, really! Fuck!

He was angry at himself, but even more angry with her.

He anxiously scanned the previous night's security footage spotting her exit through the hotel's North Tower. She entered a silver Tesla with blacked-out plates— maybe a cab, ride-share, or worse, a private car; one of thousands in the city.

Storming from the hotel, he sped down the highway berating himself for being so pigheaded, his pulse seismic. He vaulted from the car, pounding on her door with both fists before kicking it in and slamming into the foyer.

"Nick, my God! What...."

"Where did you go?"

"Go? Home, I went home."

"With whom?"

"With no one, the valet got me a cab. *I went home, just as you ordered.*"

Ignoring her sarcasm, he turned from her, feeling his anger ratcheting up to levels he didn't want her to see. How could he make her understand how dangerous this city could be? She was too damned trusting, too damned reckless.

Las Vegas was a town in perpetual motion, its population overflowing and impossible to track. Small time criminals fed off the deluge of tourists that flew in daily, bored secretaries drove Highway #15 every Friday night escaping their mundane jobs in LA while seeking to earn a quick buck from unsuspecting johns, and now, worse yet, the city was hiding a dangerous secret. A vicious serial killer was stalking the innocent. Women were disappearing, only to be discovered in darkened corners of the city, each bearing red satin ribbons around their neck, wrists, and ankles, their bodies broken. The police were at a loss, warned to keep things quiet. "Can't alarm the tourists, bad for business," were the words of his buddy on the force.

Ironically, he had known one of the victims, a cocktail waitress he had dated casually. Her battered body had been callously discarded in a dumpster, adorned with the killer's red ribbon calling card. The girl had no next of kin and he had been asked to identify the body. She was also the reason his friends in city hall shared information with him.

Nick silently formulated words of warning in his mind, calm words so as not to frighten her. Then, with one deep breath, he turned only to clash with a pair of volcanic eyes spewing fire before him.

"You don't *own* me, Nick," she screeched; but as the words spilled from her mouth, she was instantly filled with regret. She loved him, wanting now to turn back time.

He paused, shocked by her assault, grasping to control his rage. His bitter reply sliced through her. "No. You're right. Absolutely right. I. Don't. Own. You." His eyes flashed fury as he abruptly spun about, leaving as quickly as he came, tires squealing from the driveway.

She stood frozen watching his Ferrari speed away, dumbfounded, and shaking as the acrid smell of burning rubber filled the air.

"My God, what happened?" Ginny shrieked, running across the lawn, dismayed.

Unable to speak, Alaina let her tears spill over as Ginny leaned in to hold her.

"Oh, honey, what happened?"

"We… had a terrible… fight, and I said horrible things, horrible, horrible things," she sobbed.

Ginny looked into Alaina's pain filled eyes, carefully guarding her response. Nick Rusano had callously destroyed another woman, but the difference was, this one was her friend. "You really love him, don't you?"

"I do, I truly do," Alaina cried, gasping for air.

"Oh, you crazy little fool. He's a hard man to love, honey," she consoled, wiping away her tears. *Why do intelligent women always fall for the assholes?* Seeing the boxes stacked at the door, she thought to distract. "How's the packing coming?"

"I don't know. I'm thinking of staying another month. A position opened up at Desert Springs. Maybe he'll come around?"

"He will, honey, I know he will. You're the best thing that's ever happened to him." Ginny didn't believe that, but she knew that was what Alaina needed to hear. Then she stepped back and smiled broadly. "But first, let me give you a little piece of Ginny advice. Girlfriend, the best way to get over a man is to get under the next one," she beamed with twinkling eyes, "and I have just the one, sweetie cakes. I know a drummer who is extremely interested in you. Come over to my place, I'll make us some coffee and show you his picture. *He's a hottie!*"

Alaina gingerly nodded; a cup of strong black coffee was just what she needed.

#

Nick downed the double shot of whiskey as he heatedly paced the guesthouse floor, shouting into the empty space. "I don't *own you*? I don't *own you*? I own everything in this goddamned town, but I don't own *you*? Fucking bitch!" he seethed, angrily hurling his empty whiskey glass into the fireplace.

Rabbit Hole

Las Vegas is home to several festivals each year featuring performers from every genre of comedy, art, and music. Most are three-to-four-day events and fans flock to the area for drinking and partying in the Vegas sun. Nick viewed the festivals as big money makers due to the increased crowds entering the city; but he also saw them as magnets for trouble and crime.

This week's event was in full swing having kicked off the previous night. The city was packed with revelers dancing in the streets, corner drug dealers hawking their wares, drunks puking on the sidewalks, and addicts passed out in alleys.

He would need to be available 24/7 to handle any trouble that overflowed into the Royale, planning to stay in his suite instead of returning to the guesthouse over the weekend. Tonight, he stood in front of the tall windows staring down at the lights of the Strip.

Memories of Alaina in his faded Princeton crew shirt flashed through his mind. He remembered the Skyler Macent party too. She standing defiant in her one dress, angry words said between them, words he now regretted. Alaina didn't belong at that party. She didn't realize that she was the candy in the candy store. All the young women were. He slammed the window with his palm, needing to get her out of his head, but she invaded his thoughts at every turn.

"Alaina McGovern is an innocent; she needs to return to that small town of hers before Las Vegas devours her," he cried aloud, trying to free himself of her ghostly image. Would she venture out, he wondered, unaware of the danger? "Of course, she will!" he hissed, again speaking to no one.

"She needs to marry a fireman, have a pack of kids, join the PTA and spend her summers on a beach somewhere chasing after babies," he yelled, continuing the argument with his own silent reflection in the cold, black window.

His internal battle raged on. *Why do I even care what she does? Why do I need to protect her? She's an adult, she can make her own decisions—decisions and mistakes. Maybe she's gone, left town, up in Canada, drinking, fucking.* That thought angered him even more, igniting his jealousy. "You're a grown man arguing with yourself about a naive little girl from your past. *Get a goddamned grip!*"

But there she was in the front of his mind again, and again, and again. His attempts to vanquish her futile. Her soft siren song called to him, her bewitching eyes beckoned. Envisioning her image laying peacefully in his arms, he blindly reached for her finding nothing but emptiness as his subconscious took control.

"No, no, no!" he screamed, tightly closing his eyes, and pressing his fingers to his forehead. "Who am I, her goddamned Ulysses? I'm losing my sanity over a skirt!"

But there was no denying… the witch was in his head.

He called downstairs instructing the valet to bring his car around. He would just slip out for a quick ride, get some air and clear his head, but soon he found himself on her street, staring at her empty driveway. *SHE WAS OUT!* He parked a few houses down and waited– midnight, 1am, 2am. At 2:20 his cell phone rang, there was trouble in the craps pit.

#

He returned to utter bedlam, seeing a crowd of fifty unruly tourists cheering as a topless woman danced atop a table in the center of the casino floor. Four very drunk, slovenly dressed frat boys were adding to the chaos tossing beer and money at the young woman as they chanted obscenities. Nick's rage hit a tipping point.

"GET HER DOWN, YOU FOOLS!" he bellowed to his hapless security staff, before attempting to vault onto the table himself. It was then that someone gripped his shoulder, forcing him to turn sharply about. Nick was face to face with a foul-smelling male in an ill-fitting cowboy hat; his flannel shirt undone, revealing the vomit-stained undershirt beneath. The stench of his breath was appalling.

"Hey man, let the bitch dance," he yelled, revving up the crowd.

"Dance, dance, dance," the growing crowd chanted as Nick's furor rose and the images surrounding him grew hazy. He stepped back, sending his iron fist to connect with the offender's jaw. A loud, sickening crack echoed, followed by a shower of blood and teeth raining onto the craps table, causing dice and chips to scatter. The frightened crowd screamed, some quickly grabbing a handful of chips as they scurried away. Nick assessed the damage. The cowboy was passed out cold, slumped over the rail of the table, blood streaming from his mouth, jaw broken. The incident would surely make the morning news.

Vegas is a rabbit hole for the innocent; dark and deep. Only a few are capable of clawing their way out. *Where was she?*

The Ugly

Dark days prevailed with Nick's heightened anguish continuing, his soul sinking to bottomless depths. He had pushed Alaina from his mind allowing vehement anger to win out, but the fact that some low life had breached their security and caused his father to suffer repeatedly tore at him. He punished himself daily, drowning his guilt in hedonistic debauchery.

He had taken care of Chicago immediately after the attempt on his father's life even though he was still healing from the gunshot wound. No one would dare make another attempt at the old man's life after the carnage he had left behind. The one innocent victim of that retribution was Little Paulie; and Nick vowed to take care of the baby daughter Paulie had left behind.

It was Archer who finally brought him around, confronting him one morning after a night of heavy drinking. Nick had been staying in his hotel suite, too drunk most nights to drive back to the guesthouse after his shift. Last night he took another showgirl to bed but this morning he couldn't even look at her. "Get the hell out of here," he sneered.

"Well, you look like shit!" Arch began, stopping to laugh as the half-naked girl ran past. He threw up his hands, exasperated, "Enough is enough! You can't blame yourself forever. None of this was your fault. Christ, you saved the old man. If you hadn't walked in, he would be dead for sure. Nick? You listening to me? That old man needs you; he can't do this alone. It's too much. You think you almost lost your father; well, he's worried he's lost his son. He's hurting just as much as you."

Nick leaped from the chair, grabbing Arch by his shoulders, eyes wild with anger. "He'll never lose me, never! You hear me? Never!"

The two men stared off for several seconds before Nick's sanity returned. He walked to the window and looked down at the Vegas Strip, silent and contrite. Arch remained quiet, waiting, hoping.

"What day is it, Arch?"

"Thursday, November 22nd."

As if stunned, Nick turned with eyes wide, meeting those of his friend. "You're right, it's time. Let me shower."

#

Nick entered his father's office, clean shaven, fresh shirt, fully sober. It had taken two months for him to release the guilt of failing to protect the man he so deeply loved. The Old Don sat surrounded in strength by his underboss and two of his men. He nodded to his son and Archer, motioning them to sit. Nick assessed the great man noting ominous physical changes. He appeared worried, more fragile, his strength waning. It was obvious the incident had taken a toll on them both.

"I need you in Spokane, Sammy W's take was short this month. Spokane's having trouble resolving the matter. Go remind Sammy who the *Boss* is. On your way back, stop in Sacramento and pay respects to Big Howie's widow. Make sure she's financially secure then meet with his crew but before you go, decide who *you* want running things out there. I need you back by Wednesday, have some people coming in."

Nick nodded and stood, preparing to leave but the Old Don abruptly raised his hand to stay him. Rising stiffly from his creaking chair, he moved from behind the desk to stand in front of his son. He wrapped him in a firm hug then gingerly touched his healing side.

"Good?" he asked.

"Good," Nick replied.

Fireplaces Make Terrible Therapists

Nick stared into the cold fireplace, replaying the latest confrontation with his friend. Arch had stopped by the Royale with some paperwork, eager to share his good news—Daniella was pregnant again. The conversation spiraled.

"So, when are you going to settle down, start a family, get rid of these bimbos you're running with?" teased Archer.

Nick shot him a venomous look, "I'm doing just fine, thanks. I've got no problem in the fuckin' department, having a good time with the bitches, that's the way I like it."

"Are you, are you really having a good time?" Arch countered, all joviality gone. "What I saw running out of here last week doesn't tell me you're happy with your life. Maybe it's time you met a real girl, a decent girl."

"Yeah, right, decent girl!" Nick spat back, "A decent girl would never understand what we do, and you know it. Maybe you should go over to the Old Country and hand pick me a girl, huh? A nice quiet Italian girl? How about church, think you can find me a decent girl at church?"

Arch saw the anger escalating between them and tried to defuse it, raising his hand defensively, "Hey, just lookin' out for you, buddy. Thought maybe it was time, is all, nice girl, couple of kids, sorry."

Nick tossed the papers back at Archer. "Yeah, well I pay you to be my lawyer, not my fuckin' matchmaker." He regretted those words the moment he said them, seeing the hurt in Arch's eyes. They had been best friends since college.

Arch was right, of course; he always was. Arch was the sensible one, giving careful counsel, calculating the consequences of the second step, guiding him, always there. But above all, he was Nick's one true friend. He recognized the truth in Arch's taunt, knowing he was still abusing his body with too much alcohol and too many women, those words echoed in his mind. Alaina kept toying with him too, a seductive tempest dancing through his memory. He remembered their mornings on the boat, her head resting on his shoulder, the lavender scent of her shampoo. He recalled the feel of her body nestled into his as they warmed themselves on cold mornings by the fireplace, sharing stories and laughter. She had been his respite. *A DECENT GIRL!*

The attempt on his father's life had given him a reason to force her away. Convenient! That was the lie he told himself; but he had pushed her from his life before that—afraid to commit—afraid to relinquish a lifestyle that now was giving him no damn satisfaction.

He had deleted all her calls except for the last, still not understanding his reason for keeping it. She would have said it was fate. He clicked his messages and played it back, remembering.

"Nick, it's Alaina again. I thought I would call one last time; take a chance and roll the dice as you would say. I don't understand what happened with us, but I refuse to believe that what we shared was meaningless. Call me if you want, if not, I get it." Her voice hitched just slightly at the end, but he heard it.

That afternoon, he drove to the Big House to visit his mother.

"Ah! My son comes to see me!" she chuckled, pinching his cheek like a little boy. They sat for hours drinking grappa as she rambled on about Aunt Sonja's arthritis and Uncle Bernie's indigestion, but he didn't hear a word. When he finally rose to leave, she turned to him, "So, did you work it out?"

"What's that, Mama?"

"Your problem?"

"I think so, Mama," leaning in to kiss her head.

He phoned Arch on his way to the car, "Meet me at the club, 4 o'clock."

Who Are You?

Arch shook with trepidation; their last meeting had not gone well. He would tread lightly. Nick was wired, volatile, pacing and staring blankly at the streets below. Suddenly he halted, spinning around, his quick movement surprising Arch.

"I want you to do a thorough background check on Alaina McGovern. Find out everything you can. Understand? I want to know her fuckin' shoe size."

Arch nodded, inwardly smiling, maybe his friend really was listening.

Three days later he returned with that report, and they sat leisurely reviewing the information over several glasses of whiskey.

"Raised by a single mother in tenement housing."

"Tenement housing?" Nick questioned, eyebrows up.

"Yeah, you know, government assisted housing."

Nick nodded, "Go on."

"Anyway, catholic schools, good grades, worked throughout high school and college, couple boyfriends, nothing serious, a handful of close friends. Earned a nursing degree from the local college. Took a job at a nearby hospital, had a brief affair with a doctor there, a Dr. Rhys Ravikumar. Didn't end well. They had a big blowup in the hospital parking lot, witnessed by several coworkers. He was married, she apparently wasn't happy about that."

"Mom passed away and she never looked back. No other family that I could find. She signed on with a traveling nursing agency, been all over the country. Has over $40,000 in the bank. Doesn't spend much, mostly books, wine, and essentials. Good credit score, pays her bills in full each month. Bought her car with cash from her savings account. But… works like she trying to put something behind her; I'm not sure what yet, but I'll keep digging. Could be connected to someone she's searching for, someone named Frenchie, seems they were close. Other than that, Internet's clean, nothing weird."

"After the incident at the Big House, the agency temporarily assigned her to (he looked down at his notes) the Oncology ward (that's cancer) at Desert Springs Hospital. That assignment's coming to an end, her next post will be Northwest Medical Center, Tucson, but I haven't been able to verify that yet. Oh, and ah..., she wears a size 7 shoe."

Nick chuckled, "Still in town then?"

"As far as I know, yes. No activity on her credit cards, no gas stations, no tolls." Arch pushed, "Did she tell you any of this, did she lie?"

"No, didn't lie. Didn't tell me everything but didn't lie."

Arch cautiously gave it one more shot. "Well, your dad liked her. He wanted to be sure it wasn't 'the little one' that betrayed the family. Of course, I can always go over to the Old Country for you," teasing, he shot Nick a wink.

"Get the hell out of here. Don't you have some paperwork to do or something?"

They both laughed, their relationship repaired.

Battle with the Devil

The driveway was empty. Where was she? Calling wasn't an option. He needed to see her eyes, needed to know if he could save what he had so cavalierly tossed aside. He was surprised it had come to this. Marriage! Geez! Never planned on marriage, never even thought about it. But this was a girl you married.

He sat across from her empty driveway, nervously waiting. He knew she wasn't working today having already called the agency. Cora cited privacy issues, refusing to give him Alaina's whereabouts; however, Nick tried coaxing more information from the woman stating that his father might require future care, asking if Alaina would be available. But even after pouring on all his charm, Cora only revealed that Alaina's contract with Desert Springs Hospital had ended. *Nothing more.* Nibbing at the back of his mind was an angry thought. Could she be with another man? *No, she's still in love with me. Maybe?*

"All this over a damn *skirt!* What the hell am I doing?" he yelled, his frustration reverberating off the console as he hit the steering wheel with both fists. But she was more than that. He couldn't get her out of his head, surrounded by her voice, her laugh, her smile. He could still smell her perfume on his crew shirt— why hadn't he washed it?

Deep down he knew the answer. When he was with her, he was able to live beyond the concrete barrier that shielded his mind from the violence. Visions from the horrid acts he had inflicted on his enemies faded away when she was near. She vanquished the memories that haunted his dreams like a priest absolving a sinner. Her gentle touch calmed his heart, her quiet voice soothed him, her smile brought him peace.

Removing the ring box from his pocket, he stared at the diamond within, still wrestling with the demon that tormented him. "This is wrong," said the demon, instilling words of doubt. "She'll never understand what you do, never accept it. She's nobody, just another woman. Go fuck a couple dancers, down some whiskey, drown out the memories of that little bitch."

Angrily snapping the ring box shut, he flung it onto the car floor, his mental energy depleted, and soon he lapsed into a fitful sleep as his mind's battle raged on, pulling, tugging, pulling, tugging.

A blaring horn assaulted his ears, jerking him awake as a large yellow moving van pulled into her driveway followed by a beat-up Volkswagen bus packed full of boxes and toys. Three small children and a scruffy terrier gleefully piled out followed by two weary parents. *What the hell!*

The answer to his internal battle was now evident. He needed her, he just needed to find her.

Reggie's House of Cards

Reggie McGahn and his wife, Monique had saved up forty thousand dollars over the past four years through hard work and sacrifice. Reggie worked two jobs, the first as a maintenance man at the local community college followed by night shifts at the neighborhood convenience store. He had been robbed three times, the last at gunpoint. His wife worked as a home health aide accepting every shift available, adding every spare nickel to their savings. Their dream was to own a home of their own away from the crime of the inner city where the drug culture reached out to their ten-year-old son around every corner.

Every Sunday Monique circled the real estate ads hoping to find something they could afford. The banks were not helpful, their down payment was not enough, their credit history poor.

But Reggie had a plan, a flawless plan. For months he had studied every book he could find on the game of poker, unbeknownst to his wife and son. He combed websites each day exploring strategies to improve his play. He begged his coworkers to practice with him during every lunch and coffee break. He was confident he could win big and buy Monique the home of her dreams, seeing visions of his family's adoration as they joyfully celebrated holidays and birthdays together in their own home.

Reggie excitedly put his plan in motion, secretly calling in sick to both his jobs.

A one-day poker tournament can last ten to twelve hours and the Royale required all players to register their financial information, ensuring they never exceeded their available funds. He proudly deposited the $10,000. entrance fee. He would be competing against two hundred players for the day's no limit Texas Hold 'Em tournament.

Early play proved promising; he was winning hand after hand, confident in his skill. Inexperienced players were already dropping out, the competition dwindling. Reggie surveyed the room. It was easy to spot the professional players and they in turn were watching him, knowing he was an amateur, soon to fall.

As the afternoon wore on, Reggie's luck slowly turned; his winning hands became fewer and fewer, forcing him to make reckless decisions, bet poorly, and withdraw more and more funds. By the fifth hour, he had lost every dime that he and Monique had saved. His bank account was empty, forty thousand dollars gone in one short day, all hopes and dreams shattered. He had failed.

The call came through to Nick's private line at 1:45am. The Royale had a jumper. Reggie McGahn had thrown himself off the ninth floor of the Royale parking garage.

Longshot

Nick drove straight through from Vegas to Tucson; probably should have been stopped for speeding but no one bothered him. He knew he had to find her. He had no address. Arch was frantically working on that, but he could easily locate the Northwest Medical Center.

He cruised the employee parking lots until he spotted her car, then he chose a nearby slot so he could watch for her when her shift ended. He hadn't slept in over thirty hours, the paperwork and police reports from that troubled poker player had delayed his departure. Nick understood gambling addiction, but incidents like this always bothered him. How many desperate souls came to Vegas risking every dime hoping for that one *big win*? How many blew their brains out in a low rent motel room or jumped to their death to the concrete below? Scenes of that suicide plagued his thoughts throughout his entire drive. He just needed to shut his eyes for a few short hours.

Arch's call roused him. "Hey, buddy. I have that address for you."

"No need, I'm at the hospital, found her car in the lot. Hopefully, she'll be out soon."

"Great, great, well, good luck."

Nick chuckled, "Thanks, something tells me I'm gonna need it. I'm facing a Banshee Irish woman who probably won't be glad to see me."

"Nah, buddy, just turn on your charm. She'll fall right into your arms."

Nick hoped that was true, but he knew it unlikely. He was anxious. He hadn't seen her in months, ignored her phone calls, cut her off. He had hurt her.

3pm shift change

It wasn't long before he saw her walking out with three other nurses, all talking casually. There was that smile and that squeaky little voice he had come to miss. Well here goes, he thought, exiting his car, and heading in her direction. One of her companions spotted him first, drawing the group's attention and causing him to stop advancing. Her face revealed nothing, neither anger nor joy. Had he lost her? Was she no longer his?

Alaina halted abruptly, her breath catching. Nick Rusano stood in the distance; tall, broad shouldered, more handsome than she remembered in a perfectly tailored charcoal gray suit and mirrored sunglasses. He was leaning casually on her car, arms crossed, looking as if he were expected, simply there to drive her home. She told the others to go on without her, but they surrounded her in a protective stance, peering at him over their shoulders.

"Are you sure?" Nick heard the male nurse ask.

"Yes, he's a friend."

Forty feet separated them, and Alaina fought the urge to run and jump into his arms. "Don't make a fool of yourself," she murmured, so low he couldn't hear, as a chill shot through her despite the heat of Tucson's sun.

Did he see happiness in her eyes? He still couldn't tell as she slowly edged closer.

"Nick, what are you doing here?" she asked as casually as her nerves could manage even though she was shaking internally.

"I need to talk to you."

"Okay," she answered, just as one of her companions shouted from her car window, "Are you sure you're all right?"

"I'm good, thanks," waving her on.

Nick looked at her quizzically, "What do they think I'm going to do?"

"Well, you could be an ex-husband, a jilted lover, she doesn't know. You are a scary dude. It's the cuff links, babe," she smirked, sneaking a peek at him while desperately groping for control.

His mind raced backward momentarily, reeling with confusion. *Wait, did she just call me babe?*

"Is there somewhere we can talk, in private?" He was nervous enough and this was not what he envisioned.

"Um, I… I think we can cut through here," pointing toward the right. "There should be a visitors area around this bend… sorry, I'm still learning my way." Her heart was pounding. He looked so good, strong and muscular. She longed to reach out and touch him, to have him touch her.

She led him down a winding path lined with fragrant gardenia shrubs and stone benches, stopping beneath a regal cherry blossom tree in full bloom, it's sweet scent filling the air. They were alone, far from all others, tucked beneath a canopy of tender pink petals. This is good, romantic like, he thought.

"Nick, what is it? Is your father ill?" she asked, concern written across her face.

"Dad's fine, it's not about him." Turning to face her, he reached for her hand. "I just needed to talk to you, clear some things up." *Wow, that was dumb, try again.* Taking a deep breath, he continued, "I know I messed up. I know I hurt you and I'm sorry. I'm… I'm asking you to forgive me for the way I treated you."

He was stammering, so unlike the Nick she knew. She waited, then she slowly placed her palm on his cheek. "It's okay, really."

Immediately, the magic of her touch pulsed through him like a soothing balm, slowing the ever-erratic beat of his heart and cleansing his soul of the previous months despair. He rushed to place his own hand over hers, fearful of losing the connection. "No, no it's not okay. I know you think I played you. It was never that. I… I…."

She felt her throat closing, her tears rising, knowing she was losing the battle to control her emotions. She was too close to him, and she tried to step back but he reached for her elbow, holding her fast.

"I'm no good at this, Alaina, I'm no good at words," he choked, his eyes looking deeply into hers. "But I know that I love you and I'm hoping you still love me. I know you did once."

She heard the pleading in his voice and could no longer hold back her tears, letting them burst forth. "Damn you, Nicky, damn you," she cried, lunging forward, fists pounding into his shoulders.

"I'm sorry, baby, I'm so sorry," he whispered, pressing her face to his chest. "I never meant to hurt you." *Courage, you need courage, say the words you came to say.* "I need you to marry me. I'm asking you to marry me." Releasing his hold, he gently pushed back, cradling her face in his palms. "Will you marry me?"

She couldn't move, she fought to breathe, not believing what she was hearing— tears still flooding her face—her heart beating wildly.

"Ma…marry…you? Yes…yes, yes, yes, yes, yes," she cried before jumping into his arms.

Relief coursed through him as he pressed her tightly to him unwilling to let her go. Then lifting her face to his, he kissed her deeply, feeling her tears still streaming down.

"Is that a yes?" he chuckled, wiping her tears with his thumbs. But she could only nod, still unable to speak.

Jubilation filled his core as he awkwardly fumbled for the ring.

"Oh Nick, it's beautiful, absolutely beautiful," she gushed, gazing in wonder at the shimmering three-carat diamond surrounded by amethysts mounted atop a platinum Art Deco setting.

"If it's not what you want, we can exchange it."

"No, no, it's perfect, just perfect."

"Then let me kiss the hand of the dazzling woman who will wear it," he replied, slipping the ring onto her finger, and lifting her hand to his lips. Then folding her into his arms again, he kissed her lips, slowly, passionately.

A loud 'ahem' jolted them from their embrace as an elderly couple walked by, the gentleman winking at Nick.

Looking into Alaina's eyes, he whispered, "I think we need to get a room."

Do Not Disturb

They attacked each other with sheer abandon, both so hungry for the other's touch that clothes flew to the floor the minute the door closed. She needed to feel every inch of his hard body: his chest, his back, his cock deep inside. He needed to own her body, to taste her, to satisfy her in every way he knew how, to make her beg and scream for orgasm.

Their first round of sex was rough from the moment he threw her onto the bed. She gasped when he entered her, remembering how huge his cock was, how much it filled her. They were both still panting, engulfed in their rapture when she pulled his face to hers. "OH love, I missed you, I missed you so damned much. I love you." One tiny tear escaped as she looked up at him. "I've always been yours."

Smiling, he brushed a tendril of hair from her cheek, tenderly wiping away the fallen tear.

"Shh, no tears, my *Madonna*, not now. We are together, we are right where we need to be and always will be. *Together* is when we are both at peace. I love you too, woman. It just took me a while to understand what I was feeling. I'm no good without you. I need you by my side."

His tender words erased all memories of the past months' heartache bathing them both in love's euphoria before he released a soft chuckle. "Woman, you have been messing with my head for months. I saw you everywhere, around every bend and corner. I even chased you down a corridor once. Felt like a fool, frightened some poor tourist to death. You drove me mad!"

"What?"

"Uh-huh, you haunted me, calling to me in my dreams like some mythical siren. I cursed you for the witch you are."

She burst into laughter, "Well, if I'm a witch, who are you?"

"Hmm, I'm the devil in your bed," he answered, his mouth twisting into a lecherous sneer. Releasing a guttural growl from deep within his throat, he plunged toward her, ravishing her neck with savage wet kisses, and sending her pulse skyrocketing, igniting every nerve. The devil danced in his eyes as he rolled her onto her back, hovering menacingly above. She knew this move well, answering with a smile. Role playing had always added to their fun and games of domination fueled his desires.

"Sounds like the devil wants to play," she whispered demurely, portraying the innocent captive. "Are you a demon, kind sir, or a fallen angel come to ravish me?"

One more low growl escaped his throat, before he stood and deftly gripped her hips, yanking her to the edge of the bed. She answered with a vixen's laugh, gleefully wrapping her legs around him as he placed his hand beneath her buttocks, circling her nub with the tip of his enormous shaft, increasing her hunger. She arched her back, breathless in anticipation as he slowly entered her, relishing the feeling of fullness. They watched each other, moving together, pounding deeper, rougher; mutual bliss pouring from their eyes with every thrust. His wicked smile teased, bringing her to the edge, then purposely slowing. He needed to hear her plead, needed to command her body, needed to be her master. She cried out, begging for him to plunge harder but he slowed even more, making her wait, making her beg, owning her completely.

"Damn you, Nicky, you are so *evil*," she yelled, pounding his bicep with her fist, each plea adding to his arousal.

"Here I come, baby, here I come," he answered, his gaze drunk with pleasure.

Then with three more hard, penetrating thrusts they both gave in to utter ecstasy, suspended in orgasmic fulfillment.

They lay exhausted, legs entangled, facing each other on the pillows, his hand reverently stroking her hair. "You're going to cripple me, woman," he joked just as a loud knock on their door ripped them from their revelry.

"Mr. Rusano, hello, Mr. Rusano?"

"What the hell!" Nick quickly wrapped himself in a towel and threw open the door.

"Excuse me, sir. I'm… I'm Milo, the hotel manager. We've had a report of a woman screaming. Is… is everything all right?" A small man stood in the doorway, nervously staring up at Nick's large presence.

"A woman screaming?" Nick repeated with delighted astonishment. "Look, ah, we're newlyweds, and, ah, well…."

"I understand, sir, but I would just like to make sure that the mrs. is all right, for her safety, sir, please. I'm sure you understand."

Nick could barely contain his laughter. "Honey, throw a sheet over yourself and let this fine young man see that I'm not trying to kill you." He held up his hand to the hotel manager blocking his entrance. "You ready, baby?"

"Yes, okay, I'm ready," she meekly replied, sitting completely covered.

Nick motioned for the manager to enter.

"Hi, I'm fine, thank you," she squeaked, giving a small wave to the little man as she pressed her lips together to stifle her laughter.

"Thank you, thank you, Mr. and Mrs. Rusano. Maybe if you could keep it down a little, it would be greatly appreciated by the other guests," he stammered, eyes wide.

Nick's smirk was palpable. "We'll keep that in mind," he replied, closing the door, and returning to her, as they both burst into laughter.

"Oh my God, I'm so sorry," she cried through bright red cheeks.

"Don't you dare say you're sorry. That was the highlight of his day, you vixen." Laughing, he pulled her from the bed and smacked her ass with the towel. "Let's go get some dinner, give the guests a chance to sleep."

Every woman has a tell when they reach true orgasm. Men don't usually notice this or don't care as long as they themselves are satisfied. Most women fake it anyway. With Alaina, her tell was her trembling hands, most often her right.

Rules of Play

"I'm not having a long-distance marriage."

"I know."

"You're not traveling all over the country."

"I know."

"You need to quit your job."

"I know."

He was about to make another statement when she interrupted, "I KNOW."

A smirk crossed his face. "Are you trying to tell me this is not what I need to be saying on the night we got engaged?"

"Smart man," she replied, squeezing his hand across the table. "However, since you are laying down terms, let me state one of my own. Don't you ever humiliate me again."

He looked at her, quizzically.

"Rub a dub dub, three tarts in a tub. I'm referring to your bimbo hot tub stunt."

He roared with laughter, "Not my best moment, but as I recall it was you, my lady, who threw down the gauntlet that evening." Then, without warning, his mood grew solemn, "I want us to have a normal life, Alaina. I want our children to have a normal life, a life like other families with BBQs and birthday parties, with bedtime stories and trips to the zoo. I want to watch our children play and hear their laughter. I want us to create a home where they will feel secure, unafraid to express their thoughts and fears, where they know they will be heard and supported. Tell me we can do that."

That night, he purged his soul, slowly letting slip his warrior armor, and she listened, knowing she was his release. He talked of the attack on his father explaining it as rivalry among business associates—he omitted Chicago. He told her of the investigation to determine which nurse was involved, how she was also suspect, confessing his misplaced anger. He told her of his destructive behavior, the demon he pushed down, the alcohol abuse—he omitted the women. The sincerity in his voice was almost palpable and as the hours passed, she saw a man who idolized his father and sadly, only knew coldness from his mother. He drifted into a tranquil sleep around 3am; his strong, hard features transforming into that of a small boy at rest.

#

Alaina remained in Tucson to fulfill her sixty-day contract while Nick accompanied the Old Don to New York for a mandatory meeting with the Commission. The issue of most concern was an impending union revolt at a Bronx job site. As a rule, bosses preferred to handle their own territories and asking for help showed weakness, but current tactics had proven ineffective.

"My son will handle it," the Old Don volunteered.

All agreed that Nick Rusano's intervention would guarantee a quick resolution to the situation and Don Angelo knew the value of having east coast bosses in his debt.

Additionally, a rookie senator from South Carolina was blocking a bill to legalize gambling in his state. Bribery had failed thus far. The group again requested help and Nick's powers of persuasion were found to be the best solution. A thorough background check might get the needed result, Nick thought. After all, there were skeletons in everyone's closet, no one is ever squeaky clean. Finally, Don Carlos from Rochester was ailing, and the group approved his son as successor.

When the New York business was finalized, Don Angelo suggested a quick two-hour drive south to Atlantic City. He was feeling nostalgic, wanting to visit with old friends from the Ducktown neighborhood.

#

"Oh, things are not the same, we all wish you would come back." Old Bongiovanni shook his head remorsefully. "The young ones, they run the neighborhood now. Reckless, violent, no respect, there's no reasoning with them," the old man bemoaned, sorrow in his rheumy eyes, his gnarled hand reaching out.

Don Angelo listened to the litany of complaints from more of his old friends and it saddened him. He slowly surveyed Mississippi Avenue, observing its deterioration, and noting the peeling paint and clogged gutters. But he was no longer the ruling don of this area, he had no authority here.

"Let's take a stroll on the boardwalk, Son," he suggested, but as they walked his sorrow only deepened. "It could have been great; this city could have been great but look at it. They were afraid, formed some control commission, issued licenses, background checks! They didn't want us: no Mafia, no Mob control, no bright lights, no waving cowboys." The Old Don laughed, "But we were already here, had been for decades. *We* know how to run a casino. They were such fools! Said they wanted their casinos to be *tasteful!* Does this look tasteful to you?" The old man scanned the storefronts hawking ninety-nine cent souvenirs and three-dollar tee-shirts, shaking his head in mockery.

"You're right, Dad," Nick concurred, standing at the rail looking out at the pristine white sand of a vacant beach. The once famous boardwalk was empty, save for a few dozen stragglers and a handful of panhandlers begging for coins. He thought of Vegas knowing that at this very moment, the Strip would be crowded with throngs of tourists packed shoulder to shoulder, eager to spend their money.

His father spoke the truth, foolish men had let this city die. Atlantic City had wasted the financial opportunity of a lifetime. It was a great place to grow up, but he was glad to be gone.

Senator Chad Boyd

Nick Rusano flew into Columbia, South Carolina on a balmy spring morning. He was met by Joe "Sis" Cinchoni, an underboss in the Dixie Mafia. Nick reviewed the current situation, finding it unchanged from the New York meeting the previous week. The South Carolina legislature had still not approved legalized gambling, the vote being held up by one very vocal and pious Senator Chad Boyd.

"How hard can this be? Why can't you handle this yourselves?"

"We can't get next to this schmuck," Cinchoni retorted. "He's clean, too clean, a friggin' altar boy."

"All right, all right. Tell your people to get me an appointment tomorrow morning. I'm an outside interest wanting to make a large donation to his re-election campaign. And remember, the west coast will expect you to return the favor in the future."

#

"Senator Boyd, nice to make your acquaintance." Nick offered his hand while assessing the young senator—29 years old, sandy blond hair, sharp eyes, wearing a cheap, wrinkled Brooks Brothers suit, loafers, no socks.

"Please sit," replied Boyd. "I understand you are interested in the future of our great state of South Carolina. What can I do to assist you in that matter, Mr. ah...Rusano?"

Nick noted the attempt by Boyd to take control—presuming superiority. This was a boy playing a man's game.

"I understand the vote to legalize gaming is coming before the state legislature again."

Boyd tried to interrupt but Nick held up his hand, intimidating the young senator.

"It is in my interest and that of my associates that this particular legislation be passed. We intend to invest a great deal of money and effort in your beautiful coastlines and cities. Obviously, that would not only benefit your constituents with increased employment opportunities but also increase revenue for *all* aspects of your state's economy. We, of course, would be willing to make a sizable contribution to your upcoming reelection in order to ensure that positive outcome."

"That's why you're here, who are you?" The senator postured, trying to maintain some small amount of decorum. "The answer is *no, absolutely not!* I am adamantly opposed to casino gambling." His voice was rising. "My daddy was a compulsive gambler and a drunk. He lost the family fortune and left my mother penniless. I've had to claw my way out of poverty to get where I am today. You can take your offensive offer and leave my office, *now*."

Nick remained seated, emotionless.

The senator grew red in the face, fingering his shirt collar, sweat forming on his brow.

Nick stared steadily allowing the senator's discomfort to increase.

"I understand, Chad, that you are married to a lovely young Charleston girl, Shelby, is that right? Comes from a very prominent founding family, a true lady of the south."

"That's right," his voice still rebellious.

"And you recently became a father, twin girls?"

"Yes, right, right, where is this going?" more wary.

"I also understand that you recently found it necessary to replace your secretary, is that correct? Seems the previous one disappeared—*suddenly* disappeared. Her name was Cayla, correct? And the two of you were having an affair of which your wife was unaware. Do I have my facts straight, Chad?"

Boyd was beginning to tremble, both hands beginning to shake. Removing a handkerchief from his pocket, he wiped away the sweat from his brow. *Who was this stranger?* "I… I don't know what you're talking about. I never had an affair with that girl, never!"

Nick removed a small black and white photo from his pocket along with a hotel receipt for a local third-rate hotel. "Is this her? She was a pretty girl, I must admit."

Boyd was silent, fumbling with a letter opener on his desk, sneaking short looks at the photo before him.

Nick returned the photo and receipt to his pocket. "You also own a boat, correct? I enjoy boating myself, gives a person a feeling of total isolation and freedom. Some believe you can get away with just about anything while out on the water. The problem is… isolation doesn't exist in today's world; Marine Police and harbor patrols track every vessel on the water, GPS can track you also. For example, on the evening your secretary disappeared, you traveled to a particular set of coordinates four miles off the coast. I have those coordinates right here in my pocket." Nick reached into his breast pocket retrieving a folded paper. "Curiously though, immediately before that trip, you purchased a large red and white cooler. Catch a lot of fish, do you?"

The senator was fiercely trembling now, sweat dripping onto his desk.

"You can't prove any of that, not any of that," he yelled, knocking over his chair as he attempted to stand.

"Quite frankly, Chad, I don't need to prove it. I simply need to raise suspicion with local law enforcement —turn over a few pieces of evidence. I do hope you gutted her before dumping her. If not, the body blows up with gas and floats, gets messy. Were you aware of that? Coolers sometimes pop open. It only takes a dive team to give that poor girl's family some long overdue closure."

Nick took a moment to pause, seeing Boyd's entire body now shaking in fear, his face and neck bright red. "We look forward to your endorsement of the casino legislation unless, of course, you require another visit."

His business concluded, Nick flew back to Vegas that evening, anticipating Alaina's return.

#

"You goof!" Alaina laughed as he handed her a huge, overstuffed bag of saltwater taffy from his Atlantic City trip.

"Hey, it's your souvenir," he replied, grinning like a child. "Welcome home and girl, you better be staying home this time. You have a wedding to plan."

They sat in front of the fireplace that night, locked in each other's embrace, laughing, talking, at peace. He felt the tension of the last few weeks vanish the minute her palm crossed his chest, forever erasing Chad Boyd and the Bronx from his mind. Her gentle touch vanquished his demons, her fingers his salve. All was well in his world.

Shattered Wings

The Old Don was delighted, giving his immediate blessing when the young couple shared the news of their engagement. He had hoped to cement an east coast alliance with one of the powerful New York families by convincing his son to strategically wed one of their daughters, but alas, he was thankful the boy was finally settling down. He knew Alaina McGovern to be honest, compassionate, and discreet; hopefully, she would be the solid anchor his playboy son needed. No doubt, his son would teach her what a woman's place was and what it was *not* in a Mafia household.

Alaina wanted a small, private ceremony because she had no family, but Nick let her know that was impossible given the size of his own family and the business associates that would need to express their good wishes. She did, however, insist that they be married before God by a Catholic priest; so, Nick conceded, arranging for them to exchange vows at a small private chapel the evening before the wedding. He made a sizable donation to a forward-thinking priest whose parish needed a new roof, eliminating the six month wait time nonsense. He wanted to be married as soon as possible.

He teased her as they entered the little chapel, "You realize, angel, if I step inside a church, God will send lightning to strike me down."

"Oh, you're silly," she replied.

But when they stood in the candlelight as this man of God pronounced them man and wife, they both felt the gravity of the moment. Their union filled them with an inner peace neither had ever felt before.

Following their vows, Nick led her into an adjacent rose garden. "I have a wedding present for you."

She stared in awe at the dazzling pair of waterfall diamond earrings sitting atop a velvet sapphire cushion.

"*You* are my diamond, Alaina Rusano. I have never felt this way about anyone in my life. I truly love you. Honor me by wearing these tomorrow."

"Oh, Nicky, you are too good to me," she breathlessly replied, before a conspirator's smile crossed her lips. "If I put them on now, could we elope tonight? That sweet little priest just pronounced us man and wife."

Chuckling, he looked to the heavens, "Tell me God, how could you have sent me such a silly woman?"

#

The following day the main event took place. The ballroom was a glittering display of white and gold, filled with the delicate scent of hundreds of magenta and white spectator lilies and dozens of pink cherry blossom garlands—the bride's favorite flowers. Sparkling crystal chandeliers glistened from above and cascading water fountains filled every corner, adding to the elegance. Nick had spared no expense wanting this to be a perfect day for his lady.

The Old Don escorted Alaina down the aisle, proudly handing her into the waiting arms of his son. Nick reached for both her forearms drawing her to him, the warmth from his touch traveling the length of her body, their pulses beating as one. They saw only each other from that moment on, oblivious to all surrounding them as the music and guests faded into the air. This time was theirs and theirs alone.

The wedding vows were simple.

"Today you take my name," he declared, "and with that comes my protection. Sail with me as we set off together. Let me shelter you from the bitter winds and trust that I will love you always."

"Let me guide you through rough waters," she replied, "and steer you through the storms. Let my beacon bring you home on starless nights and trust that I too will love you always. Sail with me."

The second the official pronounced them man and wife, Nick released a loud whistle, lifting her high above his head and twirling her around, sending her shoes flying through the air. The crowd cheered, joining his gleeful outburst with shouts and applause. His parents rejoiced, having never seen their somber son so filled with happiness. She will be the perfect wife, the Old Don thought, as long as she remains clueless about the family business.

Two naysayers clouded the day but went unnoticed by the celebrants. Dominic was drunk at the reception and his toast to the couple was another example of his continued jealousy. "To my brother, who always takes the best of everything even though he doesn't deserve it."

The Old Don and Nick took note, but Alaina was too caught up with love for her husband to even hear the words.

Ginny also made her feelings known although not publicly. Inserting herself into Nick's arms on the dance floor, she smiled broadly pretending to enjoy the dance.

"If you hurt her, I know a drummer that will give her a good life."

"A drummer?" Nick repeated, incredulous.

"Yeah, a drummer. He's a good guy; not a lying, womanizing prick like you."

Nick drew in a sharp breath at the assault but kept his voice low, "You think a drummer can give Alaina more than I can give her?"

"It's not about what you can give her, Nick. It's about the amount of pain you will cause her. What I know is that you can't keep your dick in your pants. That's what will hurt her." Her eyes exploded in venomous hatred as she twirled away, still smiling.

#

4 am

The call shattered the quiet serenity of their wedding bed, jerking Nick awake.

"You better have a damned good reason for calling me on my wedding night," he screamed at the offender.

"Boss, I'm sorry, really sorry, but we have a body… and it's bad." The dour voice at the other end of the line belonged to Marco Simonelli, Nick's Chief of Internal Security, a no-nonsense, six-foot tall, retired police captain with a calm-as-still-water personality. Whenever Simonelli reported an incident there was no speculation, just the cold, hard facts.

"I'll be right there."

Minutes later the two men stood solemnly alongside the nine-foot marker of the Royale's rooftop pool. The local police had already been called, unnecessary staff dispensed, and innocent bystanders placated with free drinks at the lounge. They stared down at a partially clad young woman in the middle of the pale blue water. Long wavy dark hair fanned out around her skull creating the effect of a thick twisted halo. A faint trail of crimson blood curved and bobbed snakelike in the shimmering pool eerily reflected by the underwater lights.

"Do we have a name yet? Know if she was a guest?" Nick inquired.

"No, Boss, too soon to tell. Security found her on routine rounds. Pool closed an hour ago. Place was locked up tight. No one's touched the body yet."

A dive team from the local state police barracks was already hard at work, gingerly raising the corpse from its watery tomb.

"Yep, she's dead all right," the female diver announced. "Looks like a good-sized gash to the forehead and some bruising around her neck but we'll know more after the ME examines the body. Sick bastard did this one," the diver continued, pointing to the scarlet red satin bows circling the victim's neck, wrists, and ankles.

Nick knelt down for a closer look as Marco snapped pictures of the face and body hoping to identify the woman from in-house surveillance.

Marco might stick to just the facts, but Nick knew this only meant one thing, *the killer had awakened.*

Don Angelo's Iron Control

Nick had longed to show his bride the beauty of Italy's Amalfi Coast, planning to spend as much time as possible on its glittering sapphire waters. He had chartered a small private yacht that would meet them in Civitavecchia and slowly meander down the southern Italian coastline for fourteen luxurious days of peaceful solitude. It was a fairytale honeymoon fit for his queen and he wanted no one to interfere with their time together.

The morning incident was now in the hands of the police, and Nick hoped he and Alaina would still get away on time. However, the Old Don had plans of his own. He summoned his son to his office, handing him a black velvet drawstring pouch. It was heavy and Nick was curious, hesitating, but knowing never to ask questions.

"Open it," his father ordered.

Nick untied the string, tilting the contents into his palm. One hundred sparkling diamonds of various weights shined up at him.

"You are to *hand* deliver those to an old business associate of mine. He lives in the town of Catanzaro, a mere five-hour drive from the coast. A car will be made available. I have arranged for you and your bride to stay at an exceptionally beautiful hotel during the last three days of your trip. You will complete this task during that time. Who travels with you?"

"Enzio and Saul will be protecting us," Nick replied.

"Your bride, she is aware?"

"No, of course not. They will remain invisible."

"Good, I trust you will never share our business with Alaina. The less the women know, the better."

"I agree, Dad."

"Take Saul with you and leave Enzio to watch over her. This task will consume one day of your honeymoon. One day apart from your bride will increase her hunger for you."

Nick deeply resented this intrusion into his life, but he didn't question his father. This was obviously family business.

Homecoming

The couple continued to reside at the guesthouse and, as a wedding gift, the Old Don purchased a piece of property five miles down the road from the Big House for construction of their own home. He then gave orders to transfer all his personal holdings from the Royale Casino to Nick thus ensuring the couple's financial security.

Nick was the dependable son, the enforcer, the one relied upon to do all the dirty jobs throughout the years. He understood the family business and was unafraid to use violence when needed. He had earned his father's trust. Within the Mafia's hierarchy, he had risen to the rank of *Man of Honor*, a *made* man, having killed for the Commission ten years previous. Since then, he had been called upon several times when situations required his unique methods of persuasion. He was respected by all dons and associates across the country. It was expected that he would assume his father's place, ascending the throne as Boss of the West Coast when the Old Don passed.

Dominic, on the other hand, was a disappointment. He had no sense of loyalty, had a nasty disposition, and was disrespectful to all surrounding him. The Commission viewed him as a weakling and an embarrassment to his father. The Old Don, however, recognized the need to protect his wimpish son. He directed his consigliere to purchase the Calypso casino, a small, underdeveloped property on the other side of town with the intent of separating his two sons. Nick would continue to oversee the Royale and Dominic would manage the Calypso.

"I want no trouble between these two over a woman. It's bad enough."

Nesting

Alaina quickly realized that being married to Nick was even crazier than dating him. Each morning, they would share coffee and breakfast, before he rushed across the lawn for marathon meetings in his father's office. He would then go directly to the Royale, not returning until after 4am. Her counsel that he slow down went unheeded. She was working at Sunrise Hospital on the evening shift. Stolen hours on their boat became their secret luxury.

Nick lavished her with gifts, anticipating her every need. One day, when leaving for work she was surprised to find Bobby waiting in the town car, "I'm driving you today, Miss. Boss sent your car for maintenance." When she returned home, a brand-new white BMW convertible sat in her parking spot topped with a giant red bow.

"Nick, you bought me a car?" she exclaimed.

"Like it?"

"It's gorgeous, but honey, I didn't need a new car."

"Sure, you did, your car had too much mileage. Promise me you won't drive too fast; it's got some kick."

"You are too good to me."

"I can never be too good to you."

Having never lived with a woman before, Nick found the changes surprisingly tranquil. The guesthouse was no longer an empty place where he just slept but now a refreshing oasis filled with her warmth. Relaxation penetrated his soul from the minute he stepped across the threshold. She was the elixir erasing his stress. Her delicate hand over his heart instantly calmed him; the unexplained power of her touch magically healed him.

Alaina was also happy in their union, finding stability at last; no longer moving from town to town and living out of boxes. She welcomed the chance at domesticity, determined to make their small abode a comforting nest. She celebrated every holiday: decorating with paper hearts and flowers on Valentine's Day, making papier-mâché rabbits in spring and forcing him to bite the ears off chocolate bunnies on Easter morning. She baked King Cakes for Mardi Gras and adorned the front entryway with pumpkins in the fall. The St. Patrick's Day meal was decadent with her corned beef melting in his mouth along with the one tablespoon of cabbage she demanded he swallow for good luck.

In the morning, she fed his ego with words of admiration while watching him dress, likening his body to that of a god with firm, rippled muscles, sculpted shoulders, and rock-hard abs. In her mind, his smooth tanned skin and deep blue eyes gave the appearance of a present-day Ares from Greek mythology, calling out for her touch, seducing her. Being late for meetings became routine, as her spidering fingers teased his broad chest, and tickled his muscular arms, resulting in her being dumped back onto the bed for another round of morning sex more often than not. In the bedroom, she let him lead her into more adventure as they enjoyed each other's bodies.

"You're the only woman I've ever known who laughs and cries in bed," he said one night.

"Well, sex should be fun, don't you think? Sometimes we laugh and play, but other times the emotion is so intense that it makes me cry— good tears, happy tears," she replied, "I love you, Nick Rusano."

Lowering his face to hers, he placed soft kisses across her forehead knowing how lucky he was to have found her and silently vowing to keep his dark side forever hidden.

Cold Concrete and Neon Lights

"Hon, can you come up here and get this mess off the bed? I'm trying to take a nap."

Alaina heard his irritated call the minute she opened the front door. She was exhausted, her hospital shift was jumping, too busy for even a dinner break.

"Sure, wait just a sec, I just got in," she replied, quickly climbing the stairs.

Nick sat on the corner chaise smiling broadly, the ruse clearly written upon his face. Two gaily wrapped boxes sat upon their bed, silver bows atop metallic fuchsia gift wrap.

"What's this?" she excitedly questioned.

"Open them."

She gasped as she lifted the delicate gossamer gown, awed by the shimmering material flowing like liquid silver through her hands. The shear bodice glistened with rows of shining crystals, and pearl beading dripped from the sleeves sending rainbow prisms dancing across the bedroom walls.

"Oh Nick, it's exquisite."

"You like it?"

"Oh yes, it's gorgeous," she gushed, still running her fingers over the gentle fabric.

"Good, these match. Try them on for me, beautiful." He handed her the second box containing a pair of silver stilettos with rhinestone ankle clasps while keeping a third box hidden.

Minutes later she proudly stood before him, elegant as a runway model, the silken fabric accentuating every curve. "I've never seen a more beautiful dress. Thank you so much. Are we... going somewhere?" she shyly questioned.

Laughing, he pulled her onto his lap. "When was the last time you celebrated your birthday?"

"I usually work on my birthday."

"I figured that, but this year, sweetheart, *we* are going dancing."

"Dancing? You're kidding, you're taking me dancing? Oh love, where… where are we going?"

"Up on the rooftop, you remember the hot tub?" he chuckled. "Thought you might be missing Skyler," continuing to tease her, "and Myra."

"What? Stop, you're bad," she scoffed, lightly hitting his shoulder.

"We are going dancing in the moonlight on the Royale rooftop for your birthday. I've arranged for a private orchestra to play for us while I dance with my beautiful lady under the stars."

"You are so romantic. I don't know what to say. You treat me like a queen."

"Well, that's what you are, my *Madonna*. But the outfit is not yet complete."

With trembling fingers, she gingerly opened the third gift. "Oh love, it's so beautiful," she screeched, fingering the double row of glittering diamonds. "You are too good to me," she whispered, drawing him in for a kiss.

"Never, baby, never."

#

The evening was storybook perfect; the moon was bright, the air was warm, the stars sparkled above. Alaina was radiant in the gossamer gown shimmering softly against her body, and Nick stood handsome in a matching silver tux and black silk bowtie. They shared champagne and kissed with abandon regardless of their audience, both their bodies melting together. She was living a Cinderella dream; never having imagined such a perfect birthday.

#

"Do you have a quarter? Please?"

They were crossing over the concrete bridge to their car when Alaina heard the faint voice of the small girl half hidden in the shadows.

"Please?" She was young, maybe 15 years old, dirty, barefoot, and bruised.

Alaina bent down. "I'm sorry, what did you say? I couldn't hear you well."

The weary face looked up, a world of hurt behind her pleading eyes. "A quarter, do you have a quarter?" the girl repeated, her voice trembling, barely audible.

"Yes, yes, I have a quarter." Alaina fumbled through her purse searching for cash as the girl warily extended her hand. "Oh sweetheart, are you hungry? Do you need help?" The girl nodded, her eyes brimming with tears.

Alaina felt Nick's hand on her elbow, lifting her.

"Honey, what are you doing?" he questioned, trying to steer Alaina toward their waiting car.

"Oh Nick, look. We can't leave her here like this. Someone will hurt her."

"Sweetheart," he cautioned, "she's a runaway. Hundreds of runaways come to Vegas every year. She'll be all right, c'mon, let's go home. The car's here."

"No, Nick. She's just a child. We must *do* something." Alaina quickly returned to the young girl, bending down, and reaching out for her trembling hand. She noticed fresh scratches on her forehead and an old crusted bloody patch on the underside of her wrist. Alaina stood, "Nick, we need to call someone."

"Honey, no. These runaways are everywhere, as I *just* said. They flock to Vegas every day looking for a handout. Don't encourage them."

But Alaina shook her head, adamantly standing her ground, belligerence in her eyes. "How much did this tux cost?" she questioned, fingering his lapel. "How much did my heels cost? Don't you see? That little girl must have had a reason to run away, an abusive stepfather, a drunken mother." Alaina stamped her foot. "There but for the grace of God...."

He sighed, noting the insistence in her eyes. "I love you, angel, but you drive me crazy, you are relentless sometimes." Begrudgingly he walked over to the girl, bending down to examine her arms for needle marks, but finding none. He stood, staring down at his wife, "Okay, okay, let me think." He turned his back to them for a few brief moments before Alaina heard him making a call.

Lieutenant Joe Sinclair and Officer Renee Murphy arrived just minutes later. Nick briefed the lieutenant on the situation as Officer Murphy bent to gently question the girl.

"Honey, this is Joe Sinclair, a friend of mine with the local precinct. Joe's going to take her over to Sister Mary's convent. She'll be safe there for the night, be given a hot meal and a warm bed. Tomorrow he'll get social services involved. She'll be okay."

"Thank you so much, Lieutenant. I guess I'm being a nuisance, but I just couldn't leave her," Alaina responded with sincere gratitude.

"No problem, ma'am, you did the right thing."

Never Trust a Man in a Cheap Suit

Harry Donahue was *The King of the Cheap Suit*. His bloated, pockmarked face plastered every television channel, his ads littered highway billboards, his grating voice screamed from every radio station.

"Come see me today, every suit in the warehouse $99. If I don't have it, you don't need it."

But Harry Donahue was a problem for Nick that no catchy jingle could fix. He was a degenerate gambler heavily in debt to the Royale, and grossly behind on payments. Harry wasn't loyal to any particular casino, now currently in debt to several along the Vegas Strip and throughout the country. He was running his business into the ground, teetering on bankruptcy, and accumulating more debt by the hour.

Most people dislike carrying large sums of money when they travel to Las Vegas, so casinos have devised a convenient system offering gamblers a line of credit based on their personal finances and credit history. The gambler must first prove that he has readily available funds accessible to the lender. Casinos prefer cash assets, not homes, boats, etc. The player is then asked to sign what is called a marker or a binding IOU. Casinos prefer players settle their markers before leaving town but occasionally a player's debt will be extended over a thirty-day period. If a player fails to meet his obligation, the casino *can* submit that IOU to the bank for payment. Markers are interest free, temporary spending money, and can become a disastrous trap leading to financial disaster for some.

Harry Donahue was playing a dangerous game. He had manipulated that system to his advantage by signing markers with multiple casinos across town. He was withdrawing money from one casino, spending just a little, then moving on to another casino, signing another marker, withdrawing money, spending just a little and repeating the process down the Strip. Those in the industry call that *walking a marker*.

But Harry was in trouble, addicted to dice and unable to stay away from the tables, his luck was running cold. In debt to the Royale for $450,000, he had made no payments in the last six months and was currently standing at the casino cage demanding additional credit. He was causing a scene on the casino floor, berating the clerk behind the cage window, cursing the floor supervisor, and screaming for "his friend," Nick.

The call came through to Peggy, but Nick had already been alerted by his credit office.

"Send him up," he ordered, already annoyed by Donahue's audacity.

Several minutes later, Harry barreled into Nick's office, soggy cigar in place, and lowered his 300lb girth into a chair.

"What's the problem, you don't like my money anymore?" he roared, immediately confrontational.

Nick remained calm, "Of course the Royale likes your money, Harry. The problem is we would like to *see* some of that money."

"See some of that money, see some of that money? I make more money than you'll ever see in your lifetime, kid. Now let me sign that marker and let me get the hell out of here."

"I can't do that this time, Harry, not until you settle your current debt."

Harry's face flashed red and sweat beads formed across his brow. "You'll get your money next week, kid, now let me sign that marker."

"Sorry, Harry, not this time," Nick replied, rising from his chair, and extending his hand.

But Harry also abruptly rose, slamming his beefy fist down onto Nick's desk, "I need that credit, kid, and you're going to give it to me, or I'll tear this joint down. You hear me?"

Nick never riled easily and was not surprised by Donahue's outburst. He took a step back and returned to his seat, showing no reaction.

"I would have preferred you hadn't done that, Harry. We now need to establish more stringent payment terms. Sit down!" Nick met Harry's glare with ominous icy eyes, raising an eyebrow until the big man slowly lowered himself back into his chair. Nick sat silently for several minutes perusing a folder on his desk, then he began. "It says here that you currently owe the Royale a sizable amount of money, $450,000.00 to be exact."

"Yeah, well you'll never see that money now, not after the way you just treated me, not one red cent."

"Oh, I think we will," Nick calmly replied. "We have our ways."

"You can't do anything to me, gonna set your goons on me, are ya?"

"No, nothing like that. I don't believe in violence, Harry," Nick's tone a veiled threat. "You see, your file is quite thick, it contains a great deal of personal information. For instance, your wife's name is Harriet, correct? You were married right here in Vegas about ten years ago, anniversary coming up?"

"Yeah, what about it, she can't help get your money."

Nick continued, "Your two daughters go to Holy Rosary Elementary School. Your mother is still alive and lives at 555 Roosevelt Square, apartment 3C."

Harry cut in, "So you got some info, kid. What's it gonna do ya?"

"Hmm… I'm confused though, Harry. Says here you and Harriet live in Cleveland, but this other page tells me you live in Detroit, your wife's name is Marilyn, and you were married four years ago at the Detroit courthouse. Are you married to two different women, Harry? Ah, children with this wife too. Little girl named Gabrielle, cute little thing." Nick flashed a picture of a smiling blond toddler on a tricycle. "I'm not seeing any divorce records?" Nick paused, watching as sweat dripped from Harry's brow.

"I, I don't know what you mean, no, no, that's not right," he sputtered, "not right!" Color raced up the big man's neck and his eyes began to twitch, his arrogance dissipating. "Where… where did you get that picture?"

Nick kept his matter-of-fact attitude. "The Royale will expect payment by the end of the month. If not, we will use this information. Don't let your callousness force us to take actions that might upset both Harriet and Marilyn, not to mention your sweet little daughters. Bigamy is illegal in this country; did you know that? End of month, Harry. Not one day more."

Harry, King of the Cheap Suit, left Nick's office in a daze, his trembling fingers barely able to press the elevator button.

Cherry Blossoms

Cherry blossoms come early to Vegas, spreading their beautiful soft pink blooms, and heralding spring's arrival throughout the city. Several major hotels along the Strip celebrate with a change of décor in their public spaces but to truly welcome the season, a trip to the famous Botanical Gardens is imperative.

Nick had surprised Alaina by taking a rare half day off. His purpose for their garden excursion twofold, the first being her happiness. Convention season was gearing up, meaning the tourists would be packing the casino floors and he would have less time with his bride. He was also in the throes of building their new home. He knew she loved weeping cherry trees, but this trip would give him knowledge of the exact species of tree to plant. He also planned to present her with a memento to commemorate their first anniversary.

They strolled along the winding garden paths hand in hand, admiring the artistry of the tall, manicured sculptures and the beauty of the majestic cherry blossoms. Her joyful face lit up among the fat branches of rose pink as a gentle shower of petals floated to the ground around them. She bent to pick up a handful, taking in their delicate scent and presenting them to him before tossing them above his head with a devilish sparkle in her eyes, laughing as they fell upon his hair.

They were crossing a wooden bridge when she stopped him abruptly, placing her hand on his chest. "Oh honey, look," she whispered, pointing to a small group of women on a path below. "It's a wedding." They watched as the bridal party made its way to a temple garden tucked into a quiet alcove.

"Oh Nick, isn't she beautiful? Japanese women have such flawless skin," Alaina commented as they watched the processional carefully climb the small grassy hill. "I hope her marriage is blessed and that she will be as happy as we are."

Reaching out, he drew her into his arms. "No woman is more beautiful than you are in my eyes, mia amata." Then gallantly lifting her hand to his lips, he placed soft, gentle kisses across her knuckles before slipping a glittering ring onto her index finger. She stared down at its brilliance reflected in the afternoon sun. The jeweler had created a true masterpiece with seven carats of round pink diamonds forming cherry blossom flowers nestled among a meadow of twisted rose gold vines.

"Oh my god, Nicky it's magnificent," she cried.

"You're happy?"

"It's absolutely exquisite, love," she uttered, standing on tip toe to kiss him on the forehead.

"Good, happy first anniversary, sweetheart." He smiled down at her, still encircled in his arms as a gentle breeze showered them in pink petals from above. "Now, I will let you be my geisha later, but right now I am starving. How 'bout we go for sushi?"

"But you don't like sushi."

"They'll make me something, but I still don't understand how you can eat raw fish."

#

Two towering Japanese stone lions greeted them at the entrance of a cozy little restaurant far off the Vegas Strip. A dazzling seventy-foot waterfall along one wall added to the ambiance, its gentle sounds filtering through the quiet darkened room. They sat together tucked into a secluded booth, sharing shots of warm sake before ordering. Naturally, Nick was acquainted with the owners and, instead of sushi, they made him a plate of Wagyu beef off menu. The sushi chef, however, proudly presented his artfully decorated creations to Alaina, delighted by her obvious appreciation of his talent.

Nick stared down at her plate. "Really, hon?"

"No, no, you can't knock it 'til you try it," shaking her head in response to his disapproving stare. "This, for example, is unagi, one of my favorites. Bite?" she teased while holding a masterfully made piece of dragon roll stuffed thick with freshwater eel between her chop sticks. Wrinkling his nose, he jerked back.

"Tsk, tsk! Allow me to dazzle my *master* with a culinary history lesson," she began. "The Japanese are credited with first making sushi, but it actually originated with the Chinese. They made a dish named narezushi dating back to the second century BC. Naturally, there were no refrigerators then, so the Chinese salted the fish and wrapped it in fermented rice. Sushi didn't come to Japan until around the eighth century. It is the ideal food, it is healthy, it is portable, and is a perfect finger food allowing you to pop it in your mouth in one bite," she declared, deftly placing a piece in between her lips.

"How do you know so much about food?" he asked, laughing at her antics.

"I told you; I worked in restaurants when I was a teenager. I learned about sushi from a crazy chef named Arlo; he was such a cranky old fuss pot. But... you'll like this, I once worked a special nyotaimori event where nude female models were hired as buffet plates... yes, really. Diners could circle the tables selecting different sushi pieces right off their bare bellies as they lay naked around the room, very decadent." She held up her hand, "Before you ask, *no!* I wasn't one of the models, but it was certainly entertaining. Quite the aphrodisiac for those lust filled men ogling those naked young bodies!"

"Really?"

"Yep, now can I pop just one piece into your mouth?" she teased, her witchy eyes smiling up at him.

"Nooo… behave."

Snuggling closer to him, she put her hand on his thigh, her playful eyes dancing. "Are you sure?" she asked, placing one bite on her tongue with the chop sticks before removing it again and bringing it close to his lips while tickling his cock with her fingers.

"Alaina… sweetheart, not a good idea," he warned, one eyebrow cocked.

"Hmm," continuing her play under the table.

"I might need to embarrass you and take you right here in front of all these people," he threatened before wrapping his hand around her wrist and guiding the sushi back to her open mouth. Their eyes locked together as she allowed the sushi to sit on her tongue while feeling his cock enlarge beneath her palm. Quickly drawing his lips to hers, she forced her tongue into his mouth just long enough for him to taste the spicy unagi sauce. His eyes lit up and she felt his cock grow even harder beneath the tablecloth. Again, she withdrew her mouth but this time he held on for just a few seconds, gently biting her lower lip.

"We need to leave, my little witch," he said, pressing her hand against his hardness.

"But I'm not finished eating," she replied, coyly.

"Oh, yes you are."

They barely made it to the parking lot before he wrapped her in his arms, pressing her hips into his body, his hardness flush against her. "Do you have any idea what you do to me?" he whispered. "Home, before I lay you out on the hood of the car."

But home would need to wait.

"Damn…woman, you're going to make me run off the road," he cried, with both hands gripping the steering wheel as she continued to massage his swollen cock inside his unzipped pants.

"Must have been that teeny, tiny taste of sushi," she teased before withdrawing his cock and lowering her lips to taste him.

"Alaina… baby, no… honey, no! I'm gonna slam into a tree," he exclaimed, trying unsuccessfully to stop her tongue from driving him mad.

"Hmm…."

Placing his hand on her neck to steady her, he frantically made a sharp right turn into a familiar empty driveway, that of their half-built home. Fortuitous! It was the weekend, and no construction workers were present.

"Over here, right here, right now!" he ordered, pushing the seat back to allow her room as she gleefully mounted him, their need for each other boiling beyond convention. Reclining with a sigh, he submitted to her devilish play, enjoying the view of her exposed breasts, and feeling her tight grip pulsing around his cock. Holding her waist, he matched her motion, thrusting deeper and deeper until he could no longer hold back, before crying out in ecstasy with ragged breath.

Cupping her cheeks in his hands, his eyes twinkled with laughter. "You are going to get me thrown in jail someday, woman. I can see the headline now,

NICK RUSANO, CASINO BOSS ARRESTED FOR LEWD BEHAVIOR IN PUBLIC."

“Then let’s go home. I need more of you,” she teased.

Fallen Wings

"Boss, it's Marco, you're... not gonna like this."

"Do I ever like hearing from you?"

"Right. Well, we've got another body. Meet me on the roof." Simonelli knew better than to bother Nick with the small stuff. This was *not* the small stuff.

Both men stared at the lifeless brunette bobbing face down in the crystal blue water of the Royale's rooftop pool. A trail of crimson blood snaked ominously behind her. Same as last time, different year.

Guests from the party hours earlier were long gone, now safely tucked away downstairs in their drunken stupor beneath the Royale's crisp linen sheets. Custodial staff had cleaned the entire area immediately after the event, all signs of the revelry now gone. That at least would give the police a timeframe.

"What the hell?" screeched the rescue diver.

Nick and Marco turned toward the team heaving the body upward. The hapless diver held a fistful of dripping brown hair into the air. It was a wig loosened from the wearer's head as she was lifted onto the cement.

"This sure is one sick bastard," the diver announced, dropping the tangled mass into an evidence bag.

The group surrounded the body, leaning in for a closer look. The victim was Caucasian, in her early twenties with short dyed red hair and multiple piercings along her eyebrows, ears, and nipples; an ugly jagged gash slashed her forehead, a second gash tore across her abdomen, and several areas of bruising could be seen throughout her torso. Familiar red satin bows adorned her wrists, ankles, and neck exactly as before. The killer had struck again leaving behind another victim to tumble into the Las Vegas abyss.

A cold chill shot up Nick's spine.

The Seed of Distrust

Nick scanned the blueprints spread across the breakfast table, triple checking measurements and scrawling endless notes in the margins. Construction was taking longer than he would have liked but their home would be perfect, bigger than his father's with more enhanced security. Thankfully, he was able to consult his dad about flaws and mistakes the old man had previously made.

Alaina was pregnant with their first child and the safety and comfort of his family was his primary focus. She had requested little, preferring a kitchen table instead of a counter, a jacuzzi tub for two in their bathroom with a skylight above, a nursery and playroom next to their bedroom, and a small sunroom overlooking the garden allowing her to read by natural light.

His dream was much larger. He planned for a pool with a cabana house, a fully equipped gym so he could continue his daily workouts, and most importantly, a state-of-the-art surveillance system covering every corner of the house of which Alaina would be kept unaware. The Old Don advised his son to place hidden cameras in every room and record all phone conversations and computer activity so that Nick always knew what was occurring under his own roof. He acknowledged the need to record all business in his private office, but he questioned his father about the additional security.

"Not sure I need cameras in my own bedroom, Dad," he argued.

The Old Don vehemently disagreed. "This is not paranoia, Son. This is how I learned that Dominic, my *own* blood, lied to my face so many times. *I listened!*" The old man was emphatic. "Do not make the mistake of trusting those around you. Watch your brother, your bodyguards, your help, *watch your wife.* Alaina is in love with you today. Tomorrow she may turn to another, perhaps even an enemy of yours," he warned.

Nick thought about his father's words. If she ever did cheat on him, he would kill both her and her lover. It was that simple. It was the way of the families.

"Baby, can you stop by the construction site today, say around 1pm? I want you to look over the kitchen specs," he asked over morning coffee.

"Oh, silly, we'll only have a kitchen because it comes with the house. I don't intend to use it."

Laughing, he leaned down to kiss her baby bump. "Your mama is the silly one."

#

Four hours later

Alaina stood immobile staring up at the nearly completed three-story dwelling, and, although Nick had taken her to see the progress several times in the past few months, it now appeared much, much larger. She had never really lived in a house, always moving from apartment to apartment in her childhood and again in her work life. But now her dreams took flight seeing a home brimming with love; with babies peacefully sleeping in cribs and children climbing to the sky in backyard treehouses; with flowerbeds bursting with color and Christmas mornings filled with revelry.

"Hey woman, didn't hear you pull up. What do you think?" Nick sidled up behind her, wrapping his arms around her blooming belly.

"Honey, it's so big, my goodness!"

"Quick, come see the inside. Wait till you see the fireplace," he enthused, leading her across the threshold.

After a hurried tour, Alaina sat down with Nick and the foreman, reviewing kitchen appliances, counter tops, paint colors, and several final decorator choices. Nick observed her closely, she was his Alaina, vibrant and friendly. Men were drawn to her, but she remained oblivious to their attention.

"I'm hoping to move in before the baby arrives," she told the foreman. Then, looking to Nick, she placed her hand on his forearm, innocently asking, "Do you think we can do that, honey?"

Nick, however, noticed the admiring way the foreman gazed at her, the seed of distrust now firmly planted.

Life's Little Changes

Don't ever let anyone tell you that mobsters are not kind, caring, and compassionate. They idolize their wives and cherish their children even more deeply than most men. Life has more value to them, every day spent living is a gift, every breath a pearl.

Two years to the day after the wedding, their first son came into the world. The baby was christened Jackson Nick Rusano. Jackson was Nick's middle name and the name also honored Alaina's beloved grandfather, Jack McGovern.

"I've never seen him happier," Arch commented, watching Nick proudly hoisting his newborn son high into the air and presenting him to the group of family and friends who had gathered for the homecoming.

Three years later, the jubilant family again rejoiced when Baby Luca was born. Both boys resembled their father, strong and handsome with pitch black hair and dark, soulful eyes. They were the pride of Nick's life, and he happily watched them grow, delighting in every milestone. He also continued to worship Alaina, always remarking on her beauty, and making sure she felt his love each day.

Henry and Hildy Roman, a young childless couple from Germany, joined their household as domestic staff and, soon after, Nick hired Mimi, an aging widow from Atrani, as a live-in nanny. Mimi doted on the children ensuring their mastery of the Sicilian tongue and enchanting them with an endless array of Italian folktales and stories of Atrani's legendary fire breathing dragon. Nick continued assisting his father with Mob business and overseeing the daily operations of the Royale.

Dominic also experienced changes. The Calypso Casino was prospering, and he was planning an expansion. He had sent for a young bride, Angela Amorino, from Sicily. Angela was forever pregnant, having a child every year since their marriage.

Carnation Pink

Alaina sat on the edge of the tub, Nick's shirt in her hands. She stared at the carnation pink lipstick on the collar—definitely not her color. That's what you get for fishing through the hamper for that missing sock, she thought, tears welling in her eyes. She was not about to let this breach slide.

They had just celebrated their seventh anniversary and she was heavy with their third child, but he had been in a foul mood of late robbing her of the joy of the anticipated birth. A torrent of anger coursed through her, making her fruitlessly tear at the fabric.

Some men are too handsome for their own good. That described both the Rusano brothers, too handsome, too charming. They were surrounded by temptation every day with an endless number of showgirls, dancers, and cocktail waitresses at the ready. She once spotted Dominic out with a tall blond; thankfully, he didn't see her. When she mentioned it to Nick, he merely blew it off. 'He has a girlfriend, several girlfriends I think, and a mistress,' was his only comment. She wondered if confronting Dominic that day would have mattered. Would it make a difference if the same were to occur with her own husband?

The next morning, she placed the tainted shirt neatly on the bed. Nick would notice it after his shower. He didn't react, instead he returned the shirt to the hamper without comment.

On the second morning she did the same.

"Damn it, Laine! You made your point. Enough! It was just a fuckin' skirt!" he yelled, as he threw the shirt from bed to floor.

"Just a fuckin' skirt? Just a fuckin' skirt?" she cried.

"Are we doing this now? I'm already late," he protested.

But she stood belligerent, not letting him pass.

"Alaina…, it was nothing. It was just a fuck. That's all it was," releasing a deep sigh, defiance in his retort. "*A fuck* has no emotion, no… passion, no love. *A fuck* is just an act," he shouted, his frustration rising. "I'm Sicilian, for Christ's sake, Sicilian men have stronger sex drives," pausing, he stared coldly before throwing his hands into the air. "This is what I get for marrying a crazy Irish Catholic."

"Did you really just say that?" she shrieked. "For God's sake, I'm pregnant with your son, look at me, damn it! Am I not giving you enough sex right now?" she countered, eyes clashing with his as she cradled her belly.

"Um… no… yes," he stammered, shaking his head. "Honey, I don't know how to answer that. I'm having a little trouble getting around… *that*," he said, his eyes on her oversized belly.

"Damn you!" she screamed.

He turned from her, seeking composure, grasping for words. Two-three unending minutes passed before he was able to face her again, this time noting the tears streaming from her eyes. She was fragile, too fragile right now. She was always more emotional when she was pregnant.

"Sweetheart, you're tired," he said softly, taking her hand and leading her to the bed. "Let me help you relax."

"No, Nicky, no," she sobbed, pushing him away with balled fists. "Sex isn't the answer to everything!"

"No, it isn't. You're right, but sex doesn't cause pain either." Bending to kneel upon the carpet, he wrapped his arms around her belly, drawing her into a soft embrace, "This is love, angel. This is not sex, there is a difference." But looking up, he saw her slowly shaking her head, not understanding. "Come sit with me. Let me hold you, let me hold our son. What is it you always say, the baby can hear our voices? Let's not let him hear our fighting."

Leading her to the sofa, he pressed her head to his chest, massaging her back and stroking her hair as he waited for her tears to subside.

"I know *I'm sorry* won't be enough; I never meant to hurt you," he whispered after a while, but she remained quiet. Gently lifting her face to his, he searched for forgiveness, but saw only the pain that he alone owned and he felt great shame.

"*Io ti adora,* I love you, sweetheart. You are my *Madonna,* my only *Madonna* and you always will be. You are the *only* woman I love. I need you to hear those words in both your mind *and* your heart." Stroking her cheek, he wiped away her tears before cupping her face in his hands. "No one will ever take your place. Please believe that, angel. Know that I worship you," he whispered.

But with eyes spewing both anger and pain, her reply tore through him like a dagger, "Go to work, Nick."

Double Trouble

Nick scrupulously reviewed the latest expenditures report from his food and beverage department; something wasn't right, but he couldn't quite pinpoint it. His phone rang, disrupting his concentration.

"Hey Boss, you gotta see this." Steve Corson was calling from downstairs.

"Yeah, what 'cha got?"

Corson was among Nick's most loyal employees, having been entrusted with the daily workings of all table games on the casino floor for the past twenty years.

"We got ourselves a set of twins, and ohhh baby, they are something. Meet me in surveillance."

"Be right there," Nick chuckled, his curiosity piqued.

#

"Well, hello ladies, aren't you both so cute?" Nick stared at the security monitor, as Steve stood behind him, arms crossed, broad grin plastered across his regal Sicilian features. The monitor was aimed at a no limit craps table, center floor where a silver haired, 70-year-old inebriated cowboy, overweight for his six-foot frame and sporting an ill-fitting Stetson and ten-inch-wide silver belt buckle, filled the screen. With dice in hand, he was recklessly adding $500 chips to each bet and his enthusiasm grew with each winning toss, attracting a crowd, and adding to the chaos.

Two 5'8" twin blonds flanked the shooter, the only difference in their appearance being which side they parted their waist length wavy locks. Both were dressed in identical scarlet form fitting dresses, necklines cut to their navels. Masters at distraction, they occasionally bent forward for maximum cleavage entertainment and, as one rubbed the cowboy's buttocks, the other blew on the dice before each toss allowing his face to be inches from her uplifted breasts.

The pompous cowboy was unaware that his two lovely companions were actually *rail thieves*. With every roll of the dice, one twin would distract him as the other pocketed a chip from his winnings. In a high energy craps game, all eyes are on the shooter, once the dice leaves the shooter's hand, all eyes turn to the opposite end of the table to see the outcome of the roll. That is when a rail thief strikes, stealthily lifting one or two chips unnoticed.

"Who's the mark?" Nick asked.

"Conventioneer by the name of Howie Pierson, in for the cattleman's convention, room 8505, with us for the next three nights. Plays 21 and craps, he's dropped $175,000 since arriving last evening. Just signed another marker for $100,000. The girls latched on to him about twenty minutes ago. He isn't their first of the night, either."

Steve Corson knew his gamblers, maintaining an extensive file on repeat visitors to the Royale. That file included: personal facts and preferences, net worth and solvency, and gambling habits and history. Pierson was a whale; a high roller who bets high, loses high, and doesn't care. He was a Royale regular, and it was Corson's job to keep Pierson happy.

"Do we know the ladies?" Nick asked.

"No, not in the book, must be new in town."

"Were you able to get a freeze frame of the theft?"

"Right here, Boss." Steve enlarged a frame on the camera feedback clearly showing red lacquered fingernails clumsily palming two chips from the cowboy's winnings.

"Great, print that and let's have a conversation with these two darlings. Oh… and let's take care of our Mr. Pierson. He won't be happy with the Royale's hospitality if he finds he's been robbed. Send Manny over to pacify him after you pull the girls off. The usual comps should suffice, supplement his losses with additional credit, upgrade his room, send him some *entertainment*—maybe two from the stable," Nick ordered. "Put our clumsy thieves in the gray room. Get their IDs, pictures for the book, the usual. I'll let you take it first, then I'll come in."

Generally, Nick didn't get involved with incidents like this, preferring to leave it up to his security staff, however Steve Corson thought his boss would enjoy this one and he was right.

#

Nick watched the initial interview through the two-way mirror. The twins were posturing, proclaiming their innocence as Steve began his interrogation. Jack Angelini, a casino heavyweight blocked the door; no one was leaving the room.

Steve began, "Ladies, welcome to the Royale. Glad you could join us tonight."

"You can't hold us, we have rights, you know," one of the twins yelled, eyes wild.

"Can I have a cigarette, or something?" the other added, boredom in her tone.

He had already confiscated their drivers' licenses and taken facial photos. Ignoring their theatrics, he continued. "So, which one of you is Carly?" One twin raised her hand, rolling her eyes. "Great, that makes you Candy," pointing to the remaining twin. "And looks like you are both from Dallas? All the way from Dallas to gamble at the Royale?"

"I want a lawyer, this is kidnapping or, or… imprisonment or… something like that." Carly challenged, loudly cracking gum and smiling defiantly.

"Well ladies, that's where you're wrong. I absolutely do have a right to detain you. I don't know how much you paid for these," fanning the drivers licenses in front of their faces, "but they are some of the worst fake IDs I've ever come across. Unless the two of you cooperate with me, you will both be spending the night in the Clark County Jail. So, let's start again, what are your real names?"

After the initial interrogation, Steve ascertained that the sisters' names were Naomi and Maryann Henderson from a small town in western Kentucky. They were both underage and had taken the bus to Las Vegas, 'hoping to have a little harmless fun.'

He then confronted them with the theft, displaying the still frame as proof of their guilt. The one twin burst into tears while the other screamed, lashing out at Steve, "I'm gonna sue, I'm gonna tell them you raped us, you'll be the one in jail, not us. I know my rights."

Nick chuckled from behind the mirror and chose that moment to make his entrance.

"Ladies, welcome to the Royale. Let me introduce myself, I'm Nick Rusano, owner of this fine establishment. I see my associate here is giving you both a tough time. Steve, Steve, how could you be so unkind to these sweet, innocent young ladies?"

Corson smiled, knowing the schtick.

"Now let's get down to business, shall we? Obviously, you are both very smart young women, and because of that, I'm going to present you with two options, *your only two options.*" Nick continued, "Number one, we can press charges and allow you both to experience the renowned hospitality of our Clark County Jail, not... such a nice place. Anyone able to make bail tonight? Can you call your Mama?" Both girls turned away, staring at the metal table, mortified.

"I'm guessing that's not an option, hmm," he continued. "Okay, let's move on to option two. We can pack you both up on the next bus back to Kentucky with your promise, of course, that neither of you will ever again darken the doors of the Royale Casino. Now what's it gonna be?"

The crier again burst forth with a torrent of tears, "I wanna go home, this was her idea, I wanna go home, please let us go home."

Nick leaned in, handing her a box of tissues. "We can arrange that *but first*, you will need to return what isn't yours. Come on, give them up."

Before long, a dozen Royale chips lay on the interrogation room table along with another ten chips from a downtown casino.

"Have someone put them on a bus for Kentucky," Nick ordered, "and give them some tee shirts or something, cover up that mess."

Nick slapped Steve on the back as they walked away, "Best laugh of the week."

Steve chuckled, "Thought you'd enjoy it, Boss."

Naomi and Maryann Henderson were indeed put on a bus in route to Kentucky but they exited at the first rest stop hoping to hitchhike their way to another casino town, maybe Reno.

The Birth of a Ferrari

Nick strolled past the ROYALE PATISSERIE on his way back upstairs spotting tonight's featured dessert in the showcase—tiramisu cheesecake. He smiled, remembering a night in the not too distant past when he and Alaina had smeared that decadent dessert over each other's bodies, pleasuring each other in sensual decadence until dawn. His smile faded then recalling this morning's argument. His words had been hurtful, his actions even more so. She didn't deserve that. He would take her some cheesecake, but just as he was about to place his order, his phone buzzed.

'Get home, baby's coming.'

Nick sped down the highway, breaking triple digits with Alaina beside him. She was struggling for comfort, changing position from sitting to reclining to no avail.

"Hey, remember what the nuns always told you, keep your legs together," Nick joked, eyes big.

"Right," she replied, "should have taken that advice months ago." She didn't remember the car ride, minutes passing at harrowing speed before they screeched into the ER driveway. Panicked faces flashed by and strangers' words echoed, but it was Nick's gentle voice that comforted her. "I'm with you, baby, I'm with you. I love you."

Baby Rusano barreled into the world less than ten minutes later. He was in a hurry. The sounds of the busy ER faded, and all Alaina could see was his tiny pink body laying atop her stomach and Nick's overflowing jubilation as he reached for his newborn son.

It had been a difficult pregnancy, fraught with fatigue and anxiety. It was also the first time she was faced with her husband's infidelity, but as she listened to his words, she knew she had not lost him, his love was genuine.

"Ferrari, I think we should name him Ferrari," he chuckled. And so they did indeed christen their third son, Matteo Ferrari Rusano.

PART TWO

The Curtain Falls

On a bright, sunny morning in May, Don Angelo Rusano was found dead at his desk by his consigliere. His heart had failed. He died alone having given no indication of pain the previous day.

Alaina had given birth to her third child only three months earlier, but an unexplained sense of foreboding continually overshadowed her joy and the frantic preparations for Baby Matt's christening brought only limited relief. On the day of the event her father-in-law was jubilant, cradling his latest grandson at the baptismal font, before reluctantly turning him over to the arms of his godparents. Later he took claim to the baby again, refusing to share him even with his wife. Nick was puffed up with pride telling anyone that would listen how Matt was nearly born on the seat of his brand-new Ferrari.

His father teased, "How many more do you need for a baseball team? I'm expecting a full club house."

But once again Dominic tried dampening the occasion by rudely interjecting, "Don't worry Dad, I'll give them to you. Nick's probably firing blanks."

Coldly turning to reply to his brother's retort, Nick found Dominic smiling, Alaina the focus of his attention.

There are those that believe that a newborn's first gasp for breath steals that of another living soul; for each being that enters the world, another is taken away. The week before the Old Don's passing Alaina's sleep was troubled, seeing a continuous picture of her father-in-law holding the sleeping newborn. She mentioned her unease to Nick who scoffed, attributing her feelings to unfounded Celtic superstitions. Undeterred, she baked a batch of her father-in-law's favorite cookies and delivered them along with a surprise visit from his new grandson.

The unexpected loss of his father devastated Nick but he remained stoic—never shedding a tear. He sat at his father's desk for hours as Arch fielded the unending calls of questions and condolences. Dominic, on the other hand, looked forward to life without the old man whom he felt had always held him back.

Tradition dictates that the new Boss or Don can only be appointed by a ruling of the Commission. This happens very quickly. Not only had Angelo Rusano ruled over the west coast's massive criminal network, but he also had ascended the Mafia's hierarchy by exerting his influence throughout the entire country. He achieved that power through cunning and brutality, his oldest son being his main enforcer and it was expected that Nick would assume his father's position.

"Wow, don't you look handsome," Alaina exclaimed as her husband exited the dressing room wearing a perfectly tailored charcoal gray Brioni suit. But the weight of his father's passing was heavy in his expression, his deep blue eyes weary and sad. He looked with regret upon his naive wife as she assisted with his cuff links. She had no idea how much her life was about to change. He had successfully managed to keep his Mob ties hidden from her throughout the years but today might prove tricky—too much exposure. He needed to keep her in the dark a while longer.

"Sweetheart, listen," he replied, taking her hand, "today will be extremely long and tiring. You might see some things; maybe hear some things you won't understand. Just follow my lead. I'll answer any questions you have when this is over. Bobby's going to take you home immediately after the church service."

"Home? What about the guests? I need to stay for the repast. Your mother needs me."

"No, everyone knows we have a newborn. Our son needs his mother. Go home and get some rest. I'll be late tonight, don't wait for me."

#

Hundreds attended Angelo Rusano's funeral, the majority of which Alaina did not know. She stood dutifully by her husband as he and Archer greeted each of the men by name, thanking them for attending.

During the repast, Nick was summoned to a private upstairs meeting with the Commission. When he emerged hours later, an icy reverent silence penetrated the room as all eyes watched him descend the stairs. Nick Rusano had just been named Boss of the West Coast Crime Family. Alaina was not witness to this, having left hours earlier per his orders.

#

Life at home changed quickly. Security increased around the house and at the front gate with several of the men openly baring long guns. Alaina voiced her concern for the children, but Nick's reply was gruff.

"Woman, this house is a fortress, the boys are safer here than anywhere beyond these gates. This is merely a transition period."

Nick appointed a subordinate to oversee some of his duties at the Royale, only going into the casino twice a week. He monitored the finances daily since a share of the Royale's profits went directly to the Rusano family. He conducted all other business from his downstairs office during the remainder of the week. Visitors arrived each day entering through the private downstairs doors where hushed meetings occurred. Archer quickly stepped in as Nick's consigliere and, even though Archer was not Sicilian, the Commission approved his appointment based on his years of service to the Rusano family. Business *must* continue uninterrupted.

Although Nick was home more, Alaina saw him less. He often worked into the evening. The office was off limits to family and Alaina knew never to interrupt unless there was an emergency. Nick came into their bedroom late, if at all, sometimes choosing to sleep in his suite at the Royale.

His stress level soared; his temper was short. Alaina often heard his screaming through the office door, shouting a name she did not recognize along with a string of expletives. Archer occasionally came into the kitchen to refill the coffee urn but avoided conversation. Alaina viewed Archer as a saint calming the waters of Nick's violent temper.

Within months, Nick realized that his father had been covering for Dominic's mismanagement of the Calypso, and he was forced to cover the debt. It would only be a matter of time before the Commission learned of the ruse and he feared for his brother's safety.

He traveled more, going away for three or four days at a time on trips to Chicago, Detroit, and Los Angeles, never discussing business with her. She mostly saw him at morning coffee as he silently perused the Wall Street Journal. On the few times she did have a question, he was brief, wanting her to handle all family matters. He grew more distant, there was occasional sex, but his mind was elsewhere, his eyes veiled. Alaina felt their love slipping away. She missed her husband.

Yet there were still moments when she witnessed the depth of his tenderness. Once, in the early morning hours, she felt his hand lightly touch her shoulder as she paced with their sobbing newborn. The baby was teething, hot tears soaking his reddened face, nothing seemed to soothe him. Nick lovingly lifted his son into his arms, gently patting his little back and comforting him while she massaged his gums with brandy to relieve the pain.

"I'm sorry," he whispered.

She looked lovingly into his eyes and lifted her hand to his cheek. "We'll get through this, sweetheart; our love is strong."

He saw the misplaced hope in her eyes, knowing she didn't understand. "I never expected Dad to go so soon. I thought we would have more time. This is not what I wanted for us, not yet. You need to remember that I love you. I will always love you and I will always love our children."

The baby calmed, reaching for his father's face, instantly melting the tension from his burdened eyes. "Put him in bed between us. I want to watch him sleep."

But only minutes passed before exhaustion overcame them both, sleep overtaking father before son. Alaina gazed at her snoring husband on the pillow beside her. His sleep was fitful at first before he drifted further away. He looked worn as if he had aged ten years in the past six months. Silver graced his temples, peppering his once pitch-black hair and his brow bore deep furrowed lines even at rest. Whatever he was doing, it was draining him and each day his appearance crept closer to the Old Don's.

Having an absent husband can be a detriment to some but Alaina was determined to keep her promise of providing their children with a normal life. She attended every baseball and soccer game, lined up summer camps, and helped with homework. But more importantly, she created a mecca of love and support—always present and available—allowing them to grow strong and confident, the three boys forming an inseparable bond. Occasionally Nick found the time to drop in to a raucous birthday party or Thanksgiving dinner, giving her his nod of approval.

She often visited with Nick's mother, listening to tales of the old days while drinking anisette and baking cookies. Angela, Dominic's wife, sometimes joined in, but she was mean-spirited and forever pregnant, often teasing Alaina about the difference in their number of offspring. Angela tried hiding her jealousy of Alaina, but she had quickly recognized her own husband's desire for his sister-in-law, fueling her animosity.

As the years passed, Alaina became more involved with Mama's friends and the older women of the community. She planned Christmas parties and backyard BBQs, held monthly bingo parties, and formed a gardening club to assist in beautifying their yards. She organized an annual block party to celebrate the Feast of San Gennaro and every season she delivered holiday baskets of her homemade eggnog, breads, and jams to their homes. But more importantly, she listened to their stories; so many had suffered challenging times and they were grateful for an empathetic ear. The women quickly came to appreciate the wife of their Don.

No Good Deed

Alaina wound her way up the driveway, happily reminiscing. This house held so many wonderful memories: playing chess with the Old Don, Nick's first kiss, their engagement dinner, cooking with Mama. But this was Dominic's home now, having moved his family in soon after his father's death. Alaina purposely chose to limit her interaction with Dominic, visiting only when she thought he would be working but with Mama living under the same roof that proved difficult. She was uneasy in his presence, frequently feeling his lecherous stare.

She rang the bell, jumping back when Dominic threw open the door. She had not expected him to be home.

"Well, hello beautiful." His eyes slowly scanned her body, making her feel exposed in her leggings and tank top.

"Dom, I didn't realize you were home," she replied awkwardly.

"Obviously, princess. Come in," he sneered, reaching for her wrist, and guiding her into the polished foyer. "We can... talk in my office. I was on my way out, but I can certainly take time for my favorite sister-in-law." His hand moved across her arm from wrist to elbow, drawing her closer and letting his eyes linger on her breasts before raising his predatory gaze. He was too close; she could feel his breath on her face.

"No, no. I was just dropping off some custard for Angela's morning sickness. It always helped me," she stammered. "I… have another appointment so I can't stay." Fearing she had placed herself in a dangerous situation, she searched for control.

"*ANGELA*," he screamed, never releasing his gaze. "Alaina's here." His voice was shrill and threatening as it echoed up the staircase. "*ANGELA!*" he called again, louder and more insistent.

Alaina could sense his growing annoyance; Rusano men were quick-tempered. She scanned the foyer feeling a palpable coldness infused by its owner. It was too quiet, not at all like her own home which buzzed with children's laughter, the smells of baking and cooking, and the flurry of the staff attending to chores.

Dominic had not released his grip when Angela stumbled into view at the top of the stairs clutching her nightgown, disheveled, her hair tangled. She gripped the rail for steadiness, leaning over but not attempting to descend, her expression woeful.

Twisting his lips to reveal his disgust, he moved past Alaina, brushing his hand against her buttocks as he exited.

Field Trip

Tourism was booming in Las Vegas and the Royale was experiencing enormous success under Nick's exacting watch. With the family's share of the profits, he was investing in the stock market and local real estate. He expected both Jax and Luca to learn the inner workings of the casino business and they eagerly complied, working every summer and school holiday. Their relationship with their father flourished. They were maturing quickly, often listening in on office meetings and accompanying him on business trips. Nick was grooming them for the Mafia lifestyle.

The Ranchero Lake Casino was 90% complete, only the high-rise tower remained. The foreman had placed an urgent call to Nick's office a week earlier. He was having trouble with the local Ironworkers Union. Construction was behind and there were rumors of a work stoppage. The Ranchero would miss opening day. Nick sent his underboss forward to investigate. Money was money and lost revenue did not bode well when answering to the Commission.

The ironworkers had a legitimate beef, a sizable share of their hard-earned union dues had disappeared. Nick hired an accountant to investigate the complaint and the findings proved the ironworkers correct; monies were being filtered into a private personal bank account owned by none other than the project foreman himself who had cleverly opened the account in his mother-in-law's name thinking it untraceable.

Nick flew to Seattle in the early morning hours, convening with his underboss and capos before daylight. He planned on arriving at the construction site before the work crew reported for duty, assuring those with grievances that Nick Rusano was there to right the injustice. Jax, now fifteen years old, and Luca, twelve, accompanied him. Both boys had been briefed on the situation and the necessary outcome. Today would be the first test of their bravery— and their stomachs.

Nick and his entourage met with the disgruntled ironworkers high atop the city at sunrise. The thirty ninth level was incomplete, its bare metal rafters giving the appearance of a skeletal erector set. The wind howled through the open space as forty angry men stood on a makeshift floor anxious to hear what Nick Rusano had to say. They wanted their money.

Jax and Luca flanked their father as he extolled the events of the missing funds, guaranteeing their money would be returned by end of business that very day. In addition, a handsome monetary bonus would be distributed to each. Enzio made the rounds among the men dispensing bundles of cash from a black leather briefcase.

"However, our business is not complete, gentlemen." Nick went on, as all eyes watched, awaiting his hair trigger temper to ignite. "Only yesterday was I able to confirm the name of the guilty party who has been stealing your money for the last six months," he paused, ensuring everyone's attention. "Are any of you curious as to who that lowlife is?" he paused again, revving up the crowd. "Do you agree that some form of retribution is warranted?"

The union workers rallied, their outrage intensifying as every minute passed. Fists flew into the air; thunderous cries arose throughout. Not surprisingly, the foreman rallied right alongside them, inwardly laughing, secure in his deceit.

Nick raised his hand for silence and addressed the group again. "This cowardly scum," he blazed, "thought he was smarter than all of you. He filtered your money into an account under an assumed name, not his *own* name, someone else's name." Nick's eyes pointed toward the foreman, who was now beginning to sweat, quietly shaking from within, pulse rate quickening. The ironworkers rushed forward but were immediately stopped by Nick's men.

"Now gentlemen, I think it only fair that each of you reaps your revenge in one way or another, be it with a punch, a kick, or even a *shallow* knife cut, but when you have exacted your pound of flesh, the final act of reckoning is mine. Fair enough?"

The group screamed agreement, arming themselves with sticks and chains. Nick signaled for two of his men to restrain the now writhing foreman whose eyes filled with terror as each ironworker stepped forward in turn, doling out justice on the thief's withering body. Most passed makeshift weapons from hand to hand while some chose to viciously kick the fallen man with their steel-toed boots.

When the spectacle ended, Nick again took the stage, approaching the pile of bloodied and bruised flesh that lay in the middle of the floor. The foreman was barely breathing, blood gurgling from his shattered windpipe. The crowd fell eerily silent, standing motionless, their eyes glued to the pathetic little man who had stolen from them all. Nick bent forward, ceremoniously lifting the broken man by the scruff of his neck and parading him in a circle before dropping him back onto the floor.

He turned to his sons, both raptly engaged in the scene when suddenly the gentle scent of lavender strangely encircled him and her soft voice echoed in his mind. *"Nicky, don't do this, don't hurt this man. Bring my babies home."*

But the devil's voice was louder, drowning out her plea and he gruffly called out, "Jax and Luca, join me."

The boys quickly jumped in to assist their father as he hogtied the choking foreman with a thick, heavy rope. Neither hesitated, enjoying their role, their vengeance gene firmly intact. Nick tugged on the rope checking for tightness before yanking the broken body off the floor. He turned back one last time to look at the blood thirsty crowd, each man salivating. Allowing his inner demon to take control, he walked to the edge of the platform releasing a thunderous savage cry and heaved the limp bloody mass down the empty elevator shaft of the thirty-ninth floor. The foreman's gurgled howl echoed throughout the structure for several seconds sending chills up the spines of all present.

Nick calmly turned, seeing the fear-filled faces of those that had witnessed the horror. "Thank you for your attention gentlemen, I expect work to resume immediately."

Third Time

Alaina scanned the crowded room, her smile plastered in place, the perfect hostess. It was Mama's seventieth birthday party and the drinks were flowing, the band was playing, all were merry.

Nick and several out-of-town associates were gathered in a private upstairs room using Mama's party as an excuse to meet, but really paying homage to their Don. Several hours had passed with only the wafting smell of cigars escaping beneath the door.

Dominic sat brooding at a side table drowning his sour mood with too much alcohol, having been purposely omitted from the meeting. He reached for Alaina's arm as she passed.

"Sit," he ordered.

She quietly obeyed, recognizing his brewing resentment, seeing danger if his temper erupted.

He stared at her breasts for several seconds then raised his reddened eyes to hers. "You look beautiful tonight; we haven't seen each other for a while."

"I'm sorry Dominic. We must have you and Angela over to the house for dinner."

He lowered his eyes to the table, contemplating her ambiguity. "You know you married the wrong man. You were meant to marry me."

Alaina was stunned. "Oh Dom, don't say things like that. You have a wife who loves you, beautiful children. What more could you want?"

"I could want you," he scoffed, eyes rising to meet hers and pressing his thigh to hers.

"Dom, please. Let's not do this, not here, not now, please." Alaina started to rise, but he quickly tightened his grip on her arm.

"My brother doesn't appreciate you; I would have worshiped you," he sneered.

"Stop, you don't mean that." She could hear the desperation in her own voice knowing she had to escape.

"Don't tell me what I mean!" he raged, banging his fist on the table, and causing liquor to slop over his glass. "Look at my wife, she's a pig!"

The room grew quiet as several guests turned in their direction, making it imperative that she defuse the situation. Lowering her voice, she placed her hand atop his, "I implore you, Dominic, do not start trouble tonight, it's Mama's birthday."

But just then, she heard Nick behind her. "Little brother, do you mind if I dance with my wife?"

Dominic threw his hands up in surrender, the scene witnessed by the shocked onlookers.

She felt the firmness of Nick's touch as he led her to the dance floor, felt his icy eyes ripping through the fabric of her dress, even heard the frenetic beat of his heart but his voice was low and even.

"So, tell me, what were the two of you talking about?"

"Nothing, it was nothing," she replied, hoping to deflect.

"Really? Nothing? Try again." His piercing glare continued to cut through her.

"It was small stuff, trivial. Dominic was just being Dominic. He's been drinking."

The concrete smile remained but Nick's eyes were glacial. "Third time," he threatened, his voice deepening.

Alaina swallowed, turning her face from his, not knowing how much of the conversation he had heard, "He said I should have married him, that he would have treated me better."

Nick inhaled deeply, controlling his reply. "Round up the boys, we're leaving."

#

Nick's office at home

"I don't want you near him. Do you understand? Tell me you understand," he screamed, pacing the room as she sat before him, his eyes black with anger.

"Nick, please, obviously, I didn't plan for this to happen. I try to avoid your brother whenever possible. *You know that*," she implored, hoping for reason. "He cornered me at the party. He was drunk, I was trying to quiet him, to stop others from witnessing his foolishness. Nothing happened!"

Nick turned, hurling his glass against the wall, sending whiskey and glass shards flying, his rage growing. "Nothing, nothing?" he yelled. "Where were you Thursday? Tell me!" he demanded.

Alaina looked at the floor, shaking her head. Thursday? Thursday? Was he having her followed, watching her? She couldn't think. Thursday? Then suddenly realization hit her.

"I took custard to Angela; I thought it might help with her morning sickness," she stammered. "I didn't realize Dominic would be home, I assumed he'd be at work. Nick, please, nothing happened, nothing is going on." She paused, meeting his eyes with quiet resolve while compiling her strength, her voice even, "There is *nothing* between me and Dominic. I am repulsed by him, always have been and I've never understood this baseless obsession of yours. This conversation is ridiculous, *you are being ridiculous*."

"*Ridiculous!* You think I'm being ridiculous?" he boomed, his voice even louder than before.

"*YES!* Yes, I do. Look at yourself, unjustly accusing me of wrongdoing with no evidence. You are acting like a fool, and you need to stop this *now*!" she shrieked, rising from her chair, and standing to face him. "I am your wife, *not* one of your men and I demand your respect. I will say this one more time, there is *nothing* between me and Dominic. There never has been and there never will be!"

They glared at each other, she defiant in her stance; his eyes still brimming with fire before he abruptly turned toward the window, his back to her. Several silent minutes passed before she started toward the door.

"Stay," he commanded, releasing a heavy sigh, his tone more subdued.

He turned back to face her, all anger now gone, before crossing the room and dropping to his knees before her. Drawing her to him, he rested his head against her thigh in penitence. "Please, my angel, I beg your forgiveness. I was foolish to have doubted you and I am sorry. It's just that it drives me mad whenever someone touches you and seeing you with him tonight pushed me over the edge."

Feeling the searing heat of his torment, she stroked his head before coaxing him to rise and cradling his face in her hands. "Oh love," she assured, "no one on this earth could ever tear me away from the man I love, and that man is *you*. You are the only one whose touch I desire."

"I remember a girl who once told me that I didn't own her," he said, bringing her hand to his lips and kissing it gently.

"You remember a foolish girl who spoke foolish words when her only wish was to be owned by that man."

"And so it is," he uttered, before his grave expression returned. "But honey I need you to listen to me. My brother is extremely dangerous right now." She started to interrupt, but he placed his finger to her lips to quiet her, "He could hurt you, sweetheart; he could hurt our family."

Seeing her bewildered expression, he drew in a deep breath, measuring his words. "Angel, you know I never discuss my business with you but this one time I will share hoping you'll understand. A few months ago, I stumbled upon a very lucrative business venture, and I presented it to a group of my *associates*. I vouched for Dom, and the others agreed to include him in the deal. We were about to close when, for some unknown reason, he pulled out right before the deadline. Those of us that still wanted to move forward were forced to increase our buy in. I offered to cover his share, but my *associates* wouldn't have it. The deal turned into a goldmine. We won, he lost. He is angry, possibly vindictive. Understand, sweetheart, that in our business a person's word is his bond and when you go back on your word, you lose respect. Dominic is being viewed as weak by some very powerful men and soon I won't be able to protect him. He has become reckless, endangering us all."

His voice softened as he took both her hands in his. "I don't want you to put yourself in danger. I'm trying to protect you. Please stay far away from him. Do not see Angela, do not go to their house. Do you understand?"

"Yes, of course," she replied, trying to digest his words.

"Good. I need to run out, I won't be long. Go to bed."

But she held fast to his hands, hesitating, "But… no, wait. Are we… done fighting?"

"Yes…, what's on that devilish mind?"

"Well…, *this* was not how I expected the evening to end, in fact, my plans were quite the opposite. I was hoping to model that little gift you sent this morning," allowing a coy smile to cross her face.

"Gift?"

"Oh, *Nicky!* Don't tell me you forgot. The red lace teddy and heels?" She playfully circled his lapel with her finger. "I just adore the shoes, the little snowman bobbing up and down in the heel is so precious. I'm going to wear them to the Christmas party; the shoes, not the teddy," she giggled gleefully.

"Oh…, yes honey. I'm sorry, so much on my mind," quickly recovering, and steering her to the door. "Go put them on; I'll be twenty minutes at the most, I promise."

Nick knew he had not sent a gift, maybe La Perla had sent something over unprompted. No worries, just so she's happy; the bill was probably somewhere on his desk.

#

2am Dominic's home
Nick rang the bell several times before angrily pounding on the door.

"Been expecting you," Dominic smirked when he finally answered.

Then without a single word, Nick raised his fist and slugged his brother in the jaw, sending him sailing across the foyer floor.

Four Kings

The loud rumble of a motorcycle assaulted her ears disturbing her early morning ritual. *Odd, visitors usually arrived in limos or town cars, never motorcycles.* Alaina continued potting the begonias, knowing their bright pink petals would be a perfect addition to her new flower bed and would bloom in time for summer.

She could hear Nick in a heated conversation with a female. It was a young voice, but she was too far away to hear clearly. The commotion continued for close to half an hour, a mix of male and female voices, loud at first then muffled. Did she hear the words, 'you owe me?' She continued her task until the roar of the motorcycle pierced the quiet peace of the greenhouse again, ending her reverie. *Time to go in.*

She heard Arch questioning Hildy about her whereabouts as she removed her dirty Wellies in the mud room.

"Arch, do you need me?"

Arch looked worried, "He wants you in the office right away."

Nick stood behind his desk staring out the window, his back to the room, his frustration apparent. "This is Sam, he'll be staying with us for a while."

Alaina scanned the room before her eyes alighted on the tiny figure of a child trembling in the leather office chair, his body dwarfed by its size. He was thin, tear streaked and dirty. His sneakers had been mended with silver duct tape, his dirt-stained jeans were two sizes too small, and his ragged sweater had several holes and missing buttons.

"I need you to a...," Nick turned, waving his hand, at a loss for words, "to do what you do."

Alaina looked from Nick to Arch and back to the frightened child. She was confused, about to reply when she heard a soft whimper and the sound of a child's clogged nose. Their little visitor was congested, gulping for air. She gave Nick one last puzzled look before turning from him and kneeling to face the child. He was shaking; his little hands tightly gripping the arms of the chair. He kept his head low, still groping for breath as a single tear rolled down his reddened cheek.

"Hello... hello Sam." Alaina spoke softly hoping for a reply, but the child would not meet her eyes. "I'm Alaina." She looked to Nick who nodded his approval just as a flood of tears erupted from the little boy.

"Oh, no, no, no. It's okay." She gently stroked his little hand making tiny figure eights with her finger. "You don't need to be afraid. No one will hurt you."

Her simple circular motion seemed to hypnotize him, and he felt a reassuring warmth emanating from her fingers. He cautiously peeked at her through tear-soaked lashes seeing soft green eyes– quiet eyes, not angry eyes. Then he heard her gentle voice.

"Sam, are you hungry? I'm *sooo* hungry. Do you like chocolate chip pancakes? I would really like to make chocolate chip pancakes, but I can't reach the chocolate chips. I'm *tooo* short. These big guys laugh at me because I'm so short. Do you think you could help me?"

Little Sam gave just the smallest of nods.

"Oh, thank you, Sam. Thank you so much. Sam's going to help me." Alaina exclaimed, looking at Arch. "I'm so hungry. Here, take my hand and we'll go to the kitchen together."

One hour later Nick sought her out, finding Little Sam happily wolfing down a pancake from his right hand and twirling a half-eaten piece of bacon in his left. Alaina stood at the refrigerator refilling the boy's milk. She shot Nick an angry look.

"Is this your child?" she whispered.

"What? No, no!" He hesitated defensively. "Come into the hallway, let me explain. Hildy, will you watch Sam for a minute while I talk to my wife?"

"He's Selena's boy, Paulie Gordon's daughter. Sam is her son."

"That doesn't answer my question," she countered, still with an angry tone.

He held up his hands, "No, no. Honey, *you* are the only mother of my children. Geez, please believe that. That little boy is Selena's son. She dropped him off this morning, screaming, blaming me for... for her father's death. Then she took off with some scumbag on a bike. Sam is *not* mine." He paused, "What could I do? There he was, and she was gone. Look, it will just be for a week, two at the most. Arch is already trying to find a home for the kid."

"Are you telling me she just dumped him?"

"Yes… honey, the girl's been nothing but trouble ever since Paulie died. She's gone down one bad road after another, addicted to drugs, been with an endless trail of losers. I've bailed her out of jail so many times, paid for countless rehab clinics. I'm… out of ideas." Flustered, he ran his fingers through his hair, "Please, can you just do what you do? You're a great mom. It won't be for long."

"All right... all right." Alaina knew Nick felt some type of obligation for the death of his friend, although she was not aware of the specifics. "How old is he?"

"She said he's three."

"Three! He can't be three. Do you see how skinny he is? That child is nothing but skin and bones. He's already wolfed down four pancakes and three pieces of bacon. He's still wearing a diaper and... I think I see bruises."

Nick shook his head, pleading. "Just do whatever you can, you know I love you."

Relenting, she nodded, placing her palm on his cheek, "Let me get back in there."

Nick pecked her on the forehead. "Thank you, angel."

"Hey, little dude, what 'cha doing here?"

Alaina heard the voice of her youngest son whose first stop after school was always the kitchen. Matt was the most flexible of her children, with an easy-going, not a care in the world personality. He was never serious, always joking, the reverse of his two older brothers, who were mirrors of their father, all business. She rushed back in, seeing Little Sam staring wide eyed at the stranger.

"Matt, this is Sam, he'll be staying with us for a few days."

"Oh, cool." Matt turned from the open refrigerator, "Need more milk, dude?" he asked, before ruffling the little boy's hair.

Alaina quietly pulled him aside, "I need to put him in with you for a few nights, so he isn't frightened, okay?"

Matt saw her worried look, "That's cool, Mom. No problem."

"Oh, you are such a good son. I love you, sweetie."

"Yeah, yeah, Mom. Is there more bacon?"

"Cool." A tiny voice squeaked from behind making them both turn in surprise.

Alaina called Henry asking that he retrieve Matt's old toddler bed from the attic along with some pajamas and toys. Matt's bed was shaped like a racecar, bright red with chrome trim. *Sam should like that.*

"Already started, ma'am. Where would you like it?"

"Let's put him in with Matt. I don't want him to be alone. And, Henry, do we have a stuffed animal or a teddy bear laying about somewhere just for tonight? I'll go to town tomorrow for a new one, but something for tonight, something snuggly. And… we'll need diapers."

"Yes, ma'am, I'll see what I can find."

"Thank you, Henry. Poor little guy, I want him to feel safe. Could be a rough night."

The child was hesitant to allow Alaina to bathe him but then relented when he saw the mountain of bath toys Henry had retrieved from the attic. Sadly, she was correct, there were fresh bruises on his arms and finger shaped bruises on his back and ribcage where someone had held him too tightly. She reported this to Nick.

Sam slept soundly that night, but it was apparent that trust would be an issue as he was confronted with so many new faces. He shied the following morning watching Hildy with hooded eyes until she flipped two dinosaur shaped pancakes onto his breakfast plate causing squeals of delight. Even Nick chimed in, giving each dinosaur a chocolate chip eyeball before kissing his wife on the forehead and retreating to his office.

New shoes were a priority so a shopping trip was planned. Sam was noticeably apprehensive when meeting Bobby, who still served as Alaina's personal driver and bodyguard. He cowered, grabbing ahold of Alaina's dress, fearful of the tall, dark-skinned giant. But Bobby had a smile that could melt hearts which he purposely hid from others, and with a flash of that smile and a mischievous wink, he presented Little Sam with a toy truck for the journey gaining the child's trust.

#

Their first stop was the toy store where Sam released a gleeful squeal seeing the massive wall of brightly colored stuffed animals. Bobby swung him high into the air allowing him to choose his favorite—a purple and blue stuffed dinosaur with a long curly tail. Clutching it tightly to his chest, Sam chattered nonstop to his new fuzzy friend in that secret language of children for the next hour and Alaina wondered if he had ever owned a comfort toy to call his own, thinking how fortunate her own children were.

Later they sat on a bench listening to a street musician and devouring french fries dipped in vanilla milk shakes—Sam's little legs swinging to the beat, his trust building. Her wistful heart betrayed her then. For years she had longed for another child, but passion evaded her bedroom and time had slipped away.

Bedlam resulted when a harried clerk tried unsuccessfully to remove Sam's new superhero light up sneakers. "Leave them," Alaina laughed, "we don't need the box." But she was unable to rein in his enthusiasm when they returned home and he raced around the house showing everyone his shiny new shoes, even loudly banging on Nick's office door.

Two months later

Nick scanned the surveillance cameras, unable to locate his wife after several of his calls went unanswered. Her absence tweaked his radar.

"Honey where were you?" he questioned when she finally appeared.

"Oh, Henry and I were sorting inflatables in the cabana house. I want to take Sam in the pool this afternoon. I don't understand why I didn't hear you."

"No bother, probably a glitch," he replied, realizing there were no security cameras in that area, a flaw that would need to be remedied.

Arch was seated in his usual spot, his desk covered in papers.

"Alaina, good news, I was able to find a placement for Sam. Sorry it took a little longer than I anticipated but I had some trouble finding the boy's birth certificate. I think I've found a good home for him; one that should meet with everyone's approval. I've worked up all the necessary legal documents, discussed it with Nick, and I want to advise you of the specifics."

But Alaina stared blankly, barely hearing his words, overwhelmed at the prospect of losing the little boy she had grown affection for.

Arch's voice droned on in the background. "It's a young couple, living on the east side. Marilyn and George Enders, they're raising three other foster children, ages 12, 8, and 6. Their names are..." He was shuffling papers but again Alaina was lost in thought, his voice a mere echo.

Nick observed his wife. She was troubled, not focusing.

"Alaina? Alaina?" Arch was calling.

She looked up, startled, before hearing Nick speak. "Arch, can you give us a moment?"

Arch looked quizzically but quickly left the room as Nick rose, moving to his wife. He knelt beside her, reaching for her hands.

"Angel, look at me, what's wrong?"

"Um… I... I think Sam should stay with us," she stammered, pleading in her eyes.

"With us?"

"Yes, with us. Nick, please, I don't want to... to lose him. He... he's doing so well with us." Pausing for a few seconds, she tried to formulate a convincing argument. "I don't think we should disrupt his life again. He's just an innocent child. We can give him a good life here. He's thriving. He's eating healthy food, he's gaining weight. He just adores Matt; he follows him around like a puppy. Matt is teaching him about baseball. He's... Nick?"

She was rambling and he stopped her, squeezing her hands, but still confused. "Honey, I didn't think you wanted more children."

"I... I don't do anything to prevent children," she choked, blinking back tears.

Hesitating, he weighed the gravity of her words before cautiously replying. "All right, sweetheart, calm down. Do you want Sam to stay with us?"

She nodded, her brows stitched, her heart beating furiously.

"Then he will stay with us. Stop your fretting. Let me get Arch back in here."

"But what about Selena? He's her son."

"Let me worry about that. Let me talk to Arch and see what can be done." Lifting her from the chair, he gave her a firm hug, "Relax, woman, leave everything to me."

Tino and Zander

The call came through to Nick's office from the front gate security station. Archer answered, curious; business was finished for the day, and no one was expected.

"Mr. Macland, there are two gentlemen down here asking to see the Boss. They're holding a letter of introduction but say it's only for Mr. Rusano's eyes." Mikey reported.

"Mr. Rusano's eyes? Keep them there, I'll be right down. And Mikey, be ready in case there's trouble."

Arch cautiously eyed the two overly large men crammed into the silver Toyota Corolla rental, wondering how the driver managed to get behind the steering wheel considering his girth. In the passenger seat, a gentleman of similar size tightly clutched a sealed envelope refusing to relinquish it. He first spoke to Archer in Sicilian and then in perfectly accented English.

"We are here to see Mr. Rusano, only Mr. Rusano. Kindly tell him Constantine and Alexandro Talerico from Catanzaro are reporting for work. If you would be so good as to pass on that message, it should clear up any questions." With that, he handed Arch both their passports.

Arch returned to the security station and called Nick explaining the situation. Nick recognized the last name.

"Let them up with an armed escort," he ordered. "Check the trunk and undercarriage first before they pass through the gate. You know the drill."

Nick stood in his office surrounded by his underboss and bodyguards watching the two visitors painfully unfold their bodies from the clown car Toyota. He greeted both men in their native language as they entered. The atmosphere was tense, bodyguards at the ready. The shorter of the two nodded, handing Nick the well-guarded letter. Then both stood shoulder to shoulder taking a humble stance of respect, eyes lowered to the floor. Nick read the letter and slowly raised his eyes to the two giants standing submissively in his office.

"Gentlemen, please welcome two new members of our family, Constantine and Alexandro Talerico," he announced, extending a warm handshake.

Nick watched as his men warmly welcomed the newcomers before returning to his desk to reread the letter. That small pouch of diamonds that interrupted his honeymoon decades ago had served as payment to a corrupt Italian official ensuring decreased prison sentences for the two. Constantine (Tino) and Alexandro (Zander) were guilty of committing crimes at the behest of their own father, an Italian Mafia boss. Nick had placed those diamonds directly into their father's hand as instructed. In exchange, the brothers had taken a solemn vow to serve Nick for the rest of their lives, traveling to America immediately upon their release from prison. They would stay in one of the guesthouses on property as members of the family.

Angelo Rusano had protected his son even after his death. Nick turned to the window, silently thanking his father.

Cornerstone

Vinnie Mozzetti arrived on Nick's doorstep early on a cloudy Tuesday morning, hat in hand. He was a small man with thinning hair, darting eyes capped by wiry eyebrows, and oversized ears. He had made an appointment but was visibly nervous by the aspect of standing in front of the Boss. Archer met with him first since Nick was still finishing his morning paper.

"What's this about, Vinnie?" Arch inquired, "We don't normally bother the Boss without some prior reason for the visit."

"I know Mr. Macland, but I was afraid to say on the phone, afraid someone was listening." Sweat poured from the little bookkeeper's brow and his hands began to shake as he unsuccessfully attempted to light a cigarette. Archer intervened, then forced a double whiskey into his hand.

Arch's eyes widened with every word of Vinnie's story, realizing the weight of his words. He threw up his hand, bringing the little man's trembling voice to an abrupt halt. "I'll be right back, stay here, don't move." He poured another double shot into Vinnie's glass before exiting the office and summoning Nick.

"You need to hear this; there's trouble in Portland."

Nick listened attentively as Vinnie Mozzetti retold his tale, his drink spilling onto the office carpet due to his nonstop tremor.

"I was looking through the invoices, and... and the numbers just weren't adding up. I was searching for the discrepancy and that's how I caught it, money missing," he stammered, "money, money missing. So, I... I found it, you see Boss, not the money, the mistake. I traced it. Didn't want you to think it was me. I'm innocent, that's why I'm here."

Vinny continued, explaining how he unearthed a careless scheme orchestrated by Augie Forenzo, the construction foreman of the mob's latest acquisition, the Lusterlights Casino.

"He's buying m30 grade cement but he's billing you for m45 and pocketing the difference. I followed the money, Boss, we need the 45, got to have the 45 for safety, Boss. You being from Atlantic City and all, you know that, right, Boss, for safety? It's dangerous, Boss. It's dangerous. People could get hurt. Bad things could happen. I spoke to some of the men who said they're not shoring up the columns enough either. They're behind, gonna miss the deadline so the men feel rushed. They're not waiting long enough for the cement to cure. They're not waiting the 28 days like you ordered. Forenzo's pushing the men, and everyone's scared."

The veins in Nick's neck pulsed, recalling the Tropicana parking garage collapse in 2003. Four good men lost their lives that day and dozens of others were injured. No amount of settlement money could ever make up for their loss of life or for the suffering of those loved ones left behind. Nick's fist slammed the desk, and he shot from his chair immediately screaming orders to Arch. "Get me on a plane *now*. I want a crew ready to leave within the hour. Tell that engineer to meet me at the airport. Call Luca and have him meet me at the worksite. And for God's sake, get those men out of that building. I don't care what it costs, get them out of there!"

Vinnie cowered, shielding his face, and falling from the chair before he realized he was not the target of Nick's rage. He was invisible now.

Nick was barking orders to Freddy Zee, one of his Portland capos, his anger now replaced by retribution. "I want you to go to the Lusterlights site immediately and restrain Forenzo. Don't let that SOB get away. I'm sending Luca, he's in Salem, he'll arrive before me. And… Freddy, *be sure there's a concrete pump available. I have something special in mind.*"

#

Portland

Nick was met by the site engineer at Portland Airport who validated Vinnie Mozzetti's report. From there he moved on to the construction site, finding Forenzo securely restrained in the office trailer. He grinned, seeing the man's smashed face, missing teeth, and shattered kneecaps, the result of Luca's handiwork. Men still shook whenever Nick walked into a room knowing his penchant for violence and fearing for their safety. His sons were developing the same thirst for blood, cementing the no nonsense Rusano reputation.

Forenzo began to plead, begging for his life as Nick sat facing the trembling man. "Did you *really* believe you could cheat me, Augie? Where's the money?" he asked, his voice dangerously calm.

Forenzo sobbed, pointing to a small corner safe with his bloodied hand. Nick signaled Benny who fired off two shots from his weapon shattering the safe door. Inside were several stacks of neatly wrapped one-hundred-dollar bills.

"Looks like about three hundred thousand, Boss," Benny called out.

"Is that it?" Nick questioned, eyeing Forenzo. "Should I visit your wife and see if she agrees?"

Forenzo shook his head violently, "I swear, I swear, it's all there, every... every dime. Don't hurt my wife, please, I beg you."

"Benny, go pay Mrs. Forenzo a visit, make sure she understands that Augie won't be home for supper tonight. Freddy, find me some rope and hogtie this scum." Nick then turned to Luca, "Start up one of the concrete pumps. I feel the need to do some wet work, might need a backhoe, too."

Again, the scent of lavender surrounded him and he heard her voice, *"Nicky, do not do this. Come home."*

"Get away from me, woman," he yelled, his mind already set.

Augie Forenzo would never be seen again, imbedded deep beneath the Lusterlights cornerstone. Nick Rusano had buried him alive, suffocating him under two tons of wet concrete.

Enter the One-Eyed Jack

Matt sauntered into the kitchen, happy go lucky as always, whistling after baseball practice, "Mom, Coach thinks you're hot."

"Just what I need, a baseball coach that thinks I'm hot," Alaina replied, giving her son a look of warning, her eyes discretely pointing to Nick across the room.

"What? My entire team thinks you're hot, all the guys but especially Coach," Matt responded, incredulously.

"Oh Mattie, stop, you're being silly, go take a shower," she scoffed, shushing him toward the kitchen door. "And use soap!"

Nick glared at his son as he departed before turning a questioning eyebrow on his wife.

"Don't be ridiculous," she answered with a raised eyebrow of her own.

"Mommy, are you hot?" Little Sam questioned.

"Hot? Oh no, no. In fact, your daddy calls me popsicle toes. Your mama is ice cold," she joked, quickly grabbing an ice cube, and dropping it down the child's shirt.

"Eeee," he squealed with delight.

But Nick was not laughing, recalling the anonymous package delivered to the security station earlier that morning. Beneath the gift wrap and red satin bows lay six pairs of red thigh-high silk stockings and a matching garter belt adorned with sequins and pearls. No card, only Alaina's name scrawled across the label. She would never see that gift, never even know it existed. Thoughts of his wife's possible infidelity were his constant torment. He rose from the table intent on scanning her recent computer activity and what he read made his blood broil.

Recent conversation

Coach *"Hi, it's John, John Kelly, Coach Kelly."*

Alaina *"Hello."*

Coach *"I was wondering if we could meet for coffee."*

Alaina *"Coffee? Is there a problem with Matt?"*

Coach *"No, no. Matt's a great kid, just wanted to talk."*

Alaina *"I don't understand."*

Coach *"I actually wanted to ask you to dinner but thought maybe you would be more*

comfortable with coffee first."

Alaina *"That's not a good idea."*

Coach *"I thought you might need someone to talk to. You always look so sad. I think   you're   beautiful. Does your husband ever hurt you?"*

Alaina *"I appreciate your concern, but we need to keep our relationship professional."*

Coach *"I admit I'm disappointed. We could just sit somewhere quiet, private."*

Alaina *"No."*

Coach *"All right, well, will I see you at the awards luncheon?"*

Alaina *"Of course, for Mattie."*

Coach *"Maybe we can talk about it then."*

Alaina *"You don't understand, I love my husband."*

Coach *"Does he love you?"*

Alaina was unaware of the extent of Nick's surveillance. She had no idea that all her computer and phone activity was recorded, and that Nick reviewed them frequently. However, she was intelligent enough to know that predators came in all shapes and sizes. Adult men knew how to lure vulnerable women and she was determined not be a victim.

Broken Wings

"Aaaah, aaaah!"

The woman's scream echoed off the tiled floor and throughout the hall leading to the pool. Millie Zorez was part of the Royale's custodial staff assigned to clear away the remnants of tonight's late-night pool party. Unfortunately for Millie, she had returned a few hours later frantically searching for a lost bracelet, a gift from her granddaughter. The pool entrance had been securely locked but a maintenance worker allowed Millie to re-enter.

The battered female body lay peacefully at the bottom of the pool, eyes open staring up toward the starless Vegas sky, another victim of the serial killer. She had been savagely beaten. Dark purple bruises circled her neck, arms, and abdomen, and a nasty four-inch gash across her skull trailed dark crimson blood throughout the sky-blue water. A lock of dyed orange hair peeked out from beneath a wavy brunette wig and the now familiar red satin bows adorned her wrists, ankles, and neck.

Simonelli, however, wore a broad grin, informing Nick of a possible break in the now well publicized 'ROYALE MURDERS', and pointing to a crooked twenty-foot path of the victim's blood trailing from the water's edge to a nearby cabana changing room. Copious pools of dark red blood covered the blue tile floor and splattered the walls within, leading police to conclude that this was the site of the attack. Investigators speculated that the killer may have been interrupted by Millie, not allowing him time to clean up.

Nick looked over at his visibly shaken employee as she was being interviewed by local detectives. He knew her well, often stopping to chat with her while making his rounds. She was a hard worker struggling to raise three grandchildren, always cheerful and friendly. Millie Zorez didn't realize how lucky she was.

He returned to his upstairs suite and stared out into the darkness. *What was different, what was similar between the three murders?* All occurred after closing, between midnight and 3am, but the time of the year was different leading him to rule out a visiting conventioneer. The women were, as of this date, unidentified, possibly runaways or street prostitutes. They were young, between 15 and 25 years old. All were severely beaten with bruises throughout their bodies, all had choking bruises around their throats, all had head wounds. But why, why them, why his hotel? What was the connection?

The pool area was cordoned off for twenty-four hours while lab technicians scoured the cabana house for evidence. Once released, Nick chose to keep the rooftop off limits for an additional night, allowing him to do his own inspection. He timed his search for precisely 2am the following evening wondering if the killer might return.

The cabana seemed eerily quiet when he entered as if someone were there, watching. Nick could feel a menacing presence but, of course, the room was empty. He walked slowly, stepping around the congealed blood, purposely scrutinizing every corner and crevice. He felt along the walls, bending to examine the area where the concrete met the tile floor. *Nothing*, the room revealed no clue, but as he turned to exit, the slightest hint of color caught his eye. A small black object was wedged beneath a cracked shower tile. He bent to retrieve it, using his cuff link to pry it from the spot. It was a button, a simple, black, four-hole plastic button.

The Queen of Diamonds

The annual awards luncheon for the city's high school baseball teams was being held this year in Ballroom A of the Royale Casino Hotel. Matt was excited knowing he would be awarded the trophy for the Highest Batting Average on his team. It was a prestigious award.

Nick told his son he would try his best to be there, but he had previously scheduled a business meeting conflicting with the time slot. Still Matt kept his eye on the door.

He soon spotted his father hurrying toward the ballroom, and he rushed out to meet him just as a tall blond caught up with Nick and looped her arm through his, kissing him on the cheek. Her lips lingered for an uncomfortable amount of time as she whispered something in his ear.

Gwen Rosen, the Royale's Marketing Manager and Nick's current mistress wore a tight-fitting red silk suit with crystal button enclosures, stiletto heels, and bright red lipstick. She was the niece of an east coast underboss, to whom Nick owed past favors. Hiring Gwen was part of that repayment.

Matt stood six feet away, witness to the exchange, watching his father separate himself from the stranger and wipe the lipstick from his cheek.

Turning, Nick was surprised to see his son, "Mattie, am I late? I tried to end my meeting as quickly as possible."

"Oh, my goodness, are you Nick's little boy? You look just like your father. Oh Nicky, he's so cute." The woman stepped between them, feigning friendliness; her fake, syrupy tone apparent, as she reached to touch Matt's cheek. "You are just adorable, sweetie."

Matt hesitated for only a second before defiantly looking into her green feline eyes and spitting his reply, "No, I'm Alaina's son." He turned his indignant glare back onto his father before retreating into the ballroom.

Nick was unable to mask the volcanic fury that rose within him. "What do you think you're doing?" he raged, towering over an obviously satisfied Gwen.

"Why, I was just being sociable, Nicky. Don't you think it's about time I met your children? After all, we have been together for two years now."

Nick's venomous tone spewed daggers, "Know your place, woman."

He stormed into the ballroom, catching sight of Alaina across the room in a friendly conversation with Bryan Russo, a rival casino owner. Bryan's son played on the same team as Matt. Nick's jealousy vein triggered immediately and his fists clenched as he observed Russo's wanton smile and his hand upon Alaina's forearm.

Angry and humiliated by his rebuff, Gwen Rosen remained near the entrance partially hidden from view. She watched as Nick approached the stunningly attractive brunette, placing his hand on her buttocks and drawing her in for a casual kiss. *So that's the pretty little wife.* She seethed, taking measure of Alaina. *It's about time I dispose of her; one call to my Uncle Vito and that bitch will disappear. Get ready, big boy, little Gwen is about to rock your world.*

But Gwen Rosen's venomous eyes were not the only ones watching the dazzling couple that day.

Nick Rusano eyeballed Coach Kelly as he stood at the podium presenting the team trophies. When both men made eye contact, Kelly stammered, briefly losing concentration. Nick nodded with satisfaction. Just one week earlier, he had made a generous donation to the school's athletic department in exchange for a guarantee that Kelly's contract would not be renewed for the following school year. Time for that coach to move on.

Matt accepted his trophy with pride. He had worked diligently all season, earning this accolade; but as he sat at the table with his father, the scene in the hallway replayed over and over in his mind. There was no denying what he saw, and the hatred he felt for the man sitting beside him multiplied with each passing minute.

#

Nick arrived home a few hours later and immediately sought out his son. Both Matt and Luca were loudly battling each other in a spirited video game in the entertainment room.

"Matt, can we talk for a few minutes, man to man?"

The boy stared straight ahead, his jaw locked in anger, before slamming down the video controller and turning to his father.

"What you really want to know is, did I tell Mom? Well, the answer is *no*. I wouldn't want to hurt her. It's a shame you can't say the same."

He turned to his brother, "Tell Mom I'm having dinner at Chris's."

He then briskly walked past his father, purposely banging into his shoulder, his eyes filled with disgust, "We have nothing to say to each other."

Nick watched the boy retreat knowing better than to continue after him. All his sons had inherited their father's volcanic temper, Matt a little less but it was still there.

Boundaries

Ginny had retired from the stage three years earlier, taking a job as a seamstress in the Royale's tailoring shop. She could no longer bear the weight of the thirty-pound headdress and no amount of alcohol dulled the pain in her neck and back. She knew of Nick's infidelities, never sharing that knowledge with Alaina. She especially disliked Gwen Rosen, his latest distraction, and today she was unable to mask that scorn. She chuckled as the nasty condescending shrew abruptly turned on her red stiletto heels and retreated from the repair room, anger exuding from her eyes. *Yep, another written reprimand for unprofessional behavior will be coming my way before this day's done. Not like my folder isn't bulging already. Oh well.*

#

Nick's office

"What is wrong with that *bitch* in tailoring? I want her fired!" Gwen screeched, storming into Nick's office without even a nod to Peggy.

"What's going on?" he moaned, already annoyed by the intrusion.

"I ask her to do a simple hem on a skirt and sew a button on a jacket and she wants to know if the items are *'hotel property'*. Of course, they aren't!"

"What's her name?" he sighed.

"Ginny, Ginny… something."

Ginny Monroe, of course. Ginny never could mask her disdain. He remembered her threat at the wedding. 'If you hurt her, I know a drummer....' She and Alaina were still close, taking Zumba classes every Thursday.

"You don't fire people for doing their job, Gwen. She's right about the policy, no personal items. The woman makes such little money as it is, I'm not going to fire her. Don't take advantage."

"Arrrg! How can you take the side of a peon?" she yelled, throwing up her hands.

"Can you lower your voice?" his cold eyes meeting hers. "However, I'm actually glad you stopped by."

She hesitated, noting the sarcasm in his voice.

Nick continued, "We need to set a few boundaries, clarify a few rules. I need you to understand your *place* in our relationship. Don't ever, ever go near my sons again. Do not speak to them, do not even look in their direction. Am I clear?" His voice was calm, but she could hear its icy edge.

"Oh Nicky, I never meant to upset your little boy, really, I didn't. Forgive me, lover," she cooed, insincerity evident in her honeyed response. She tried stepping behind his desk in an attempt to rub his neck, but he waved her off, annoyed. "My, you are touchy today, sweetheart. Are we still on for tonight? Maybe I can massage away some of that tension." She smiled coyly, attempting another ploy to placate him.

"No, my wife and I have a dinner date." Surprise flashed across Gwen's face; her jealousy apparent as he continued. "You really have your bitch face on this week, Gwen, and it isn't pretty. Don't you have some work to do?"

She froze, at a loss for words just as Nick's intercom buzzed.

"Sir, that call you've been waiting for from Macau is coming through now," announced Peggy.

Nick pointed at the door silently directing Gwen to leave; unable to mask his smile as she slammed out. He stepped into the outer office. "Thank you, Peggy."

"No problem, sir. It was getting a bit loud. Can I get you a fresh coffee?"

"That would be wonderful, thanks."

He'd had enough of Gwen. He needed to end this, but just as quickly another thought entered his mind. His confrontation with Gwen might just prove fortuitous.

"Peggy, get Ginny Monroe up here right away."

Ten minutes later Nick had no doubt the tornado had arrived, hearing Ginny storming toward his office, spewing a string of expletives that would make a truck driver blush. *Why did I send for her?* he asked himself, his blood pressure already ratcheting skyward. Ginny was a viper on wheels, and he avoided her whenever possible but today maybe, just maybe, she might be of some help.

"I'm fired, right? That bitch you're fucking just got me fired. Well, I don't give a damn. Fire me, I don't care. Fuck you!" Ginny spun to leave, just as quickly as she had entered, murmuring more curse words as she reached for the door.

"Sit down!" he bellowed. He was determined not to lose his temper, but this woman continuously tested his patience. He would have dismissed her years ago were it not for Alaina's intervention.

Ginny stopped abruptly, eyeing him with contempt; belligerence written in every muscle.

"Ginny, sit down and shut up. This is not about that. I have something more serious to discuss; I need your help." Nick motioned to the chair.

Still not trusting, she cautiously complied.

"Good, let's start again." Nick placed the black button he had retrieved from the crime scene on the desk between them. "I was hoping you might be able to identify this."

She stared at the button then looked up, confused. "It's a button, an ordinary black button. I don't understand."

"Have you ever seen this type of button before?"

She hesitated, slowly nodding, "Yes, we have that type of button in tailoring. We have hundreds of them. We use them on the dealers' vests, the waitresses' uniforms, repairs for the clerks and bellhops. I still don't understand."

Nick looked toward the tiny object with defeat, his futile hope in its value diminished.

"Boss, what is this about?" She was puzzled, watching him become uncharacteristically solemn.

He released a heavy sigh, debating how next to proceed, before withdrawing the crime scene photos from his top desk drawer.

"Have you heard about the incidents at the pool?" he asked.

"Um… sure. They say some girls died up there."

Nick nodded, "I found this button in the cabana house where the police believe the murders took place. It's the only clue I have to possibly finding the killer."

Realizing the gravity of his words as he turned the pictures face up, she slowly lowered her eyes to the three 8x10 color photos, each showing a naked, badly battered woman with multiple wounds to her face and skull. Her first reaction was shock, momentarily jerking upward; then she regained her nerve and returned her gaze to the photos.

"Whoever did this was meticulous, the button is the only mistake the killer may have made and I don't even know if it was his." Nick was talking in the background, but her eyes were glued to picture #3, the most recent murder. "Ginny? Ginny, you okay?"

"Yeah, yeah, sorry. I… I was just thinking that they all sort of look like... Alaina, especially this one." She stuttered over the words, pointing to the gruesome image as a frightening coldness coursed through her body.

"Alaina? What? No, Alaina's home, she's fine. That's a wig, they're wearing wigs."

Ginny slowly nodded, still shaken. "Sorry, that was stupid of me. I know it's not her, we just had lunch yesterday. Sorry, Boss, sorry."

"It's okay, I probably shouldn't have shown you these. If you think of anything, call me and… Ginny, I didn't tell you about the button."

#

Gwen Rosen ended her workday at precisely 5pm every day. After her little stunt, Nick thought she deserved some payback. He knew she would walk past the Keno lounge as she exited, unable to avoid his planned retribution.

Laughing heartily, he stood in her path engaged in a lively conversation with two newly hired, very well-endowed cocktail waitresses; his arm around the waist of one while the other seductively hung on his shoulder. Gwen's fiery eyes met his from across the room as she observed the scene and he noted with satisfaction her look of seething indignation.

Message received.

Ghost from the Past

"You can't have him, he's mine. Give him to me."

A shrill female voice screamed from the far side of the lawn startling Alaina as she watched Little Sam run the bases for home plate, loudly cheered on by his older brother, Matt. Three years had passed since Sam came to them. He was a happy little boy, excelling in school and loving the game of baseball.

"He's mine, you witch. Give him to me. Sam, come to Mommy," the woman shrieked, storming across the grass.

The intruder inched closer, her demeanor frightening. Heavy black eyeliner, dark burnt red lipstick, and jet-black spiked hair added to her alarming appearance. Alaina was shaken, her first reaction being that this could be a lost runaway that had somehow stumbled onto the property… but she was wrong.

Sam ran to Alaina, cowering behind her and she quickly picked him up, folding him tightly against her chest.

The woman continued forward, her arms extended, calling to the child, "Come to Mommy, Sammie, come to Mommy."

"Matt, get your father!" Alaina yelled, backing away and tightening her grip on Sam whose face was now buried in her neck. Frightening seconds ticked by before five massive bodyguards thundered in, forming a protective barrier between her and the intruder.

"Selena, step back!" Nick's thunderous voice boomed from behind, making Alaina's body quake.

Turning, she saw Luca and Jackson running toward her along with Nick and three additional bodyguards, all with weapons drawn. *This crazed girl is Selena Gordon?*

Nick signaled to Bobby who quickly took Sam from Alaina's arms and rushed him into the house. Just as quickly, Luca grabbed his mother's arm hurrying her to safety, gun squarely aimed at the intruder. Alaina glanced back, witnessing Jackson wrapping his arms around Selena's waist, encasing her in his tight grip before lifting her off the ground as she struggled, spewing an endless string of profanity.

Alaina could still hear the girl's screams minutes later after she and Sam were secured in the playroom with Bobby standing guard. She observed her little son, now busily playing on the floor with his toy trucks, the incident forgotten. He was bewildered and frightened during the event but had not recognized his own birth mother. Hours later she was still unsettled as Nick attempted to comfort her, enclosing her in his arms and stroking her hair, his voice soothing.

"She wanted money, that's all. I paid her off and put her on a bus. She will never bother you or the boy again. Now, I don't want you to think about it anymore."

"But..."

"Listen to me, sweetheart, please. Her goal in coming here was extortion. She wanted money for drugs and, in exchange for that money she signed Sam over to us."

"But what if...."

"Shh, what did I just say? She won't be back. Now, no more talk, try to get some sleep."

#

The following day

"You took care of that situation?" Nick questioned Jackson who stood before him in the downstairs office.

"Yes, sir."

"Any problems?"

"No, sir."

You waited to be sure?"

"Yes, sir."

Selena Gordon's body was found by an unsuspecting housekeeper at a low rent downtown motel the following morning.

OFFICIAL CORONER'S REPORT

The cause of death was determined to be a deadly mixture of heroin and cocaine, commonly known as a speedball. The deceased had a history of substance abuse resulting in several previous arrests.

New Shooter

"New shooter, new shooter coming out," barked the stickman behind the crowded craps table.

The casino floor was busy with hordes of tourists packing the Vegas Strip eager to spend their hard-earned cash on booze and cheap thrills. Jackson and Luca were both working, enjoying every minute of their busy schedules. Casino life was exciting to the young men. Both were living a bachelor's dream, plenty of spending money and plenty of playtime surrounded by gorgeous women willing to jump into bed whenever they crooked their fingers. Showgirls, dancers, cocktail waitresses were abundant and more than willing to please the handsome brothers.

Nothing is a secret in the casino world; casinos are cities unto themselves. Everyone knows who dates who, who sleeps with who and it was common knowledge that Luca Rusano was seeing a slim, sexy craps croupier named Valentina, her uniform barely containing her generous breasts. Jax was playing the field and, much like his father, lived by the philosophy of a different beauty every night, no strings attached.

With both boys home for the summer, Nick was spending more time in his home office only going into the Royale one day a week and allowing his sons to stretch their wings. Tonight, he was deep in concentration, reviewing the specifics of an upcoming real estate merger. His phone jolted him back to the present.

"Boss, don't mean to bother you but I've got something you need to see." The caller was Steve Corson, his trusted floor manager. "Can you come down, the sooner the better?"

Nick heard the urgency in Corson's voice and arrived a short time later. "What's going on?"

"We have a problem with two of our craps croupiers, Valentina Abramov and Stefan Lange. Boys in the eye alerted me. I've already pulled them both off the table. You're not going to like it. This is a nasty one. Let's go down to surveillance, I captured a few things on tape." Steve shook his head; it was going to be a *very* bad night, better get ready.

Nick glared at the camera footage in the surveillance room and at the still photos spread across the desk. His anger catapulted.

"Stupid, stupid kid!" he yelled, slamming his fist down on the table.

"I wanted to alert you, Boss, before I called the kid in." Steve knew his boss's temper, knew the roof was about to explode. He worried for the boy's safety.

Nick's eyes were black with rage, his face bright red, temple veins throbbing. Then he grew silent. Steve recognized this as the proverbial quiet before the storm.

Opening his cell phone, Nick calmly called the casino floor. "This is Nick Rusano, would you please have both Jax and Luca Rusano report to surveillance immediately. Thank you."

Steve took cover.

Nick's hands were flying, his eyes ablaze as he paced the room. The decibel level of his screams reverberated throughout the floor, sending employees scurrying even though they were not the offenders. Both boys cowered in their father's presence having been shown the proof of their negligence. The offense was clearly visible, both Valentina and Stefan were working with a third party to defraud the Royale.

"Are you blind? Are you fucking blind? Too busy looking at her ass to miss the fact that she's hiding the dice in her tits. What the *FUCK* is wrong with you? Do I need to give you both a lesson in shaved dice?"

Four employees are needed to control a craps table: one stickman, and two croupiers, with a box man sandwiched in between whose job it is to monitor activity. It is an exciting fast-moving game, and Valentina and Stefan were using an old tried and true ploy. Valentina would introduce a pair of shaved dice onto the table while Stefan made sure to overpay their coconspirator with each successful roll of those dice. With Valentina's ample bosom, she could easily hide the offending dice at will, inserting and returning them as needed. Not only was Luca a novice at the conspiracy but he was enamored by her charms, and she knew how to distract him. The theft was blatant, but the disturbing question hovered. How long had this been happening? How much money had the Royale lost?

Nick looked at both his sons. "I suggest the three of us adjourn to my office." Nick directed Steve to keep Valentina and Stefan under wraps for the time being and to see if the third player in the scam could be located.

Both Jackson and Luca knew it would now fall on them to resolve a problem they had created. Nick stared out his office window, his back to them. "I'm waiting," were his only words.

#

It was decided that Jackson and Luca would deal with Valentina and Stefan whereas Nick would handle Sammie Balakin, the not so lucky dice shooter. Balakin, was quickly located at a dive motel a half block off the Vegas Strip. Jackson and Luca accompanied their father, watching as Nick dispensed of the cheater with one clean shot to the head, no questions, just business.

The Royale kept a warehouse several miles out of town for incidents such as this, incidents where a form of punishment was deemed necessary. The building was soundproof; its walls lined with various pieces of torture equipment such as chain saws, hammers, vises, pliers, welding equipment and metal pipes.

Nick had sent his men ahead and when the three arrived, they found Valentina and Stefan shackled to opposing metal posts midway down the main aisle. Valentina spat at Luca as he neared, cursing at him in her native Russian.

Luca released a loud, sinister laugh, "Bitch, you won't have a mouth to spit from when I'm done." He was especially enraged since this girl had humiliated him in the eyes of his father. He would take pleasure in her every scream.

Nick pulled up a chair, his part of the retribution was finished. He now wanted to observe his sons, ordering his men not to interfere.

Jackson was only there to play but he would enjoy tonight; it had been a while since he tasted blood. He especially enjoyed working alongside his brother when wet work was required. He knew that Luca wanted Valentina for himself so before the party started, they both agreed that he would deal with Stefan while giving the devious bitch a birds-eye view of the entertainment. They attached a wide leather work belt around her waist secured with a heavy metal chain before looping that chain around a pipe in the ceiling. They bound her hands and feet, then hoisted her writhing body into the air twenty feet above them, laughing as she screamed.

"Save your breath, bitch. There's no one within fifty miles that can help your sorry ass," Luca joked.

Jackson then took his turn, starting with something simple, a nail gun. Sweat poured from Stefan as he sobbed, his eyes wild, begging forgiveness. Jax was oblivious, drawing out the moment, letting the young man's fear build. Slowly he approached his victim and one by one, he fired the nail gun into every joint as Stefan screamed.

"Oh, c'mon, wimp. That's no more than a bee sting," Jax chuckled. "Let's try this."

Trading the nail gun for a circular saw, he tightly grabbed Stefan's bound arm and quickly sliced off the man's right hand. Columns of blood gushed skyward as Stefan's howls echoed against the warehouse rafters. He began to lose consciousness, but Jax would have none of that.

"Don't get blood on the floor. Maid doesn't come in til morning," he cackled. "Let me cauterize that for you. You don't want to miss any of the entertainment now, do you?" Jax hoisted a nearby blowtorch and held it to Stefan's wound ignoring his agonizing screams as the smell of burning flesh permeated the air. He then moved to Stefan's opposite side, relishing the moment, and tasting the man's fear. Lowering the saw again, he sliced off Stefan's arm below the elbow.

Urine showered from above and chains rattled revealing the petrified puppet aloft who had just witnessed the carnage, knowing she was next.

"Oh bitch, are you scared?" Luca roared, lowering Valentina to the floor, and retying her to the warehouse post as she spewed obscenities in Russian before spitting at Luca again. He released another deep, throaty laugh before grabbing her forehead and slamming her into the pole, sending arcs of blood spurting from a four-inch gash in her skull.

Luca sneered with satisfaction, "Funny, I always admired your pretty face, doll; but now I want to make a few minor adjustments." He reached for a portable belt sander and grabbed Valentina by her hair forcing her to remain upright. Her eyes grew wide with fear seeing the purring machine and she released a blood curdling scream as he held the tool near her ear letting the ominous sound rachet up her terror. "Such a pretty girl," he murmured, gently stroking her chin, and running cool fingers up her neck as her screams continued. But he was undeterred, holding her head erect with one hand and moving the sander over her cheek and jaw with the other. Layers of mangled flesh peeled away in a hideous display of torture, sending bits of ragged dermis and blood flying across the room.

Stepping back, he assessed his work, not yet satisfied. He wanted to destroy the face of the girl who had embarrassed and deceived him.

"Shall we do the other side?" he joked. "You know, for symmetry."

Jackson intervened, stepping forward and gallantly bowing to his brother, then ceremoniously handing him a welding torch. Waves of delight crossed Luca's face as he held the glowing red-hot tool in his hand, admiring its possibilities before moving it closer to Valentina's eyes for her inspection. He then lowered the torch to the same cheek but this time he paid special attention to her lips and jaw. Valentina screamed in agony… until she could no longer scream.

"Not so pretty now, are you?" were the last words she heard.

Nick did not interfere, never leaving the chair until both boys stepped back to assess the carnage. "Finished?" he asked.

"Yes, sir," they replied in unison.

"Satisfied?"

"Yes, sir."

"Good job. Take them out to the desert, let the vultures finish them off."

Fallen Petals

1 pm

The air was still, too still. Not a single breeze swayed the branches of her towering cherry trees that stood silent, motionless, grieving. Alaina raised her eyes admiring the pink canopy bursting with rosy petals, knowing they wept along with her as they floated to the ground below. Her thoughts returned to that day at the Botanical Gardens so many years ago. Where had that time gone? Where had he gone?

Dominic's words hammered her nonstop; her encounter with him hours earlier shattering her Stepford wife cocoon.

"He's never been faithful to you, sweetheart. Do you have any idea how many women he's been with since you said those fated words, 'I do'? I can name you a few. There was Juliette, Suzie, Angélique. Ahh, Angélique, now that was the one; she was a centerfold before she came to the Royale. Better yet, ask him about Gwen. He's been with her a while now. I told you before, toots, you married the wrong guy. Wake up!"

Standing on the side of the road, she stared wide-eyed, digesting her brother-in-law's venomous words as one small tear escaped down her cheek.

"Stop, Dominic, please stop. I can't hear this."

"You need to hear this," he shouted, tightening his grip on her arms and shaking her as her tears burst forth.

Gulping in a breath, he stepped back, recognizing the brutality in his words; his goal had never been to hurt her. He loved her, *he loved his brother's wife.* He always had and he awoke to that tortured reality every day of his life for the past twenty years. *He loved her!*

He gently reached out, wrapping his arms around her as she quietly wept against his shoulder.

"Come home with me," he whispered. "I will take care of you. You know how I feel about you. I have always loved you."

"Don't, don't say those words, Dom, please don't. You know I can't… I can't just walk away, I have children."

He puzzled at her response, "Why not? That little boy isn't yours. Can't you see that you deserve a better life, a life that I could give you. My brother has never treated you right. He doesn't know what love is, but I do."

She shuddered, looking up at him, shaking her head in denial, "No, no you don't. That isn't true. My life would have been no different with you. I've seen you out with other women."

"They weren't you, Alaina," he quietly answered, stroking her hair.

He could feel her shivering; each car that passed pelted them with the cold. But he waited silently for her tears to subside, gently holding her head against his shoulder. "I want to take you away from him, come with me now, tell me you'll come."

"Dom, I can't, you know I can't," she sobbed.

He drew in a breath, unsure what words would convince her, unsure of what to do. "You aren't ready; but you will be soon, I'll wait. I will wait for you, my love." He gently wiped her eyes with his handkerchief, barely able to refrain from kissing her lips. "I'll wait," he assured her. Her sobs continued as he helped her into her car, still hesitant to release her hands from his. She was leaving and his world was imploding.

Frozen and frustrated, he watched her taillights recede into the morning mist. His declaration of love had failed to move her and now she was running back to HIM, his no-good cheating brother—his brother who had everything. Rage erupted within him and his fist savagely struck the roof of his Lamborghini. *You frightened her, you fool!* But it needed to be done, and for a few brief moments she had been in his arms. He held his handkerchief to his lips still wet with her tears. The scent of her perfume still lingered. He could still feel her cheek against his.

#

The cherry trees brought no solace now, her thoughts barreling past like a runaway train moving toward an inevitable wreck. She was so hurt, so confused, so betrayed. Infidelity is like an ever-growing stain on your favorite dress, spreading further and further the more you scrubbed. It's always there, never fully gone, always tainting the fabric, always staring back in the mirror.

Nick had never been faithful, she knew that. She was cursed with a nurses' nose. She could smell another woman's perfume immediately. She could smell sex on him immediately. She should have acted years ago but she was too weak, too in love, willfully blind. Was she too weak now? She had grown into a strong bitch, far from the lovesick girl she once was.

Did she have a reason to stay? Her children were grown. The older boys were finishing college, Matt was in high school, busy with a different sport every season, strolling in for dinner occasionally. Nick had just bought him his first car, a metallic red Ferrari, naturally. Sam was the only child she needed to consider. She had pleaded to make him a part of their family, knowing how disrupted his early life had been. She was his mother in heart. Could she walk away from him now?

Her mind returned once again to the Botanical Gardens as another shower of pink petals christened her from above. She still loved Nick Rusano and right now, *today, this very minute,* she hated herself for it.

5 pm

"Alaina, can I have a word?" Archer crossed the lawn, approaching quietly, his stance unusually aggressive. "Did I see what I thought I saw this morning?"

"What did you see, Arch?"

"I saw you kissing Dominic on the highway. I drove right past you, I nearly hit the brakes and turned around to confront you both. Tell me I'm wrong!" he demanded.

"No, my God, no. That is not what you saw," she stammered. "Dominic… Dominic stopped me in the road. There was no *kissing.* I was upset, he was consoling me."

"Well, that's not what it looked like," he raged. "What the hell, Alaina. I've been friends with Nick for over thirty years. It looked to me like you're having an affair with his brother."

"No, Arch, *no.* You have it wrong; it's not me, please. Dominic was telling me about Gwen, Nick's mistress." She was exasperated, shaking with disbelief. "I am not the one having an affair, damn it! It's not me."

Arch drew in a deep breath, considering her words. "I want to believe you, I really do, but I know what I witnessed and you better hope that no one else did the same because if so, Nick already knows. If Enzio saw you or somebody else, he already knows, and God help you. He will kill you; do you understand? You have never witnessed even the smallest hint of his temper, but I have. He will explode, he will kill you both and believe me it won't be pretty. It will be slow and ugly. You better be telling me the truth because this will fall on me too if he thinks I knew and didn't report." Arch hesitated, looking down at his watch. "I need to get back, but heed my words, you will not escape if you are lying. That man is a monster."

Alaina sat in the garden a while longer, she would confront her husband in the morning.

No Coffee for You

"Lain, can you grab me more coffee?" Nick sat at the kitchen table reading the day's Wall Street Journal.

Alaina was busy helping Little Sam tie his shoes. "You have stinky little feet," she teased, tickling his toes and making the boy giggle and squirm. "Oh yes you do, they be *stinky*. Phew!" She leaned into his feet, scrunching up her nose. "Phew, phew, phew, when was the last time these piggies were washed?"

Nick waited for a pause in their play, enjoying the interaction between the six-year-old and his wife. "Lain, coffee?"

Silent minutes passed with no response.

"Lain... Alaina," he tried again to get her attention as she moved to the refrigerator.

"Mommy?" Alaina turned to the little boy, seeing him pointing to his father. "Daddy wants you, Mommy."

But she turned her attention back to the kitchen counter, her back to Nick.

He rose, realizing she was purposely ignoring him, and slammed the coffee cup down next to her hand. "Can you refill the coffee?"

She gazed briefly at him then turned to walk away without answering, but his firm grasp stopped her, forcing her to face him.

"What is this about?" he growled; his question met with cold silence. "Ok... let's take it in the office." But she stood firm, causing Nick to lower his head to her ear. "Alaina, I don't know what is going on here, but do you want to do this in the kitchen, because I will?"

Knowing he was right, she relented.

#

Nick's office

"Now, tell me what this is about?" he barked, backing her against the interior door of the office, his stance threatening.

"It's about you not coming home and stinking up the sheets with cheap perfume when you are home."

Releasing a heavy sigh, he stared into her eyes. "I don't have enough on my schedule, woman? On top of it you're coming at me with petty female jealousy."

"Right, let me go."

"No, damn it, we'll settle this now so I can get a damn cup of coffee in my own damn house."

"You want to settle it? Well, how about adding this to that busy schedule of yours. *Item 1- choose* between wife and mistress."

He paused, weighing his reply, anger rising.

"Who am I married to?" he demanded; his face close to hers.

But Alaina met his eyes with belligerence, not answering.

"Ah, there's that fuckin' defiant look I know so well! Who... am... I... married... to?" he roared, banging his fist on the wall.

"Me, you're married to me."

"Who do I live with?"

"You live with me."

"Who is the mother of my children?"

"Oh..., is that the criteria? No children with Gwen or isn't she the motherly type?"

Nick jerked, backing away. She had caught him off guard. "Is that from Ginny?"

"Oh no, no. It comes courtesy of your own brother, your snide brother who practically ran me off the road yesterday. I thought some lunatic was behind me, Nick, slamming on his horn and riding my bumper. That smug bastard took *great* delight telling me what a hypocrisy our marriage is, sharing tales of your exploits, naming woman after woman—Angélique and… Juliette and…, and…," her voice seethed in frustration.

"Alaina…"

"Don't!" she snapped. "Do you know how hurt I am? Have you any idea how humiliated and embarrassed I am? Do you, Nick?" Inhaling deeply, she forced her eyes shut, seeking composure but she felt him moving closer. "Don't! Don't come near me!"

"Alaina, they were women from long ago."

"Long ago? But while we were married?

"Yes, but," he paused, exasperated, "they were just a fuck, that's all."

"*They were just a fuck? REALLY!*" she screamed, disgusted by his cavalier response. "JUST A FUCK!" She struggled to continue, searching for breath before spewing her defiant reply. "Maybe that's exactly what I need, Nick. Just a *fuck*! What would you do if it were me—if I were the one getting *just a fuck?* Don't you think I've had opportunities?"

His eyes darkened, her words awakening the demon within, tipping him over the edge. He quickly moved forward, pinning her against the door with his Goliath strength, his voice blaring. "You are my wife, don't ever forget that. I will kill any man that touches you, do you hear me? I will kill that fuckin' baseball coach or whoever it is. No one touches you, no one! Understand?" His wild glare restrained her for brief seconds before he pressed his mouth to hers kissing her roughly and imposing his power over her as she struggled against him.

"Get off me," she screeched, ripping her lips from his. "You're hurting me. Get *off me*."

Her frenzied gasp surged through him, and he sprang back, releasing her. His mind stumbled, frantically searching for words, knowing how wrong his actions had been. "Laina, please, baby, please, I'm sorry. Those… those women meant nothing to me, nothing."

"Nothing, really? Well, every one of them meant something to me, damn it. This Gwen, does *she* mean something to you?" she yelled, each word spewing fire.

"Hell, no!" Standing before his wife, the very thought of Gwen brought shame to him now. "She's a chit."

"A what?"

"A chit, a marker, a debt owed, a debt paid."

Alaina starred in disbelief, "I don't understand."

"I'm indebted to her uncle for a past favor, the girl needed a job."

"And that payment included sleeping her?"

Seeing his wife's look of disgust, he lowered his eyes, struggling to remember the last time he had sex with Gwen or anyone else. Had it been months, maybe years?

"I cannot even fathom the level of depravity in what you just said," she raged, shaking her head and gulping back tears. "How could you do this to me? How could you hurt me like this? We've been married for over twenty years, and I have never been unfaithful, never even thought of being with another man. I love you too much to disrespect you in that way; but you think nothing of disrespecting me. You have *dishonored* me, Nick; you have *dishonored* our marriage vow." Her words were beginning to slur whether from her rocketing emotions or her injured lips. She felt it too, finally losing control as the dam broke and a torrent of tears burst forth.

"Why, why, tell me why," she screamed, angrily lunging for him, and pummeling his chest with her balled fists. "Why?"

"Alaina, stop," he cried, shoving her fists away. "Honey, stop, stop," grappling to control her movements. But her anguish only catapulted, seeing the futility of her assault on his rock-hard chest. She was breathless, her eyes crazed, her face scarlet, and he knew he had to stop her before she injured herself. "Stop, honey, stop," he yelled again, continuing to bat away her hands until finally he wrapped his fingers around each wrist, forcefully pinning them between his chest and hers. "STOP!"

They stood face to face as her tears streamed down and she choked out airless gasps.

"Let… let go, you're... you're hurting me," she sobbed, the pain from his viselike grip sending burning arcs from her wrists to fingertips.

His eyes widened with disbelief, and he bolted back, releasing his grasp, his remorse immediate. He had hurt her; my God, he had hurt her. He turned, unable to face her, his guilt insurmountable. She was still raging behind him, but he could no longer hear her words, trapped in the horror of his actions. He had lost control, unable to shackle the monster within, the monster he swore she would never see. Her terrified eyes flashed before him; her gasp drummed in his ears. He leaned onto the desk staring down at his hands, aware of the pain they could inflict. His head was throbbing, shooting shards of pain behind his eyes; his heart was racing, pounding out all sound. She was rambling in the background and minutes passed before her words slowly seeped into his consciousness.

"I'm done as soon as Jax graduates," her voice faltering. "Until then, I'm moving into the guesthouse so I can be here for Sam's schooling. Bring in Gwen or one of your other bimbos for all I care, but know this, I'm taking Sam with me when I go. I know you'll fight me, but he is really my child. Have Arch draw up the papers."

Releasing a painful groan, he turned to face her, seeing her fists still clenched with fury, her face bright red, fresh tears streaming down her cheeks. The shame of hurting her weighed heavy on him, each tear that fell a dagger piercing his heart.

He spoke softly now, all anger gone, "Alaina, stop. That is not what I want."

She narrowed her eyes, her mind still broiling with fire, "Well what exactly do you want, Nick? You can't have it both ways, not anymore. I won't stay the ever-faithful wife while you're out fucking your painted bitches. Our marriage vows are nothing more than a joke to you."

He stood penitent, hands clasped before him, seeing the woman he loved standing strong. Her voice still trembled as she spouted more angry words, but her eyes spoke only sadness.

"What you're saying is true, and I have no excuse, no rebuttal. I know I have sinned in your eyes and to you my actions are unforgivable but hear me, honey, those women were meaningless." He reached for her, noting her fear as he moved closer before he gingerly placed his hands on her shoulders, gently drawing her in. "You are the only woman that I love, the only woman I have ever loved. I… never meant for you to be hurt. As for Gwen, she'll be gone today. She means nothing, never has," he pleaded.

"If she means nothing then why is she even in our marriage, Nick?"

Because with Gwen I don't need to hide; she was raised in the life, she knows who I am. Staring down at his naive wife, he knew his day of reckoning had come. She deserved to know the truth, but—not today.

He searched for words to delay this conversation before gently wrapping her in his arms. "Baby, this was never about you; it's about me desperately trying to shield you from my temper. There are days in this office when the pressure is unbearable and my anger escalates to unthinkable rage, consuming whatever good is left inside me. I've… been forced to make decisions that hurt people. I've done things, horrible things that you would never understand and when that happens, I can't face you. I'm so entrenched in self-loathing that I can't even look myself in the mirror let alone the sweet, innocent eyes of my wife."

"When that rage hits a breaking point, I recognize the danger and I run, escaping out the office door for fear of hurting the people I love. I can't take it upstairs to you and the kids, don't you see? I'm afraid, afraid I'll step on a toy and lash out, punch a wall over spilt milk… or worse. I've never been worthy of you, sweetheart; you represent everything good and I'm ashamed to let you see the man I have become. You are my angel, my beautiful porcelain angel and… I'm so afraid of breaking you. I know how it looks, I know how it sounds, but it's the truth. God help me, it's the truth."

Wiping tears from her swollen eyes, he spoke softly, weighing his words. "I know you don't understand but what's important right now is that you know that no woman on this earth could ever take your place."

The sincerity of his words thundered in her ears, spiraling her into a chasm of confusion and vanquishing her fire. She clutched his sleeves with both hands, her anguished pleas tumbling forth. "If… if the pressure is too much, why don't we leave? We could walk away, start again. You… you could do anything, design houses, be a … a carpenter, anything, I don't care."

"Honey, we can't leave," he replied remorsefully, fearing her response. He watched her expression morph from confusion, desperation, and finally sorrow as she grappled with his answer.

"Then you're going out the wrong door, Nick," she whimpered, placing her hand on his cheek. "I'm waiting for you upstairs. Let *me* quell your anger; you know I can. I miss you. I miss my husband, I miss the man that I love, the man that I *still* love." Her voice trailed away to barely a whisper.

He looked at his beautiful wife with heartfelt anguish. He had broken her, something he feared. "Shh, no more. We've hurt each other enough today," he softly replied, stroking her hair. "Let me look at you." His fingers faintly traced her swollen lips, assessing the damage. He then raised both her wrists, kissing them lightly and seeing the bruises already forming. "I didn't mean to hurt you, baby. I'm sorry, so sorry." His words were tender, his eyes contrite, as he caressed her temple and she saw his sorrow pouring forth. "You will never feel my anger again."

She was drowning, and could no longer control her emotions, her love for him shattering all turmoil. That long lost feeling of melting in his arms washed over her, erasing her pain. With trembling fingers, she reached to touch his cheek; and he gently cupped her hand guiding it to his lips. "Forgive me, Madonna, forgive me. I beg you."

The feel of his huge cock against her thigh triggered her shameful yearning. It had been too long, her need too great. His eyes met hers, mutual craving betraying them both. Angry words slipped away, past hurts vanished, all consumed by the intensity of their shared desire. She pulled his face to hers, encouraging his stronger embrace. His fiery kisses traveled from her lips to her throat in hungry unbridled passion. Lowering her to the floor, he frantically tore at her nightgown, feeling for her wet center before plunging his swollen cock inside as she gasped in pleasure. The room disappeared between them as he moved deeper, harder, his rhythm becoming quicker and she met each thrust with her own breathless motion, their eyes never leaving each other. She gripped his shoulders, no longer able to hold back her orgasm, hearing the echo of her own voice calling his name. With one final deep plunge he burst forth, collapsing on her, both panting in their ecstasy.

"Baby, baby," he whispered, cupping her face in his hands, "I can never lose you; do you understand? I can never, ever lose you. I love you too much."

The crunch of driveway gravel shattered their lust, ebbing away at their thirst filled emotion.

"Damn, that's Arch," he exclaimed.

Alaina quickly scooted out from beneath him, but Nick pulled her back for one quick final kiss. "I need you, baby, remember that," he called as she glanced back before closing the door.

She inwardly chastised herself as she retreated up the stairs. *How could I have been so weak? How could I have let that happen? I need to stand my ground, make him live by my terms or nothing will ever change.* But the memory of her surrender was still fresh in her mind; his kiss still sent sparks through her body; his touch still made her tremble. She loved him; she knew she would always be his.

The day wore on with Archer pulling more and more papers from his briefcase. Nick was distracted, not hearing half of his consigliere's words.

"I need to take a break; in fact, I need to take a few days," he finally announced.

"A break? We have the meeting with McQueen on Tuesday."

"I know, write it up the way you think. I'll review it when I get back. Right now, I need to make things right with my wife." Nick looked at Arch, his meaning clear.

He sat in solitude after Arch left; the burden of hurting the woman he loved drowning him in a sea of torment. How could she ever forgive him if he couldn't forgive himself? If only he had let her vent; the result would have been so different. He needed to atone, to beg for clemency knowing he alone was to blame. Every word she spoke was true, he had been with other women; but each was meaningless, each unsatisfying, he couldn't even match the name to the face. Even he didn't understand why, but what he did know was that Alaina was the one woman he could never lose. She was his peace, his comfort, and—his weakness.

He also wasn't foolish enough to believe that one quick tumble on the carpet had resolved the issue. He needed a plan and it started with ridding himself of Gwen. He had inwardly laughed when Alaina suggested Gwen move in, that was the last thing he wanted. The two women were complete opposites. He rued the day Gwen first arrived at his door. Her goal was to be the next Mrs. Nick Rusano, she wanted the lifestyle, the social standing. Ridding himself of her would be easy, explaining it to her Uncle Vito might prove tricky. As for Dominic, he would deal with that bastard later.

He reached for the phone, putting his plan in motion. "Peggy, I'm coming in this afternoon, need some letters typed."

"Yes, sir, of course. Is there anything I can prepare in advance of your arrival?"

"Yes, as a matter of fact, pull up Gwen Rosen's contract and check it for a severance clause. I'll be there within the hour."

"Yes, sir, already on it. See you soon."

"Oh, and I need you to send something to my wife."

"Roses, sir?"

"No... something more... more personal. Um..., I had a greenhouse built for her birthday last year, something on that line maybe? She likes to tinker in the dirt... soil, it's soil, she would correct me there," he laughed.

Peggy hesitated, "I … think I can come up with something, sir. Perhaps some orchids? They are quite beautiful, and some are exceedingly rare. Maybe two or three?"

"Perfect. Thanks, and get that Rosen paperwork on my desk as soon as possible."

"Of course, sir, right away."

#

Peggy McKillop had been Nick's secretary for over 20 years. She knew his faults, knew when he was tired, when he was angry, when to stay away from the door, when it was safe to knock. *Today might prove interesting.*

Nick scanned the severance agreement, nodded to Peggy, and immediately summoned Gwen Rosen. Within minutes the tall, haughty blond strutted in, garbed in a formfitting ruby red dress and four-inch stiletto heels; her bracelets jangling and her cloying scent filling the room. Nick despised both noisy jewelry and heavy perfume.

"Hello, darling. I was wondering if we were getting together this week." She immediately moved behind the desk, raking her long red fingernails through his hair.

"Sit," he commanded.

"Okay, honey. Just business today?"

As she took her place in the chair opposite his, Nick placed the severance agreement on the desk between them along with the key to her apartment. Gwen stared at the two items, puzzled.

"I... I don't understand."

"Nothing to understand," he replied. "I am severing both our business and our personal relationship, that simple. Sign the paper, or... don't. Either way, clean out your desk by close of business today."

"What! Oh no, no, no," she squealed, slamming her palm on the desk, red nails flashing. "You can't just walk away from me, Nick Rusano. There'll be consequences, you'll see. I'll make you pay for this. My uncle will make you pay." But her outburst received no reaction.

Peggy smiled, watching as Gwen stormed out, having heard every word. That ignorant, condescending bitch had finally been brought to reckoning.

Next, Nick called the boat yard instructing the owner to immediately take his cabin cruiser out of dry dock and put it in the water, ensuring it was prepped and ready. He ordered the fridge stocked with three days' worth of food, several bottles of Macallan whiskey and Alaina's favorite wine.

Having executed his plan, he was home by 6pm.

Two tall Miltonia orchids sat in the foyer—bright colors of pinks and whites—their citrus scent filling the room. Peggy had pulled through; he knew Alaina would be pleased. He followed the sound of laughter, finding her sitting on the floor playing a board game with Sam. Silently, he observed the love between child and mother before Sam noticed his presence.

"Daddy!" he squealed, jumping into Nick's arms.

Alaina's greeting was much more subdued, her eyes vacant, "The orchids are beautiful, thank you. I'll take them out to the greenhouse tomorrow."

"No, tomorrow we're going to the cove," he replied, handing her a copy of Gwen Rosen's termination letter.

They motored to their old spot early the next morning, the sounds and smells enveloping them even before he dropped anchor. Watching the stress melt from her shoulders as she absorbed the vista was proof he had made the right decision.

He poured two glasses of Macallan, motioning her to join him on the chaise. They sat in therapeutic silence, allowing the water to decrease the previous day's tension.

Finally, he spoke, his voice solemn. "I've done things in my business life that I'm not proud of. I've done things in my marriage that I'm not proud of. But beyond any of that, I am not proud of the man that I've become, the man that hurt you." He lifted her wrist, lightly running his thumb across the now dark purple bruise—the result of his grip the previous day. For all the violence he had inflicted on people in his business dealings, he had never hurt Alaina. He felt genuine shame.

She pressed her lips together, not responding, avoiding his eyes.

"Baby, I am deeply sorry. I never meant to get physical. I cannot say I am sorry enough—cannot beg for your forgiveness enough. You know I'm not an abuser, I've never hurt you. I just lost my mind when you talked about other men, about leaving me; but… I know that doesn't justify what I did." He paused, hoping she would speak but she remained silent. "Laina, please, I will make this right. I will make us right. Give me the chance to fix this. Don't just end our marriage; don't just walk away. Please baby, I'm begging you to find it in your heart to forgive me."

"Would you forgive me, Nick? Your actions yesterday proved the answer is *no.*"

He nodded, acknowledging her pain, and keeping his voice calm. "You're right, I know you're right, but I also know you have a more forgiving heart than I will ever have."

Placing his fingers under her chin, he gently turned her face to his. With soulful eyes he looked deep into hers, the emotion almost tangible. "I can't lose you, baby, I can't. I can lose *everything, everything* I have, but I can't lose you. I won't survive it. You are the only person that keeps me from slipping into the darkness." He drew in a breath, knowing he needed to tell her the truth, to stop hiding who he really was; but not today, maybe tomorrow but not today.

She moved his hand from her chin, but his fingers clung to hers as she struggled to tamp down the increasing pressure in her chest.

"Alaina please, talk to me."

She felt herself beginning to tremble and knew he saw it too. Her voice faltered; her breathing clipped. "Nick, I… I came here today to listen, to try to understand. After twenty-three years of marriage, I feel you are deserving of that although I cannot imagine any plausible explanation you might offer for your behavior and the pain you have caused me. I love you deeply, but I can no longer live like this. It hurts me far too much. I need to maintain some level of my own dignity. Infidelity is never acceptable in a marriage, *never* and I cannot look at you every day knowing you've been with others." She paused, turning to face him as he lowered his eyes. "As far as the excuse of hurting our children, I don't believe you would ever do that, I know how mentally strong you are. But know this, if you ever did hurt them, I would take them from you. Do you understand?" She waited as he nodded, affirming her words. "I also know that if I had not confronted you yesterday, you would continue with Gwen and we would not be sitting here now."

"No, baby, you're wrong." Again, lifting her face to his, he continued, "I have plans for us; plans I've been working on for years. I will make this right; I will make us right. I am *begging* your forgiveness. Please believe me, it's always been you, never anyone else." His eyes locked onto hers, refusing to release her before he slowly lowered his mouth to hers, kissing her gently. "I need you," he whispered as his fingers caressed her cheek and tenderly circled her eyes, pulling her closer to his chest.

A gentle mist rolled down the hills briefly blanketing the cove in sorrow before the morning sun chased it away and the soft sounds of the water did its job, soothing her anger. She wanted to forgive him, wanted to believe his words, but her heart was broken.

"Will you swim with me?" he asked, cautiously smiling.

"Yes… of course." Then a mischievous grin crossed her face, "Last one in," she screamed, quickly leaping from his arms and jumping into the lake.

"Oh, you little..." he yelled, diving in after her.

"Oh, my God, it's freezing," she gasped when the temperature of the water enveloped her. She quickly jumped into his arms, more surprised by her own actions than he was. She was facing him, both hands tightly gripping his shoulders, her legs firmly wrapped around his waist. Her eyes opened wide, and she burst into laughter realizing her physical predicament as the tension between them slipped away, both recalling the many happy days on these same waters so very long ago. He clasped her tightly, pulling her firmly against his chest, not wanting the moment to end. The warmth of his body chased away the chill and she sighed, feeling his lips upon her neck, his tender kisses finding the weak points he knew so well. Then he suddenly pulled back, his smile turning to a devilish grin as he deftly unhooked her bikini top and tossed it behind him.

"Nick! Oh..., you are impossible."

"Hmm...," he murmured, his lips once again buried in her neck, his fingers tugging at her bikini bottom.

"No, no. Stop! I have more to say." Pushing back on his shoulders so they were face to face, her mood grew serious, "I love you *too* much, and that love clouds my judgement at times preventing me from doing what must be done. So now it's your turn to hear me. I will leave you if your behavior doesn't change. If you're not home every night, I'm done. Jax graduates in two months, and as your brother so viciously said, *I* no longer have a reason to stay."

He froze, wounded by her words, and hurt poured forth from his eyes. "I know you don't mean that. Please say you don't mean that," he begged.

Her heart wrenched within her chest immediately regretting her cruelty, and her own emotions erased her resolve as she grabbed for him, pulling him tightly to her. "No, no, I don't. You know I don't," her harsh words now melting to sorrow. "I love you, Nick Rusano, I truly love you, I always have. I... I don't know how to be angry with you, but I can't quell this pain."

Relief coursed through him, "Oh, baby, I love you, too. I beg you, give me a chance. I never meant to hurt you, never ever meant to dishonor you. Please find it in your heart to forgive me." Tears began to form in her eyes as he reached for her, crushing her to his chest, "I won't allow myself to lose you, baby. I love you too much."

That night he made love to her slowly, as moonlight filtered in above them, but she exacted her revenge, letting him see that it was *just a fuck* to her. There was no passion, no emotion, no love, just the mechanics of sex—the emptiness in her eyes exposing her repayment. When they finished, his somber words reflected the silence between them. "I feel your coldness, Laina. I understand. I'll wait for you to want me again." She stared coldly, making no attempt at a reply before turning over and silently hiding her tears.

Sleep didn't come easy. He sat in the blackness on deck, whiskey in hand, as she slept below. Thoughts tore through his mind in rapid succession smacking him with the consequences of his selfishness. *Even a player's best game plan is vulnerable to attack.* That was the crux of it, the chess master had not protected his queen; he had lost focus, and she had slipped away. For years he had planned, slowly moving the pawns on the board, selling a piece of property here, moving money there with the intent of ending his ties with the Mafia. He wanted a life with her, wanted to build her a castle high in the California mountains; the place she once talked about, far away from Las Vegas. She was the only woman he ever really needed, and he wasn't about to lose her. He would calm her down, he would prove his love.

They pulled anchor the next morning, motoring to one of her favorite little towns along the water. They lingered, play acting, young lovers hand-in-hand, strolling past the gaudy storefronts and cluttered sidewalks filled with tacky swimsuits and cheap souvenirs. They shared a paper cone of fried clams, laughing and smearing tartar sauce across each other's chins, then they perused the used bookstore exiting with an overstuffed bag of cheap treasures. She was smiling, happy, talking to strangers— the Alaina she always was, the Alaina he loved. Perhaps her retribution last night had given her some satisfaction, he didn't know. They would have dinner tonight at her favorite dockside restaurant. He would hold her as they danced to tunes belted out by some cheesy band. He was on his way to repairing this. He had to.

"Look at that!" Nick pointed to a Formula 350 Crossover Bowrider docked below them as they strolled the marina. It was a sleek model new off the yard in two tone blue and bright white. Its silver trim added to the crisp elegant look, reflecting in the noon sun. "I think we're due for an upgrade, don't you, honey? Trade ours in for something just for us?" Winking, he gave her a squeeze just as a dapper, deeply tanned gentleman came up from the galley below.

"Good morning up there, beautiful day." The elfin little man had a friendly face with clear blue eyes, a small salt and pepper mustache and full ruddy cheeks the result of the half empty whiskey glass held casually in his hand. "Care to come aboard, take a look at my latest toy."

"Love to," Nick enthused, jumping at the offer.

"Name's O'Toole, Michael O'Toole, from Sidney we are originally. Wife wanted to see the states so here we are. Come on up here, Marion. Meet these fine people."

Before long, the men were merrily chatting about the cruiser's specs: the advantages of a 6.2 Liter engine, the horsepower, fuel capacity, and bridge clearance all the while sharing whiskey and cigars. Marion gave Alaina a tour, proudly showing off the comfortable sleeping area and galley while stirring up a pitcher of spicy margaritas and the afternoon soon slipped away over tales of their travels and children.

Alaina felt some discomfort, however, seeing Marion's eyes frequently returning to her ever-darkening bruises, now shades of gray and purple. Finally, the woman leaned forward, whispering softly, "Honey, do you need help? Should I call the authorities?"

But just at that moment, Alaina heard Nick's signal to leave, offering his business card to Michael and extending an invitation for the older couple to visit the Royale. He thankfully had not heard Marion's question.

Alaina smiled, drawing close to the woman's ear. "No, that won't be necessary, not at all. You see, the two of us enjoy... bondage." She winked as Marion rapidly brought her hand to her chest, gasping at the revelation.

"What did you say to the wife?" Nick questioned as they continued their walk along the docks, his arm wrapped tightly around her waist.

"Oh... well... she couldn't take her eyes off my wrists so... I told her that we were both into bondage."

"You what!" he roared, bursting into laughter before gently cradling her wrists in his palms and kissing them both. "Baby, I am so sorry for hurting you, I will never, ever hurt you again. I swear."

And he never did.

Unloading and Relieving

On the third morning he motored back to the cove, hoping the tranquility of the crystal blue water would soothe any lingering unease between them. Last night had worked its magic. They had shared plates of garlic crabs and golden crisp oysters, bottles of Modelo and too much cheap wine. He'd held her tightly as they danced—their bodies melting into each other no matter the tempo of the song. They talked, they laughed, they even kissed; both clinging to memories of years past when their love was still young. He wanted desperately to make her feel loved— determined to make amends—to save things. He didn't attempt sex, although he longed to; instead, he held her as she slept while his mind spun a movie reel of his mistakes.

His thoughts turned to the many times he had glimpsed her shadow across the lawn, heard her whispers on the wind, her laughter on the landing as he was about to order a vicious act, her unknowing intervention causing him to stay his hand and reverse course. She was his angel shielding him from the abyss and he feared being without her.

But now Charon beckoned, extending his hand, demanding payment. The time for deceit was over; there were truths that needed to be said. Would his revelations only hasten her departure? Would she run when he told her of his Mafia ties?

With extreme trepidation, he began, "Sweetheart, we don't own the Royale outright, not 100%. No one person could own that monster totally. I have… business partners, business partners that are dangerous men, very dangerous men." He paused, allowing his words to sink in before meeting her eyes. "*I*... am one of those very dangerous men." He waited several minutes before continuing. "Do you understand what I'm saying?"

"I think so," she affirmed softly.

He took a breath, returning his gaze to the water, knowing she did not comprehend his meaning. "You sell your soul to these people, Alaina, they never let you go. They demand absolute loyalty, coming first even before a man's own family. Every year they tighten their grip, pulling you in deeper until escape is no longer an option. I was born into the life, and I've lived by their rules since I was a teenager, surrounded by them every day." He laughed lightly. "You talk about that town you came from with Christmas parades and homecoming bonfires, that sounds perfect to me but it's not how I grew up. My path was determined before I took my first breath."

"For years I've shielded you from this, fearing your judgment, afraid of letting you see who I really am. But when my temper overflowed onto you the other day, I crossed the line between the two worlds that I have worked so hard to separate and… you suffered." Lifting her wrist, he gently ran his thumb across the darkening bruise. "I'm not making excuses, not for my absences, not for my temper, not even for my infidelity. I *know* there's no excuse that is acceptable, especially to a woman like you."

He turned, unable to read her eyes before reaching to cradle her face in both his hands, "You represent the opposite of that world, it's total antithesis and I admit to being blatantly selfish, wanting you but knowing I was never worthy of you. Every day I cloaked myself in your innocence and I absolved my sins with your purity but now that selfishness has brought us here. I need you to stay with me. I'm begging you to stay with me. Any hurt that I have caused you, I will atone for. You said it yourself, Jax will be home soon. Things will ease up, you'll see. I spoke the truth, I have plans for us, for you and me; but those plans will take time. I know you don't fully understand, and I can't think of a single reason why you would stay after what I've just said but I *need* you with me. Stay with me, baby. Just wait, wait a while longer. Give me the chance to prove that I'm the man you thought you married."

Her eyes revealed nothing, and she remained silent as a cold fog rolled in shrouding their craft in sorrow.

Waterloo

Archer paced, raking his fingers through his ever-receding hairline. He needed to hear from Nick, but then again, *he didn't*. There had been no messages, no emails, and his imagination was bombarded with lurid scenarios. After the incident in the garden, he worried that someone else may have spotted Alaina with Dominic. If so, no one, not even he would be able to reign in the carnage. He jumped each time the phone rang, envisioning Alaina's body at the bottom of the lake and his best friend in jail charged with murder. Hard to defend.

"So, how was the lake?" he ventured, observing Nick's pensive mood on his return.

"The lake, hmm, not sure," Nick replied while reviewing the McQueen contract. "Looks good. Change this wording on page 34," pointing to an area, "otherwise we're good."

Arch noted Nick's avoidance and cautiously redirected. "Listen buddy, I'm your friend, first and always. Tell me *what* the hell is going on."

Nick's eyes revealed nothing before he stood and opened a fresh bottle of whiskey, placing it on the table between them.

"She's threatened to leave me when Jax comes home. She moved into the guesthouse last night," he paused, "gave me an ultimatum, home every night or she's gone."

Arch raised his eyebrows, "And… are you going to abide by that?"

"I am. I can't let her leave, Arch, I can't lose her," he answered, pained by the consequences of his actions.

"Talk to me, buddy."

Nick shook his head in shame, replaying the event. "You remember me telling you about Dom's visit last week, how he stormed out of this office after I refused to advance him more money? Well, he must have spotted Alaina on the road and flagged her down. Asshole shared some information about Gwen and a few of my *past indiscretions*. She came at me raging the next morning, I've never seen her so upset. She was carrying on and... I lost my temper."

"You what?" Arch raised his voice, eyes wide knowing how violent Nick could be. "But I just saw her in the kitchen."

Nick nodded, contrite. "She's... bruised...sore, but I can't roll back that clock. That's the *biggest* problem. I hurt her. I physically hurt her, Arch. Never, never in all these years have I ever touched her. I just... lost control. I swear I never meant to go as far as I did. Pinned her wrists for thirty seconds and... their black." He stared down at his hands, the scene flashing through his mind. "Said she was going to ask you to draw up separation papers and I don't know what to do. I won't survive losing her, Arch. You need to help me; I'm begging you to help me."

"Whoa... buddy. She didn't say anything. Um, I'll let you know first thing, but you need to fix this. Let's, let's fix this. Tell me what exactly happened at the lake. Details, buddy."

Nick released an exasperated sigh, "I don't even understand what happened at the lake. She's got me so damned confused, one minute she was in my arms, the next... her eyes were filled with loathing."

"Hmm... could be she's seeing ghosts," Arch suggested, pondering Alaina's ambivalence.

"Ghosts?" Nick's brow furrowed, "What the hell are you talking about?"

"Um," Arch was stumbling, looking for a plausible explanation that Nick would understand. "I went through something similar with Daniella years back. Once she found out about my *affairs*, she became obsessed with jealousy. Every conversation was accusatory, every woman was a threat." His sorrowful eyes met Nick's and he shook his head, "Bottom line, bud, no matter what you do, take them to their favorite restaurant, take them out on the boat, whatever—they think you did the same with another woman."

"What! I never took another woman on my boat."

"Yeah, but she doesn't know that. She could be seeing the ghosts of other women just like Daniella did and they're haunting her. You make love to her, and she sees another woman reflected in your eyes as you're fucking her."

Nick stared for several seconds, comprehending Arch's words. "*Fuck!* So how do I fight a ghost?"

"You don't. She feels betrayed, you've lost her trust. She's not hearing your words of remorse, not seeing your gestures." Arch nodded toward the brightly wrapped gift box at the corner of Nick's desk, "Nothing will work, not jewelry, not flowers, nothing. Material gifts just devalue her pain. You need to wait and see what *she* does. I tried, believe me I tried but there was no forgiveness, every ounce of civility was drained. I had to move out, the situation became untenable. So, now I'm with Janie, peace and quiet, no hostility." Nick knew Arch's mistress; he and Janie had a son together.

Nick fingered the present weighing Arch's words, his face a myriad of emotions. "*Pearls*, she loves pearls, had them sent over this morning. She probably won't accept them. She's refused guilt jewelry before, but I'm still gonna try. I'll try anything, I just know I can't lose her."

He stared morosely recounting more of his wife's conversation. "She asked me *why* and I couldn't answer. I don't even know myself, control, maybe power."

"No, no, I couldn't tell her that. I told her a half truth, part of it really is my temper. I go down to the club when the pressure gets too much. I'm afraid to take it upstairs, afraid I'll snap, hurt the kids. She doesn't believe I could do such a thing, but she's never seen that side of me… until now. I'm sure you would agree there are nights when it's better for everyone that I don't go upstairs, better I drink with the devil than be in anyone's company."

Releasing a painful groan, he sank back into the chair, staring up at the ceiling. A twisted smile crossed his face, and he began to reminisce, his words barely audible. "We were happy once, really happy, two babies running around, a third on the way. Then the old man sent me on a job," he turned back to Arch. "You remember that punk I dropped off the eighth-floor balcony in Henderson, the one that stabbed old Giorgio in the heart?"

"Sure, I remember, punk deserved to die; old Giorgio never hurt a soul, good earner, too."

"Right, well I was so wired that night that when it was over, I didn't go home; went to the club instead. Fell into bed with a dancer, blowing off the steam of the kill. Alaina knew, I saw it in her eyes and instead of being a man and talking it out; I ignored her. A few months later, different job, different dancer. I avoided it like it never happened. I knew she was hurt, and I just went on being the selfish prick that I am. I let my pride stand in the way, knowing there were words I should have said, things I should have done. Then when Dad died and the Commission appointed me Don, I became obsessed, drunk with the power, thinking it gave me some twisted right to do whatever I wanted. Men were bowing to me; women were falling at my feet. My weaknesses ruled and I slid right back into my old lifestyle. Thought I was a big man living by the code—having as many women as I wanted— self-absorbed macho *crap*." Sadness painted his eyes as he leaned forward, "I turned my back on her, Arch. I hurt the only woman I've ever cared about, and I have no fuckin' idea how to fix it."

Arch was about to refill the whiskey glasses when Nick's angry fist slammed down onto the table between them, "I *know* if I would have gone to her back then, we would have worked it out. But now, with all this being shoved in her face, I'll be lucky if she isn't already packing." He opened his palms, shaking his head, his voice pleading, "And the irony of the whole situation is that not a single one of those women ever meant a thing to me. I can't even remember their faces, nothing but meaningless one nighters. A quick fuck, that's all they were, never anything more." Rising from the chair, he began to blindly pace, his anger rising again. "It's not like I've ever gotten any satisfaction out there. *Hell no!* There's not a damn thing out there I want, nothing but fake hard tits and fake hard souls. I don't want Gwen; I don't want any of them. What I want is that woman upstairs; I want the one woman that *now* doesn't want me!"

"Nick, I'm sure she'll come around. Just give her some time."

"Ha, you don't know her," he scoffed, raking his fingers through his hair. "Thursday morning, that little hellion released the Banshee inside her; went up one side of me and down the other. She told me I dishonored her. *That* was the word that brought me to my knees, *dishonor…* and she's right, I did, and I feel nothing but shame and disgust. *Dishonor!*" He shook his head, returning to the chair, his voice a whisper now. "Best thing that ever happened in my life and, of course I destroyed it because of fucking macho selfishness."

They sat silently for several minutes before he chuckled, "Little bitch paid me back too, tried making love to her at the cove and… nothing. She knew exactly what she was doing, I saw it in her eyes, little female power play. Made me feel like I was paying for it."

Arch smirked, "Oh sorry, bud," gingerly topping off their drinks.

"Yeah," releasing another heavy sigh, "I've been a fool, and I can't figure my way around this. How does a man explain being so self-indulgent and selfish? How does a woman forgive that?"

"How about another baby, keep her busy?"

"No, that's not the answer; besides, I don't think she can have any more." Nick shook his head, inhaling deeply, "This is a war on two fronts, my friend. First there's my asinine temper and then there's the women. This is about the value she places on fidelity, and I've mocked her with my actions. I was a damn fool to believe I wouldn't someday face the repercussions of my actions. No, I need to build back her trust and find some way to make up for *hurting* her."

Arch felt a sudden shift in the air as Nick's angry fist slammed down onto the table once again, sending jets of whiskey spilling over the glasses. "I've *never* understood why fidelity is so *damn* important to women!" he boomed. "Hell, my father kept a mistress all his life, *two* in fact. My mother never cared; she was glad when the old man stepped out. Why can't some women understand that those encounters have no weight?"

"Hmm, now you're asking for an evolutionary shift. Women these days view infidelity as the ultimate betrayal."

"Hmph!"

"I'm sorry, buddy, but I'm missing the problem," Arch dared. "Why not replace her? One woman's no different from another. Hell, you could move any number of them in here tonight." problem."

A violent storm crossed Nick's face and he lunged from the chair, grabbing Arch by the lapels, "I don't want just another woman, what I want is that one upstairs."

Arch gulped in a breath knowing he had overstepped.

Nick's eyes instantly filled with remorse, releasing his hold. "She's the only decent woman I've ever known. I was never worthy of her to begin with; you know that. All that charity stuff: the women's shelter, the safehouse for runaways, that's all her. She drives me crazy with her causes, but deep down I know every one of them makes this town a safer place. You'll laugh, this year she's got me handing out turkeys for Thanksgiving."

Unable to control himself, Arch burst into laughter, eyes tearing before he released a resolute sigh. "Look, buddy, there's no shame in admitting you love your wife and that you're afraid of losing her."

Daggers flashed from Nick's eyes again, only to be replaced with humble resignation seconds later as he recognized his friend's truth. "I *do* love my wife but it's far deeper than that, something I've never shared with you." Minutes ticked by before he raised both palms in quiet appeal, speaking slowly, his voice barely a whisper. "This… this is gonna sound… irrational but ever since I met her, she's had this strange *eerie* grip on me. I couldn't pull away from her, and I… didn't want to. I sought her out, lusted for her, craved her—like a damn drug. She cradled me in tranquility and no matter what atrocity that old man sent me to do, I could walk in that door, and she would wash it all away—vanquish the stress, erase it from my mind like it never happened." He hesitated, noting the skepticism on Arch's face. "Think about it, I've cut the throats of what five, maybe six men, shot dozens in the head, never thought twice. It's because when I'm with her, it all disappears. Her touch, her tenderness seeps right through my skin and… and cleanses my soul."

"Sounds crazy, right? But Arch, I swear there's something there, something I've never understood. You know I've never gone in for that mystical nonsense but there's a strange aura that radiates from her. When she's close, I'm blanketed in her warmth and my heart slows, my anger dissipates. When we're apart I feel her tether drawing me home; it's haunting I tell ya. I've denied it, I've scoffed at it, but it's real. She knew the old mas was dying, had a premonition weeks before he passed, and I mocked her. She knew Matt broke his leg skiing thirty minutes before the phone rang."

He lost focus for a few seconds, tamping down the sharp pain that traveled across his chest before he continued. "On the altar I vowed to protect *her* but now I know it was just the opposite; she was sent to protect me. It's like she's some kind of angel shielding me with her wings, like in one of those old-time movies. It's eerie, but I've learned when that angel speaks, I listen." His lips curled, inwardly laughing at his feeble attempt to explain, as Arch's puzzled expression morphed to compassion. "I turned my back on that protective shield and now when I open that upstairs door the warmth is gone; I feel only naked coldness. I can't let her leave, Arch; I can't let that angel go. I don't think I could do what I do if she weren't upstairs. She puts her palm across my heart, and it gives me the strength to come back to this office every day. And as God is my witness, I miss her touch so much right now. All these years, and she's never shown me this amount of disdain."

"Geez, buddy, why didn't you ever tell me this?" Arch asked, seeing his friend's anguish. "All this time you've been holding this in. Brother, there's nothing, nothing you can't tell me. Our bond runs deeper than blood, you know that."

"I couldn't, it makes me sound weak. I'm the Don for Christ's sake and she's my fuckin' Delilah!"

Nick released a desperate sigh, his frustration mounting again. "I just want to march across that lawn, toss her over my shoulder, and carry her back into the house; lock her in the damn bedroom if I have to, show her who's boss. I already gave the order that she's not to leave the property."

Arch's hand shot up, "No, no buddy. That's the worst thing you could do. That's… that's unlawful imprisonment according to the law. For God's sake, keep your temper in check. You listening to me? You're talking crazy."

"Yeah…, I know you're right, but I don't know which way to turn. I just want to disappear with her, buy a boat and sail away; give her the life she deserves, not the one I destroyed."

"All right let's think about this logically. You need to regain her trust and prove you're not running around anymore. Get rid of Gwen for starters. I never trusted that bitch."

"Hell, I did that last week. Sent her back to her Uncle Vito. As far as other women, I haven't stepped out in years. Dom just filled Alaina's head with names from the past." His expression then morphed from sadness to stone cold resolve, "We need to get out, Arch, out from under the Commission's thumb."

"Out?" Arch was stunned. "You're serious?

Nick nodded, "Totally out, all of us, you, me, the boys, out of this town, out of this life."

"Nick, that's never going to happen. No one gets out, you know that."

"I know but I've wanted out for a long time." He began to pace again, slamming his fist onto the desk, "So, what have I done instead? I put Jax and Luca right into the life, and they love it just like I did. They live for the blood. Makes no fucking sense, and what makes even less sense, *she has the same effect on them*. I send Jax to do a job, and where does he go after reporting back, straight up to the kitchen for milk and cookies with his mother. *SHE'S A DAMN DRUG, I TELL YA!*"

Arch laughed, "Well, you could kill her."

"Don't think I haven't thought of that. I've called her a witch so many times, I swear she puts a spell on me with just her touch." He again lowered his head, falling back into remorse.

Arch looked pitifully at his broken friend; a man with iron fists and a heart of stone—now brought to his knees by a woman. "All right first let's fix your marriage then… ah, we'll talk about the other. Let me think on this overnight. In the meantime, don't go anywhere near the guesthouse and no caveman moves. Go upstairs, talk to her."

"Talk to her? I've been talking for three days; I don't have the words she needs to hear. I'm too afraid."

Options

"Mommy, Mommy, I'm home."

Archer watched from the office window as Little Sam bounced from the car, lunch box flying. Perfect time to catch Alaina in the kitchen, he thought, knowing the child would need an after-school snack.

He grabbed the coffee urn sending a wink to Nick, "Let me test the waters." But he returned defeated within minutes.

"She talk?"

"Not really, just casual. Did you go upstairs last night?"

"Yeah, watched the game. She put out a spread, made a deflated football cake. Boys were there. She was herself, screaming for the Saints to win, but later she slept in Sam's room, little guy had a nightmare."

Arch recognized the pain in his friend's face. "Stop your worrying. I've got this, bud, trust me. Have a few ideas that might fix this, but first, let me ask a question. How much does she know? Is there anything she knows that could incriminate you?"

"No, nothing."

"You're sure? Nothing a lawyer could use, nothing she could take to the feds?"

"No, I've kept her in the dark all these years. The most she knows is that I have some shady investors."

Arch nodded and his legalese kicked in. "As I see it, you have four options. Number one, resign your position with the Commission, tell them your family will no longer do their bidding, liquidate your assets, and sail off into the sunset."

Nick laughed, pouring them both a whiskey. "Yeah, and the minute I do, I endanger everyone around me. I already have a target on my back."

"Exactly. The second option is divorce. I can work out a settlement that would probably be agreeable to her. Divorce is going to cost you big, you realize that, right? She has plenty of leverage, but… she came here with nothing; we can use that to our advantage."

"No, I know her, she'll probably just walk away. She never cared about money."

"Are you kidding, any lawyer that got his hands on this would see big numbers, buddy. You'll be lucky to get out with the shirt on your back. And ah… she might already be moving in that direction. A credit check came through the wires this morning, she's applied for an apartment in that new hi-rise downtown."

Archer watched as anger rose in Nick's eyes and his jaw tightened.

"What's three?" he bellowed.

"Three… um, three is reconciliation. It's your best option, least expensive, too. Placate her, calm her down. Get your house in order or… get rid of her. These are dangerous times, Nick. You said it yourself; you have a target on your back and your territories are highly desirable. Remember what happened with the LeBritzzis." Arch paused, letting his words take weight before continuing, "New York is imploding right now; everyone's unhappy with the way the new boss is running things and it's a powder keg, ready to blow. Guys are jockeying for position; maybe planning a move. Gwen Rosen could have been a pawn, part of a scheme to get close to you. They won't come at you head on; you're too strong. Trust no one, buddy, or the next pretty face that comes along just might stab you in the throat while you're sleeping. And don't think for a minute that the Commission will just hand things over to Jackson, he's not ready. You need to stay vigilant or all the planning we've done will be for naught. Which… brings me to my next point, if you're serious about getting out and I sure as hell hope you are, then we need to strategize. Let's start increasing your personal investments, move some more money, and pick up more real estate. Who knows, with some smart planning, you might just sail away with that woman yet."

Nick sat back, considering Arch's advice. "What's the fourth option?"

"Kill her, get her out of your head."

"I *like* four!" Nick chuckled, refilling the whiskey, and clinking glasses with his friend.

"Look, really, I have an idea. Alaina loves the water, right? I know a great place for just the two of you, romantic place—took Janie there last year. Take a look at this." Arch accessed a website on the computer featuring a luxury resort in Playa del Carmen. "Place has these private cabanas built on stilts right over the ocean. A butler delivers breakfast every morning plus drinks in the afternoon, gourmet restaurants, infinity pool—quiet, real isolated. Time, she needs time, Nick, time with you, just the two of you. Listen to what I'm saying. I'll cover for you, buddy."

"Nah, won't work. What am I gonna do, have Enzio staring as I make love to my wife, pistol drawn in case of trouble?"

"No, no, I'll cover for you, no one needs to know you're away. Three days could save this, buddy—just you and her, three days. You never need to leave the cabana, climb down the ladder and you're in the ocean. Little bit of schmooze, little bit of charm, she'll love it, trust me."

"You sound like a used car salesman," but Nick stared at the screen. "All right, yeah, maybe."

Dominic's Comeuppance

Nick barreled into Dominic's office, unannounced; but in true Dominic fashion, he found his little brother in the embrace of a tall buxom brunette.

Nick smirked, "Get rid of the bimbo, we have business." He waited as the girl rushed out before slamming the door and confronting his brother.

"You hurt my wife. Wives are off limits. You know that; it's the code. I don't bother your wife; you don't bother mine."

"The code, the code, oh, c'mon! Did I upset your pretty little wife? Have a fight, did you?" Dominic was gleeful, smiling ear to ear.

"No, actually quite the opposite, she fell on my dick like the sex hungry animal she is," Nick countered. Only he knew the lie, only he knew the extent of Alaina's pain, pain that he owned.

"I know that's not true; I saw her face when I gave her some of the details. I saw her eyes." Dominic gloated.

"Really? Let me tell you about my pretty little wife. Makeup sex with her is wild, that girl can rattle the rafters. Sometimes I start an argument just to hear her beg." Nick slammed his fist on the desk, "That, little brother, is the woman you don't know. That's the woman who is devoted to me." His eyes darkened before a devious lie crossed his lips. "Fact is, she gifted me these cuff links just this morning," gloating and pulling on his shirt sleeves. "Devoted, brother, devoted."

Dominic was bewildered, stammering, "You don't deserve her. You never did. I would treat her right, dress her up, show her off."

"No, no, no," Nick smirked. "Let's be honest here, you would beat her. You beat all your women. She's no Angela. You don't even know the real Alaina. She's a strong bitch, too strong for you. You would beat her within a week. Frankly, little bro, I have never understood your obsession with her, except that you want her because she's mine. She's not some train set that I got for Christmas, and you covet. She's my wife, for God's sake. Stay out of my marriage!"

"Oh, and one last thing. I'm pulling out of the Forest Avenue deal. Good luck getting backing without me." Nick knew the bank would never approve a loan for the Calypso without his signature. His brother would be forced to grovel to the Commission, and they viewed him as a weakling. Soon they would replace him, turning control of the Calypso over to him. Dominic was unaware that Archer and Nick had formed a shell company months earlier and were stealthily purchasing land parcels surrounding the property— another master move on the chess board. He had cut his brother deeply, essentially boxing him in and destroying any plans for expansion while securing a future empire for his sons.

Checkmate.

Floating

The lights of Vegas welcomed him as he descended the stairs of the small Cessna. Turning, Nick surveyed the sleek jet from ground level, realizing that his muscles didn't ache, and his legs were not cramped. He ticked off the conveniences of the private charter: he controlled departure times, the price was reasonable, the seating was comfortable, and he could enjoy his preferred brand of whiskey. Another key factor—his firearm was not subject to TSA rules. This is the answer, he thought, knowing that he and Alaina would be traveling on two long flights from Las Vegas to Princeton for Jax' graduation and the Dad Vail Regatta in just a few short weeks.

Every year they attended the Regatta; a prestigious two-day rowing event held along Philadelphia's majestic Schuylkill River where over one hundred college and university crew teams convened hoping to claim the coveted trophy. Nick had competed while at Princeton and now his sons were following in his footsteps. This year, Princeton was favored to win.

Nick's relationship with Alaina had warmed since the cove although she had not invited him into her arms, and he desired her touch. He didn't want to rush her, he wanted passion and emotion, not the coldness she had deservedly shown him at the cove. She was standing firm in her convictions, but watching her retreat to the guesthouse each night was crushing him.

#

Three weeks later

"Oh, Nicky, am I late, you said 10 o'clock, right? I made a quick batch of Luca's favorite cookies for his birthday; I just need to pack them up."

He smiled watching her breathlessly dash down the stairs, sandals dangling from her fingertips. She was stunning in a flowing white silk dress emblazoned with large tiger lilies and he couldn't help but appreciate her beauty as she floated toward him. His breathing momentarily hitched, seeing the pearls he had left at her bedside weeks earlier adorning her neck. *Could that be a sign of forgiveness?*

"No, sweetheart, no rush. Go pack your cookies."

She looked at him quizzically. "What time's the flight?"

"The plane leaves when we get there. I hired a charter."

"A charter?"

"I flew to Chicago a few weeks ago with a private service, thought you might enjoy it. I sent Zander ahead so it's just you and me, beautiful."

Awkward seconds of hesitation passed between them as she shied from his penetrating gaze before retreating to the kitchen, unsuccessfully vanquishing the wanton urges rising within her. She longed to embrace him, to feel his arms around her again, to feel his lips on hers. This was the man she loved; she could no longer deny it.

#

The interior of the Hawker 400 jet was spacious with wide comfortable reclining leather seats and a concealed cockpit allowing for privacy. They settled in across the aisle, she with her book and he with a contract needing review. Eventually he nodded off, two glasses of whiskey lulling him into deep dreams.

He didn't hear her at first, her soft voice filtering through the haze of sleep, trying gently to awaken him.

"Nicky, baby." The voice was barely audible. He was dreaming, envisioning her face on their pillows at home, dreaming, falling, dreaming.

"Nicky... honey, wake up just a little."

His consciousness threaded between ethereal worlds hearing her airy voice beckon. He felt something tickle his ear, then a delicate finger traced his hairline, barely skipping along his brow. A velvety tongue brushed up his neck, placing light kisses from collar to ear.

"Nicky... Nicky." A feathery breath touched his eyelids demanding a response.

"Alaina... baby?" He slowly opened his eyes, seeing his beautiful wife bending before him. He reached out, still groggy, slowly passing from dream to reality.

She was smiling, her bleary image coming into focus. "I need my husband," she whispered.

Was he understanding her? He placed his hands on her waist drawing her to him, "Oh, baby, your husband needs you." Euphoria pulsed through him as he watched her climb atop his body, straddling his thighs. He pulled her face to his, still questioning before their eyes locked together teeming with love, lust, and forgiveness. He warily ran his fingers through her hair then lightly traced her forehead, her cheeks, her chin; her welcoming smile warming his heart. Wrapping her tightly in his arms, he felt her exhale, releasing her pent-up anger and a surge of relief washed over him. She was silent, lost in time, her head pressed against his chest, and he rode that wave with her, suspended in the curl, needing to hold her forever.

Their first kiss was rough, burning with passion, breathless and intense. They each struggled for control, overwhelmed by emotion, pulling and biting on each other's lips. With wolfish hunger his mouth traveled down her neck awakening her senses and making her tremble in his arms. He paused, gently pushing back on her shoulders; allowing their eyes to meet, "Are we... doing this?" he asked, never releasing her eyes.

"Shh," she cautioned, holding her fingers to his lips.

For weeks he had longed for her, his arms aching to caress her, but holding back, waiting. Was he still dreaming or was this reality? He felt his cock stir as her thighs straddled his, their clothing the only barrier between them. His hands began to tug at her dress, releasing the buttons one by one until he leaned back, breathing deeply, appreciating her breasts barely restrained within her lace brassiere. She guided his hand to the front snap hastening their freedom, allowing them to fall into his cupped hands. Savagely burying his face in her cleavage, he pressed her breasts to his cheeks, inhaling the scent of her perfume and surrendering to her witch's spell.

Her teeth found his shoulder and her cat-like bites traveled up his neck, making him shudder as her delicate fingers snaked beneath his shirt, sending frenzied palpations to his heart. She hesitated then, drawing in a breath when her fingers reached a bandaged area, but he cupped her hand, casually moving it away, his lips still buried in her breasts, kissing each nipple. He heard her moan with pleasure as his lips traveled back to her neck, a spot he knew so well, her weakness.

Her thighs continued to gyrate against him, their passion growing. His fingertips skipped along her thigh barely brushing her skin as he pulled her dress up and ran his fingers along the edge of her panties, making her nerves drum uncontrollably. Releasing a heavy moan, he withdrew his lips, "Baby, you are driving me crazy, I am rock hard, ready to burst."

But she only smiled, her haunting eyes hypnotizing his senses as she reached for his zipper, releasing his engorged cock into her hand. She rose to position herself, guiding him into her soaked pussy, pushing him deeper with each gentle sway of her hips, her lust filled gaze never leaving his. She picked up the pace ever so slightly letting his hands hungrily clutch her hips. Their rhythm increased with each thrust, faster and faster. She placed her hands atop his shoulders giving her more leverage as he plunged deeper and deeper, groaning louder with the pleasure at each thrust. The heat between them intensified, hearts throbbing as one, until he lurched in tremendous climax before collapsing in exhaustion.

Slowly he raised his eyes to hers, still panting but penitent. "I've missed you woman."

"And I've missed my husband, for a long time now," her meaning clear as she gently stroked his face, her siren trance still enslaving him.

"I will never stray on you again, I love you too much, please believe that. Come back to me; come back to our bed, never leave me again," he begged, his voice trailing off in breathless whisper.

But she didn't answer, knowing she now had control. Instead, her eyes moved to the bandage on his shoulder.

"What is this? Are you hurt?" she quietly questioned as she lay in his arms.

"I'm only hurt because I've hurt you," he replied, remorsefully. He reached for the tape, carefully removing the gauze, revealing a freshly inked tattoo across his left shoulder. Her fingers gingerly traced the words.

Alaina, the only woman I will ever love until my dying breath.

Her hand rose to caress his cheek and he held her gaze before turning his lips to kiss her wrist.

"Baby, sometimes a shining knight slips from his steed and falters in the eyes of his lady but now that knight is firmly back in place and will never fail his lady again. I love you, Alaina Rusano. I truly love you." His words were solemn, his eyes overflowing with sincerity.

The cab ride to the hotel was quiet. They sat bodies close, thighs touching, still adrift in the ecstasy. She had shocked him; their impromptu lovemaking filling his heart with hope. Reaching for his hand, she guided him to the pearls encircling her neck.

"Thank you," she murmured, and he drew her hand to his lips.

#

The windows of the small boutique hotel looked down on the beauty of Philadelphia's Boathouse Row with a magnificent view of the Schuylkill River. She stared at the rippling waters where her boys would be racing in the morning and a gentle calm permeated her being. She was at peace now.

Nick hustled the bellboy out the door knowing a serious conversation with his wife was imminent. He moved toward her, hesitantly meeting her eyes, "Are we ... good?"

"Well..., I want to believe that what happened on the plane was simply a prelude of better things to come," she replied softly, the glow of passion still emanating from her eyes. "So, I would say we're very, very good and that my knight still wears the colors of his lady."

An overwhelming sense of relief rushed over him from just her simple words. He reached for her, crushing her body tightly to his and kissing her deeply before gently cupping her face with his hands.

"Baby, I was so afraid I had lost you. I know this was all my doing. You don't know how sorry I am. I, I don't know why..."

"Shh, my love," she replied, placing a finger to his lips. "Don't talk, just listen." Inhaling deeply, she gathered the courage to say her practiced lines. "I've spent endless hours thinking of what it would be like to not have you in my life, and I don't think I could bear it. What I know is that I feel a deep enduring love for you, and I never want to be without you." She hesitated, briefly looking away before her eyes returned to his, "But if you've already decided to move on, I will understand. I was the one who set the terms, after all."

He stepped back, reaching for her hands as his eyes began to tear. "I made my decision twenty-three years ago, woman. I will love you until my last breath, I promise you that. I will never again hurt you, not physically, not emotionally, never," he vowed.

Dinner with their sons would need to wait, tonight was theirs and theirs alone.

Alaina cheered as her boys raced their shells up the river the following day; their muscles hard, their bodies tanned and healthy. They were the image of their father, their handsome wonderful father whom she loved.

She drifted into a deep sleep on the return flight lulled by visions of her boys triumphantly crossing the finish line and awakened only by the harsh crackle of the pilot's voice.

"Welcome to Playa del Carmen, folks, where the weather is a balmy 88 degrees."

"Nick?" she questioned.

"This is for us, sweetheart, just us. Only Arch knows where we are. No meetings, no phone calls, no bodyguards just seventy-two uninterrupted hours where I'm not letting go of you for a single minute." Smiling, he wrapped her in his arms, where she remained for the next three days.

The Vow

Alaina gazed upon the shimmering turquoise water rippling under the pale orange sunset, allowing the calm to penetrate deep within her soul. He was hers again, he was her Nick, the man she loved and always would. She knew she would never leave him, her love for him was too strong. On the first morning, they made phone calls home only to find the world spun on without them, causing them both to laugh. Three luxurious days of white sands and warm waters awaited in their secluded bungalow perched above the crystal waters of the Caribbean. It was a couples paradise allowing for complete privacy with an open-air porch and jacuzzi looking out onto the placid horizon. An attached ladder led to the water below where they swam and held each other, turning back the clock to happier days. At night he wrapped his arms around her as they danced to the soulful rhythms of Calypso music, sharing dinner under a Mexican moon; later renewing their passion for each other for endless hours beneath the stars above.

Arturo was assigned as their personal butler delivering a breakfast of steaming sweet buns, eggs, tropical fruit, and large carafes of strong, hot coffee each morning. He had a joyful personality standing tall and proud in his crisp black uniform and bow tie with dancing amber eyes and deep smile lines framing his mouth. Nick let him know they didn't want to be disturbed and so Arturo only visited twice each day, once for breakfast and again before dinner delivering the daily cocktail.

On the third morning, Nick hurried off to run an errand, returning two hours later. "Hey gorgeous, I bought you something." Stripping her of her bathing suit, he slipped a floor-length snow-white chemise over her head. She was confused, seeing that he also wore new clothes.

"You look beautiful," he announced, unclipping her hair, and letting it fall to her shoulders. "Wait right here, don't move."

He rushed to open their bungalow door allowing a smiling Arturo to enter trailed by a small entourage of islanders: an attractive young woman dressed in a bright coral and yellow dress and matching headwrap, an official looking gentleman with small mustache and spectacles sporting a white three-piece suit and pocket watch, and finally, two gaily dressed musicians. Smiling broadly, he led her onto the outside deck; then he dropped to one knee and looked into her eyes. "Alaina Rusano, will you marry me again? I promise to get it right this time and I solemnly vow never to stop loving you. Believe my words to be true and please say yes."

Her eyes filled with tears, looking down upon the man she so deeply loved before lifting him to his feet and wrapping his face in her hands.

"I *believe* my answer is the same. Yes, yes, yes, yes," she squeaked, leaping into his arms.

"Is that a yes?" he teased.

"You know it is, you crazy fool."

The joyous rhythm of soft Calypso music and the gentle splashing of ocean waves filled the air as the dapper gentleman quickly stepped forward to officiate their second ceremony. Arturo and his female companion sang softly in the background, but as with the first time, they only had eyes for each other as they repeated their vows from years ago.

Reaching for her hand, he slipped a dazzling five carat aquamarine ring onto her finger, its color a perfect match to the sea. "When you look at this, I want you to remember this moment and the promise I just made."

Napa

Nick sauntered into the office, a smile emblazoned across his face and Arch couldn't help but grin.

"Everything went well?"

"Better than well, can't thank you enough, buddy. She's good, we're good, all's well upstairs. What's going on here, anything?"

"Everything's quiet, no worries. Old Sergio asked to meet; his gout is worsening. I set him up for Monday; probably wants to ask permission to hand the Seattle operation over to his son."

"Little Serge ready?"

"Yeah, kid's been running things for a while now."

"Good, anything else?"

"Nothing, but let me tell you, Tino and Zander were none too happy having you out of their sight. I feared for my life."

Nick chuckled, "They're good men. All right, I want you to clear your calendar for at least a week."

"A week?"

Nick nodded, "Did some thinking while I was away and you're right, we need to speed up the investments. I want you to fly to California and scout the Napa Valley for development opportunities, decent size properties, maybe a horse farm or a winery. Nothing that can be touched by our *friends*, something totally ours. Understand? Put out some feelers. I'm envisioning a first-class resort, a place where we can gather our families for Christmas and holidays every year, celebrate like normal people do with Thanksgiving dinners and New Year's parties." Nick was wired, quickly firing off ideas, hands flying. "Maybe we let Matt and Joe run the place. What do you say? Go in with me, buddy, let's form a partnership on this one. I'll front you the buy in, I owe you that much. I figure we buy now and sit, watch the value increase."

"Whoa, wait a minute, slow down. You're going to California?"

"*We're* going to California. You're coming with me, right?"

Arch was confused but excited, "Absolutely, just say the word. A consigliere goes with the Boss."

Nick's eyes instantly saddened, "I would rather hear you say you'll go as a friend."

"*Jump, just say jump.* I'm with you, buddy, always." Arch assured him.

"I'm getting out of this town, and I believe… thanks to you, I've been given a second chance at my marriage. Let's take a good look at the numbers and start increasing those investments *together*. I've got plans, Arch, plans for our future, lots of plans for your family and mine. Ten years, buddy, we're both out of here."

Arch grinned. "I'm in. I'm all in. I'm ready."

"Good. Find the Napa property first," he directed, "then you and I will ride north. Alaina tells me Northern California is some of the prettiest country she's ever seen. We need to find a large enough property for both of us. You understand what I'm saying, right? Once we break away, you're safer with me."

"For life, Nick, for life," Arch affirmed.

Nick nodded, the silent bond between them unsaid. "We need something isolated, invisible to the eye; quiet and peaceful, a place where we can settle down, smoke cigars, and drink good whiskey." He chuckled then. "Hell, we might even take the women… maybe… if they behave."

Arch pondered Nick's words. He loved Nick like the brother he never had. Both men knew the value of their decades-old friendship and he would stand beside Nick until his last day. That was the job of a consigliere but the bond they shared was much deeper than that. California sounded perfect.

#

Six weeks later

Both men secretly set out together on a weeklong ride along the west coast. Arch was eager to show Nick two properties in Napa Valley he had found, hoping for approval. One piece of land was owned by an aging vintner anxious to return to Spain but in dire need of capital. The other by an elderly couple who had established a small bed and breakfast on the property. One property abutted the other presenting an ideal opportunity for future development, and Nick quickly approved the purchase. The Napa enterprise would be a partnership with both men owning an equal share of 50%. The investment would be secured for both their offspring, hidden from any Mafia association.

With that task complete, they drove north, acquiring a massive piece of land high in the California hills overlooking a sparkling crystal blue lake. They would build their dream homes there, far away from the lights of Vegas, far away from their criminal activities, where they could spend their final days in peace.

Walking the Plank

"*En Garde*," the little boy screeched, his face stern and challenging as he pointed his plastic sword at Nick ascending from the downstairs office. "I am Captain Goodheart and you, sir, are the lowdown pirate, Blackbeard, the scourge of the seven seas. Over there, you scurvy hornswoggler, while I decide how you will die." Little Sam pointed to the corner of the foyer, gently poking his father with the tip of the sword.

"Yes, sir, Captain, right away, sir," Nick complied, gingerly taking his place beside Alaina on the floor. "Who am I again?" he whispered as they watched Sam battle an invisible foe, merrily careening back and forth along the polished foyer floor.

"You are the wicked cur, Blackbeard and I am a damsel in distress," she replied, placing her hand on her chest, and crying out, "Oh help, save me kind sir," in dramatic fashion. She then leaned in close to his ear, "And by the way, my wicked pirate, I'll model that sexy lace corset you sent when I can be alone with my dastardly Blackbeard," she winked, tickling him under the chin.

He laughed heartily, giving her a lecherous squeeze, but dread coursed through his veins knowing he had not sent a gift. However, that puzzle could wait. He wanted to be in the moment, watching the spirited play of the little boy with eye patch and bandolier proudly wearing the pirate outfit they had purchased in Playa del Carmen.

Alaina had come back to him there, back to his arms, forgiving him.

8pm

Nick could hear Alaina's voice as she read a bedtime story to Little Sam down the hall. Tonight's apropos selection was *Treasure Island.*

He quietly lifted the lid of the white box on his wife's dresser, the red ribbons already untied. Inside lay a blood red satin corset with matching stockings. He stared repulsed watching the satin morph into hideous pools of dripping blood before slamming his fist down upon the table.

Cheerios

Happy little cereal, Alaina thought, smiling at the bobbing oat rounds floating in the bowl. It was 2am and sleep had evaded her as it had the last three nights. Tonight, she would need to tell him before he guessed the obvious. Months had passed since their trip to the cove and memories of their conversation now felt like a tightening vise slowly nipping away at her oxygen as she pondered tonight's response.

Nick had been true to his word, coming upstairs every night, their passion for each other renewed, at peace with their union. Both boys were home now. Jax was fully immersed in the family business, managing the Royale by night, and attending business meetings by day, as Nick had done with his own father. Having Jax by his side had noticeably decreased Nick's stress. Luca was also working at the Royale although he would return to Princeton in the fall. Both boys were living in one of the guesthouses behind the main house. They were best friends, always had been, unlike Nick and his brother.

But her unease continued as Nick's words repeated in her mind, *his plans, his plans.* She removed the lease for the downtown hi-rise from her pocket, staring down at the blank signature line. She didn't want to leave him, but if this baby interfered with *his plans*, she would take that apartment and raise this child on her own. She prayed that would not be tonight's outcome, her trepidation growing.

Both men were working late, reviewing blueprints for the Royale's new entertainment complex. Alaina heard the front door, and she braced herself.

"Hey Mom, what 'cha doin' up?" Jax asked, leaning down to kiss her forehead.

"Couldn't sleep, there's pie in the fridge if you're hungry."

"Nah, too tired, catch you tomorrow."

Nick had taken a seat next to her when they entered, placing his hand over hers. He turned to her expectantly, "So... when are you going to tell me?"

"Tell you?" she apprehensively replied.

He smiled, stroking her hand, "That you're pregnant."

She slowly drew in a breath, "Tonight? I was going to tell you tonight. I wasn't really sure until this morning; I've been so irregular this past year." She hesitated, searching his eyes. "Nick, I know we talked about your plans."

"My plans?" He paused; confusion written across his face. "What? Honey?" Then realization hit him. "No, no, no, sweetheart, no. You know how I am when we're having a baby, nothing gives me more joy. Where is this coming from… wait… are *you* happy?"

"Oh love, yes, I am. This baby is a gift from God, our gift from God. I was just worried. Our conversation at the cove…"

"No, no, come here." He pulled her to his lap, hugging her, massaging her abdomen. "No, no, sweetheart. *Our* plans will just include another baby. *Our* plans won't change."

Relief washed over her, and she snuggled deep in his embrace, releasing her worry, "I love you; you know that?"

"Oh, angel, I love you too... another baby, ha! *We're* having another baby!" he chuckled.

Quickly lifting her fingers to his lips, she fretted, "I am worried about my age though, Nicky."

Stroking her brow, he reassured her, "No, no, babe, we will get every test possible and... no matter what, you know we will love this baby."

She lingered in his arms; all worry now released. This was what she had hoped for.

"Wait," she hesitated, "how did you know?"

"Hmm, darling, you're forgetting I know every inch of your body," teasing as he snuggled his face in her bosom, "plus the Cheerios, of course."

"The Cheerios?" She looked at him, confused.

He chuckled again, still embracing her. "Sweetheart, you have a tell. Whenever you're pregnant, you eat Cheerios in the middle of the night."

She had been caught out and burst into laughter.

"Now finish up, I want to make love to my woman."

They climbed the stairs, his arm wrapped around her waist as he mused, "Cheerio Rusano, I like it—has a good ring to it, you think?"

"Oh, don't be silly," she laughed.

"What? Matt's middle name is Ferrari. He almost christened my front seat."

"Then perhaps Miles would be more appropriate for *mile high*," she countered.

Coinman Marcus

Mel Belenz slammed the $100 Royale chip onto Nick's desk, shaking his head in disbelief. "He's at it again, Boss. When will that old man ever learn?"

Belenz, a trusted ten-year employee, managed the Royale's fraud department. He was an expert in his field and his many skills included the ability to detect a counterfeit chip from one hundred feet away.

Nick carefully examined the disk, first fingering the offending object then tossing it into the air, testing for weight. "How many?" he inquired.

"Three so far. Came in last night, new girl at the window."

Nick released a heavy sigh, knowing this was a conversation he would not enjoy. "Get me the old boy's address and we'll take a ride."

"Boss?" Belenz hesitated, causing Nick to look up.

"No, I'm not going to hurt him. Rest easy, can't hurt the old cogger, not today and… reassign the girl."

Defrauding a casino is a dangerous game and manufacturing counterfeit chips is among the most popular if not futile methods. The color of chips indicates value and have now become standardized throughout the industry; $5 chips are red, $25 are green, $100 black, $500 purple, $1,000 and $5,000 may vary. What the general public does not realize however, is that all chips have particular designs or logos showing their casino of origin; and those designs incorporate special paints and UV inks. Many also contain RFID devices imbedded into that logo enabling casinos to track their location. This is particularly beneficial in a robbery; casinos keep additional sets of chips secured within their safes which can quickly be switched out, rendering stolen chips valueless and aiding in apprehension. That $500 chip in your pocket can travel down the street to the corner coffee kiosk and the casino knows its exact location.

Nick studied the tiny ebony disk, an artful forgery made with care by a skillful counterfeiter. This was definitely Coinman's creation. He admired the old man's craftsmanship and his *chutzpah*.

Coinman Marcus kickstarted his life of crime as a casino shill decades ago luring unsuspecting tourists to increase their bets at blackjack and poker tables. He'd been running small time scams ever since: manufacturing coins from blank disks for use in now defunct slot machines, creating special metal devices to trigger payouts, and fabricating counterfeit chips. Although Coinman was on the no trespass list, security rarely noticed the doddering octogenarian who deftly evaded them, laughing all the while.

#

Nick pulled into the run-down trailer park located just a few short miles from the glamour and glitz of the Vegas Strip. He surveyed the littered driveways filled with rusted out cars, overflowing trash containers, and broken glass. At the end of the lane a dozen squealing children with sticks tormented a pack of mangy dogs. He shook his head, in a town where thousands of dollars hinged on a single roll of the dice, these people were barely getting by.

Both men stared at #18, a dilapidated blue and white single wide mobile home built in the 1950s. Lace curtains decorated the windows and a handful of red geraniums struggled for life in the tiny patch of dirt near the door.

A small woman in a neatly ironed housecoat greeted them as they approached, but a look of apprehension quickly replaced her smile the instant she recognized the visitors, feebly calling for her husband before inviting them in.

Nick studied the interior; it was clean, but signs of low income were apparent with threadbare throw rugs and worn furniture. Coinman Marcus was noticeably nervous, hand twitching, sweat forming across his brow.

Nick placed the chip on the wooden coffee table between them, "I can't have this, old man. You know I can't have this, not in my place."

"Yes, sir. I... I know. I'm... I'm sorry, Mr. Nick, I'm sorry," he stuttered, avoiding eye contact.

"He didn't mean no harm, Mr. Nick, really he didn't." Flossie beseeched, but Nick raised his palm, silencing her, his icy stare boring into Coinman.

"What do you suggest I do about this, Marcus?" Nick asked.

"Please, Mr. Nick, please, I swear it won't happen again. Please don't hurt us, please. Flossie here got sick; we ran out of money, no money for her medicine, you see. I just needed a little bit. Please don't... don't hurt us."

"How many of these did you make?"

"Twenty, I made twenty, please Mr. Nick, please, I'm sorry, I'm sorry."

Nick leaned back, staring into the old man's pleading eyes before turning to Belenz. "Go through the house, confiscate all the equipment, check the yard for anything buried."

He then turned his attention back to Marcus, swiftly slamming his hand down upon the table. "Come through my doors again and I will break both your wrists and dump your body in the desert. Do you hear me, old man?" he roared.

Coinman quaked, nodding his understanding.

Nick drew in a breath and retrieved the counterfeit chip from the table's surface. He waved it before Coinman's rheumy eyes, made a fist with his massive hand and crushed the disk in his palm allowing the broken bits to fall upon the table between them.

Standing to leave, he locked angry eyes with the quaking old man, "Heed my words, Marcus, don't cross my threshold again." He then reached into his pocket and tossed a one-hundred-dollar bill on the table between them, "For her meds."

Cashmere and Beignets

In March, the Commission called a special meeting and since St. Patrick's Day fell on the chosen date, all agreed the meeting should be held in Chicago. Bosses and Underbosses from all coasts gathered. The primary topic on the agenda was Macau, the Las Vegas of Asia. There was money to be made on China's southern coast and the Mob wanted their share.

Nick had grown to despise these meetings, viewing them as necessary burdens. He was particularly resentful this weekend, already missing Alaina's melt in your mouth corned beef, and preferring to be home rather than watching fat old Dons drink whiskey, smoke cigars, and play with painted whores. But he saw the value of this gathering. The Royale had recently added a costly wing onto its casino floor offering several table games favored by Asian high rollers. Pai Gow Poker and Baccarat were two of Nick's biggest money makers, especially in the no limit private rooms. Investments in Macau could expedite his retirement plans.

Jax now traveled with Nick on all business trips. He proudly stood beside his father cementing his position as the tough son of the Boss of the West Coast crime family. In addition to acting on behalf of his father in their own territories, he had been called upon by the Commission earlier in the year to carry out several jobs, all benefiting his reputation.

Both men arrived in Chicago one day early at the request of Nick's longtime friend, Emile Monserrat. The older men planned to meet for drinks on the evening before the scheduled Commission meeting.

As father and son rode the limo to the hotel, Nick spotted a Henri Bendel boutique. Bendel's was one of Alaina's favorite shops, having the well-earned reputation of supplying upscale luxury goods nationwide to its discerning customers. He would buy her a small gift before his meeting.

#

The atmosphere when entering Bendel's is always welcoming. Uncluttered aisles are lined with elegantly designed displays, their glass showcases flush with exquisite merchandise. Bendel's prides itself on providing individualized customer service, which was precisely what Nick encountered as he entered.

A tall, thirty-something brunette quickly approached taking note of his handsome physique and immediately assessing his wealth from his appearance.

"Good afternoon, sir. Is there anything I can do for you?" she posed; the innuendo evident. Nick had to admit, she was attractive, with deep green eyes and full red lips, but he had no interest in responding to her lame flirtation.

"Thanks, I'm looking for a gift for my wife."

"Perfume?"

Nick smiled, continuing to make his way further into the store. "Not unless you carry Byredo."

"No, sorry, sir," she pouted, following him. "Perhaps a leather handbag or wallet?"

"No, I don't think so." He turned, moving on to the next area where a debonaire male clerk sporting a blue paisley bowtie awaited.

"I'm looking for something special for my wife."

"A fine scarf perhaps, sir?"

"No, that won't do, she has so many." Alaina frequented Hermès in the Royale Promenade every spring and fall when the new collections were released.

"I see, something splendid then," the clerk nodded with understanding. "If you'll allow me, sir." Gesturing to a glass showcase, the obliging gentleman retrieved a luxurious oversized pashmina shawl in gradient shades of purple. "These exquisite wraps are imported directly from Nepal and are exclusive to Bendel's. The soft cashmere fibers are blended with silks of the finest quality resulting in the lustrous, rich appearance you see here. When your lady wears this, she will be enrobed in both warmth and glamour."

Nick ran his hand across the silken shawl; it was baby soft, an ideal gift to keep Alaina comfortable on cool evenings.

"Perfect, but the blue and turquoise will be more to her liking. Wrap it and deliver it to the Waldorf, suite 4, Rusano."

"Of course, sir."

With his purchase complete, Nick made his way to the exit, again noting the wide smile and flirtatious wink from the tall brunette.

#

7pm

Nick exited the elevator planning to enjoy a whiskey at the bar before his meeting with Emile. He spotted Jax across the room already in a head-to-head conversation with a petite blond.

"Well, hello again, handsome." The honeyed voice came from Bendel's brunette as she crossed the lobby. "Buy a girl a drink?"

He smirked, not at all surprised by her intrusion, "Thought it was clear I had a wife."

"Oh sweetheart, I'm not trying to be your wife, I'm just trying to keep warm on a cold, windy night," she answered coyly, lips in full pout.

Laughing, he replied, "One quick drink then, but I am meeting someone."

Her pout deepened but she quickly looped her arm through his as he escorted her to a table. She reached for his hands, encircling them in hers, red lacquered nails flashing. "I was hoping we could get to know each other better. A man with such large, strong hands surely has...," her voice trailed off as she lowered her eyes to his groin.

Nick smiled, before discretely catching the eye of his son across the room and nodding toward the brunette. Jax immediately understood, and shrugged in agreement, pulling a third chair over to his table.

"I really do have a business meeting tonight, but my son there in the corner would be happy for you to join him. Trust me, he is endowed with the same *large* hands."

The woman nodded her understanding and quickly crossed the room to join Jax, turning back to blow Nick a sultry kiss as she departed.

Minutes later, Emile entered, jovial as always, greeting Nick with a firm handshake and hug. Emile Monserrat was Boss of the Dixie Mafia, his territories spreading its tentacles from Dallas to New Orleans. He was a powerful looking man, with a hard muscular build and a dark southern tan, who held tight rein on his businesses. Both men had been friends for decades making their bones during their youth.

"I have a proposition for you, my friend and I hope it will be agreeable," Emile began in his accented voice.

"I'm listening."

"I have a low life that owes me a great sum of money. He is refusing to make good on the markers he has accrued in one of my Bourbon Street establishments. Ordinarily I would handle this myself as you know, but he has mocked me in a most abominable way. He roughed up one of my company girls, my very favorite, my sweet little Ava. Sent me pictures of her shattered face before dumping her body in the Mississippi. I grieved for this one, it was a personal affront, you see."

Nick nodded, "What are you asking?"

"Your boy, he needs to come up, yes, make his first sanctioned kill?"

"He does."

"Will you do this for me, my friend? I propose we present this at the meeting tomorrow. If approved, he will be a *made* man by the end of the month, you agree?"

"I accept the job but, as for Jackson being raised up, some may challenge his bloodline, my wife is Irish."

"Bah! Demand a vote! I need the job done and I have chosen your boy. I will meet anyone's challenge and, when all is done, Uncle Emile will sponsor him."

Nick leaned forward, clasping his friend's hands, "We will take the job no matter what their decision."

"Ahh, good, you are a faithful friend. I am too close to this, you see, and when emotion gets in the way of business, mistakes are made."

"Curious, though, how do you intend to recoup the debt?"

"Ah, that, my dear friend, is better left unsaid. Are we in agreement then?"

Nick nodded, both men sealing their contract with a jovial handshake. He glanced at his son across the room knowing the deal he had just made would heighten the boy's status within the Commission. Tipping his glass to Jackson, he watched as his son exited the bar arm-in-arm with both the blond and the brunette.

"The boy will have a busy night, yes?" Emile joked, as they passed. "Am I keeping you from your own enjoyment, my friend?"

"No, not at all. Sadly… tonight I am missing my wife."

"Ah, I understand. It is a blessing from our God if we find one true love in our lives, yes?"

Nick smiled, agreeing as Emile continued.

"It's almost a year since my own Celeste passed. The cancer devastated her once beautiful body and she suffered," Emile lamented.

"I'm sorry, old friend," Nick commiserated.

"I still miss her greatly and… I have been abusing my body ever since," he laughed, patting his stomach. "So, it is time to drink. We will forget our troubles for tonight, at least."

Both men sat with their whiskeys for the remainder of the evening, reminiscing on the days of their youth. He would review Emile's proposal with Jax in the morning.

A Box of Stars

Nick viewed her from the doorway as she lay dozing on the veranda; her hand atop her slightly swollen belly in a protective posture, the warm sun giving her face a delicate glow. He had left Chicago as quickly as possible, wanting nothing more than to be away from the endless drone of old men complaining they weren't yet rich enough. He also wasn't the only one at the meeting that recognized the tension between the New York families. Arch had been warning him for months that trouble was brewing on the east coast.

But for now, preparing Jackson for his New Orleans assignment was his foremost priority. This would be his first kill and Nick was well aware of the mental toll that would exact on his son's psyche.

"Mommy, Mommy," Sam shouted barreling up the stairs and careening into his father's arms.

"Shh," Nick put his fingers to his lips as he hoisted the little boy into the air, but it was too late; Alaina stirred, looking to the doorway.

Sam wrangled himself free and ran to his mother. "Look, Mommy, look. Teacher gave me a gold star *and* a sticker *and* a lollipop." The little boy proudly presented his latest spelling test, thrusting it into his mother's hands.

"Oh, look at this! How wonderful, we need to frame this," she exclaimed, kissing his sticky face, lips still tightly clamped down on the treat.

"Yep," he beamed, red lollipop drool spilling from the side of his lips.

Nick lowered himself to the side of her chaise, reaching for the sticky hands of his son.

"Did I ever tell you about the trick I pulled on your grandpop?"

Little Sam shook his head, eyes big with merriment.

"Well, one day Sister Mary Benedict gave me a silver star for *my* spelling test. I was so excited, I ran home to show Grandpop, just like you. Grandpop reached into his pocket and rewarded me with a quarter. Soooo… I got to thinking, I could go down to the store and buy my own box of stars. Yep, I thought, I could make a million dollars. So that's what I did, I bought a box of stars and started gluing them on all my school papers, sometimes I even put on two stars."

Sam's eyes grew big as saucers, "You did, really, Daddy?"

"Yep, but Grandpop was too smart for me. He caught on quick, no more quarters for me. He sent me to my room and took away all my comic books. It was awful."

"Ohh, poor Daddy," Little Sam replied, sticking out his bottom lip.

With that, Nick stood tall, reached into his pocket, and mimed the voice of an old man. "So here, young man, is your quarter. Don't buy a box of stars."

Little Sam burst into laughter, drool flying.

"Now go find Mimi so she can wipe that sticky face," Nick laughed, pecking the child on his head.

"I can't believe you did something like that, deceiving your sweet father," voiced Alaina, astonished.

"What? I was a little entrepreneur even back then," smirking and presenting her with an elegantly wrapped box. "Brought you a little something from Chicago."

"Bendel's, you went to Bendel's, my favorite!" she exclaimed, excitedly unfolding the tissue. "Oh love, it's *so* soft, my favorite colors, too. It's beautiful. Thank you so much and thank you for the other gifts too although I don't think they will fit for a while. Is that a tease for after the baby?" Alaina pointed to a white gift box with red satin bows already untied.

Nick hesitated, crossing the room, and lifting the lid as a cold chill ran down his spine. A seductive pair of red satin panties and matching bra lay beneath, another anonymous gift.

"Yes, sweetheart, for after the baby," he answered, turning, and winking.

Lagniappe Ante

Jackson Rusano was puffed up with pride, his mind racing with possibilities. The Commission had approved Emile Monserrat's request assigning him to make his first independent kill. There was more to it of course but he dared not ask questions. That was part of the code, you did what the Commission commanded, end of story. Jax recognized the significance, knowing it would advance his standing within the organization, earning him more respect. He would no longer be given the petty tasks of collecting money from deadbeat gamblers or roughing up longshoremen; those jobs would go to the lesser young men still coming up.

These days he stayed by his father's side whenever possible, learning the ways of the families, doing whatever was needed to keep the West Coast machine running effectively. He was hungry to make his bones. He loved the control, the power—everything about the life. *He loved the blood.*

Jackson stood before his father now, anxious to begin, listening, learning, respecting the powerful man behind the desk.

Nick's counsel was stern. "You never hurt a citizen; they are not involved in our business and harm should never come to them. It is a cardinal rule within the families: never hurt women, children, or innocent bystanders. Our business dealings must remain invisible. You only target the offender. This man owes a debt to the organization, both financial and personal, that is the reason for the kill. That's all you need to know. Are you good?"

"Yes, sir."

Nick softened, "I have prepared you for this all your life, Son, you are ready. Once you have completed this assignment, you will be elevated to the rank of *Man of Honor*. It is a position of high esteem that most men never achieve, and it will follow you throughout your entire your life. Do you understand?"

"Yes, sir."

"Good. A private plane is waiting to take you to New Orleans. I have sent Tino ahead. He has been scouting the area for the past few days. This is the name of the offender, and here is his photo. His boat is named the Lagniappe Ante. He docks at the Municipal Harbor Pier on Roadway Street. He goes fishing every morning, usually at 6am. You will need to rig the dynamite and detonate it from a burner phone just as Tino taught you. Be sure you are a safe distance away and that you both observe the kill. That being said, what is most important to me is that you return safely. Questions?"

"No, sir."

"Excellent." Nick stood and shook Jackson's hand. "Call me as soon as you're clear."

He watched his young son drive away fully aware that a harder man would return and that his life would be forever changed.

Mean Man

Wedding bells rang out above the towering spires of the Church of St. Mark as the young bride and groom recited their vows. Bella Atanio was marrying her childhood sweetheart and young mafioso enforcer, Rico Patrizini. A private reception immediately followed at Genovaro's restaurant.

Nick was conducting business in a private room upstairs as was always the case when the families gathered. Alaina sat at one of the tables conversing with two of the cousins, Mario and Geneva. The boys, Luca and Matt, were enjoying the party, dancing with the many young ladies in their finery. Jax was absent, having been sent north by his father on business. The younger ones, Little Sam included, dashed about squealing with laughter and playing children's games. The party was in full swing.

Dominic watched Alaina from across the smoky room hoping to steal a few minutes alone with her. He continued to lust after his brother's wife. She remained beautiful whereas his own wife had become more an embarrassment with every passing year.

He approached the table and sidled in next to Alaina to the surprise of the cousins.

"Mr. Rusano, sir, what a surprise! Do, do you need to talk to me?" stuttered Mario, visibly nervous.

"No, kid, I need you to get lost."

"Yes, yes, sir." Mario nearly toppled his chair in his haste to leave.

"Dominic, you scared those poor kids," Alaina laughed.

"I came to talk to you, not them. So, tell me, how you are, beautiful? What are you pregnant again?" Dominic gaped.

Alaina answered joyfully, "Yes, I am."

"What the hell for? Kids are nothing but brats," rebuked Dominic.

"Oh no, Dom. Nick and I are elated. This baby was such a surprise and we're both so happy. Where's Angela? I don't see her."

"Sent her back to Sicily, back to her mother," he grumbled. "Your husband approved it."

"Approved it? I don't understand." Alaina was shocked, questioning his words.

"Well, he is *head* of the family, I had to get his permission. But don't worry, beautiful, I did it for us. One big happy family, if you get my meaning."

Alaina was speechless, stunned by his utterance.

"Mommy, Mommy," a giggling Sam came bounding onto her lap, "Mommy, Luca is chasing me."

"He is?" she replied, unsuccessfully trying to corral the child.

Sam stared up at Dominic, cocking his head for just a moment before giggling again and placing his hands on Alaina's stomach.

"Mommy has a baby in her belly," he announced.

"I can see that," Dominic replied.

"When I grow up, I'm going to marry Mommy."

Dominic sneered, "No, kid. I'm the one who's going to marry Mommy."

Little Sam froze as if stung before hopping to the floor and running smack into the open arms of his big brother.

"Gotcha, buddy," Luca laughed, cradling the little boy, and lifting him into the air. His eyes met Dominic's with icy coldness, the hatred palpable.

"Mom, Dad's ready to go," he announced, never releasing his stare.

Alaina rose clumsily, still shocked by Dominic's revelations. Looking up she felt Nick's eyes boring into her from across the room.

The ride home was silent, fraught with tension. The only sounds came from the backseat where Matt battled Little Sam in a party favor sword fight, laughing with each pretend joust. Then suddenly the little boy paused, staring at the plastic toy. "I like weddings. I like cake. But I don't like that mean man," he declared with total childhood innocence.

"What mean man, Sam, was someone mean to you?" Matt asked.

Alaina closed her eyes hoping Nick was too preoccupied to notice. But it was too late, the powder keg was lit.

"Mommy, you know, the man you were talking to, the one who looks like daddy. He looks like you, Daddy. He said he's going to marry Mommy. He's not going to marry you, Mommy. I'm going to marry you and we'll have lots of cake. We'll eat cake all day, won't we Mommy?"

"Yes, honey, we will," she replied, seeing her husband's dark, angry eyes piercing through her from the rear-view mirror as they pulled into the driveway.

"I'll carry him up, Dad," volunteered Luca, lifting a now sleeping Sam from the car.

"No, I'll take him," Nick hissed.

Alaina watched Nick climb the stairs before retreating with her two sons to the kitchen.

"Mom, I'm so sorry," Matt pleaded, his hands reaching for his mother's arms.

"You did nothing wrong, sweetheart. It's all right." She knew her husband's wrath was inevitable, yet she never understood the basis of his jealousy.

"But it's not, I hate him. I hate him *so* much. All he does is start trouble," anguished Matt.

The kitchen door slammed open, causing them all to jump.

"What the fuck is this about? You hate who?" his father bellowed.

Matt cried out, visibly shaken, "Uncle Dom, I hate him. You can't make me like him. He… he starts trouble for everyone, and all you do is take his side, and… sometimes I hate you, too."

Nick drew in a breath, gored by the words of his young son. "Both of you, in my office *now!*"

"Nick," Alaina cried out, grabbing his sleeve but he raised a warning finger halting her.

"Just the boys, you and I will talk later."

#

Office

Luca stood tall, locking eyes with his father, young challenging old, determined to diffuse the situation. He placed a reassuring hand atop his younger brother's shoulder before stepping forward.

"Dad, you need to take a breath and listen before passing judgment. Hear me out, please." Inhaling for strength, he carefully considered his words watching the vein in his father's neck pulsate. "Mom was talking with two of the cousins and I witnessed Uncle Dom run them off. I couldn't hear the conversation, but it was obvious Mom was uncomfortable. He clearly said something that upset her and that's when I intervened. He is the one at fault, no one else. Matt is right. Anytime something happens and Uncle Dom is involved, you choose his side over your own family, and it's especially true when Mom is involved. It's *displacement.*"

"Displacement?" Nick repeated, not believing what he was hearing.

"Yes, Dad, displacement. I guarantee you that Uncle Dom purposely planned that little stunt tonight just to start trouble. Open your eyes, man. He is constantly causing trouble for our family, for our business, and especially for Mom. I see it, Jax sees it, Matt sees it, we all do, but you're blind to it. Geez Dad, brotherly love is one thing, but you refuse to see his scheming, and his manipulation, and… and his treachery. It's hurtful, Dad, hurtful to all of us." Luca fiercely met his father's eyes, ending with this, "And the last time this exact thing happened, you and Mom had a big fight, and you took off to your girlfriend's house for a couple nights."

Nick looked between the two boys, "My girlfriend?"

"Yeah, probably that lady with the red lipstick," Matt blurted out.

"Matt...," cautioned Luca.

An uneasy silence fell across the room as their father's expression changed from anger to uncertainty. He abruptly turned toward the window, raking his fingers through his hair. Tense moments ticked by before he released a loud sigh, turning back to face his sons, "In case you haven't noticed, your mother's pregnant."

But Luca burst into laughter, "So…, that means what? How does that change *your* response?"

Nick stared unsettled by the two young men standing before him, mature, strong, defiant. They were defending their mother, firm in their beliefs. He raised both palms while searching for words to reassure them, his voice softer. "Look, your mother and I are good; you don't need to worry," he paused, drawing in a deep breath, and measuring his response. "I know I show anger and… and jealousy when it comes to Uncle Dom and your mother but that is... my devil to fight. Matt, there are no more girlfriends. I know you may not believe that, but it is the truth. The lady with the red lipstick was a mistake, my mistake. I never meant to hurt your mother. She has forgiven me, and I hope you will also."

Matt did not reply, staring defiantly for several seconds. He loved his mother greatly; she was his confidante, always supporting him, always listening. He would protect her, and he wasn't sure he could ever forgive his father's actions.

Nick noted his son's nonresponse before turning to Luca, "Tell me more about what Uncle Dom's been doing. Sit, both of you."

Sensing he now had his father's attention; Luca relayed a series of incidents. "He comes onto the pit floor, tells the workers we're not treating them right, not paying enough, that they would be more appreciated working for him. He questions the payouts, slows down the play. He fondles the waitresses, it's disgusting. And remember that poker dealer we caught stealing last month? I think he was reporting to Uncle Dom, I think he was put in our place to spy." Luca took another deep breath and diverted his eyes ending with this, "and he told me last week that I should have been his son."

Nick looked in disbelief between both young men, seeing Matt nod in agreement, feeling their pain. Contempt passed over Nick's face. This was unnecessary cruelty purposely meant to hurt his loved ones.

Luca continued, "One last thing, Dad, and this might be important. Last night I took Jessica to see that show she's been talking about at MGM. I spotted Uncle Dom downstairs at the bar yucking it up with the Canale brothers from the Bronx. He didn't see us."

Beyond the office doors Alaina was pacing, arming herself for an angry confrontation with her husband, but she heard no screaming, no thrown glass—only the muffled words of the three men. More than an hour passed before they finally emerged.

Nick noticed the fire in her eyes. "Relax woman, you know I would never hurt my children. Boys, go to bed," he said quietly, "I need to apologize to your mother for my bad behavior."

Alaina looked at her sons, receiving a reassuring nod from Matt and a thumbs-up from Luca.

"Forgive me, Madonna," he began. "I behaved badly. Sometimes I act the fool, blind to the wealth before me."

"Very true, big man," she concurred, seeing the dark clouds of worry in his eyes, "come to bed, you're tired."

But sleep evaded him.

The Donna

"I'm here to see the Donna; not the Don, the Donna, you idiot. Do you speak English? The Donna!"

Mikey called up to the office from the security station. "Mr. Macland, there's an old lady down here, a Signora Veneto, asking to see the Donna."

"The Donna, you sure?"

"Yep, wants to see only 'the Donna,' nasty too."

Arch looked to Nick, watching as he scanned the house cameras, finding Alaina playing with Sam in the garden. "You have an appointment, honey? No? Well, someone's here to see you, we'll put her in the sunroom."

Alaina quickly changed her clothes and greeted her visitor, instructing Hildy to deliver espresso and cakes. Signora Veneto, an eighty-year-old widow dressed in traditional black dress, sat admiring the view. She was a small woman, heavily wrinkled with age but her eyes still danced.

Her gnarled hands reached for Alaina's swollen belly. "Ah, my Donna, you carry a son. He is strong."

Alaina wrapped the old woman's hands in hers, smiling warmly. "He certainly is that. Some nights he won't let me sleep with all his kicking and squirming." Both women laughed, erasing the generations between them before the old woman continued.

"You must forgive me, my dear, for taking you away from your children. I feared bothering the Don with such a small request."

"Of course, how can I help?"

With quivering lips, Senora Veneto told Alaina of her older brother, Tessio, who was dying of cancer. "He is refusing to let the visiting nurse into his home. She's a stranger, you see. I know he's not taking care of himself; he's not eating. I take minestrone, he doesn't eat; I take torta barozzi, he doesn't eat. I don't know who to turn to. If you could just visit him, you being a nurse and wife to the Don, he would never turn you away. Please, say you will do this for me. I worry so much about him," she begged, nervously fingering the gold cross around her neck.

Alaina squeezed her hand, feeling the woman's despair and noting the tears falling upon her wrinkled cheeks.

"Of course, tomorrow morning, 10 o'clock?"

"Oh yes, dear! Thank you, thank you so much. I will meet you out front, I have a key," exuberant in her reply.

Arch looked at Nick as they viewed the conversation on the office surveillance. Nick nodded his approval, then held up his hand after thinking further on the matter. "Send her a few things once in a while, small stuff," he ordered.

And so, it began. The women came to Alaina from that day forward with their requests and Alaina plunged in full thrust. She started by visiting each woman in the community to assess their needs, bringing baskets of wine, food and supplies, all gifts from their Don. Nick added a small office off the sunroom so she could conduct business in comfort, and before long she was scheduling transportation for food shopping, cleaning services, and doctors' appointments.

She found some were behind on their mortgage payments, and others needed help with home maintenance, and painting. She immediately went to Nick, and he, in turn, renegotiated their mortgages with the local bank and sent a team of workmen to paint and make necessary repairs. One morning a half dozen women arrived at the gate requesting an emergency meeting with their Donna. They were in a panic: their favorite Italian bakery was closing due to foreclosure. Where would they buy their sfogliatella? Again, Nick intervened, allowing the bakery to remain open and causing the women to rejoice.

"Remember, if the grandmothers of the community are happy, then everyone is happy," Alaina schooled Nick one night; and indeed, their community was thriving and their love for their Don and Donna deepened.

Arch pondered the recent changes. Nick kept an iron grip on all his criminal responsibilities, never hesitating to order retribution against anyone falling out of line, sometimes even inflicting the violence himself, still enjoying the game; but since his revelations to Alaina of the true family business, he was less volatile. He was the Don of a major criminal empire and she had accepted that.

Tell Me No Secrets

Luca nudged the blond cocktail waitress sleeping beside him. "Get dressed, need you to go." The girl moaned but he was already out of bed, tossing her fallen clothes onto the sheets. His father needed him, having just called his cell phone moments earlier.

Luca smiled, envisioning the possibilities, already tasting the blood. *It's going to be a great spring break!* He relished the wet work, craving more and more, always getting pleasure from the terror-stricken eyes of his tortured victims.

#

"Son, need you to get out to Miss Lily's right away. She's having a problem with one of her girls." Annoyance was clearly written on his father's face. "Seems we have a singing canary. Little lady's been nibbing into the personal business of some of our clients. Don't know if she's acted on any of that knowledge yet but she needs to be stopped immediately. Could be dangerous to us. Understand?" Nick looked up as Luca nodded.

"Good, take her for a ride. You okay with that?"

"Yes, sir," Luca responded, delighted by the assignment.

"And, Son, treat yourself while you're out there." Nick winked, knowing of Luca's special relationship with a cute little ranch girl named Jazzy.

Prostitution is a lucrative business in a town like Vegas, where money flows freely from conventioneers and cheating spouses looking to escape their mundane lives back home. Nick owned three upscale pleasure ranches on the outskirts of the city, this one overseen by one of his favorite employees.

Miss Lily was an exquisite beauty standing only 5'3" tall but never seen without her four-inch stiletto heels. Shoulder length platinum hair, a flawless complexion with accented beauty marks, green eyes, a full bosom, and an hourglass figure added to her allure. She was the type of woman who never aged even though Nick knew she was approaching fifty. She had personally pleasured him several times throughout the years.

Lily ran a tight ship enforcing strict house rules, ensuring the protection of both her girls and her diverse clientele. She happily opened her doors to state senators and local farmers alike and, because of that, strict confidentiality was required. That was the reason for Lily's call to Nick. She had received two separate complaints from high power clients that one of her new girls was asking too many questions behind closed doors and one client was concerned about potential extortion. Nick assured Lily that her problem would disappear by end of day.

Four hours later

"Any problems?" Nick asked as Luca stood before him.

"No sir, all taken care of. Miss Lily sends her thanks." Luca smirked knowing the girl's battered body would never be found, dumped deep within the Mojave Desert. That little canary would never sing again. He had sliced out her tongue.

In Charge

After the incident at the wedding, Matt began to watch his father more closely. Jax was immersed in the family business now, acting as his father's right hand and when Jax wasn't attending meetings or out of town on business, he was at the Royale. Luca had returned to Princeton.

This gave Matt more time to observe the relationship between his parents. His mother was redecorating the nursery, jubilant about the new baby. His father had purchased a new boat, christening it the *Cheerio*; strange name, but, oh well. They seemed *'good'* just as his father said. They often touched each other in small but intimate ways; he gently stroked her back; she caressed his cheek before a small kiss. Once Matt interrupted a passionate embrace between the two in the kitchen and one night, he saw them dancing in the garden, tightly wrapped in each other's arms, music playing in the background. But the most embarrassing moment occurred one morning when he was rushing to school. He needed an important paper signed for an upcoming field trip and, of course, he had waited until the last minute. He banged on his parents' bedroom door then barged in unannounced.

"Mom, Mom?"

Hearing water running, he ran toward the bathroom, mortified at finding his parents *together* in the shower making love. They were deep in a kiss, unaware of his presence. Retreating into the bedroom, he bolted from the room, paper unsigned.

His anger festered unable to comprehend his parents' relationship. He watched, he listened, he waited; searching for proof of his father's sincerity and filled with concern for his mother.

A few weeks passed before he found himself observing them once again outside their partially open bedroom door. He slowed seeing them kissing, talking, passionately kissing, talking.

His father's hand was on his mother's stomach. "Promise me you'll rest while I'm gone," he said, obvious concern in his voice.

"I will," she softly replied.

"No, no. Don't give me any lip service, woman. I know you. You're exhausted, you need to rest. Promise me."

"I promise," his mother affirmed, placing her palm on his father's cheek, and lovingly looking into his eyes.

"I'm going to check. I'm putting Mattie in charge; I know he'll take good care of you." One more kiss. "I'll be home in a couple days. I don't want to leave you, you know that."

"I know."

Matt quickly and quietly descended the stairs, his parents unaware.

His father entered the kitchen minutes later. "Matt, I need to attend a funeral back east, look after your mother for me, will you?"

"Sure Dad, sure."

"Good. Take care of her, Son. I'll be back on Friday. Jax and Luca will be with me, but Uncle Arch will be available. Call if you need anything."

With that he was gone.

Tunnels and Mazes

The funeral mass for Don Sabatini was held in New York City's St. Patrick's Cathedral. Sabatini was an icon, loved by the community. City dignitaries and Mafia hierarchy alike were in attendance paying their respects. The Commission convened the following day, all members agreeing to appoint Sabatini's oldest son as don of his father's massive criminal network.

Nick scanned the room seeing Jackson deep in conversation with the son of a Brooklyn don. The young men were coming up; tough, strong, ready to take control. For that, he was grateful, wanting his tough guy years to end. He would be there to guide his sons just as his own father had done for him, but he felt satisfaction knowing that a similar meeting would take place in the future giving his sons control of his vast empire.

One more day of business and he could fly back to Alaina. He was worried, this pregnancy was not going well, not as easy as the last three. He wanted to get home, glad to be leaving before dinner tomorrow.

He felt his phone vibrate. Could only be Arch, he thought. He stepped into the hallway seeing Tino rushing toward him, "Boss, we need to go."

"What's going on?"

"There's been an accident. Mr. Archer ordered me to pull you from your meeting right away. He's on his way to the scene so he'll tell you more, but we need to leave *now*."

Nick checked his phone seeing the ominous message from Arch, 'CALL NOW, we've been hit, Alaina missing, get home.'

An angry nor'easter was assaulting the east coast slowing New York traffic to a crawl. The weather window was narrowing, but the pilot assured them they would still be able to depart if everyone hurried. Nick's nerves were raw, his thoughts only of his wife and unborn child. He was five hours away, on the other side of the country and no amount of money or power could get him home sooner.

Arch quickly relayed the harrowing news, "Bobby's dead, shot in the head. Blood all over the front seat. Windows all shattered. The car has severe rear end damage. There's a small amount of blood in the back, but I don't think she was shot, maybe hit her head, some blood on the seat. Her bag's here with her phone inside, but no sign of her. Need to tell you this, Bobby called back to the house just a few minutes after he and Alaina left the complex, told Zander he thought he was being followed by a black sedan with tinted windows, didn't want to alarm Alaina. Zander ordered him to turn around. We sent a backup car right away, but we were too late. One good thing, we were first on the scene, so no police involvement. No one knows she's missing. I'm manning the phones, waiting for some kind of contact. Nick..."

"Find her, Arch, find her. I'm stuck up here at 40,000 feet, just find her. This was planned. Whoever did this knew I was called to New York. Find her!"

Arch could hear the anguish in Nick's voice. It was the quiet before the storm.

Nick paced the planes' interior, his brain racing. *Who of his enemies would do such a vile thing? Could it be a takeover? Could it be the rooftop killer?* He had no answers as he prayed for the plane to fly faster, but instead they hit pocket after pocket of turbulence, forcing him into a seat. With blatant disregard for FCC rules, he kept his cell phone on, waiting, hoping.

Suddenly his phone sprang to life; a video call was coming through. He stared at the flickering grainy image, the transmission poor. It was Alaina, tied to a bed, purple bruising across her neck, a bloody scrape across her forehead. IV tubing was taped to her arm infusing a white solution. Her eyes were closed.

Nick heard a man's muffled voice through the static, watching his gloved hand push his wife's shoulder, "Say it, say it now," the captor demanded.

Her voice was barely a whisper, her words slurred, "Nick, Nick don't come," her voice grew louder with each successive word, "don't come, he wants to kill you, don't..."

"Why, you bitch, that's enough," the male voice commanded, striking Alaina with the back of his hand. "Well, looks like the lady has some fight in her. Wasn't at all what I told her to say but nonetheless you should come soon. Right now, I'm sedating her but tomorrow, she's mine. Better hurry."

Nick could see Alaina struggling in the background. She was pale, bruised, and barely conscious. He screamed into the phone, losing all control, with both Jax and Luca holding him back. "Who are you? What do you want, you bastard? *What do you want?*"

"Want? Why, I want *everything*. Most of all I want your life. Your pretty little wife is only the start. Better call your bank." The voice was venomous, relishing the moment.

The video blacked out, but Nick continued to stare at the phone.

#

Arch was also staring at phones willing them to ring as the hours crawled by in the Vegas office. The worst part about a kidnapping is the waiting. Security was doubled around the complex and Zander and Enzio were at the airfield awaiting their boss's arrival. Others were combing the city desperately seeking information.

Nick stormed into the office, eyes black with rage. He called an immediate war room meeting, gathering his men around him and listening as each offered up theories and possible plans, all awaiting his command. The atmosphere in the room was tense, but the phones remained silent.

There must be something, some clue, something. He scanned the outside street cameras hoping to identify the sedan Bobby had spotted, he dumped Alaina's bag on the table, searched her phone, the house computer feed, *nothing.* He replayed the video of his wife repeatedly, wincing each time the kidnapper struck her. There was nothing identifiable in the background, no noise, no music. He tried focusing on the abductor's voice, his words.

Pretty little wife, Pretty little wife. Where had he heard those words, who talks like that? Think, think! Then suddenly it hit him, a brick wall slamming him in the face with horrid reality. He drew in a sharp breath then raised his eyes to the group, his tight grip shattering the whiskey glass in his hand.

"It's Dominic, Dominic has her," he announced with surety. An eerie silence enveloped the room; they now knew their target.

"Find that bastard *now,* and bring him to me," he screamed as intense torment ripped through his body, and his eyes turned demonic black. "I'll tear his heart out. I'll eat his fuckin' face," he raged.

His head was pounding, blocking out all sound and a stabbing pain pierced his chest. He leaned forward blindly gripping the edge of the desk, his knees weakening. A heavy hand seized his shoulder, yet he stood alone—no one behind him. Then he heard his father's thundering voice in his ears, guiding him from the grave, 'Breathe, Son, breathe, clear your head, think'. An immediate calm washed over him then and the pain in his chest subsided.

He stood erect, calling out orders and seeing every man in the room spring into motion; some checking weapons, others circling awaiting their assignments. Jax and Luca began to strategize. Arch was screaming into the landline to men in the field sending them to search places Dominic was known to frequent: his business, his mistress, his country club, his Calypso suite.

"Quiet!" Nick's ear-piercing scream silenced the room, another video call was coming in. Alaina's blurry image appeared on the screen, her sickening moan tearing at his heart.

The muffled voice at the other end joyfully mocked him. "You'll never find us, tomorrow she is mine and I will fuck her brains out."

"I'll kill you, little brother, I will kill you and enjoy every bloody second," Nick roared.

The caller hesitated, then broke into a sheepish laugh, "So, you figured it out, took you long enough," his ominous voice sneered. "I'm waiting for you, bro. I'm taking everything, your home, your business, your money, and especially your pretty little wife. I'll even take the brat she's growing. You owe me, it all should have been mine, never yours, mine."

The phone went dead, leaving Nick to stare at a cold gray screen. He released a blood curdling scream, before Zander rushed to restrain him, shaking him back to reality.

He willed himself to think. *Where would Dom take her? Where would the little coward go to hide?* And then it came to him, the Big House. He would take her to the Big House where his father had built a series of four underground tunnels leading to safe rooms and the guesthouses behind the house. It was his perfect escape, a maze of connecting tunnels deep in the damp, quiet darkness below.

He quickly divided his men, unlocking the concealed armory hidden behind a false wall in his office, and ordering them to ready their weapons. Dom could not have pulled this off alone, there had to be others. This would be a gun battle.

"I'm going too, she's my mother."

Nick turned, staring into the determined eyes of Matt, his 16-year-old son. "No, you're staying here with Uncle Arch. I won't put a gun in your hand."

But Matt refused to be deterred. In the melee he became invisible, stealthily concealing a Glock 19 in his back waistband and joining the group in the last van, unnoticed.

#

They entered the Big House through a hidden entrance in an exterior rock face at the back of the property. Nick hoped Dominic was unaware of the door, knowing his father's level of distrust for his youngest son. It was quiet, eerily quiet. Dominic had vacated the property months ago after sending his family to Sicily; still, it was *too quiet*. He questioned himself, could he be wrong?

"You're with me," Zander ordered, grabbing Matt by the shirt collar.

The groups worked their way through each tunnel, inching cautiously across the dark spaces, each coming out into the empty first floor kitchen of its corresponding guesthouse. The radios chirped, *"Nothing here, Boss."*

"Nothing here either," another echoed.

There was no sign of Alaina.

Nick's phone rang. "No, no, no, big brother. I'm not in the tunnels, wrong as always. By the way, your wife's not doing too well, little trouble breathing but don't worry, I'm right by her side. Cute tits, by the way." The call ended and Nick's heart sank, his brother was watching them remotely. He had little time to think before a second call came in from Marco Simonelli at the Royale.

"Boss, Mr. Macland had us screening street cameras for a black sedan seen outside your place this morning. We just spotted it at a warehouse across town, 64 Bentley Drive, an abandoned building. Three vans are parked on the west end."

"Son of a bitch," Nick yelled. "Meet me there."

#

Twenty armed men descended on the abandoned warehouse as the Vegas sun lowered in the bleak desert sky. A barrage of gunfire echoed off the rust-stained gray walls shattering the murky windows and sending jagged glass shards clamoring to the floor. Those inside were quickly outnumbered, the concrete awash with pools of blood. Nick scanned the area; eleven men lay dead scattered along the two-story interior. Rico was the only one of his men injured, suffering a flesh wound to the left shoulder. Mandatory monthly practice at the range had paid off.

"Nick... Nick," a raspy voice called, beckoning with a bloody hand from behind a concrete pillar. Tino stepped in front shielding Nick as they both advanced. A bullet ridden Mickey Canale lay dying, gasping for air. "Never meant to hurt your... wi... wife," he sputtered, pointing a mangled hand to an interior door before choking out one final breath.

Nick entered first, surveying the surroundings. Dozens of rusted dust laden machines sat abandoned in the center of a massive metalworks shop. Two open staircases led up to a second level and several long empty hallways lined the perimeter. The air was eerily still. *Good place for an ambush.*

"Spread out," he ordered, motioning for Benny and Jax to take the upper level. The men divided into teams of two and began a thorough search. Zander and Matt veered off to the right finding themselves in another long empty corridor.

"Stay behind me, kid," Zander said before quickly holding up his fist signally Matt to halt. The faint sound of Puccini's *Nessun Dorma* filtered toward them. Zander's fist signaled advance, and both inched forward. Following the music, they edged along the cinder block wall before making a right turn toward a brightly lit room, their presence still hidden. Zander's fist shot up again as he observed a dozen men on patrol, each armed with an M-16 rifle. In the far corner was a four-poster canopy bed draped with silk curtains. Alaina's motionless body lay tucked beneath a snow-white satin quilt, her hair fanned out across a lace pillow. Dominic stood over her, his hand caressing her cheek.

"You're mine now, my beauty. You will never return to him. You belong to me."

"Sick bastard," Zander hissed before calmly whispering into the radio, *"Corridor C, room 109, maintain radio silence."*

Matt began to charge at the sight of his mother, but Zander restrained him.

"Wait," he cautioned, "two against twelve, big guns, wait. Your father will want a piece of this."

The boy stilled, seeing the logic. Within minutes, Nick and a group of ten men quietly filed in behind him. He assessed the scene, seeing his wife's body motionless across the room. *Is she breathing?* Her face was badly bruised but from his vantage point, he couldn't see if her chest was rising.

He held up his fingers signaling the position of the twelve men patrolling the room and assigning who of his own men was to kill each of them. He then lifted his fingers silently counting to three, signaling the fight to begin. The gun fire was deafening as bullets from M-16s sprayed the walls of the quiet room and men fell to the floor, screaming in agony and bathing the floor in blood.

Nick barreled straight for the bed, his focus on his wife just as Dominic turned to face him, oblivious to the scene unfolding around him. Both men briefly made eye contact before Dominic slowly lifted his arm, aimed his Ruger 357 Magnum squarely at his brother and fired off two rounds.

Nick stumbled, the impact from a bullet shattering his left knee; but he continued forward, his focus undeterred, struggling to drag his lame leg behind him as pain coursed through his body. Dominic again took aim and fired as Nick advanced. Grasping his thigh, he fell to the floor, bright red blood spreading across his pant leg.

"NOOO! Don't hurt my dad, nooo...," Matt's trembling voice rang out above the chaos and the world stood still. Nick raised up, watching his young son square his stance and fire the Glock striking his Uncle Dominic in the shoulder. In a blur of black steel, the gun tumbled to the floor as he ran to his father, gently cradling him in his shaking arms.

"I'm sorry, Dad, I'm sorry, I'm sorry for everything."

"It's okay, Son. It's okay."

Dominic paused, confused by the tender father-son exchange and impervious to his own shattered shoulder before drawing in a breath and turning his attention back to the bed. He angrily ripped the IV needle from Alaina's arm, lifting her in his arms. Turning to face the group, he gazed down at the beautiful face of his Alaina, her body cradled against his chest, forever his. Triumphant!

Nick inhaled sharply, motionless at the staggering scene unfolding before him. A sudden sense of icy dread coursed through his veins seeing his wife's limp body. Blinking several times, he willed the illusion to disappear but no, this was no hallucination. Bright red satin bows adorned Alaina's neck, wrists, and ankles.

He stared; his mind paralyzed, unable to comprehend the obvious. His heart was frantically beating, blood rushing to his head, his breathing halted.

Could Dominic be the serial killer? No, impossible, no!

Images of the battered bodies flashed through Nick's mind: the wigs, the ribbons, the anonymous gifts, even Ginny's words 'they all sort of look like Alaina'.

No, no, it couldn't be.

Nick lifted his eyes, seeing his brother's rage pouring forth, forcing him to acknowledge the truth.

Nick's incredulous stare met Dominic's scornful eyes as an eerie telepathic message passed between them.

Yes, it's me, I am the one.

Breaking the connection, Dom inched closer, Alaina's motionless body in his arms. She was his now and no one could take her from him. But something was wrong. His maniacal smile faded, melting into a frightened look of confusion. Alaina's clothes were drenched in dark red blood, her skin was a sickly shade of gray, her lips pale blue.

"No, noo, noo!" Dominic's tortured scream echoed off the cinder block walls, piercing the ears of everyone present as all turned to watch the scene in fearful disbelief.

"Help me, Nick, help me," he cried, and in that moment, Nick was transported back in time seeing a little boy being chased by his schoolmates down Mississippi Avenue, begging to be saved by his big brother.

The smallest spark of sanity returned to Dominic's eyes for mere seconds and Nick reached out, struggling to gain a foothold, "Wait, wait, I'm coming, little brother, wait," he called.

But it was too late, the madness again took control.

As her blood dripped down upon him from above, Dominic reverently lifted Alaina's body high into the air like a human sacrifice. A look of terror crossed his face and in one fear-filled motion, he released his grip causing her to tumble to the ground. The scene unfolded in slow motion. Hands shot up in futile pleas, voices echoed in hollow silence as her frail body plummeted to the floor—her skull making a resounding thud when she hit the concrete.

"Matt, Mattie, help me. Steady my arm." Nick tapped his right shoulder directing the boy and Matt hoisted his father into position, placing his hand under his father's upper arm. A frenzied Dominic rushed toward them, wailing and screeching, as Nick fired off three rounds striking him in the chest, his flailing body falling at Nick's feet.

It was over.

#

"Mr. Rusano, Mr. Rusano, you need to wake up, sir."

Nick opened his eyes, slowly focusing on the smiling face of the middle-aged nurse in blue scrubs, her gray hair tightly permed. Dolly was Alaina's day shift nurse.

"You really shouldn't be here, you know," she whispered, giving him a warm wink.

Nodding, he carefully slid beneath the hoses and tubes, lifting his stiff body from the tiny bed where he had slept every night tight up against Alaina. He hobbled to the chair, watching as Dolly performed the many nursing tasks surrounding his wife's care.

He had been rushed into surgery immediately following the gun battle. His patella and femur were now successfully repaired but he was told to expect a lifelong limp. Alaina had not been as lucky. With a fractured skull and cerebral edema, she lay before him unresponsive, breathing with the help of a ventilator, her body cooled by IV fluids to decrease the brain swelling, her prognosis poor. Additionally, she had lost a profuse amount of blood possibly caused by the placental abruption from the accident's impact. The fetus had died in utero, deprived of oxygen for too long, unable to survive. She was forging her own battle for life, unaware of the fate of their child. Tears formed in his eyes, knowing he was to blame for all her pain.

How could he have missed it? How could he have been so blind? He would never know how many women his brother had killed.

His men had cleared the warehouse leaving no trace of the carnage and he had attributed his own injuries to the careless cleaning of his weapon. Still, there would be investigations the worst being that of the Commission. Nothing escaped them. They could decide to strip him of the Royale and all his other holdings, but none of that mattered now. Everything he had done—every move, every deal, every handshake— had been done for just one woman, the woman that now lay before him, battered and courting death.

Dolly tapped him on the shoulder, jolting him back to the present. "She looks a bit better this morning, more color in her cheeks. Do you want to wash her face today?"

He smiled, limping back to the bed, before lovingly patting her skin and allowing his mind to strip away the dark purple bruises revealing the flawless porcelain beneath. Mesmerized by her angelic beauty, his fingers lightly traced the arch of her brow, the hollow of her cheeks, and the gentle curve of her neck, committing to memory every freckle, every line, every wrinkle and vowing to never let her fade from his memory.

Once again, Dolly's hand fell upon his shoulder, breaking the spell and ripping him from its sweet nirvana. "She can hear you; you know. Talk to her Mr. Rusano, she's listening."

He nodded, his tears falling. "Come back to me, baby," he whispered softly, "please come back. Fight, baby, fight."

Three days passed with each round of administrators and doctors admonishing him for staying with his wife each night, but he remained steadfast watching as the ventilator supplying her oxygen droned on… and he prayed.

He was lightly dozing when he felt it, her finger was brushing his cheek. He jerked, eyes opening wide, seeing her green eyes staring up at him.

"Baby, baby," he cried out, before running for the nurse. When he returned, Alaina was struggling with the ventilator tube trying to pull it from her windpipe, but he quickly stopped her. She relaxed her grip, understanding but confused by her surroundings. Her eyes returned his smile as he clung to her hand, trying his best to comfort her.

Hours later, when the tubes and hoses were removed and the parade of doctors and technicians finally left them alone, he held her, rocking her gently as she sobbed for their stillborn son, his tears joining hers in mutual grief.

Aftermath

He was pacing, anxious to take her from this depressing hospital filled with endless, blaring emergency calls and the harried faces of doctors responding to them. *How do people heal in hospitals?* She would require months of rehab due to the brain trauma and, even though her physical injuries would heal quickly, her memory had been affected. Six months, they told him. Whatever returned in six months would be the maximum she would recall. There were memories he wished would never return, painful memories he himself had caused. But that was not his call, she would remember what she could. Her brain needed to heal. He questioned his own strength and chastised himself every day for attending that New York funeral and leaving her alone.

Looking back, he realized it was the visit to the morgue that tipped her over the edge, spiraling her mind into the depths of despair. She had been adamant, demanding to say goodbye to that sweet, innocent babe that had been so viciously ripped from their lives. And so, he stood beside her as she reached with trembling fingers to stroke the cheek of their unborn son.

"Nick, he's cold. He needs a blanket."

"Hon?"

"HE NEEDS A BLANKET!"

Nick looked to the compassionate clerk who quickly retrieved a woolen cloth and, with a mother's resolve, she meticulously swaddled the babe.

"That's better," she whispered while cradling him close to her heart. "I'm sending you to your grandfather until we see each other again. Papa Rusano will keep you safe." Then with tear filled eyes, she kissed his forehead before reluctantly surrendering him back to the clerk. "Keep him warm for me, please."

"I will, madam."

But time was no salve to her pain, and he grew increasingly worried about her mental stability. One afternoon he found her in the greenhouse staring into emptiness, frozen deep within a catatonic refuge. Several minutes passed before he was able to break through; patiently kneeling by her side and softly calling her name. When he tried to help her stand, she collapsed, sobbing uncontrollably in his arms as they both inched down the wall to the cold cement floor below. He held her tightly, angered by his inability to soothe her, his own tears falling with hers.

He monitored her movements after that, scanning the surveillance cameras even during office meetings, and opting to send Jackson or Luca on all necessary business trips. He lingered longer over morning coffee, watching as she moved robotically in vacant motion.

It was Little Sam that ultimately rescued her, his pleading brown eyes breeching the battlements of her anguish. The little boy needed his mother and Nick realized that she also needed him more than ever before.

"No, Daddy, you don't understand! Only Mommy can teach me my times tables. We play hopscotch, jump the numbers, and... then I get it," he announced, twisting his lips to the side, hands on hips. "Now where is she? Mommy, Mommy," he screeched, running in search of her after school one day. And so, it was their youngest son that reached down through her sorrow. There was Sam's homework and little league practice, his nightly bath and story ritual and soon she seemed herself again, but Nick still worried.

Only a few minor incidents occurred after the greenhouse, one prominent in his memory. She was in the kitchen making kolache, a recipe passed down from her grandmother. It was too quiet, and Nick looked up from his paper; Alaina stood motionless, staring into the mixing bowl.

"Honey?"

She turned to him, bewildered. "I don't know how much yeast I need. I've made this recipe a hundred times and I can't remember," she replied, slamming her fist on the counter.

Seeing her frustration, he rushed to hold her. "Angel, angel, calm down, calm down for me. Breathe... slow."

But she only shook her head, sobbing. "I can't remember."

"Sweetheart, look at me. It's in there, it's in your head, it's there. It's just in the back of the filing cabinet. You haven't needed that memory for a while, your brain is prioritizing other bits of information but it's in there, angel, it's in there."

But instead of comfort she grew increasingly upset, striking his shoulder with her palm, "I don't want your pity, Nick!" she shrieked. "You should have divorced me, moved in one of your women. Now I'm just a burden to you, don't you see?"

"What! What are you saying?" he cried, staring down at her. "Don't you ever say that. I never want to hear those words again. Do you hear me?" He quickly raised both his hands and tore at his shirt, sending buttons flying across the floor and banging his fist on his shoulder. "What does this say? Read it to me, Alaina."

She looked up, tearfully reading the words from his tattoo. "Alaina, the only woman I will ever love until my dying breath."

Folding her back into his arms, he held her close, soothing her with his voice. "Those are not empty words to me, sweetheart. I love you. I will be with you always; I will never let you go. Do you understand that? We have been to hell and back; we have stared down the devil. Together we can battle *anything… even yeast!"

Laughter broke through her tears giving way to a smile before he squeezed her to his chest.

True Confessions

Nick assigned a new driver to Alaina after the tragic loss of Bobby, finding Gianni Brambilla to be the perfect choice. The young man was strong and quick witted but most importantly a crack shot with a pistol.

Gianni enjoyed his new assignment. Mrs. Rusano was a kind woman, and he was proud that he was among those called upon to rescue her at the warehouse. But today Gianni stood nervously before Nick, worried that he had already done something wrong while driving the boss's wife.

"Gianni, how's Mrs. Rusano treating you?" Nick asked.

"Just fine, Boss. She's a nice lady."

"Yes, she is. I need you to keep her safe, as we discussed. However, I have a question. You leave the complex every morning around the same time, where are you taking her? I know she can't be getting her nails done that often," Nick queried, laughing.

"Um, well, on Mondays and Thursdays we go to the memory doctor for Mrs. Rusano's therapy, Boss; but every day, whether she has an appointment or not, Mrs. Rusano has me take her to church," he stammered, nervously shifting foot to foot.

"Church? Mass?" Nick knew Alaina was religious, but she never went to Mass every day.

"No, Boss. Mrs. Rusano just wants me to drive her to the church. She sits in one of the back pews, sometimes for an hour, sometimes longer. I think she's praying, Boss. Although... I have seen her cry, but mostly she just sits there. That new priest comes out to talk to her sometimes, but mostly she just sits, like I said. I keep watch, don't worry, she's safe. I won't let anyone near her, Boss, ever." He paused, seeing Nick staring intensely. "Um, sometimes she has an errand, but usually I just bring her straight home after that."

Nick digested the young man's words. He was worried about Alaina, knowing she was still grieving. He needed to think further.

#

Two days later, Alaina sat in her usual pew, buried deep in reflection, seeking the comfort of her God. She felt a hand softly reach for hers, jerking her from her thoughts. Looking up she watched her husband bend to say a prayer upon the kneeler before sitting beside her and reaching to hold her. Together they silently prayed, allowing their shared grief to slowly ebb.

Alaina heard the apse door open, seeing Father Mike come from behind the altar and approach Nick.

"Are you ready, my son?" he asked, placing his palm on Nick's shoulder, and leading him to the confessional.

Nick Rusano never committed another violent act after that day.

PART THREE

Easy Money, High Price

Anger and poverty cause men to make desperate decisions. Prison systems nationwide can attest to that fact. Historically, Las Vegas casinos have been prime targets for ill-conceived robberies and numerous thefts; most unsuccessful and sloppy, performed by small time amateurs. Hollywood romanticizes this folly producing films of daredevil heists by teams of pretty boy actors claiming intimate knowledge of in-house security.

Recently a string of robberies plagued downtown Fremont Street. Two smaller casinos were targeted; the thieves assuming security was not as strong in the downtown area. A third, more brazen robbery followed soon after. Suzy Scatter's, a cozy slot parlor located on the edge of Las Vegas Boulevard was the target. The thieves boldly entered in broad daylight, allowing dozens of horrified tourists and employees to witness the event. Their disregard for human life was apparent when a hapless security guard suffered a fractured jaw after being rammed in the face with a rifle butt. That incident struck a nerve with casino owners along the Strip as they watched the thieves inch closer to the big money. Would they attempt to rob a major casino knowing their chances of apprehension would be vastly increased due to the high-quality surveillance? A sharp turn to the right onto Las Vegas Boulevard would set the Royale Casino directly in their path.

Every casino boss was nervous, rarely leaving his or her property, and monitoring internal security around the clock. Nick had not been home for two weeks, sleeping in his suite and issuing strict orders that the family was not to leave the complex. Ominous electricity pulsed in his veins, he could feel it, taste it. Blood would spill, he could smell it.

Tonight, the city was on high alert, the air filled with a jittery sweat blanketing those in the know. An anonymous tip had been received by local law enforcement, one of the major casinos on the Strip was tonight's target. The FBI reacted quickly; their agents disguising themselves in gaudy tropical print shirts and blending in with hordes of unsuspecting tourists. Dozens of police cruisers stealthily patrolled the streets, unmarked vehicles were stationed in darkened corners, and undercover detectives dressed as bums sauntered drunkenly along garbage filled alleys. Tensions were high.

And then it happened, quickly, sharply, without warning.

The ear-splitting crack of a rifle blast shattered the quiet hum of the casino floor, assaulting the ears of everyone in the room. The echo reverberated off the ceiling resonating for several long seconds. The air filled with an acrid smell singeing nostrils and assailing the tearing eyes of those nearby. Sparkling crystals on overhanging chandeliers clattered from above and drink glasses rattled on tables below, sending amber liquid spilling over the rims. All heads turned toward the sound, their bodies paused in mid motion; hands slowly lowered dice to tables below, roulette wheels spun slowly to a halt. No one spoke.

Three gunmen stood before the window of the main bank recklessly pointing their weapons at a frightened female worker, her eyes wide with panic. Their faces were covered with black and white skeletal masks, eyes barely visible through thin slits in the rubber. Each was armed with an M16 assault rifle, and additional 9mm handguns were strapped to their sides.

The leader stepped forward, firing off a second blast in an unsuccessful attempt to break the bulletproof reinforced glass. Nick had been standing alongside Marco Simonelli, his Chief of Internal Security, one thousand feet away in the poker lounge; both men deep in conversation when the unmistakable sound assaulted their ears. He quickly turned, catapulting over a brass railing, and knocking over several chairs in his path. Racing toward the cage window, he drew his own Glock 40 from its holster. The scene evolved in slow motion as dozens of his men sprinted across the casino floor from varying directions, Jackson running fearlessly alongside his father in full stride.

The robbers appeared nonplussed as they were surrounded, even chuckling to each other. "No one gets hurt if you give up the money," roared a gravelly voice distorted by a mouthpiece imbedded beneath the mask.

Nick now stood eight feet from the thief; his own pistol drawn and aimed precisely at the intruder's head. He assessed his opponent, six-foot tall, solid muscular build, military trained by the way he held his weapon. His companions were lightweights, one shaking nervously as he eyed the massive amount of firepower surrounding them.

"You'll never get out of here, put the gun down while there's still time," Nick sneered, in full command.

"Oh, I think we will unless you want to see this sweet lady's lovely face plastered all over your carpet," replied the leader, quickly tossing his rifle to his companion and grabbing a shaking female dealer from a nearby blackjack table. Using her body as a shield, he jammed the 9mm under his squirming captive's chin; it's barrel cutting into her windpipe and leaving her gulping for air.

"Now let's stop the heroics, pretty boy, and give up the money. I don't mean the small stuff either, I want the big money in the back, you know what I'm talking about."

Both men's frigid stares collided in an intense battle of unflinching power for several endless seconds before Nick spoke, his weapon still pointed at the robber's head. "You can have *all* the money, every dime as long as no one gets hurt. Let the girl go and I'll take you to the money."

"No, no, that's not the way this works. I make the rules here, money first," he scoffed.

Nick's eyes remained locked on the gunman's in a venomous duel as the white noise of the casino droned on in the background. Rows of empty slot machines continued playing their endless musical chimes. A lounge singer performed a sound check on a microphone down the hall, oblivious to the scene taking place five hundred feet away. A lonely maintenance worker swept cigarette butts from the floor, headphones shielding him from the chaos.

Outside, multiple police cruisers could be heard screeching into the driveway, their tires peeling and sirens blaring, depositing dozens of armed officers onto the casino floor with weapons drawn. But in the tight little circle of fifty men, all with guns in hand, the room remained deathly silent, all eyes riveted on the unyielding challenge of only two men. No one dared move.

"Um, excuse me, sir, I think you dropped this." The shaking arthritic hand of a crippled Coinman Marcus tugged on the sleeve of the third member of the gang, offering the nervous gunman a shiny black $100 chip from his open palm.

Bystanders froze, watching in horror as the stunned gunman savagely shoved the frail octogenarian to the floor, "Get away from me, you old fool!"

An audible gasp resounded inciting the crowd into action. Several people instinctively surged forward, crying out in protest, and triggering a turbulent riot to erupt within seconds.

Nick caught a glimpse of his son through the barrage of flying fists as Jackson jumped in front of the hostage knocking the 9mm away from her chin seconds before it exploded in a deafening blast. Terrified screams filled the air and Jackson fell to the floor, clutching his chest, bright red blood immediately soaking his suit jacket just as Nick felt a massive force connect with his own shoulder, sending his body careening to the left away from the gunman. He turned in a daze experiencing a lapse of sanity as he watched a perfectly coifed Elvis leap from the crowd in a white jeweled pantsuit and sunglasses. The King squared his stance, and fired off two shots center mass within seconds, instantly killing the gang's leader.

#

The hospital waiting room was busy with wall-to-wall tourists sporting blistered heels and sprained ankles. Nick stared at the overhead television watching talking-head newscasters fill the airways with frightening details of the robbery. The tourists weren't listening, thinking it was just another publicity stunt; their priority being a swift return to the frenzied Strip to secure their $40 photo-op with Caesar and Cleopatra.

A drug groggy Jackson lay in an ER bay awaiting surgery to repair his left shoulder. He was lucky, there was no major organ damage. He would need months of physical therapy to regain his muscle strength, but he remained in good spirits, his sense of humor intact, "Hey Dad, at least it wasn't my shooting arm."

But Nick was not in a joking mood as he sat morosely taking stock of his life. Today he nearly lost his oldest son, he recklessly stared down a crazed gunman yielding an M16 assault rifle, one of his employees was nearly killed, and his own life was saved by an Elvis impersonator. That part at least was comical.

Alaina was on her way, and he nervously watched the entrance. She had seen the news reports and his call to her an hour previous had done little to placate her. She needed to visibly see her husband and son. He jumped from the chair, catching her in his arms when she barreled through the emergency room doors, tears gushing from her swollen eyes. Her trembling hands reached for him, tracing his face, arms, and chest, giving her visible assurance that he was uninjured.

"Jackson, I need to see Jackson."

"I know, but he needs to see the face of his tough warrior mother, not her tears. Catch your breath for me first, honey."

He recognized the pain behind her practiced facade as he led her to their son's bedside, watching as she reached for Jackson's face. Her baby boy was hurt and even though a grown man lay upon those stark white sheets, Nick knew she only saw her sweet, injured baby helpless in the bed. How much more could she take before her mind again retreated to the safety of its catatonic abyss? How much more damage could this town inflict upon them all?

A familiar dull ache traveled across his chest, its duration longer than before.

Chasing Redemption

The first sign of any health problems occurred the day Alaina threatened to leave him at the cove. Her angry revelations jolted him into a reality he had not foreseen. He felt just the smallest amount of discomfort in his heart that night. It was brief, lasting only a few seconds and he waved it off. Between the problems he was having with his marriage back then, the ever-growing pressures from the business, and his criminal responsibilities, he didn't have time for medical nonsense.

Then came Alaina's kidnapping, his brother's death, and his own knee repair. During that hospital stay, his EKG showed irregularities and a blockage in one of the major vessels of his heart. He kept that knowledge to himself, sharing only with Archer.

The doctors cautioned him. He had a family history, they said. He didn't live healthily, they said, too many rich foods, too much alcohol. But in Nick's mind, he was invincible, choosing instead to ignore his body's signals and live in a perpetual state of denial.

But the bouts of chest pain grew more frequent, and his doctors agreed that triple bypass surgery was the only solution. With luck he might have five good years left. His father was already gone by this age.

Alaina was unable to attend his latest doctor's appointment due to a sprained ankle, giving him an excuse to delay the surgery. She would insist on immediate intervention, but his priorities were elsewhere. He met with Arch ensuring that all his legal documents were in order and that Alaina was protected should things not go as planned. As for his sons, he was leaving them a financial empire. He had long ago followed Arch's advice, carefully moving the chess pieces, hiding money, increasing personal investments, all to ensure the security of his children's future, all in keeping firm with his ten-year plan to relinquish his Mafia ties. Only the Commission could stand in the way of his freedom.

It is essential that a don's hospital stay be brief. There are always those who contemplate power grabs and Nick's territory was highly lucrative. His many enemies could not know of his weakened state. Security around the complex was tripled, all meetings cancelled, no visitors allowed. His sons would handle all business matters just as he had done for his own father, but Nick knew from experience that no amount of planning could stop a bullet.

Alaina remained at his side following the surgery, and within forty-eight hours he was sent home to recuperate. As with his father, Daniella visited daily to check on his recovery. Tino devised a daily exercise regimen to help him regain strength and Zander monitored his progress in the lap pool each morning. His daylight hours were filled but each evening as the sun withdrew and nightfall approached, his past deeds came calling, haunting his dreams.

"No, put it back," he cried, pushing her hand away.

"Honey, it's your pain pill."

"I know what it is, I don't want it," diverting his eyes, his reply harsh.

Sitting on the side of the bed, she questioned him, "Nick, what's wrong?"

His lower lip began to tremble, but he continued to stare at the sheets. "It makes me dream."

She had witnessed his restless sleep, his mumbling, twitching, and flailing arms; pushing each night to extend his waking hours much like a teenager begging more time.

Moving to lay beside him, she began to stroke his brow, trailing soft fingertips along his hairline and temple. "Talk to me, love, tell me what's troubling you."

Perspiration was forming above his upper lip, his eyes pools of frightening dread. He reached for her hand and pressed her palm to his heart, "I'm afraid, Laine, really afraid."

Terror rose in his eyes, as if seeing someone that wasn't there and he froze before gripping her wrist with viselike fingers, his words tumbling out in anguished pleas, "Stay with me, don't leave me, tell me you won't leave me."

"Oh honey, I won't leave you, I'll stay right here, right by your side."

"You don't understand; I've… I've done things, horrible things. I've hurt people, I've killed people, Laine."

He was hallucinating and she sought words to calm him. "No, no, sweetheart, listen to me. You are a good man, you have always been a good man, but right now you need sleep."

"No pills!"

"No, darling, no pills." Guiding him to her bosom, she cradled him in maternal warmth, gentling rocking him as mother to child and with each rise of her chest he felt his heartbeat meld with hers. "Now close your eyes, my prince."

He could barely hear her voice as she sang her lullaby; nor could he feel her feathery caress. Floating upon a blissful sea, he succumbed, allowing her inner angel to battle his demons.

Just When You Thought

Nick had long been an equal member of the Commission, a powerful don in his own right, controlling all mob interests throughout the entire west coast. He had served the Mafia his entire life, following orders, never asking questions, making his first sanctioned kill over five decades earlier before the age of twenty. How many had he killed since then, all for the advancement of the families. On the day of his fateful meeting with the other members of the Commission, he was worried, but he hoped if he were able to present his case successfully, they might be convinced to release him. He was wrong!

He sat pensively observing the crowded table of aging dons, most fat with their wealth. Some brought along their sons or underbosses, all eagerly awaiting their own advancement. It was the young ones you had to worry about, they were reckless, hungry for power. Only his friend, Emile knew of his planned proposal. He would make his request to retire at the end of business, allowing the group to debate after he left the room. They would undoubtedly hand down their decision the following morning giving him no clue as to the outcome until then. He had carefully planned for this day, having already handed most of his responsibilities over to his two oldest sons. Jackson had assumed full control of the Royale immediately upon his Princeton graduation. Then, shortly after Dominic's demise, Nick gained control of the Calypso property along with a financial percentage of the profits. It required little of his time, still being in its growth stage. He had amassed large pieces of real estate surrounding the property and he sat with Luca whenever possible outlining the expansion. His plan had neatly fallen into place allowing him to place the Calypso into the capable hands of his son a few years later. Both properties were thriving.

Nick also divided his Mafia interests throughout the west coast, ensuring that every capo in every city knew to report to both his sons, cementing their loyalty. He had built a lifelong reputation of firm control through negotiation and violence, training his sons well; they were always by his side. If anything, they had proven to be even more blood thirsty, maintaining control through fear of retribution in all business dealings. The three men together were ruthless. Nick presented his case to the Commission, citing his recent triple bypass and the doctor's five-year prognosis. He spoke of his wife's fragile mental condition and her need for constant care (untrue). She had family in California, and he wanted to move her closer to them (untrue). He outlined his plan to distribute his responsibilities between his two sons who had already pledged their loyalty to the Mafia. He ended by thanking the other members of the Commission for their time stating that he would await their decision. He then retired to his suite, made a quick call home, drank a few glasses of whiskey, and stared out at the dismal Chicago cityscape wanting only solitude. His ten-year plan was nearing its end.

The Verdict

The following morning, the Commission passed down their decision. They all agreed that his family had suffered and that he was forced to kill his own brother during the kidnapping incident. However, the Commission viewed that simply as a personal matter of jealousy between two brothers over a mere woman, having nothing to do with business. They recognized the heinous toll it had taken on his family and uncharacteristically sympathized seeing his cardiac surgery as a possible result of that occurrence. Rarely does anyone walk away from their Mafia obligations and Nick Rusano was no exception. He was still young, they said, not yet seventy years old. He had made millions, they said, because of the Mafia's skillful investing. Consequently, he would agree to oversee Mob interests in the minimally troublesome states of Oregon and Washington, allowing him to make the move to California. The remainder of his west coast interests, including the Royale and Calypso, would be divided equally between Jax and Luca. However, Nick would continue to counsel them. Their future in the organization would be determined after his death. The Commission had plans to expand its influence west of Chicago, three Rusanos would be beneficial to all. Nick was livid. He had given a lifetime of service, murdered dozens without question, padded their coffers with billions of dollars, and made numerous personal sacrifices. His jaw clenched in anger when they passed down their verdict; but he was aware that a challenge would only result in retaliation, putting his family in danger.

Jax and Luca warily watched their father during the hours-long plane ride home. Nick's eyes darkened with the intense anger they both knew well as he stared silently out the cabin window. He contemplated his next move, weighing the dangerous option of rebellion and listing his vulnerabilities. He knew he had not hidden his displeasure well; his face unable to mask his anger. He would need to lock down for a few months, increase security, see if anyone made a move against his family. These were dangerous times.

Months passed and no threats materialized. Over concern for his friend's safety, Emile called several times warning Nick of the volatile rumblings occurring within the east coast families. The Commission tested the loyalty of the Rusano family during that same period. One such test involved sending Luca to kill one of his old college buddies who was running an independent counterfeiting trade between New York City and Columbia. Luca did not flinch; he was as cold-hearted as his father when it came to business, and he carried out the hit expeditiously.

Jax' test was also personal, ordering him to execute a woman he previously dated who was about to testify against a Mob associate in Milwaukee. She had witnessed a murder inside a brewery and was currently in protective custody safeguarded by federal agents. Money can buy any type of information and her location was quickly revealed. It proved an easy body snatch after that. Jax had a penchant for elaborate violence and since he had his private pilot's license by then, he simply dropped her out of a low flying plane over Lake Erie assisted by a Milwaukee capo.

As for Nick himself, he received several visits from other Commission members and their sons just *wanting to enjoy a friendly weekend* at the Royale.

Message received.

Nick Rusano had offered up two of his sons in exchange for his freedom. It was his biggest regret. They both loved the life now, but he knew they would grow to despise it just as he did.

Life Beyond the Chains

Their anniversary was approaching, and Nick thought it an ideal time to show Alaina both California properties, telling her to pack for a week and promising a long scenic drive with plenty of stops along the way. San Francisco greeted them with a blanket of thick fog on the morning of their departure, but by the time they stood beneath the majestic redwoods, the sun shone brightly.

He proudly showcased the Napa property, detailing his plans for Matt and Joe Macland, assuring her that neither boy would ever be involved in any Mob activity. They then continued north enjoying the slow scenic drive up the coast, allowing the refreshing Pacific Ocean breezes to fill their senses, and erase the cruel remnants of Las Vegas from their minds. The sea called to them, and they lingered; watching waves break against the rocky shoreline while strolling hand in hand on the pristine shore.

His mood was solemn as he drew her close, "How did time slip away from us, Laine? Where did the years go? I look at you and I see that same young girl on our wedding day, so filled with hopes and dreams. I hear that same laugh, see that same twinkle in your eyes. I had so many plans for us, so much I wanted to show you, to give you. Tell me something, is there anything… anything you want that you don't already have? Tell me, tell me now."

"Want? Oh love, there is nothing that I *want*." She felt herself beginning to tremble, fearful of the path this conversation was taking. "You've given me a lifetime of your love; if anything, I want to turn back the clock, to relive every single day from the first moment we met."

Remorse poured from his eyes, "Oh woman, I only wish I could buy us more time. Damned heart!"

She spun from him, releasing a deep sob, unable to see the cresting waves through her overflowing tears. But he quickly turned her about, cradling her face in his hands.

"No, no, where is my Boudica, my valiant warrior woman? Shh… shh…."

"Your Boudica kneels at the feet of her Roman god, refusing to let him go, she wants to lay in his arms forever," she sobbed as he wiped away her tears.

"Hmm, my queen wants to lay in my arms, huh? What do you say we make love in the sand, shock all these young ones?"

"You're making a joke to distract me."

"Not working?"

She raised her hand to gently caress his cheek, "No, not one bit. Honey, you are going to prove those doctors wrong; you'll see. You are the strongest man I know. We will walk every day, we'll exercise. Instead of five years, you'll live ten, maybe twenty."

Nick inwardly smiled at her optimism, but he knew the truth—five years at the most, the damage to his heart was irreparable.

They continued north, each keeping the conversation light and allowing the imposing landscape to be the temporary ether to their despair. She looked quizzically when he swerved onto a dirt road.

"I think we're lost. Let's climb up the hill, maybe I can see the road and get my bearings," he replied, grabbing her hand, and pulling her from the car.

An osprey saluted them with his regal call as they climbed, and the majestic redwoods baptized them with their refreshing perfume as they climbed, but seeing her joy when her eyes alighted on the crystal lake below proved his choice correct.

"So, what do you think, should we build our dream home here?"

Turning, she saw his wide grin of satisfaction realizing they were not lost, this was part of his plan. "Are you serious? Are you saying this is ours?" she cried.

"Well, you did tell me how beautiful Northern California was. Happy Anniversary, gorgeous," he replied, drawing her in for a gentle kiss.

As they explored the property, he presented his tentative plan for the layout: the boat dock, the porch, the fireplace; but she was no longer listening, still mesmerized by the shimmering water beneath.

"Oh, love, it's breathtaking, it's… it's a mountain paradise floating in the clouds. I can't wait. How long do you think it will take?" she exclaimed; her eyes wide with glee.

"I'd like to be out of Vegas in a year, do you think you can do that?"

"I can be ready in a month," she laughed.

"Well, I suppose we could speed things up by eliminating the kitchen since you don't intend to cook but… only if you swear to become a nudist up here in the wilderness," he teased.

"I can't do that; I'll scare the bears!"

#

Construction began immediately. Nick sat with Alaina over breakfast each morning designing their dream home, a three-story spilt level with graduated stone steps leading down to the boat dock. They opted for pacific northwestern decor with beamed ceilings, tall glass windows to enhance the mountain views, and colorful Navajo rugs. The highlight, of course, was the floor to ceiling fireplace, their special place where they would still hold each other and talk into the night.

The transition was flawless, but before the move, Nick met with Jax and Luca. "I have no intention of covering Oregon and Washington, as infinitesimal as that may be. Traffic in and out of Canada alone could prove to be a problem in the future," he vehemently announced.

"We'll take it, Dad, no problem," they concurred, their voices chiming out as one.

All three men drove north to Portland and Seattle the following week cementing their authority with the local capos and establishing chain of command. Nick was still bitter by the Commission's ruling, but he cautiously tempered those feelings putting the protection of his family above all else.

Inky Skies and Wooly Socks

Nick rose early most mornings. It was his favorite time of day when he could breathe in the crisp air and listen to the gentle call of the osprey overhead. He couldn't imagine a better place to spend his remaining years. He was finally at peace, finally able to tamp down the violent events that haunted him. Alaina slept in a little longer these days but when she did wake, she would find him quietly reclining on the porch in his big, cushioned chair, eyes glued to the skies, waiting to share a carafe of coffee with her before breakfast.

They found themselves cloaked in a blanket of serenity as the tall fragrant pine trees and mist covered hills cast their spell and the days eclipsed to weeks, and weeks to months. A continuous parade of wildlife entertained them daily from the rocks below followed each evening by an aerial ballet of red-tailed hawks and fireflies dancing across the moonlit sky. They languished in the calm, drifting in the gentle nights, she wrapped in her cashmere shawl and wooly socks and he with his warm arm around her, sharing whiskey and wine.

Nick often lingered long after Alaina gave in to sleep, staring into the darkness and listening to the call of wolves, but it wasn't nature's wolves that troubled him, it was the two-legged predators from his past. Security was his primary concern even after installing the finest high-tech equipment available. He remained vigilant; he still had enemies and would until his last day. Haunting him always was the possibility of retribution from his brother's children and, although they lived in Sicily and had been silent for years, they remained a perpetual threat blaming him and Alaina for their father's death, refusing to recognize his insanity.

Zander and Tino resided nearby. Both married showgirls and now had young families of their own, but their move to California was never in question. They proudly protected Nick, having each sworn a lifetime vow. Henry and Hildy made the move also, delighted to continue to serve the couple.

Archer and Janie built their home just a quick five-minute walk down the hill. A consigliere serves for the life of his don but the two remained best friends often smoking cigars on the porch and drinking into the night, grateful to have put their Mafia days behind them. Daniella finally divorced Archer and married a prominent thoracic surgeon. Her career had always been her priority, and she never could come to terms with Arch's second family.

Matt partnered with Joe Macland and converted the Napa property into a first-class resort, naming it the Restless Roan Ranch. Two years after opening, they proudly introduced a line of fine wines from the Roan vineyards, and they ventured into the world of champion horse racing; breeding and training quality thoroughbreds. The families gathered each year to celebrate the holidays among its peaceful sloping hills exactly as Nick had dreamed.

Sam received an offer to join the minor leagues. Excelling at baseball, he credited his big brother Matt for their many hours of practice.

Sadly, word of Ginny's death reached Alaina not long after she and Nick left Vegas. Ginny never did reconcile with her rodeo chasing husband but instead left the Royale to care for her dying mother. Ginny herself passed shortly after, succumbing to cirrhosis of the liver due to excessive alcohol abuse. But Alaina's vision of her friend remained unchanged, she remembered Ginny as a hard living, flamboyant showgirl who lived every day to the fullest, truly a beautiful woman.

Nick also experienced a loss. Emile Monserrat, his longtime friend from New Orleans, was stabbed twenty-seven times and left to die in a Bourbon Street gutter. His demise was not the result of a Mafia hit, but instead that of the misplaced indignation of a drunken Mardi Gras reveler.

Vegas was behind them now. The cost of their escape was high, both physically and emotionally. Nick's cardiac problems only worsened, his heart unresponsive to myriad daily medications. Alaina's memory had long ago returned but she experienced occasional unsteadiness which doctors attributed to spinal nerve damage from the fall. Nick lovingly nicknamed her *pinball,* and he held her tightly during their morning walks as she scouted for her favorite visitors: Bright Eyes-a young doe, Tippy-a gray rabbit, and her favorite, Ginger-a three-legged fox. Boating remained their greatest joy and when the weather was good, they spent afternoons on the water blanketed in their love while watching the sun disappear beyond the horizon.

The seasons slipped away and the serene stillness of the California hills worked its magic on their souls as their devotion for each other deepened.

Sono Andati

"Hey old lady, just how old are you now?"

"What? What kind of question is that?"

"Well, you have a birthday coming up right?

"*You know* perfectly well how old I am, you fresh thing."

"Probably time I trade you in for a showgirl," his mischievous grin teased.

"What is this about, *old man*?"

"Ha!" He wrapped her in his arms, his touch still electric, "Well, I was thinking I might take my old lady dancing for her birthday."

Alaina's eyes lit up, remembering her first birthday with him. "The Royale?"

"No, no! I have somewhere different in mind," grinning and giving her a squeeze. "You'll see, I've arranged something very special for my *old* lady."

Six days later

Alaina stood in the mirror wearing the silver gossamer dress he had bought so many years ago. It was the most exquisite dress she had ever owned, having carefully preserved it, never wanting a single stain to mar its beauty. The crystals still glistened in her palm; the luminous pearls still dripped elegantly from the sleeves. I'm not the girl I used to be, she thought, staring back at her aging reflection. She walked into their bedroom where he patiently sat, looking dashing as ever in his silver tux and his eyes widened, admiring her beauty.

"I'm afraid it's a bit tighter," she sighed with trepidation.

"No, you look exquisite, woman. To me, you are Venus walking." Crossing the room, he passionately kissed her lips as the opening sounds of Vivaldi floated up from below. "Hmm, I think they're calling us, need to continue this later," he winked. "C'mon, beautiful, time to celebrate."

"Oh Nick, wait. I don't think I can wear these heels anymore, I'm afraid I'll fall." A frown crossed her face, dangling the silver stilettoes from that long ago night.

"Don't worry, you'll never leave my arms tonight," he replied, lifting and cradling her as they descended the stairs.

The garden

Magic ruled the night as they danced beneath a canopy of twinkling stars and sparkling lights strung throughout the trees. The sweet scents of honeysuckle and crisp pine perfumed the air, and a chorus of fireflies joined them in their waltz. The musicians played softly, but they remained oblivious, captivated by the spell of their passion. He held her close, hesitant to release her from his arms even when the music paused. Whispering words of love, his soft lips nuzzled her ear and kissed her neck, sending shivers down her spine.

"Oh love, how is it that after all these years, I still melt in your arms?" she breathlessly murmured.

"And you, my beautiful darling, are still able to calm me with your touch," he answered, lifting her hand to his lips before cupping it to his heart. "I've always felt there was power in these fingers. I want to hold you in my arms for eternity, *mia amata*. You forever remain my cherished angel.

The following morning
She sprang from the bed anxious to hug him, to kiss him, to thank him for such a glorious birthday, knowing he would be waiting on the porch.

The crisp air filled her lungs and icy tentacles shot upward through her bare feet, as she beheld the magnificent mountain vista. "Ohh, honey, what a gorgeous sunrise!" A majestic osprey swooped into view, and she stood mesmerized watching his aerial ballet. "Look at that!" she exclaimed, pointing upward before excitedly turning toward him.

But he did not respond. She hesitated, her mind desperately denying what her eyes revealed. Nick's head was bent into his chest, his eyes closed, his body slouched to one side.

"Nick, honey... Nick... Nick?" She rushed to him, dropping to her knees, frantically grasping his shoulders with trembling hands, desperate to wake him, "Nicky, Nicky…," she cried out.

But he was gone. His head lobbed toward her, unresponsive; his arm dropped to his side, his body was already cold. She gently lifted his face, cradling him in both palms, "No, no, my prince, no, no, no. Don't leave me, I beg you please, don't leave me." Crashing waves of vertigo overcame her, sending opposing streams of biting cold and searing heat coursing through her veins. Her breath caught in her throat, and she struggled for air as a deluge of tears burst forth and she crushed his limp body to hers continuing to beg, "Please, God, no. Please give him back to me, please."

"Madam, madam, you must come away. Madam, please, let us help you. Please, madam, you must let go."

She heard Henry's faint voice as he wrapped his hand around hers attempting to release her frozen grip from Nick's sagging form. Strong arms lifted her upward, cloaking her frigid body in a blanket, and Tino's blurry face loomed above her as he carried her into the house. She heard familiar voices, maybe Arch and Janie, she wasn't sure. There were strangers' voices too, but she didn't know who and she didn't care as long as she remained by his side. Through streaming tears, she lay next to him then, clinging to his chest, and speaking soft words of love that only his spirit could hear.

Hundreds attended the funeral of Nick Rusano, paying respect to the powerful Don feared by so many but also remembered for his multitude of good works within the Italian community. Alaina stood strong supported by her sons. She thought herself fortunate, he had loved her, cherished her, protected her throughout their years together and only she knew the bottomless depth of his tenderness.

Angry Thunder

"Mom, I still think you're making a mistake. This is not what Dad wanted," Jackson protested.

"Oh honey, we just had this discussion. I understand you're worried, but this is my decision. Now, that's the end of it. Go home, I'll call if I need anything." *He is a good son, so much like his father;* but she wanted to be alone, to be with her Nick, knowing his spirit remained in the home they both loved.

Jackson shook his head; he should have insisted that she remain in Vegas but instead he chose not to wrangle with her stubbornness. She was grieving, too lost in her pain, unaware of the reasons for his concern and the danger surrounding her. But he was fraught with tension, his mind racing with apprehension since the day of his father's burial when the past slammed into the present. Across the lush green lawn of the cemetery, he had spotted a familiar face hidden in the shadows, the face of Dominic Jr., his uncle's son. Their eyes met briefly before the ominous figure tipped his hat and quickly walked away. Jackson saw the venom in those eyes, felt the icy hatred fed by decades of malice and contempt in that brief moment of contact. Cold foreboding shook his core.

His duties as the new Don demanded his immediate return to Vegas, but before leaving he met with Tino and Zander reviewing all security procedures and doubling security. He would force his mother to come with him in a few months gambling on the hope that Dominic's offspring were unaware of her location, safely secluded in her mountain retreat. Still, he vacillated, his mind imploding with trepidation before giving her one final hug.

As his plane headed east, he lifted his eyes to the heavens, "Take care of her, Dad, until I return."

Alaina stepped onto the porch and leaned against the rail, admiring the beauty of the distant purple mountains. She was alone at last, far from her doting children and the throngs of faceless well-wishers.

BANG, CRACK!

A powerful thunderstorm suddenly sprang up across the western sky, the electricity in the air heavy on her skin. Wide bolts of lightning slashed the horizon followed by heavy drums of thunder, *Thor's thunder*. She looked toward the storm. Nick was there, she felt his commanding presence surrounding her and a welcoming warmth pulsed through her body as she imagined his strong arms caressing her.

BANG, CRACK!

She turned her eyes to the heavens, her tears beginning, "I know you're angry. You wanted me to stay with Jackson, but that's not what I want. Please understand, love, I can't let you go just yet. I need to be here with you."

Mighty bolts of lightning flashed above her once again and she felt the porch floor shake beneath her feet. "Yes, yes, go ahead, but I'm staying so...," she hesitated, "rumble all you want."

BANG, BANG, CRACK!

Explosive thunder crashed down upon her, causing her to gasp at the formidable power. Inhaling deeply, she gathered her courage, "I *can* hear you, Big Man. There is no reason for all that racket; I know you're chastising me, telling me I'm a stubborn woman, but this is what *I* want." Laughing, she lifted her eyes to the skies, "Besides, you don't know everything, so for once stop bossing me around."

With that, the storm's ferocity increased; its angry assault piercing the heavens in a magnificent display of power and strength. Enormous bolts of lightning tore across the darkening horizon once again followed by angry claps of intense thunder as heavy sheets of rain began to fall.

Drawing in a deep breath, she stepped back, bowing to his superiority. "Oh, you are a devil tonight, and I miss those mischievous eyes. I'm going to take a bath now and go to bed. Join me if you choose."

A low rumble began as she moved toward the door. Did she glimpse his shadow standing in the corner?

A Grieving Heart

Alaina knelt in the garden tending to the bright purple lupines, desperate for distraction. The days seemed endless without him, and each sunrise brought with it a renewed battle with the demons of her deepening depression. The garden was her sanctuary, cocooning her in memories of their life together. She could still see his smile, still hear his voice, still feel his touch.

His spirit remained, watching over her, protecting her. She saw his image among the trees, his shadow on the porch. Sometimes she felt his presence in the kitchen as she puzzled over which spice to use, once she thought he even rattled one of the bottles. He repositioned her shawl on the bedroom chaise, and she knew positively that he was with her at night when the scent of his cologne blanketed her as she drifted off to sleep.

"Honey, you need to stop moving things," she chided, helplessly searching for a missing garden glove. A gentle breeze caused the lupines to dance, and she laughed. "Stop teasing me, I need my glove. Where did you hide it?"

"Madam, did you say something?" Henry questioned as he approached, carrying a fresh bag of potting soil.

"Oh Henry, you startled me. I was just talking to Mr. Nick."

"Ah, and how is he today?"

"Playful, as always. You haven't come across a gardening glove on your way, have you? I seem to have lost one."

"Here it is, madam, right here on the bench."

Yes, Henry and Hildy think I'm crazy, but I know Nick is still with me.

Her sons rallied around her after the funeral, all wanting her to live with them. Jax was the most insistent, calling every other day 'just to check in.' She tried telling him she no longer needed her bodyguards, but he insisted they stay.

Good intentioned friends continued to call, assuring her that it would get easier, that her grief would subside, *they lied.* Get out more, meet new people they said, but that was the last thing she wanted. She was happy in her home, the home he built for her, enrobed in her memories. Still… she wept for him every day.

Today would test her strength. Archer was coming and she would need to don her armor and hide her tears.

"Alaina, you look well," Arch exclaimed, greeting her with a hug. "I apologize for not coming sooner. Nick had his hand in so many businesses that it's taken longer than expected to settle his estate. I hope you understand."

"Apologies aren't necessary, Arch, I know how busy you must be. Come, let's sit by the fire. Legal matters are always more palatable over whiskey, don't you think?"

She looked toward the face of the man she knew so well with his ruddy cheeks, bulbous nose, and deeply furrowed brow. His mischievous Irish smile remained but she could see the pain in his eyes still grieving for the loss of his friend. *It probably hurts to visit.*

"Thanks, it's... it's been a difficult few months. We had best get started. I've divided everything into three boxes: business, personal, and a third we'll talk about later."

The afternoon slipped by as Arch tediously presented paper after paper for her signature, explaining Nick's wishes for the financial dynasty he'd left behind.

When finally, he reached for the last box, his expression softened, and warmth returned to his eyes. "Nick labeled this box *Sakura*. I never understood the meaning there, but he must have had his reasons."

She smiled. Sakura was the Japanese word for cherry blossom, a message sent even in death.

"This one is for you alone," he continued. "Inside you'll find the keys to several safety deposit boxes in both Nevada and California along with detailed instructions and access codes. The box also contains deeds to multiple properties and investments but it's important you understand that none bear the name Rusano. These are hidden investments, hidden from Nick's ah... business associates." He stared at her for several seconds before lowering his gaze to the floor, attempting to hide his discomfort.

She reached for his hand "It's all right, Arch, you don't need to explain."

He hesitated, drawing on the whiskey, his eyes now able to meet hers again. "You always knew, didn't you..., who he was, what he did?"

"Actually, no. Up until Don Angelo's death, I thought Nick was a simple businessman managing a casino. He kept that world well hidden from me. But… I could never have walked away from him, Arch, not then, not ever. I loved him too much." She paused, breathing in deeply, inwardly fighting back tears, her words more solemn. "His father's death nearly broke him, and it was a dark time in our marriage. There were days when he was unable to face me whether from shame or guilt, but I realized he was suffering. He needed me more than ever. I was his respite, yanking him back from the throes of chaos each time he crossed over our threshold. I was his stability on the other side of the door, his gateway to the normal life he longed for. It was on days when he didn't crossover that most worried me. His mind was calling to me, but his demons held tight, and I couldn't reach him."

Her voice faltered but she continued, "We both know he never wanted what was handed to him, but he didn't know how to escape. He straddled two separate worlds every day playing a role on an unforgiving stage. So tough and hard on the outside but with me, he was gentle and caring, with me he was able to drop the mask. I witnessed his joy as he rocked his babies and his remorse when he returned from one of his *stealth* business trips, his mind paralyzed in silent torment as he lay his head upon my breasts. That was the man I knew, Arch, and I feel fortunate to have been the woman he loved."

Arch nodded, fighting to control the sadness washing over him before reaching for her hand. "Alaina, there's something more in the Sakura box. He wrote one final letter and asked that I deliver it on your anniversary. I know I'm a few days early but, better early than late."

With that he anxiously rose from the chair and leaned in to hug her, his eyes brimming with tears. He rushed toward the door embarrassed by his show of emotion, then abruptly turned back, "I… I nearly forgot. Janie's planning a special dinner to… to celebrate. Say you'll come; you shouldn't be alone."

Her eyes betrayed her and he saw her lips trembling as her hand reached across the space between them. He rushed back, holding her as she burst into a torrent of tears, her body shaking with overwhelming grief.

"I can't, I'm sorry I just can't," she sobbed, "Oh Arch, I miss him so much. I... I don't know how to live without him."

"I know, I miss him too. I still can't believe he's gone," Arch cried, his tears now falling with hers.

Found in Sakura Box.

My Darling,

This is the hardest letter I have ever written because it means that I have left you. There is so much to say, but I don't know where to start. How does a man say goodbye to a woman whose love was unfaltering? Time was always our enemy, but an endless amount would not have been enough for me to express my immeasurable love for you, knowing that you returned that love every day, with every breath. There were years when I gave you nothing but heartache and I only hope that the good outweighed the bad.

You were my angel; your strong wings sheltered me and prevented me from slipping into the darkness. I ask that you forgive me for unkept promises and remember that I loved you always.

Forever yours, Nick

She tenderly fingered the pendant within, a two-inch platinum angel wing embedded with one hundred brilliant white diamonds, his final gift.

Illusion

The call of the osprey was shrill and impatient, "Wake up, you're missing the sunrise." Still, she lingered, refusing to relinquish the nirvana of her dreams, begging the kaleidoscope of her memories to rewind. There was baby Jackson toddling merrily across the lawn in pursuit of a mischievous puppy. Daredevil Luca was screeching with joy, his tiny form gleefully cannon balling into the pool. She heard three-year-old Matt's joyful squeals echoing through the hall upon escaping the bath naked and dripping wet, and she laughed aloud seeing Little Sam's shocked face when he hit his first home run. She could see their smiles, hear their laughter; they were calling her, and she reached for them with outstretched hands.

There were mornings when she didn't want to leave the bed, unable to face another empty day, her dreams her only savior from the savage claws of loneliness. *This* was one of those mornings. The winter had been harsh with snow painting the hills in a glistening white carpet as the angry wind howled against the windows, both refusing to relinquish their tight grip and keeping her indoors. But winter finally surrendered, allowing her to resume her daily walks—walks once taken with him—where she could be alone with her memories.

She paused as she stepped off the porch, reveling at the beauty of the mountains covered in a gentle mist of pink and blue and testing her weakening legs. She would be forced to go to one of her children soon; Matt would be her choice.

Again, the osprey's call pierced the air, "Hurry now, no time to waste."

Still, she lingered; reveling in the scent of the majestic fir trees and allowing the crisp morning air to travel deep within her lungs. But it was damp, and the cold's icy tentacles bit through her shawl; nothing seemed to warm her lately. Tears began to travel down the familiar path of her cheeks and the empty hole in her heart grew larger, the pain from his loss intensifying. It would not be a good day; the pangs of her grief had arrived early.

A glimpse of terracotta caught her eye, and she spotted Ginger, the three-legged fox nudging two baby pups toward the tree line.

"Good morning, little one, how are you today?"

Ginger hesitated as if to reply, her beautiful amber eyes meeting Alaina's, but the moment was quickly broken by her mischievous pair, and she turned to coax them along, their existence quickly swallowed up by the curling mist on the path ahead.

The osprey called out once more, admonishing her tardiness, "Hurry, hurry, don't dawdle."

Alaina hastened on, determined to reach the lake with hopes its shimmering surface would conjure memories of their days on the water. But the mist grew thicker with each step, enveloping the trees and skewing the path. She inched forward cautiously questioning her ability to continue but just as she was about to turn back Ginger reappeared on the trail, a mere foot away with her furry face cocked, her penetrating stare beckoning.

"What is it girl?" she asked, puzzled by the animal's behavior.

The shrill blast of a boat's horn sounded nearby, startling her. Perhaps a stranger was in trouble on the water? She crept closer, barely able to see. A boat was moored to their dock, white with blue trim identical to the Bow Rider she had sold months earlier. She squinted to read the name...Che... Cheerio, no, no, it couldn't be.

Another blast from the boat's horn sang through the air demanding her attention and urging her forward as the gentle mist swirled atop the crystal blue lake, shrouding it in ethereal beauty. The fragrant scent of the fir trees, so strong just minutes earlier, drifted away, replaced by the woody smell of whiskey now filling her nostrils and permeating the air around her. *Not possible*. Then, from the corner of her eye, she caught the barest hint of movement, a mere shadow of a man. Fear shot through her but still she crept forward, and there, just a few short feet away, stood Nick Rusano, tall and tanned, smiling that handsome smile, a half empty glass of Macallan in his hand.

She warily surveyed this image of her husband. His hair was dark and full with no trace of gray, his eyes were bright, his face unlined. He was young and muscular, the Nick from when they first married.

"Nick?" she stammered, her eyes growing large in disbelief. "Nick?"

"Care to come aboard, my lady," he beamed, greeting her with outstretched hand. In awe, she stepped closer allowing his strong grasp to help her into the boat. He drew her near and she reached for him with trembling hands, slowly tracing his forehead, cheeks, and chin as her tears began to fall. She felt her heart beat faster, felt her lungs beg for air, questioning the vision before her.

"Are you ready, gorgeous?" he asked her in a whisper, as his hand lightly grazed her temple. "We must hurry, no time to waste."

But before she could reply a thundering boom sounded behind them and the boat was hit by a violent wake. She gasped, gripping his shoulders and his hands quickly moved to steady her. A surge of heat propelled her into his chest, and she cried out to him, groping for breath and quaking with fear. No longer able to stand, she collapsed against him, her mind spiraling into a frightening darkness.

"Laina. Laina." His soft voice echoed in her ears as if from a deep canyon, tinny and distant. Calling, reaching, calling, reaching, summoning her back.

She was trembling, feeling his body tight against hers, cocooning her in his warm embrace and her eyes flew open.

"You're safe now, my darling, forever safe in my arms," he whispered. "Don't be afraid. I'm right here with you."

Her lips were still quivering, but she felt secure allowing his soft words to lessen her fear as strange pulses of turbulent energy began to surge through her body, vanquishing her fatigue. The aches and pains of old age faded away, and she felt her weakened legs strengthening. Catching sight of her hands, she saw they were no longer arthritic and wrinkled but young once again. Her heart overflowed with intense elation, yesterday's sorrows forgotten as she raised her eyes to meet his reassuring gaze, nodding her understanding and blissfully accepting her new reality.

His hand moved to stroke her chin and his jubilant eyes looked deeply into hers.

"Sail with me as we set off together. Let me shelter you from bitter winds and trust that I will love you always," he exclaimed, pausing, and waiting for her to join him.

Smiling, she placed her hand upon his cheek, her love pouring forth as she spoke, "Let me guide you through rough waters and steer you through the storms. Let my beacon bring you home on starless nights and trust that I will love you always. Sail with me."

"We will never be apart again, my angel, never again," he whispered as he bent to kiss her lips, and she rejoiced, feeling herself melting in the arms of the man she loved, once again enveloped in his tenderness.

The Bow Rider effortlessly pulled away from the dock, silently piloting toward their welcoming sunrise. The osprey swooped down giving a final salute, and the morning mist inched closer, washing over them forever entwined in eternity.

EPILOGUE

"Jackson, it's Uncle Arch, I have news… terrible news. There's been an explosion at the mountain house. Your mother's gone, Son, she's gone. I'm sorry… so sorry."

Jax listened, hearing the quaking anguish in Archer's voice as his father's old friend recounted the scant details of the accident.

"I'm … there now, Zander's with me. He says he spotted a stranger hiking in the woods the day before last, but he wasn't able to track him. The place is flattened, Son, nothing but sticks and rocks. Your mother's body was pulled from the rubble along with Henry and Hildy, all three dead. Tino has blast burns over 40% of his body. I'll update you when I know more, but… you better come soon." His uncle released a heavy sob before disconnecting, no longer able to control his grief. Arch had sworn a solemn vow to always protect Alaina and he had failed. The old man's heart was broken.

Jax stood frozen for several minutes; groping for breath, unable to control his explosive furor. His whiskey glass rocketed across the room, shattering into a hundred glass shards as his anger erupted and the torment took hold.

Why, why did they need to hurt her, why?

He stared at the phone; his mind clawing for some small amount of composure before he dialed Luca's number to share the news of their mother's murder. An icy chill coursed through his body hearing his father's words in the hollows of his mind, 'Think Jackson, think. Plan'. Overwhelming rage gripped his soul, sending him plummeting to the floor on buckled knees, as his thunderous screams echoed throughout the building. "They did this, they did this and we're going to kill every last one of them. We're going to *war*, brother. We're going to *war*!"

The End

ACKNOWLEDGEMENTS

With deep and overwhelming love, I thank my daughter, Danielle, whose continuous encouragement, and support saw me through many days of tears and self-doubt. You were there for me in my darkest hours, helping me see that my struggle was worthwhile, believing in my passion.

Special thanks to my husband, who spent endless hours alone in front of the television as I labored to put thoughts onto paper. This forced solitude was not at all what you were expecting in retirement. Sorry, handsome.

My heartfelt appreciation goes out to my beta readers whom I allowed a glimpse into my past and very private life. I am sure I shocked all of you but, in spite of that, you each gave freely of your time. Your detailed comments and constructive criticism helped me view this story through the eyes of my audience. Shelby, I know how busy you are but still you sacrificed cherished hours of sleep to support this old lady. Ruth, you jumped at the chance to read my draft and your words of encouragement reenforced the belief that success was achievable. You are a dear friend. And Lynda, I am especially grateful to you and your husband, Bill. Your insightful critique over glasses of wine and unending laughter enhanced the narrative. Thanks for the role play, girlfriend.

I would be amiss if I did not thank the wonderful residents of my Ducktown neighborhood whose colorful characters were my inspiration. I feel fortunate to have been raised in the warmth and protectiveness of such a caring community and memories of those carefree days will be forever etched in my heart.

Thanks also to Jane who encouraged this struggling tech-deficient writer to create an author website. Your kind words were appreciated more than you know.

Finally, to my readers and followers who patiently embarked on this journey with me, thank you for giving these characters a place on the coveted bookshelves of your minds.

Author's Note

Growing up in Atlantic City was a child's dream come true. While my friends in Philadelphia could only spend summers on its white sandy beaches, I had the luxury of living in the city year-round. I have only wonderful memories of those days spent laughing and holding hands with my friends while jumping ocean waves and skipping along a boardwalk filled with amusement piers, custard stands, and storefronts packed with cotton candy, saltwater taffy, creamy fudge, and macaroons. The hawkers pitched ocean boat rides and the auctioneers lured customers into their shops with free samples of Teflon frying pans and miracle hairbrushes. The famous Ice Capades filled Convention Hall with their nightly extravaganza and the Miss America parade graced our famous boardwalk closing down the tourist season each September. The world renown Steel Pier called to me every Friday morning where I danced as a teenager with friends to the latest 45s at the record hop. It was there that I received my first kiss and watched as the Supremes, the Four Tops, and the Temptations performed to sellout crowds. For years I longed to ride the diving horse, courageously sailing from its sky-high perch to the tank below; unfortunately, that dream was never fulfilled but I would still do it today if the opportunity ever arose.

I also was fortunate enough to grow up in the Ducktown neighborhood of the city and it truly was the safest area of town where a young girl never needed fear walking alone no matter the hour. It was a tight community where everyone knew each other by name and took pride in their neighborhood. I can still recall the tempting aromas of the shops, their windows filled with hanging Italian meats and pungent cheeses and the clerks who forever flirted with my shy but beautiful mother. Pizza was five cents a slice at the Italian bakery and the best subs in town were served by the White House sub shop on Mississippi and Arctic Avenues; their walls covered with signed photos of celebrities from past visits.

Unfortunately, the city met its demise, and the slow hunger of deterioration began. Not even the casino heyday could restore the gentle lady to her former elegance. I miss the Atlantic City of old but have endless happy memories of her glory.

This novel is a work of fiction and any reference to characters or events are also fictitious. It is not meant to offend or depict the remarkable residents of my hometown in a negative light. Atlantic City will forever remain a reigning queen in my heart.

On the Drawing Board

The Four Horsemen of Perdition
Jack
2nd in the Tenderness series

Please feel free to contact me with your memories
of Atlantic City at **www.diane-zimmerman.com**